OLD UNION

Wayne Ward

Trafford rev. 06/16/2014

 www.trafford.com

North America & international
toll-free: 1 888 232 4444 (USA & Canada)
fax: 812 355 4082

God is our guide! From field, from wave,
from plough, from anvil, and from loom.
We come, our country's right to save,
and speak a tyrant faction's doom.
We raised the watch-word liberty:
we will, we will, we will be free!

George Loveless, Tolpuddle, Dorset, United Kingdom, 1834

Jack London once wrote when God finished creating the rattlesnake,
the toad and the vampire, with the scraps left over he made a scab.

Ella Rose
Tullie Mae
Eira Valentina
Aurora Delisay
. . . . four musketeers

1

2013

LAID WITH A PRECISION lost in modern masonry, sandstone blocks bedded so fine and accurate if not for slight imperfections in their quarrying the two almost identical two storey buildings, separated by a twenty foot swathe of azalea, lilac and rhododendron, might have been a single stone. Over the years encouraged for its English stately home grandeur, vigorous ivy spread its grasping suckers over the upper portions of the buildings, the Mt Osmond nursing home.

A single car width of crushed quartz passed with perfect symmetry through manicured lawns, one-way traffic managed by a three foot high circular granite pond from which rose amid flowering water hyacinths a nymph holding aloft an urn of cascading water.

Spread over six hectares, an emerald and private enclave in the midst of native bushland, sweeping lawns and garden beds, winding gravel pathways, others sealed with asphalt for wheelchair access. Jasmine choked arbours amid mature oak, elm, maple and silver birch, the logical choice of landscape architects pining for their native land. Barely perceptible at first the grounds followed the contours of the mountain, dropping away on three sides before overwhelmed by the heavily forested Adelaide Hills. Far to the east the hazy outline of the city of Adelaide spread on its broad coastal plain before ending in a dark blue strip between sky and urban landform, the Gulf of St Vincent.

Rarefied air and sweet birdsong, the pungent scent of eucalypt and acacia in the deep valleys; though birds lived their lives in the surrounding native forest, a sojourn from the heat of summer in the cool lush foliage of northern hemisphere trees offered respite.

Outdoor staffs were busy due to the promise of a sunny autumn day, clearing early rain and a light northerly wind adding a fresh carpet of falling leaves on the lawns, a bounty swooped upon by the gardeners for their compost pens. Prematurely stored away for winter, canvas deck chairs unfolded and park benches wiped clean, wheelchairs marshalled in the foyer for the frail; reprieve from the sterile confines of the wards.

About the old man nothing clearly identified a past history in Pimba, according to a new generation in the South Australian outback town a harmless old hermit or fossicker who lived alone in one of the abandoned railways houses when the Commonwealth Railways centralised maintenance facilities. The roadhouse-general store furnished a name and information he collected a pension, the money paid into a Commonwealth Bank account accessed through their agency.

Further inquiries produced records with the Commonwealth Railways, retirement and a small pension, and there the search little more than tidying loose ends ended. Endeavours to communicate with the man failed, doctors of the opinion the medical crisis that saw him admitted to Mt Osmond the probable cause. Staff attempted to communicate, but failed. A nurse noticed a faded tattoo on his right upper arm, of interest and speculation, a statement indelibly inked in human flesh. It resulted in a nickname.

Gravel crunched under the wheels of the wheelchair, the nurse avoiding ruts where ride-on mowers took shortcuts and decided to stay on the path, gripping the handles and angrily composing a memo in his mind to stop the practice. The dark mood persisted for only a brief moment as he caught site of the slim figure of a girl waving from a park bench under an elm chosen because of its early loss of foliage allowing the sun to shine spidery filigrees of warmth through it massive bows.

Paul Harris's rostered Sunday brightened, his girl waiting on a park bench taking time off from a busy weekend schedule for a picnic lunch. He spun the wheelchair around to offer his patient a view of the hazy city in the far distance, then sat down to kiss her puckered mouth. "Dear old Rosalinda in the kitchen's managed to get another of her brood out from the Philippines and is in a fine old mood, hence a grand picnic lunch."

She pouted pettishly, then gripped his hand excitedly. "Even though the credentials committee will make their decision on your eligibility on Tuesday, you can come with me tonight to the meeting if you like. It's quite within our rules."

"Wendy, I may be on an extended shift if my relief has problems with his car again. Hungry?"

"Absolutely starving!"

He reached under the wheelchair for a small hamper, placing it on the bench between them; roast chicken pieces with chunks of seasoning, sliced ham, tomato, lettuce, six dinner rolls, plastic plates and cutlery. "Beats the dining room with its odd odours. Impending death, some lark reckoned."

Selecting a piece of chicken for the old man, he removed the skin to expose soft flesh. "Would you believe the old geezer's still got teeth?"

"Has there been any intelligible communication?" she said, nibbling on a piece of chicken for a starter.

"No, the archetypical deep and silent type. Which is not an apt description for stroke."

"Not even I need the potty?" she said with a delicate tremor.

"No, all we have is his name and that he's as old as the fossils we think he might have collected. Simon's nicknamed him Old Union, suppose because of the tattoo."

She used her handkerchief to delicately dab grease from her mouth. "Couldn't he have found a more agreeable nickname other than Old Union? Burdening him with that has branded the poor chap for the remainder of whatever life is left in him."

"No more than an old Australian tradition at work there, Wendy my dearest. Simply an old tattoo and Simon's creative mind did the rest."

"Utterly detest tattoos, especially on women which seem to be the fad nowadays. Not only grotesque and disfiguring, but categorising people from a lower station of life."

Smacking his lips he prompted the old man to eat, breaking off another chunk of meat and adding a pinch of seasoning. "Have a look, darling." Removing the blanket draped around the old man's sunken shoulders he indicated a tattoo on his right upper arm. Over many years the blue ink etching faded but still palely visible in the wrinkled folds of flesh; an anchor with its cable entwined around the shank and both flukes, beneath the flukes in the shape of a scimitar the words: *Bound by Unity.*

She crinkled her nose, layering a bread roll with ham, tomato and lettuce. "Our meeting should be especially stimulating tonight with the release of the latest polls pointing to a landslide victory in September. Would you believe the arrogance of that woman to call an election months and months in the future? Utterly ridiculous!"

His mind focused elsewhere. "Only two more rostered Sundays, Wendy. Then my weekends are free for four weeks."

"I will miss our picnic lunches, but not the long drive. Paul, Mr Abbott's visiting Adelaide and we have requested for him to address a specially convened branch meeting," she said, a decision pending where to take the first bite from her roll.

"Your branch can get the leader of the federal opposition to a meeting?"

"We have the numbers to support our request, a highly active branch. We can only try, Mr Abbott being so busy and in such great demand. We will be sending a delegate to the official meeting."

"Hopefully my militant and beautiful Wendy?"

She shook her head ruefully. "Alternative. Paul, please do the poor old codger a favour and don't call him that awful name, Old Union. I thoroughly detest it."

"Name's stuck, sorry."

"Give him the benefit of doubt, the man may he have been blessed in his long life unaffected by that dreadful affliction."

"We think the tattoo of an anchor and the word unity he might have belonged to a maritime union. Oh, he also wears this little silver anchor around his neck, buried in the hair and folds somewhere. Certainly not the navy, I don't think a naval man would want his superior officers to see him as bound by unity and not strict naval discipline. Might even have been a fisherman, but are fishing boats symbolised by anchors, probably not."

Half listening, she hoped Mrs Hammersmith would become indisposed so she would take her place as delegate. Her chance to shake hands with a future prime minister, maybe even a hug. Man of the people, decisive and forceful, a leader in waiting when the dysfunctional and faction ridden Labor government finally collapsed in its own cesspool of incompetence and gross mismanagement.

She felt heartened with strong speculation within the party that Mr Abbott on assuming the prime ministership, repealing the carbon and mining taxes, would coax Mr Peter Reith, a fellow combatant against the unions in the John Howard years, to return to politics as an advisor in industrial affairs. Use his fearless expertise in dealing with recalcitrant union bosses as he did when he wiped the floor with the Maritime Union of Australia, standing side by side with a fearless leader of the stevedoring industry, Mr Corrigan, who demanded the return of his waterfront from union corruption and featherbedding.

Not that she abhorred the concept of unions, the right of free association inherent in a thriving democracy. No, only those unions who dictated with intimidation and violence, street marches with bullhorns and chanting, their terms of employment to besieged management.

The old man slowly turned his head and looked for the first time at the young girl. Thoughts did pass through his mind where probing doctors at Mt Osmond were certain none dwelled.

Through her ceaseless prattle she mentioned one name that bore deep into his conscious thought, Sir Robert Menzies. Last week she carried in her shoulder bag a birthday gift from her father, *Lazarus Rising*. She spoke with adulation about the author, Australia's second longest serving prime minister, John Howard. She continually stroked the glossy dust jacket, turning the book over to show Paul a photograph of the author; bespectacled, smiling, a face matured by long years in service to his country. Etched with wisdom and trust, goodwill and fairness, the visage of a statesman.

She offered him the book to hold. "Though Sir Robert will never be surpassed for his service to Australia as the country's longest serving and most revered prime minister, Mr Howard can stand proudly in his shadow with his own claim to greatness. Unwavering leadership, a wise and steadfast hand guiding us through the economic and terrorist challenges of dangerous times.

"The second greatest prime minister in Australia's history, his treasurer never far from his side, gave us twelve years of unparalleled prosperity and growth no Labor government controlled by its faceless factions could ever match, proof obvious as our country slides into bankruptcy. Prime Minister Howard stood firm with our allies when others faltered in the fight against terrorism, strengthening our bonds with the United States and the United Kingdom."

He agreed. "Australia can think itself fortunate for having such men to step-up and take command in troubled times. Winston Churchill is such a man who immediately comes to mind. I do not know that much about Sir Robert, shame upon me. Wendy, I am curious, why isn't there dams and highways, rivers and bridges, airports and stadiums named in honour of Sir Robert? You would think after all the years the Liberal Party and the Nationalist have been in power there would be hundreds of reminders of his greatness."

"We are reminded every second of every day in the quality of life and freedom we take for granted, and I say it proudly from my heart, Sir Robert's legacy to his nation. We are the envy of the world because Sir Robert guided us through dire times and triumphed, never faltering, veering or capitulating against great odds," she said, her voice close to breaking.

The old man remembered Menzies, he most certainly did. He lowered his head and stared into his blanketed lap, his claw-like fingers screwing up the woollen fabric. The name caused bile to rise in his stomach.

2

1935

THE SPIRIT OF THE boy though challenged many times never broke; Sam knew he could never best the spectre of a man who caused his mother to retreat into a shell, a brute who constantly beat her and him. A pitiless man hardened by years of heavy manual labour, his father offered no love or counsel for a fifteen-year-old son who worked from sunrise to dusk, taken from school at twelve to plough dry fields. Arid soil gripped in perpetual drought, fierce westerly winds blowing away the last few withered stalks of maize grown with borrowed money.

Nathaniel Wright, a heavy hand and an acid tongue, dominated a timid wisp of a wife. He ruled both woman and a boy with a broad leather strap he hung on a hook on the back door of their wattle and daub home, always visible, a symbol of fear and punishment. Bare flesh felt its searing pain, wielded by a merciless hand. Often Sam crawled to his bed in agonizing pain from a beating he could not understand why, failing to hold back the tears that streaked his face. He might have forgotten to ask to leave the table, collect nettles and other weeds for the few scrawny fowls scavenging in the yard. His mother cried often, lesser beatings with an open hand across her face with the full force of work hardened shoulders. Then would disgorge abuse for a meal not on the table when he entered the front door, or when he unsuccessfully searched for housekeeping money to buy drink.

There were good times he remembered sitting with his mother on the front porch when the summer sun so large it near filled the entire blood red horizon at last dipped beneath the horizon, times when his father visited a brother in Hay and would be gone for weeks. Together both played a game of describing what came into their minds; Maud would inevitably select clusters of wildflowers growing by bubbling brooks flowing through grassy banks, blue skies and feathery clouds remembered from childhood. Her son oddly talked of sailing ships and steamers which puzzled her as none of the family were connected to the sea, let alone seen a ship. She asked the obvious question.

His sixth grade teacher who when pointing to the farthest southern navigable landform at the tail of South America on a map of the world spoke of her father who commanded sailing ships and steamers. A sea captain who travelled the world and with her on his knee talked of all its wonders. On the blackboard Miss Spooner drew a fair resemblance of a three masted sailing ship and a steamer and questioned the fascinated class what differences were obvious between the vessels. Sam's hand darted up; wind filled canvas sailed the three masted ship, a hidden engine the steamer. He asked the teacher how a boy could go to sea, the not unexpected answer your future lies behind a plough, son. Even so a young boy moved to a far corner of his mind the chalk images, a promise to himself that would guide him down a long and eventful path.

The family survived on what the farm reluctantly gave up, rare good years when rain settled the dust and his father planted maize or lucerne. A few straggly sheep sold to the local butcher for near to nothing. Eggs when the fowls laid. The occasional day labour. A never-ending struggle to exist, the family like so many others no more than pawns of nature who ruled their miserable lives in the arid plains of outback New South Wales. In the schoolyard their obvious poverty never interfered with their games or found its way into their excited chatter. This is how people on the land lived, and if the manager of the Bank of New South Wales dwelled with his rich family in a large brick home, the disparity represented no more than a stratum of society the poor worked hard and sacrificed to attain.

Sam remembered his father confrontation with the bank; two men in suits arguing with his father on their front veranda before his father disappeared inside the house and reappeared with a shotgun. The men from the bank never returned, but the Balranald sergeant of police did and spoke at length with his father, the policeman a brave man Sam thought. Whatever came of the confrontation no one bothered to come back to the farm.

His mother died and his father buried her in the local cemetery, digging the grave himself and fashioning her coffin from whatever scrap wood he could find around the farm. He loomed over the open grave, ignoring the minister intoning the burial service, clenching his fists this woman cheated him of a vessel to discharge into and vent his rage. Sam, hat in hand, stood in the protective shadow of his uncle and aunt from Hay and cried silently. Then a grunt from his father, a shovel thrust in his hand.

He searched a bureau in his parent's bedroom for his birth and baptismal certificate, documents that legalised his existence, placed them with his few items of clothing in his canvas school bag and ran. In his mind a destination, Sydney and a ship!

≈

Sam's journey began in the dusty outskirts of Balranald, his destination 550 miles to the east. He never looked back at the red powdery imprints he left after leaving the cemetery and murmuring the tearful words for his mother to rest in peace. He followed a road with the sun ahead of him in the morning, behind him in the evening, a country highway paved with thin and potholed macadam, long stretches of hard baked rutted clay. Ever eastward through flat and featureless plains, desolate and dry localities and small towns, communities offering no welcome for him and his fellow travellers, an army of unemployed.

Narrow wooden bridges crossed dry creek beds, sometimes a river no more than a string of shallow waterholes fed by natural springs. In some towns a sign pointed to a locality, permission granted by the police for itinerants to camp overnight and be gone by daylight. Sometimes a park, mostly a weed choked paddock.

Sam's company far outnumbered the motor vehicles and horse and bullock drawn wagons travelling the highway, despondent men trudging along the narrow road shoulders with their swags weighing heavily on their sagging shoulders. Men of every calling, of every strata of society denied work, separated from their families. Men devoid of hope, of all ages, living the lie of freedom in a failed system.

For this wandering band of humanity their existence balanced on a thin edge of Christian charity or hunger. Long and silent queues outside church halls of shuffling men with lost pride, like pet animals awaiting a master's pleasure to feed them. Rarely did much discourse pass between God's providers and the hungry, sometimes a service for them to sink to their knees and give gratitude to God for their lives.

Sam kept in the background making himself as inconspicuous as possible, and if addressed by a Christian volunteer who filled his bowl with soup and handed him a slice of bread, he would lower his head and avert his eyes, a mumbled thank you. Without warm clothing he suffered in the cold inland nights, even worse ahead with the foothills of the Blue Mountains, the range rising to 4000 feet west of Sydney. Cold and miserable but never faltering in his journey, he discovered charitable clothing and blankets scarce, an army of unemployed moving like a swarm over the land preceding him. Luck would have it a girl who ladled stew into his cracked bowl smiled and noticed him shivering, from a chest at the back of the church hall offering him a blanket last used as a painter's drop-sheet.

Mustering his courage, he returned her smile, her age about his, pretty with rosy cheeks and long blonde plaits tied with red ribbons; the minister's daughter. Then the driving force of others behind him, hungry eyes never leaving a large steaming tureen, moved him on, guided him to a long table with side benches where the itinerants wolfed their food, for most their only meal for the day.

Money meant little for Sam, his only remembrance of it a few silver and copper coins thumped on the kitchen table by his father, a grating voice demanding his wife put food on the table. In the city he would need money, or he might be lucky and join a ship, the dream almost a reality as the Blue Mountains loomed on the eastern horizon, thankful for the minister's daughter's generosity.

His trek eastwards went against the flow of humanity, the city disgorging its legions of unemployed seeking work westward. In the city factory chimneys rusted, gates chained and locked. Government attempted to apply a balm to the suffering population, the worst of the financial crisis peaked and factories would soon be employing though wages offered for long hours poor. Who would complain? Certainly not those with shrunken bellies, wrenched from families left behind in abject poverty?

He listened intently to the socialist orators on the road, fiery men mostly of British origin, with loud and penetrating voices condemning their wretched plight. Others in similar oratory castigated both the Australian and British governments who in patriotic fervour called young men to arms. To save from ravishment beautiful young white virgins tremulously draped in union flags from vile Huns depicted as ink-black, cloven hoofed, hairy fiends with thick blubbering lips and leering, lascivious eyes. Some audacious critics remarked the slathering brutes resembled the Negroid race, the unjust criticism lost in the call from the Empire from far away in her hour of need.

When the slaughtering and gassing, the maiming and senseless sacrificing, the insanity and utter destruction, ended the brave young who survived four years of blood and gore came home to grand promises from those who sent them of a new world, a world of prosperity, homes and jobs. Schools for their children, wholesome food on the table, equality and freedom.

His young mind absorbed it all and sometimes asked a question of the orator, his reply not understand but stored in his memory.

Driving a small tray truck lashed with baling wire to keep its body parts intact, smoke billowing from its exhaust pipe, a journeyman carpenter offered him a lift to Lithgow. The man shared his lunch, cold baked rabbit and black bread.

Offering Sam a drink from his water bag he spoke with a thick foreign accent about a man named Adolf Hitler. Idolatrised by chanting hordes and swooned over by hysterical women, a raving maniac dragging Germany up from the abyss of catastrophic depression and national humiliation to world power. Amid mass hysteria and self-glorification the Fuhrer decreed the building of autobahns, with a sweeping hand ordered into the countryside armies of blond robotic youth armed with hayforks and shovels. With arrogance befitting an Aryan deity, the demigod accepted tributes from world leaders for his resourcefulness and zeal.

The carpenter suddenly went quite, his eyes staring ahead; though hard to hear over the roar of the engine and the rattling of body parts, his words came clear and ominous: "There is not one world leader courageous enough to stand toe-to-toe with this raving lunatic. With impunity he crushes opposition with an army of street thugs. Smashes the union movement and jails union officials and Communists, the Communists earmarked for instant death. He confiscates Jewish property and has them carted off in railway cattle trucks to concentration camps. He removes from society with brutal efficiency minorities, the racially impure, the mental and the disabled."

His final damning statement, hammering the open palm of his hand on the steering wheel, gifting industrialists the entire German treasury and workforce to gear for war, a personal guarantee from the Fuhrer your workforce will bow as one to the commands of their masters.

"Are you a German?" Sam asked, wide-eyed.

"I am a Communist!"

When the carpenter gripped his hand in Lithgow Sam felt the power and intensity of the man, the fire in his eyes. "Will the Germans fight against Hitler?" he asked innocently.

"No! Only the Communists!"

The Blue Mountains now close cast a shadow over Lithgow, their brooding presence and deep heavily timbered valleys shrouded in mist, the promise of biting cold; an early search for an abandoned building, bridge or culvert, became a necessity to survive the night huddled in his blanket. His only meal of the day came from the Lithgow Salvation Army, a thin vegetable broth of mostly peelings. Stale bread became a staple, sometimes a piece of flyblown fruit. Always the good word of the Lord came with sustenance and Sam wondered why such a benevolent and loving God spoken of in adoring words could blight the land with despair. One day he did ask the question, immediately shown the door for his impertinence, or it might have been atheism, no glint of pity in the flint-like eyes of the matron for a malnourish boy from whose mouth spilled heresy.

Crossing the mountains he encountered men heading west filled with hope. Talk of work on the railways, jobs in coal mines, farmers ploughing fallow fields. Planned new roads would need labourers, rumours of dam construction in the south of the state.

Work on the land held no interest for the young boy though he experienced a similar infection of optimism that gave his fellow travellers that extra bounce in their step, further fuelling his desire to reach Sydney and find a ship. Over the many weeks of his long trek his childhood vanished, replaced by a maturity far beyond his years. Eyes that could hold another's, confidence in his sinewy body to overcome threat to his person. Not with the brute force his father used to overcome those unfortunate to come under his menacing influence because he needed no driving hatred of his fellow man to prove his new manhood.

≈

His boots caught Sam's attention first, then the expensive but well worn clothes that clung to his gaunt frame, in better times a business suit. His boots gleamed with polish, not a frayed lace or twine to bind the soles to the uppers. Sam sat beside him on a seat outside Parramatta Railway Station, his long journey almost over if only money for the train fare jingled in his pocket.

In his mid-30s the man's face etched a sense of melancholy, sallow complexion and grey downcast eyes. Coppery hair thinned early in life, but still sufficient to fall over his forehead. Sam also noticed the clean-shaven face and fingernails clean and not broken.

With his hands folded behind his head and his legs fully stretched he turned and grinned at Sam. "My name's Baden Stewart."

"Sam Wright."

"You've just missed a train."

"No matter. I have no money anyway."

"Sadly a fact of life," Baden said resignedly. "Even more tragic, the dilemma so common."

Sam stared at his school bag and blanket in his lap, ashamed of his unclean body and filthy clothing, boots which flapped when he walked, the soles packed with paper that disintegrated in the first few steps.

"Not wishing to pry, but if you're looking for elusive work you might consider changing your clothes and having a bath."

"I cannot help how I look," Sam said, annoyed with the cockiness of the man. "Looking around I am no better or worse than others."

"Sorry I embarrassed you. It is not you and the legions that follow in your footsteps. It is the system at fault and the hot air buffoons we habitually elect to high office. All of whom should hang their heads in collective shame as a nation of idle and desperate wander hopelessly the back roads and byways. A population reduced to begging and serfdom."

"Serfdom?"

"Well, put it this way, virtual slavery. Lives held in the ruthless grip of faceless entities who decree with the power of wealth what we eat, where and how we live, how we reproduce. Who by withholding that virulent disease of mankind, money, have plunged the world into penury, torn asunder families and prematurely brought to an end that most precious gift, life."

Sam looked at him puzzled and a little uncomfortable. "Who are you?"

"In another more auspicious life I draped a wife of stunning beauty on my arm and lived in a home commensurate to my position practicing law. Maintaining the standards of society as passed down through precedents adjudged by our wisest elders to keep society from each other's throats, while of course enriching in grand style all those privileged to dispense this wisdom of the ages."

"Why aren't you doing that now?"

"Even we who once inhabited the highest of pedestals have fallen in these dire times. Put simply what you see before you is a man expensively educated and grossly overpaid, who like the multitude is now a victim, a statistic to greed. Roaming the land and fed by people who levy a fee you surrender your soul to their crucified God in their places of worship. In another life I gained entry to the bar at a young age, my good fortune a prominent law firm in Sydney sought my services. Prestige and money beckoned. Then a wife whose aura failed to penetrate deeper than her flawless skin, a home in Redfern to begin with before setting sights on the north shore. Now all gone with the bad investments of the firm, as well as a fickle creature who proved a man should not marry on face value alone."

"There is no work even for you?"

"It would seem we are a class who have bred in large numbers and legal advice, except in cases of bank robbers who have hidden their stash to pay us, out of the reach of most people. Sam, do you understand what all this misery that inflicted us like a plague is about? Why you walk in rags and near barefooted and some do not? Why you are sitting here when you should be in school?"

"On the road I continually heard men talk of things of which I have no understanding, but I wanted to listen and learn. It seemed those who spoke the loudest and angrily could offer no solutions. Nothing but words."

"You are what you are because the world is no more than smoke and mirrors, an illusion of prosperity built on paper. Quite attractive with fine ink etchings and secret watermarks, but without substance worthless. Where are you from, Sam?"

"Balranald."

"I pry because it is in my blood, but did you live the high life in Balranald?"

He shook his head. "I ran away from home."

"So many broken homes. Victims of despair apportioning what little means there is available to buy food we would otherwise feed to pigs." Baden looked closely at Sam, then added: "There is one good man of the cloth who deserves to be rewarded with the eternal glory he promises his flock, to my cynical mind wasted in a spiritual calling. With his organisational skills he should be a leader of industry, if not a trickster of supreme persuasion. Come with me, you look in dire need of the fruits of his ceaseless labours."

Puzzled, Sam followed him down the street, Baden's voice trailing behind him. "On second thought it is wrong of me associating the reverend with a charlatan, a good shepherd leading his flock through troubled waters. You won't get the gospel forced down your throat with your soup and bread, nor a tambourine rattled in your ear, but you will receive warmth and great kindness from the good Reverend Byrne."

Leaving heavily trafficked Parramatta Rd, Baden led him down a narrow street of commercial buildings, most with their windows boarded up and padlocks on their doors. In a cross street occupying a small lot stood a small weatherboard church and hall badly in need of a coat of paint, its original white gloss now no more than peeled shards exposing badly weathered timber.

Baden paused, passing a critical eye over the church and hall. "I would suppose in the hierarchy of the church this parish is considered a first step before stone and spire, bell and slate, stained glass and gold icons. Sometimes I wonder when I make my way here to help out how such an unworldly young man can wrench the heartstrings of the fortunate and wealthy in our midst."

Reverend Byrne's boyish face showed the strain of his calling, a constant struggle to fulfil an additional role in life, provide one substantial meal a day cajoled from reluctant sources. Wheedling, begging, uncaring of lost dignity; his successes filled old steamer trunks with oddments of clothing and footwear. In his flowing black robes he haunted the Parramatta markets for spoiled vegetables, local butchers for meat about to turn, bakers their stale bread and pastries. Never once in his determined mind were there any thoughts of retreat, his spiritual passion gained through the strength of the Lord, though he did admit his wife Amber by his side an indispensable partner.

Around noon every day the church hall filled with the aroma of simmering meat in a rich broth to which voluntary cooks added diced onions, parsnips, carrots and pearl barely. Others at a long trestle table cut bread at least three days old into thick slices and spread them thickly with dripping.

Reverend Byrne's long day began at 5:00am, his success measured in spoiled vegetables and fruit; today his flock would have an apple with their soup and bread, tomorrow half an orange. Clothing and footwear came from Sydney, most of it poor quality, but welcomed by those who wore even worse on their feet and backs. His wife sorted through the clothing, sewing torn garments on her machine, a sympathetic ear for clothes conscious women forced to dress their families in castoffs that with prayer the world would change for the better.

Amber imbued a sense of family camaraderie in her husband's flock, comfort for a child that ailed, somehow finding money so a family could afford a doctor, an embrace for those bereaving a lost family member. She scrubbed and cleaned and served without complaint by her husband's side, gave succour to those who queued for sustenance, their despondency hidden behind a veneer hardened by years of idleness.

Baden introduced Sam to the weary young minister, seemingly unaware of his own worn and shabby ministerial attire and that his hair hung in disarray over his forehead; today's successful forage would reap nourishing benefits for his parish with an exceptionally rich soup and bread only one day old.

"Reverend, I have a country lad in dire need of your succour," Baden said, a lilt in his voice. "Though not a rare feat these days, the boy has walked all the way from Balranald."

Reverend Byrne raised his eyebrows questionably. "Balranald is a long way. Did you really walk all the way?"

Sam hung his head and a shock of unkempt hair obscured his eyes.

"Amber," he called his wife. "We have a young man who is in obvious need of a bath and clothing as well as boots. Can you tend to his needs?"

Sam's face turned a deep crimson.

"Don't be ashamed, son," the reverend said, placing a comforting hand on his shoulder. "We all suffer this contagion, but can take heart we have survived and will emerge stronger and of greater faith. Please accept what we have to offer as a gift in the spirit of sharing, there is no shame in that."

Amber took his hand and led him out a back door to the rectory behind the church. He felt a knot in his belly, the sweet natural scent of a woman, her curly brown hair framing her heart shaped face and dimpled cheeks. Young girls he encountered he glanced at shyly, some returning his attention boldly which caused his breath to catch, to wonder what secrets these girls hid.

In the laundry she filled a tin tub with hot water from a wood fired copper. "Must have known you were coming. I don't usually light the copper until evening, but I did early this morning for something that's slipped my mind. Probably to wash a new lot of clothing, one explanation. Leave your old clothes on the floor, I will leave the new outside the door."

He sunk to his chin, emptying his lungs in one long slow exhalation as the water soaked into every pore and filled him with a sense of exhilaration. Then scrubbing with a stiff bristle brush, between his toes, a wash cloth in his ears, ashamed at the scum floating on top of the water. He dried himself and with the towel wrapped around his waist emptied the bath with a dipper, opening the door to find his new clothes in a neat pile on which sat a pair of polished boots. Boots even to challenge Baden's!

His heart pounded as he eased fresh underwear up his thighs, followed by almost new cotton trousers and shirt. The woollen cardigan though worn would keep him warm, clean and smelling of washing soap. Sitting on the laundry back step he pulled on woollen socks and his new boots, amazed at the reverend's wife's skill in matching the clothes to his size.

Skin tingling and warm, washed clean, and in his new clothes he felt like a toff as he entered the church hall to stand in line for his soup and bread, find his benefactors and thank them.

Behind the trestle table Baden assisted two elderly women spread dripping on bread; today the church would provide soup and bread for about seventy men and women and children, a number that rarely changed in the small parish.

Sam collected bowls for washing up, given a broom to sweep the hall. Baden took him aside, his chores finished with the last of the crockery and cutlery packed away for tomorrow, Reverend Byrne long gone in his continual scavenger hunt throughout Parramatta.

"Where to now, Sam? Have to say you scrub up well."

"Sydney and join a ship."

"For a country lad from Balranald, that's odd. Do you know how to join a ship? Sit at the table, I have a treat for you."

"No, I don't know. Do you?"

"I've no idea. Suppose you might ask the captain. Advising people to go to sea never arose giving legal advice. Around the waterfront would be those who would know, seamen of course. I can give you the train fare to save the leather of your new boots."

Sam's face flared. "I couldn't."

"Money is simply paper and metal invented by man to maintain order, and because of its scarcity keep the poor in their place, labouring for the rich. Go join your ship, the future awaits you."

"By what I have seen on the road do you think there is a future?"

His face saddened. "My pessimism has infected you, sorry."

"Baden, thanks for bringing me here."

"Tea and a scone before you go, which puts you in a special category as not many who pass through here get offered such luxuries, and I will bore you about the future based on the past. I spoke earlier of illusion, but it is a little more complicated than that, this awful state of affairs affecting the world."

"Would I understand?"

"Probably not. None of us do really do, we surmise and pour out fancy words to make ourselves sound knowledgeable. We all live with our personal tales of woe how the world's financial system has failed us. Why has it failed mankind? Why indeed when the world of glitz and abundance spun on its axis in deep space at breakneck speed and created unimaginable wealth, mountains of money for a fully employed populace. Money in deep pockets to buy shining new automobiles, fancy gadgets, travel to exotic places. Buy new homes and all the luxuries society craved in this prosperous world. Factories with inventories bursting at the seams, pouring their productive smoke into the atmosphere twenty-four hours a day, seven days a week."

Sam took his cup of tea and scone from the smiling lady who earlier engaged Baden in conversation, thanked her and between sips of the strong and hot brew devoured the scone spread thickly with fig jam.

Baden ignored his scone but drank his tea, then with wry shake of his head pushed the treat in Sam's direction. "We keep hearing from many sources the worst of the Depression is over, or has peaked and from now on opportunities will arise to slash the unemployment rate from thirty to thirteen percent. We witness government fiscal policy to stir the financial system into life with major public works such as the Sydney Harbour Bridge, railway construction, roads, Sydney's subway system and dams.

"The bush might beg to differ that little has changed with probably a few less aimless men tramping the roads in search of work. For farmers cereal crops are not worth planting because of a small home market and exports to the United Kingdom nonexistent since 1930. The same with orchardists forced to watch their fruit rot on the trees because the average person can't afford to buy a single a pear or an apple. It can all be explained in simplistic terms, but to simplify a world plague is the heights of absurdity."

Sam ate Baden's scone self-consciously, savouring the seedy fig jam on his tongue. Baden's words filled his mind, embedding layer upon layer of new concepts, conflicting against conservative values forced into his mind by spinsterish schoolteachers, forging a new concept of beliefs. For the first time in his life he began to comprehend, gripped by a consuming desire to decipher one simple word. Why?

"Towards the end of 1929 a new federal government gained office and inherited a prosperous Australia with its markets to the United Kingdom assured. Were not we the food bowl of the United Kingdom? Did not our wool warm the bodies of the motherland in their harsh northern winters? Australia followed the lead of the United States in investment frenzy, this mad dash for wealth. People from navvies to board chairmen borrowed barrow loads of freely available money on low interest to buy more and more property and shares. Fortunes awaited the common man and woman in the street, entrepreneurs with flare and business acumen. Streets paved in gold? Wrong. Papered in money and share script.

"Prices for Australian made goods and produce began to fall from 1930 blamed on the ensuing melee caused by the collapse of the United States share market, followed by Europe. Someone somewhere called in a debt. Someone else wanted to withdraw funds from a bank and the flimsy structure began to teeter. The value of the pound plummeted and interest rates edged upwards putting a strain on those who to make their fortune borrowed to the hilt. Internal revenue collections fell and federal and state governments found it difficult to honour British loans negotiated in times of high tax returns. Default loomed, a fate inconceivable in the minds and hearts of a young nation joined by blood to its forebear.

"With barely time to write a withdrawal form after the stock market crashed in the United States the value of Australian shares fell into an abyss. A panicked run on the banks saw the black hole grow even deeper. Factories and services closed and unemployment spiked. Federal and state governments, not withstanding their debts negotiated in times of high tax returns, faced the real prospects of being unable to pay wages and pensions. Acting on advice from a higher echelon of society, the sinister and faceless moneyed class, the government cut wages and pensions which in effect made the financial crisis worse as a major source of circulated money within the community vanished. Thousands of desperate family breadwinners deserted the cities for the bush in search of work, any work no matter how poor paying or demeaning. Families faced the real prospect if not quite starving to death, one meal a day seemed a blessing of abundance.

"The system collapsed. Governments of all persuasions controlled by the moneyed class failed through either corruption or incompetence in not regulating the new order of greed endemic throughout the developed world. Those entrusted with high office ignored the warning signals that a world without foundations, created by illusion, would fail the test of time, closing their minds to a new disease swamping the nation, the worship of wealth. Australia, a land of full and plenty, shipbuilder, manufacturer, fertile plains, could not feed or clothe itself."

Sam finished his scone and drained his tea, his eyes wide with wonderment as Baden's words sunk into his mind. More followed.

"Australia burdened with a huge debt for public works underwritten by British financiers and the Bank of England, faced the distinct possibility of defaulting even after having savagely cut public works, wages and pensions. The federal Labor government, but not the government of Jack Lang, the Labor premier of New South Wales. From the floor of his personal fiefdom, the New South Wales parliament, Big Jack Lang condemned British usurers and legislated repayments to the United Kingdom be suspended until government revenues made restitution possible. The federal government viewed this rebellious act bordering on treason with shocked disbelief and paid New South Wale's public debt from the federal treasury, sinking the federal government even deeper into debt and more wage and pension cuts.

"Teetering on insolvency the federal government invited the governor of the Bank of England, Sir Otto Niemeyer, to a Melbourne meeting to advise all Australian state treasurers how to combat the world financial contagion. Sir Otto with no hesitation stated the federal and state governments must honour their debts to the United Kingdom. Without a single twinge of compassion for the suffering, he further recommended governments again cut wages and pensions, cancel all public expenditure and government departments balance their budgets, the agreement known as the Melbourne Plan.

"The Melbourne Plan opposed the New South Wales premier's plan, the Lang Plan, a spending policy to soften the blow of the Depression in the state. Lang even introduced a new pension of one pound a week for widows which came under immediate censure from opposition parties in the state parliament who damned the measly payment as encouraging sexually active widows to live in sin and not remarry. From the Sunday pulpits fire and brimstone rained down, fingers of damnation pointed at timid widows who now with sin money lining their pockets would openly fornicate and spurn the sacred vows of matrimony. Oh yes, the entire moral structure of the world teetered on the brink of anarchy, not by the debts of thousands of millions of pounds and dollars, but by a single pound note in a widow's apron pocket supporting a brood of hungry children."

Baden rose from the table and persuaded his lady friend to make Sam a tomato sandwich with leftover bread. Returning to the table, he sank down as if he carried a heavy burden.

"Sorry if I assault your young ears with my harangue, but it is not very often I get an audience I can corner with scones and a sandwich. My stomach churns when I think of this land of abundance stagnated by world affairs not of our doing. To listen to pompous political buffoons and their slavish loyalty to the United Kingdom who view us as cannon fodder and a cheap larder."

"Aren't we poor because of drought?"

"Sam, you need to read history to fill your mind with knowledge, learn of the men and women who forged our destiny. Then you can refute what I say, cut me down to size. Drought, if only it were that simple."

"Why would I argue against you?"

"Because each of us is gifted with a mind. Consider a newborn baby, its head lightly covered in down, eyes tightly shut, and nothing inside that soft little head except two survival instincts, the ability to cry and suckle. A vacuum waiting for us superior beings to cram with knowledge. Do you want to know what happened after the Melbourne Plan became the adopted policy of the federal and state governments?"

Intrigued, he nodded.

"The Lang Plan called for spending on major public works and the circulation of new money, millions and millions of pounds pumped into the New South Wales economy. Jack Lang committed to the financial overlords he would not repudiate state debt and guaranteed payment of interest until the economy recovered. He came under bitter assault from his own party in Canberra as well as all state premiers. So what happened to Jack Lang? The governor sacked him and his elected government, then the bitterest of pills, the man and woman in the street hungry and dressed in castoffs voted him out of office in a landslide. That's what happened to Jack Lang when he dared to challenge the British hierarchy, his punishment for such effrontery not from the monarchy or the Bank of England, his own people. We will starve before we repudiate our British debts! Our children can go to their beds at night with hunger and disease, but we as loyal citizens of the Crown will never falter in our pledge to repay every single penny of our British debts. We live in honourable penury."

"Poor people did this?" Sam said, amazed.

"While standing to attention in rags and barefooted, saluting a foreign flag. The people you met on the road, what did you notice of them?"

Sam shrugged. "There were those who fought among themselves, always ready to pick a fight. Many kept to themselves. Others were angry and spoke like you, but I took no notice, that is until now."

"Most of those on the road would be approaching their forties, right?"

"Many of them, yes."

"Those who rushed in their droves to the recruitment centres in 1914, overwhelmed by an all-consuming desire of patriotism to sign their names to fight for the British Empire."

Sam understood only parts of what Baden said, confused. "What do you mean? What has the war to do with being on the road looking for work?"

"Those men were promised by politicians swamped in flags and hoarse from victory speeches a prosperous post-war nation. Guarantees set in legislative concrete by the lawmakers exultant in victory of equality, justice and security as reward for sacrificing their youth. Many of those wretched men you shared the road with suffered unseen wounds. Men again separated from the home hearth, again fighting for their existence, but this time not on foreign soil but in their homeland."

Sam experienced a despondency of ignorance previously cushioned by childhood.

Baden offered his hand, the other with a silver coin to pay his train fare to Sydney. "Sam, there is something about you which tells me all I have said might not be wasted. Read and absorb and seek out among your fellows those who can guide you successfully along your chosen path. Let them lead you and fill your mind with ideals, but never allow them smother those that dwell within you. You are your own person. Good luck in whatever your choice of profession, for you I hope the sea."

3

SAM STARED WITH OPEN mouthed wonder at the train, even more astounded when he boarded and sat at a window seat and watched the platform slowly and silently under electric traction pass by on the command of a uniformed man with a green flag and the sharp shrill of a whistle. Amazing sight after sight flashed by his grimy window as the train sped through fields, over and under bridges, banked up traffic halted at gates, with firmly applied brakes stopping with what seemed reluctance at stations crowded with passengers.

With the city skyline emerging out of a haze in the east he glimpsed the grey steel arch of a modern engineering marvel, the vision obscured as the train passed through grimy inner city masonry, and finally Central Station.

Even more wonders as he felt himself becoming one with the surge of people disgorging through barriers at the end of multiple platforms attended by stern faced uniformed men. Tingling the nostrils the sulphurous smoke of steam locomotives at the head of country trains about to depart to every corner of the state, people forever rushing and dodging coupled barrows piled high with luggage. He at last found himself in brilliant sunshine, emerging from the cavernous depths of the railway station to stand at the top of the concourse leading to Eddy Ave and Belmore Park.

As if against his will he felt himself swept down the concrete forecourt with the flow of people, wonder after wonder as he experienced the throb of the city with its trams and cars and trucks all vying for right-of-way in the narrow streets. Raging through his mind a confusion of thoughts, assaulted from every direction by rushing people seemingly oblivious to the modern marvels of city living. Of even greater impact on his reeling senses, poverty so evident in the country in the city seemed not to exist.

Or maybe, another thought, the enormity of the city overwhelmed the despair prevalent in country towns, buried it under concrete and masonry, steel and glass, people forever on the move. The city must surely harbour people clad in rags who called home back lanes, doorways and alcoves. An underclass with all their worldly possessions and bedding on display to deter covetous eyes seeking territorial rights. With these thoughts he would need to find shelter for the night, search for a meal, an afterthought that sent a wave of excitement through his body, a ship.

When he asked directions to the waterfront he mostly received abrupt unintelligible mutters, one man even shoving him aside. On his fourth attempt he received a positive response: "What waterfront are you referring to?" He might have worked in an office, his suit coat frayed at the cuffs and trousers shiny with wear.

At a loss, Sam could only stare at him.

"Millers Point, Pyrmont, Darling Harbour, Dawes Point, Blackwattle Bay, Circular Quay, Woolloomooloo? Be specific, son." Even though his staccato voice carried a distinct edge of antagonism, the man showed enduring patience with the boy.

Trying to remember one of the names, he blurted: "Darling Harbour."

"Follow George St and turn left at King St. Keep walking and you'll eventually fall in the water."

He wanted to thank him, but the man with a dismissal wave of his hand hurried off. He left the wide thoroughfare of Railway Square and entered busy and narrow George St which divided from Pitt St like a tuning fork. City office buildings cast him in a pall of perpetual shadow; he continually bumped into people, apologising and willing himself to be self-assured and show maturity, not a gawking, bumbling country boy.

Unfamiliar and intimidating streets, soaring masonry, Hay St, Goulburn St, Liverpool St, Bathurst St, Druitt St, Market St, a dread he must have missed

King St, relieved when he saw it ahead and turned left to cross Sussex St filled with hotels. At Lime St he stopped; his destination reached and his feet rooted to the spot where he stood in wonder. To the north as far as the eye could see warehouses and bond stores, wharves protected by high fences and double gates, and rising above all a forest of derricks and masts, funnels painted in a myriad of colours and symbols. He smelled the air, coal smoke.

The constant noise of a busy waterfront assailed his senses; an army of men forever on the move pushing carts and wheeling barrows, trucks passing through wharf gates, the clattering of steam winches. The spectacle ignored as a young boy stared mesmerised at the ships, only the steel arch of the new bridge rising against the skyline to the north demanding of a second look.

In perfect symmetry the finger wharves followed the shoreline of the harbour abutting a high sandstone bluff, at its base a broad thoroughfare of commerce, every wharf with a ship berthed alongside. Some flew a small Australian flag from their foremasts, the starboard halyard, others did not and this puzzled him. Later he would learn those that did not fly the courtesy flag were Australian registered, the other foreign, predominantly British.

To avoid the congestion Sam kept close to the bluff, even so failing to avoid making contact with others who either ignored him or muttered abuse. Among the hectic activity large groups of idle men gathered, sullen faced and silent. When a man dressed in a suit and bowler hat approached their eyes brighten, bodies stiffening to attention. Older men hid grey hair under their hats, flexed their shoulders and arms to give a message of fluidity of limbs. Most carried their tools of trade, hooks. The foreman with an air of aloof detachment referred to a clipboard, then pointed to those fortunate for afternoon shift selection.

Mustering his courage he left the relative protection of the bluff and approached the nearest wharf gate, two ships berthed opposite each other working cargo. An anchor hung from the hawse pipe of one of the ships, a streak of bleeding rust where it housed, her name also in need of touching up with white paint: *Macuba*. Though when he looked closer through the wire mesh fence her white superstructure shone with fresh white paint as did the two white bands on her tall black funnel. The warehouse and bond store where her general cargo disappeared into, painted in large white letters edged in black across its façade: AUSN.

The ship opposite with similar funnel colours and banding belonged to the same company, her funnel though in need of painting, the name on her bow *Mildura*. Huge ships with their derricks plumbed for cargo, the sound of their steam winches reverberating between the finger wharves.

Sam marvelled how seamen could get such heavy ropes so taut, wire breasts and backsprings bar tight. How could seamen climb masts so tall, although obviously with ladders abaft the masts seamen did? As he looked, his fingers hooked through the wire mesh of the fence, despair suddenly gripped him. Who would want a boy from the country on a ship? Secondary though to his immediate need, finding shelter.

Retreating across the road he climbed the Argyll Cut, a set of steep and narrow iron steps bolted into the weathered sandstone to reach another road running parallel to the wharf precinct. From this height he could see the entire harbour across to Pyrmont and Balmain, north to Millers Point. From his vantage point he could see all the ships berthed in Darling Harbour. Ships with different funnels than the *Macuba* and *Mildura*; one ship stood out with an exceptionally tall funnel, blue for three quarters of its length, the top quarter black; the name on her starboard bow *Rhesus*. On her stern flew the red duster and her pristine white paintwork glowed in the fading afternoon light.

Ships working cargo were berthed across the harbour at Pyrmont Bay, more now than a few years ago when the United Kingdom found it difficult sustaining its population in the ever tightening grip of the Depression. So it might be true, the financial crisis receding from its peak, the wharves of Sydney proving it. Hunger gnawed, his subconscious mind moving his feet with no sense of direction; Argyle St, adjoining streets narrow, crowded with tenements with their front doors separated from the gutter by a three foot wide footpath.

Hopelessly lost he saw a hotel on the corner, another down the street. To eat he could beg, but people passing in the street were as poor as he. Even making eye contact to portray an image of desperation and trigger a response of generosity impossible when those who brushed by did so with heads lowered; even a young boy became an object of suspicion and to be avoided. Hold out his hand for sixpence to buy a half loaf of bread, bread still warm from the oven, washed down with milk. Water would suffice, ahead a small park which would have a drinking fountain. Its band rotunda offered shelter for the night, and even if the heavy bank of dark clouds in the west brought rain he would at least be dry and warm with his cardigan and blanket.

Boisterous and jovial, staggering in the general direction of the Argyll Cut, two incredibly ugly men clung on the arms of two equally inebriated women whose long faded beauty hid behind layered makeup and fire red lips. One of the men, short and portly, a white cap perched on a mop of red hair, dressed in baggy blue dungarees and shirt, led his mate in a babbling rendition of some song with lyrics garbled in a haze of alcohol.

His singing became even more muddled, the reason either because of his disfigured mouth or because he considered suckling the thick folds of wrinkled neck flesh of his giggling, squirming companion more enjoyable. Sam stared at him, amazed at a disjointed jaw pulped when a lowering quarter block and span parted company with its gantline and the unfortunate man below never heard the panicked scream of *stand from under!* A master with delusions of medical prowess attempted to redefine the face, the ship in mid-Atlantic and weeks from port, failing dismally and leaving a speech impaired and grotesque creature to a fate of terrifying small children.

How the men were dressed caught Sam's attention, their swagger made even more pronounced by their large consumption of alcohol. He thought high spirited seamen with money in their pockets ashore from a long voyage, in company with their waterfront girls, women of dubious morals but hearts of gold. In reality not so young waterfront strumpets and the portals for many a seaman who climbed the iron stairs of the Argyle Cut to The Rocks in search of feminine company. Both probably past fifty, happy souls in their cups with not a care in the world.

The slightly more intelligible songster, though normally not an object of fear for small children, did cause some ill mannered people to look twice and give thanks for their own meagre looks. A perfectly round red face, button nose and one large ear, the other lost in a bar in South America; visible under his white cap a bristle of wiry grey hair. His love forgot to wear her eye patch, an empty socket no doubt the result of a ridge of old scar tissue marring her right cheek. Her friend, all parts intact, simply succumbed to passing years with flab, a broad rear and unruly hair like a rat's nest dyed black.

Hugh Golledge and Cliff Surtees put no credence on feminine allure or looks in their consorts, true love found in the dark reaches of the ladies lounge in the Lord Nelson Hotel. There were other more stimulating matters on both their minds heading in the general direction of their ship berthed at the Melbourne Steamship Company's wharf in Darling Harbour.

Sam nervously approached them and found his voice: "Excuse me, but are you on the ships?"

Hugh rolled to a halt, caught in mid-verse of a new mindless warble. Spokesman for the group, he chortled: "We on the ships, Cliffy?"

"We ain't on two ships," Cliff slurred through a wet flap of mouth and overhang of jaw, using his companion to steady himself. "We is on one, the *Coolana*, bastard of a job with a mate who dropped out of a camel's arse and a skipper begat from the scrotum of a mangy dog."

"Too right," Hugh agreed. "Why are you asking, going to rob us, son? Should have done that before we went to the pub."

Hugh's woman peered closer at Sam, squinting and tilting her head in her most coquettish pose. "He's a bit of a dish this boy, Hugh. Think yourself lucky you've won me or I'd be tempted to sample a bit of young stuff."

"Fucking hell, Polly! You ain't, you're heading straight for the sack after me priming you with a gallon of gin. Christ, gal, where the fuck do you and Bess put it? I just hope it ain't that big."

"How can I go to sea?" Sam said. "Can you help me?"

Hugh stiffened to his full height of five foot four inches and fiddled with his one ear; shoulders thrown back he looked like an obese emperor penguin. "You'd have to see the captain for that."

"How?"

"How what, boy?"

"Get on the ship?" Sam said, then in desperation as he failed in his search for the right words: "Climb the ship."

"Jesus Christ, you hear that, Cliffy? Son, you don't climb ships. You fall up ships gangways like me and Cliffy do most times. Tonight though we'll follow close behind these two lovelies so we can look up their clackers."

Cliff steadied himself, drool streaming down his chin. "Huddart Parker's got a ship alongside. Fucking arseholes!"

"Are Huddart Parker bad people to work for?"

"Hugh here will agree with me about those bastards, up to no good. Union's right wary of them. Want a job with that lot go stand outside their gate tomorrow, got a ship in port."

"If I do will I get a job as a seaman?"

"Might aim a bit higher, son, captain or chief engineer. Don't need much up top to be one of them." Hugh in his stupor noticed the women were amused at his baiting the young boy, himself not overly displeased with the diversion in servicing Polly in the damp and musty smelling steel box he shared with Cliff and two others. He needed a bit of a breather for the booze to wear off and get it hard enough, though remembering Polly last trip he needed to be hung like an aroused steer to even feel the sides. He bunched her dress from behind and an exploratory finger found an alternative target and she let out a shrill cry. Pleased with his preliminary foreplay, he advised Sam: "Cliffy's right, there's one of Huddart Parker's alongside, I think the *Colac*."

"Could I be a captain or chief engineer?"

Hugh's rogue finger again probed Polly's rectum, his foray this time receiving a squirm and a giggle. "Depends on what did you do before you got the urge to go to sea."

"Worked on my father's farm in the country. Balranald."

"Fucking hayseed," Hugh said with a grimace; buoyed by success he dug deeper, thwarted by her tightened buttocks. "Reckon we should lower our sights a bit here. What about cabin boy?"

"No, I want to be a seaman."

"Deck boy?"

"What's deck boy?"

"About on the level with a bilge rat or a maggot. Go stand humbly at the Huddart Parker wharf gate early in the morning. Who knows, might need a deck boy. Christ, where the fuck's Balranald?"

"West, hundreds of miles."

"The poor boy has an urge to go to sea? Isn't that sweet," Polly cooed.

"Wouldn't send me worst enemy to sea," Hugh said.

"You're at sea, and Cliffy."

"Yeah, but me and Cliffy were bred to it. How did you get here, son?"

"Walked."

"Hundreds of miles?"

"Were you looking for work, poor darling?" Polly's roused motherly instincts and smile lessened the impact of heavy facial lines, though offset by recently applied lipstick which missed its intended target, transforming her lips into a fire red gash.

"Stronger and more desperate men than me got the jobs that were available, those jobs not much anyway. I just wanted to get to Sydney, go to sea."

"Have you any money, dearest?" Polly persisted, puckering her grotesque lips.

He shook his head.

"Give the poor boy some money, Hugh."

"How generous we are with my money, sweet dumpling. Want to know something, that gallon of gin you got stored between your legs took all my money!"

Polly swung her attention to Cliff on the verge of nodding off. "Cliff?"

Bleary-eyed, he shook his head.

"Hugh, you big mean dear thing. You have some loose change in your pocket, I heard it."

He reluctantly offered Sam some coins, two glistening silver. "The last of me money! I'm in the poorhouse thanks to you, Polly."

Whether pride or embarrassment in the company of seamen he did not know, but he felt reluctance to take the money. Thankful for the advice, yes, but receiving alms from those he hoped one day to emulate, no. Hugh might have read the indecision in the boy's eyes, shoving the money at him.

"Lord Nelson's got dinner for under a bob and well worth it. Hear from the locals the beef stew will keep a starving man going for days." Though a slight exaggeration even for hard times, the Lord Nelson Hotel's fare of beef stew and potatoes and a large chunk of bread did fill quite a large hole in a hungry belly.

Sam watched the foursome stagger down the street, street lights flickering on; the earlier threat of rain petering out to sea and hopes of a dry and mild night in the band rotunda caused his morale to soar. Even more so when he thought of beef stew and potatoes he would buy with his newfound wealth.

Seamen's money!

4

A MORNING SUN IN a blue and hazy sky rimmed the tops of city buildings in a blaze of light, their glass and masonry flanks anchored in concrete still bathed in the greyness of early dawn light. Confidence filled him as he doused his face in a washbasin in the park lavatory, cleaning his teeth with salt he carried in a tobacco tin. Ignoring the rumblings in his belly he hurried down the Argyle Cut steps to join the early morning maritime bustle, searching for the Huddart Parker wharf.

He found what he sought, slowing his pace and regulating his breathing; relax, be confident, a young man willing to learn and eager to work. Impregnable warehouses and bond stores occupied most of the timber planked decking of the wharves stretching the full length of Darling Harbour. Interstate and overseas cargoes loaded and landed in nets and slings, bales and boxes, barely a cleared space between secured and protective storage and wharf aprons.

Gangs of wharf labourers worked the *Colac* with hooks, trolleys, barrows, handcarts, a constant eye for prowling foremen who in an instance and without challenge could terminate a man for slacking. Replaced by one of a large pool of desperate men still waiting hopefully by the gate overlooked in the morning pickup. Who like themselves willing to work their hands bloodied and raw, toil mindlessly to impress their overseers. Who could have their shifts extended without notice, sometimes upwards of twenty-four hours with no sustenance.

Proud men suppressed by the system and a union decimated from endless confrontation. Here on the Sydney waterfront the shipowner and his foul mouthed standover henchmen ruled with iron fists, the worse threat of all, blacklisting. Hundreds of men daily swarmed around the waterfront gates of the shipping companies, begging for work. Chosen like cattle in a saleyard, herded into three distinct labouring groups according to where a man lived; foreign, interstate and local.

With the day's allocation of labour picked up another group of men began to congregate by the wharf gate. Sam moved closer to them, possibly seamen he thought because among their number some were dressed like Hugh and Cliff in pale blue denim and white caps. He counted twenty, another nine standing apart aloof from the main group; firemen, trimmers and greasers.

He found it impossible to keep his attention focused, one new revelation after another, his eyes though continually drawn to the ship and the teeming multitude of labouring men who invaded her. On the wharf, on her decks, the rattle of winches and the whipping sound of wire under tension. Her starboard anchor and a dozen links of cable hung from her rust streaked bow above faded boot topping, Roman numeral draft figures barely readable. Even her name which she should have bore proudly in white paint reflected neglect in difficult financial times.

The ship's immensity staggered him, its three island construction; focastle head, bridge and poop. Slabs and tarpaulins maintained watertight integrity, No.1 and No.2 hatches in the forward welldeck, No.3 and No.4 likewise aft. The hatches serviced by single sets of five ton union purchase gear, the gear rigged with chain and span to the foremast and mainmast from which rose exceptionally high topmasts.

The poop, due to union resistance to open focastles, accommodated twenty-one deck and engine room ratings in four berth cabins, two bathrooms, two messrooms, the accommodation accessed by narrow alleyways and steep companionways. Well-found accommodation suitable for uncertified ranks and considered by management in shipping circles as sumptuous pampering. With no more space available within the claustrophobic confines of the poop with its tiny portholes, exposed overhead pipes, low deckheads and concrete decks, marine architects pondered where to put the heads for twenty-one men. Ignoring the fact of extreme weather and exposure, a dash from the steamy warmth of the accommodation, agreeing a narrow deckhouse with the capability of satisfying the bodily functions of three men at a time either side of the poop with direct discharge over the side.

Wind howling around the curvature of the poop and quartering seas proved folly this solution with raw sewerage caught in updrafts splattering the accommodation block, a task of the deck boy before greasing the rod and chain steering gear and relieving tackle to wash down the cable trays clogged with faeces.

Befitting their status in the structure of responsibility the bosun and donkeyman accommodated amidships with the officers, engineers and catering, their tiny cabin overlooking the after welldeck.

Chaos seemed to reign on the ship and wharf confines, this far from fact as the labour force worked under the rigid supervision of foremen stevedores who with a glance could send a man into panic. Slacking punishable by instant dismissal, severe reprimands for a hand in a pocket, even a brief respite for an aching back sitting on a sling of potatoes waiting for the hook cause for a finger indicating termination.

Sam noticed one man in particular, aloof from the turmoil about him; mid-twenties, tall and bareheaded, a shock of fair hair. He condescended to wear a suit but left the top button of his shirt undone, his crumpled tie loosely knotted. Clean shaven Sam thought him cocky, a mischievous grin never far from his face; he approached him shyly, nervously fumbling with his blanket folded over his schoolbag.

"Take that to school for your afternoon nap?"

Sam hunched his shoulders, lowering his head near overcome by a feeling of inadequacy. "I want a job, but I don't know how."

"You would have to be a first trip deck boy, right?" The threatening smile broke on his face.

"I don't even know what a deck boy is."

"Super sailors will never admit it, excluding matelots, we all start as deck boys. I'm Charley Kirk. You're not from around here, what I mean Balmain, Rozelle or Millers Point, those prolific breeding grounds of seamen."

"Balranald. My name's Sam Wright."

"Then, Sam Wright from Balranald, prepare yourself for the waiting game." Charley drew a pocket watch from his pocket and studied it at arm's length. "Normally if there are jobs the master will make his illustrious presence known by 9:00am, but it's well past that now so either he is late, still servicing his tiger, logging someone, drunk in his bunk, or there are no jobs."

"Do you know if there are jobs?"

"Those paying off are usually pretty boisterous about it in the pubs hard times or not, the way of seamen who get it in their heads to throw their hands in. Though being on the Sydney Hobart run most tend to extend their stay on the old heap of shit. Did hear along the traps there might be a job in her, better than the *Mildura* and *Macuba* a few wharves up. Full of AUSN bulls and others of suspect character. Melbourne Steamship's *Coolana* is a horror, and if she's doing a survey or painting masts her old timers go on leave."

"AUSN?"

"Australian United Steam Navigation. On the threshold of a seagoing career are you considering coastal or deep sea?"

"What is deep sea?"

"Well, the waters around the Australian coast are quite deep, by deep sea I man foreign-going. Though with the gift of our Commonwealth Shipping Line to our British competition, shipping out deep sea is now almost nonexistent."

"I never thought about leaving Australia."

"Then don't because all you'll get from British shipowners is slow starvation and endless work for pennies. Learn your profession on the Australian coast and get decently paid for it as well as fed, above all the protection of the union. You know what a union is?"

"I heard talk of unions on the road, good and bad ones."

"Federated Seamen's Union of Australasia, none stronger or more militant. Its resilience proved by being and able to drag itself out of the mire of defeat in 1927. Held in dread by the black hearts of shipowners and their toadies."

"Would I be able to join the union?"

A wry smile spread over Charley's face. "Yes, I would strongly advise you join the union. If not your career at sea might well be exceptionally brief, maybe the fate given those who differed from the union in 1927. We still have remnants of those men within our ranks, though their number fewer owing to being invalided out of the industry for a number of unfortunate accidents at sea and on the wharf."

Striding with purpose an elderly man in a navy blue suit and black tie emerged from the milling workers on the wharf, causing Charley to remark cynically: "That gentleman might well be the master of the *Colac*. A man with an eye for a feather in a hatband, a newspaper folded under an arm, a handkerchief in a lapel pocket, other visible means of identifying a man recommended from a higher order for the job. I see obvious signs among us which can be defined as drawing notice to one's presence amongst these hopefuls so this could be quick."

Charley's prediction proved correct.

Captain Harold Finch completed the business of selecting an AB, an old hand with a copy of the *Sydney Morning Herald* folded under his right arm. The master likened the selection process to a cattle market, though with long experience able to pick the ruffian or habitual slacker from the hardworking seaman. Today differed a little with the chief and second engineers occupied with vital engine room duties, his deputising for their responsibility enough to peeve.

"Engine room ratings form a line." He ran a disapproving eye over four men who stepped out of their group.

"One trimmer for the *Colac*," Captain Finch said distastefully, not overly impressed with what offered for employment. "Stand closer in line there you lot." An experienced nose twitched for the sour tang of alcohol saturated breaths, instantly dismissing those with bloodshot eyes, tremors, and faces blotched with liver spots. His choice made he paused with a cursory glance at a young boy with a school bag and blanket. "Deck boy?"

Sam's heart pounded, struck dumb!

Charley shoved Sam so he stumbled three steps forward. "Here, Captain, you got yourself a first tripper from Balranald with straw still stuck in its hair."

Captain Finch thought it probably more prudent to wait a few days, the ship not due to sail until the weekend, a chance of signing on a deck boy with a discharge.

"Strong lad, Captain," Charley persisted. "Breed them tough in the bush. Work them from dawn until dark, good value for the mate."

Captain Finch relented. "Name?"

Sam choked, replying in a croak: "Sam Wright."

Sam Wright, sir, would have been more appropriate, he thought, but then what could one expect from the lower orders. "Wright, present yourself to the mercantile marine office to sign on. You will of course be obliged to be medically examined."

"Where is the mercantile marine office?"

"If you can't find it you're of no use to me or the ship." He glanced witheringly at Charley. "Whoever you are, point the boy to the shipping office." The commencement of his day close to being ruined by his association with this surly mob loitering outside his company's gate, he imagined more pleasant thoughts such as sampling the Sydney manager's fine old Scotch he kept in a cabinet in his office, though he held suspicions the crafty old devil of late to save company money watered down the elixir.

Sam looked at Charley desperately.

"Millers Point, under the bridge. There are some fossils of a mind the whole thing will fall down in a year and be the demise of the shipping office, or its more official name, the mercantile marine office."

"The man said a medical examination."

"Lesson one, that man is not a man, he is the ship's master and never forget it. Off with you, lad, destiny awaits you."

"What of you?"

"Nothing doing here, maybe the *Mernoo* due this afternoon next to the *Coolana* at the Melbourne Steamship Company wharf."

≈

Sam's medical examination arranged by a clerk in the shipping office consisted of a cough, a cursory glance down his throat, a cold stethoscope on his chest, medical history of any past life threatening diseases and a request to read the bottom line of a Snellen chart on the wall. His wiry but strong frame might prove to be of use for a shipowner extracting the maximum of labour for the least sustenance. The doctor thought nervous and possibly a little backward, but suitable for employment at sea.

Buoyed by passing his medical, his return to the shipping office quickly dissipated any newfound confidence in the musty reality of officialdom, the power and authority and discipline vested in the articles of agreement opened on the counter. Clause after clause of punishment and enforced order, the master's supreme authority and sustenance measured by pint and pound. The marine superintendent at times intoned the articles of agreement to seamen, the dull monotone meaningless to those hardened to officialdom, for a first trip deck boy signing his name to the articles, a tremulous occasion.

At last free of officialdom a sense of euphoria filled him as he strode the streets of The Rocks with his shoulders thrown back. If anyone stopped him he could proudly boast the name of his ship and that he, Sam Wright, signed on as deck boy. He even thought a young girl probably playing truant glanced at him and smiled, though he could have imagined it. He would give his blanket to the bearded old man clothed in tatters stretched on a park bench close to the rotunda, the derelict's home. Not his schoolbag though, that he would keep for his personal papers and most importantly his discharges needed to count his sea time along the pathway to becoming a master.

Taking the steps of the Argyle Cut three at a time and entering the wharf precinct, he headed for the Huddart Parker wharf, the gate now his to enter as a seaman on the *Colac*.

As if silken rope with teased tassels for the delicate hands of regal personage, he gripped the grimy manila manrope rove through the bottom stanchion of the gangway, then placed his foot on the lower platform. Even with the rusted thimble loose in the seized eye, the tail frayed, mattered not as he looked up the steep gangway. Every so often his foot would catch on a loose tread, stumble but never impeding his momentum ever upwards.

Rubbish and old newspapers and a distinct smell of oil and coal smoke, a dank cloying odour emitting from an open door beside a tarpaulin covered small hatch, the fiddley and starboard bunker pocket. Where to find the chief officer and report for duty?

He reminded him of a fierce and intimidating animal tensioned to spring into furious action, his confidence fleeing as he dared to look in the man's challenging face; a seaman dressed in baggy blue dungarees and sleeveless grey flannel from which sprouted a thatch of grey hair, the same hair that filled a greasy once white cap on his gruesome face. Scarred and brutal, the recipient of ruthless punishment over its fifty odd years, gnarled fists evidence of giving as much as the lean body received.

Paddy Fenton thrust his face close to Sam's. "Are you who I think you are?" he growled, his voice like coarse gravel underfoot. "With a schoolbag? Good Christ!"

Sam swallowed forcefully, wondering if he should offer his hand.

With a curl of his lips the bosun looked the pitiful creature up and down, his expression no more contemptuous than if something offensive clung to his boot. "Where's your working gear?"

"I haven't any."

"Then you'll work in what you stand up in. Where it will rot off your scrawny back, fouled with rat shit from the bilges, wire rope oil and grease in the winch beds."

He knew instinctively he must show no weakness. "In the shipping office the man said I should report to the chief officer."

"What the hell would he know? You report to me, not the mate, you hear plainly!" His growl became even more deep throated and menacing. "Mate's got nothing to do with whelps like you! You answer to the bosun and the delegates. Me who shoves your head down bilges, sends you squealing like a little girl aloft. You make my bunk and you clean my cabin. You draw the mob's stores and kits from the galley. Scrub with sand and canvas the messroom tables until your hands bleed, no sympathy as you dig out winch beds, scale rust in the chain locker, vomit down a bilge. You will never open your mouth to complain or talk back because I have a big boot which will fit nice and snug up your arse. Understand?"

Sam nodded, feeling his façade of strength crumbling.

"Now I made mention of the delegates, both who will want to have a word or two with you, to set you straight on a number of matters, the first being on articles you don't count. There is no one lower than you except if we are wet nursing an apprentice, and as such you will remain if you haven't run crying to your mother until you become an ordinary seaman, even then most of them are still useless on deck."

He could only stare at the deck.

"Go aft and find your cabin. Starboard side top bunk. When you do and have claimed it with your school bag, come forward to me."

"Starboard and forward?"

Paddy jabbed a finger aft, then forward. "Make it fast and watch your step."

Advice well given as he negotiated a steep ladder accessing the after welldeck, cautiously edging sideways through a narrow passageway between hatch slabs, landed beams and the coamings. Four winches being driven with full heads of steam deafened, whipping runners and the metallic clang of hook and monkey face slamming into the coamings discharging wire banded Tasmanian hardwood stowed in the wings, its pungent odour of weeping sap tingling to the nose.

A portly hatch man at No.4 hatch with a sweat stained felt hat pulled down over his ears blocked his progress, glaring at the nervous young boy whose eyes implored to grant him passage. He did so begrudgingly, irked at having to squeeze his large belly against the coamings to allow Sam room to pass, and then climb another ladder with badly warped handrails to the poop.

Stepping over a high stormstep he entered a sour smelling subterranean world. A steep companionway disappeared into a twilight void, a hacking cough and the shuffling of heavy stokehold boots proof the space inhabited by humans. A man emerged from below in grimy dungarees and sleeveless shirt, a sweat rag knotted around his throat and another formed with four knots for a cap. He brushed past Sam without a word, a trimmer.

In this cramped space formed by the counter stern the crew slept, ate and bathed; seamen, firemen, trimmers, greasers, ordinary seaman and deck boy. Sam found a starboard cabin with a top bunk unmade, folded linen at its foot. Between the double bunks two dressers and two double door metal lockers, on the concrete deck a coir mat.

On one of the dressers the photo of a young girl and something else that imprinted in his mind, a pound note heaped with silver. There for the taking or did this symbolise trust in the honesty of fellow shipmates? The formidable bosun said he wanted him back on deck as soon as he found his cabin, but he could wait; he needed to try his bunk and climbing a steel four rung ladder at the foot he stretched full length.

Four inches from his nose a six inch pipe with an inspection elbow joined another of larger diameter, a few inches above that the deckhead sprayed with cork insulation. Touching it his fingertip came away damp and he noticed patches of black mould. The foam mattress contoured around his body, for warmth a blue dyed sheet counterpane and a thin army surplus blanket, for privacy a bunk curtain. Light filtered through a small porthole with the deadlight resting on its dogs obscuring most of the natural light.

Aft and a clear division of deck and engine room cabins were two tiny bathrooms with shower cubicles barely the width of a man's shoulders, hand basins and metal tubs fitted with steam pipes. Serrated tiles on the deck, some missing and others cracked, exposed slimy concrete beneath. Overhead pipes with leaking flanges, loose lagging and electrical cable clamped to deckheads permanently beaded with condensation, prevalent the musty smell of slow running wastes.

Sam found the bosun talking to two men at the after end of No.2 hatch marrying a new runner to an old mangled in the gear cogs of the winch due to riding turns, the occasional frosty glance at the winch driver enjoying an enforced break.

"Lad, I'd send you forward for a bucket of fish oil and a wad, but I got this feeling you're so dumb you haven't your white card or you would have shown it," the bosun rasped. "The union rooms are not far up the road, get confused ask someone. Tell them who you are and you're there for your white card. Prove to be a village idiot and the delegates will have severe reservations signing it when your month's up."

Finished marrying the runners with seizing wire, one of the men signalled the winch driver to heave slowly. "Us two will be signing it so don't take the bosun's words lightly. I'm Wilfred Birch."

Sam shook his hand, a man of slight build but with an aura of strength and reliability in his weathered face; mid-thirties, dressed in paint splattered dungarees and grimy white singlet, a deck knife sheaved on his belt. His mate clearing the new runner flaked over hatch slabs and beams as it slowly rose with its married partner to run freely through the gyn block introduced himself, Raymond Murray.

"There may be a solution to your lack of working gear, son," Paddy said, a little less aggravation in his voice, his attention on the old runner being run off from the winch barrel, a deep mistrust of shore winch drivers. "When that idiot deck boy Rufus bolted before I got my hands on him I reckon he might have left gear in the drying room. I'll check. Go get your white card. Something else, you got a habit of sneaking in pubs making out you're a man forget it. Get caught in a pub and you're down the gangway."

≈

His heart beat faster as he stepped into the dark and narrow foyer of the Federated Seamen's Union of Australasia's office in Sussex St. Even the momentous occasion of putting his signature to the articles of agreement earlier in the day paled in the dingy confines of this office. A sense that in this place men of the same calling joined minds and purpose and became a single voice, not always agreeing but the vibrant force of strength.

Five men on the other side of the counter stared at him, not challenging but more of annoyance at his intrusion breaking their conversation. Men who wielded authority, he thought, maybe delegates like Wilbur and Raymond. Men whom his father reviled; Sam felt he should feel similar repulsion, a dominant father's influence implanting in a pliable young mind a virulent condemnation of unionism likened to a pestilence upon the land. Especially the malignant shearers union who demanded with threats and thuggery excessive high wages and conditions squatters could ill afford even in good times.

Though he and his family struggled to survive like most small farmers in the district, Nathanial Wright's eyes would reduce to pinpoints, his face drain of blood at the mention of the word union. Working conditions demanded from the farm gate for silk sheets and hot water baths. Three course meals served on fine bone China, paid time off for delegates on union business and compensation for malingerers. Unions! A hell put on this earth to crush the initiative of hardworking men to negotiate with their employer.

The men returned to their conversation, one coming to the counter. "Yes?"

"My name is Sam Wright," he said nervously. "I am deck boy on the *Colac* and have been sent by the delegates for my white card."

The man planted both hands on the worn and scarred counter. "Have the delegates informed you the importance of your white card, that you will be on a month's probation and if found unsuitable you will be denied membership? You are only young, but have you belonged to a union before?"

"No."

"Father?"

Sam made a courageous decision, he told the truth. "My father spoke bad things about unions. I never believed him because I saw the large landowners in Balranald living in grand houses, driving cars and wearing fine clothes. Shearers and labourers dressed like me by their gates asking for work. I knew my father wrong."

The man folded his hands across his chest. "Well said, son. In a month's time I hope we welcome you into the union."

Only when hurrying up Sussex St did Sam look at his precious white card and the signature: *C. Herbert*: Sydney Branch Secretary. Federated Seamen's Union of Australasia.

5

TRUE TO HIS WORD the bosun left a pair of split at the knees and poorly washed dungarees, woollen check shirt, singlet and a holed pair of socks on his bunk, the last deck boy's abandoned gear in the drying room. Sam returned to the ship at 5:00pm; Percy Cox, the reluctant ordinary seaman impressed by the bosun into the role of peggy, carried three tea towel wrapped kits from the amidships galley. With a smirk he relinquished his task to its rightful heir, instructions for the deck boy to strap up after the AB pigs finished scoffing, him with better things to do like servicing a bit skirt up the road.

The messroom smelled of hot food and fresh coffee brewing in a steam percolator. Pork chops, boiled potatoes and broad beans. Did he have to pay for this sumptuous feast? Percy, stuffing a whole potato down his throat followed by a chunk of bread plastered with butter, couldn't let the opportunity pass; chief steward lives amidships and he's the bloke to see, and of course if you're broke he'll strap it up until payday. Or ask the captain now having his dinner in the saloon for a sub.

Wilbur put an end to the prank, choosing a less fatty pork chop, two boiled potatoes and a spoonful of broad beans. "Listen to one word from the bucko and you'll end up a moron with the attention span of a stick insect. Paddy's given up trying to find a brain in its head."

Percy's oafish grin exposed a broad gap of two missing front teeth; Wilbur's voice held no rancour, closer to affection; he saw the slavish expression in Sam's face and advised: "Make sure you leave some for your shipmates."

Sam met his three cabin mates; ABs Ben Putney and Roy Bow both twelve to four watch, AB Uriah Reid, four to eight watch. "You, my lad, are a day worker and we are watchkeepers which means one simple word, quiet," Uriah said. "Tiptoes and no slammed drawers, understand?"

He didn't. "We all work different times?"

"Those keeping watches do," Uriah said with great patience.

"Watching what?"

"Lookouts and steering. On call and general duties during daylight hours."

"Seamen steer the ship?"

Uriah sighed. "Yes, seamen steer the ship, not the captain. We take the helm entering and leaving port. Seamen do lookouts on the wing of the bridge or monkey island, some the focastle head and even the crow's nest."

Sam with a multitude of questions received a weary rebuke from an AB with working gear to scrub on the deck with a hard bristle brush and sandsoap. "Son, you are now part of a distinct world with little relevance to ashore. Everything onboard has its own name and place in the maritime scheme of things. Ships are self-sufficient and demanding, unforgiving of those who ignore the dangers of the marine environment. Wholly self-sustaining and giving succour to those who sail in her. Put in simple terms, a ship never rests and at any given time those who serve her will be on duty."

"How can I learn all that?"

"Prove to be a twin of idiot Percy and you won't. Simple advice, watch, listen, learn, support your mate and get your hands dirty. Seamanship is a craft passed down by seamen like Paddy, a top seaman, a good man and a clean past."

"Clean past?"

"Paddy has nothing to hide from 1927."

"1927?"

"Scabs." Uriah yawned, not relishing the hands and knees ritual of scouring his working gear. "Time later to learn what a blackleg is because unfortunately you'll come across a few and be exposed to their vitriol, that's those who haven't slunk away and hid the yellow streak up their spines."

Sam desperately wanted to learn more. "Is a scab a man who went against the union?"

"Who deserted his fellow workers and sided with the shipowners. Let me give you some advice, in the future you may not agree with the union and if so make your voice heard loud and clear. Stand to be recognised, but if your comrades vote in the majority you take your position at their side."

"Blacklegs don't do that?"

"Blacklegs receive crumbs tossed them by shipowners while striking unionists and their families starve and have their chattels thrown in the street by landlords. Unfortunately our union still has remnants of such vermin."

≈

Paddy allocated Percy to show Sam his morning duties from 7:00am to 10:00am. With a small wooden box and accompanied by a trimmer, Percy swaggering and boasting of his latest conquest, Sam drew two tins of condensed milk, two loaves of bread, one tin jam, two pounds of butter, sugar, dry tea and a four pound block of cheddar cheese from the miserly looking chief steward.

Three wooden messroom tables became a point of interest as Percy thumped down a bucket of sand and a wad of canvas. "Bloody ABs will kick your arse if it doesn't gleam white. Paddy wore out a good pair of boots kicking the last deck boy up the rear end. Hey, I tell you me sheila went down on me. Could hear this stud hollowing like a rooting bull from the ship. Bitch lives just up the road near the pub."

Sam heard such boasts many times on the road. He would need to fill a bucket with water, stopped when Percy shook his head. "First you've got to make the bosun's bunk and make it his way or else get a kick up the clacker."

"Is there a special way of making a bed at sea?" Sam frowned, puzzled.

"Course there is. Just as well the mate reckons I'm the best seaman on the ship and can show you so saving your first trip rump from Paddy's size fourteen boot."

"You know the size of the bosun's boot?"

"Cranky old bastard. Wouldn't be game to kick this bloke's rear, can tell you that."

"Where you from, Percy?"

"Balmain, mate. Breed 'em tough there."

"Tougher than Paddy?"

"Puh! Wouldn't stand a chance against me old man and uncles. Any of them joined this ship Paddy would bolt."

The bosun and donkeyman's double berth cabin and petty officer status afforded them the comfort of a narrow settee, dresser and duel wardrobe. Percy pointed at a wire basket. "That's got to be emptied every day on the lee side. Know where the lee side is?"

"I thought the only sides were port and starboard."

"Nah, there's lee and weather. Just watch where the pansy steward throws the officers shit and go on the other side. Ain't got a clue that poof, always the weather side. Just make certain you go to the lee side or it's the bosun's boot, mate."

"How do I make his bed? What about the other one?"

"Bunk, mate. Christ, bloody first trippers. Making the donkeyman's bunk is breaking down the deck boys award, let him make his bloody own." Percy with arms outspread grasped the top sheet and counterpane; he paused, befuddled, wondering which way to fold the linen, deciding to do so in the middle. Sam frowned, even the ordinary seaman's muttered expletives failing to make reason of his bed making, but not the voice in the doorway.

"Oh dear God, I have made a terrible mistake. I should have sent to the zoo for a baboon to show the deck boy how to make a sea bed. God help me and forgive me." Paddy grabbed Percy by the scruff of the neck and dragged him bodily out the door. "Get a scraper and a bucket of kerosene from the storekeeper and if I can't see my face in the windlass bed by the time you knock off you're as good as dead!"

Released from the bosun's vice-like grip, Percy let out a yelp as he shielded his buttocks with both hands and ran for freedom.

"Son, what the cretin masquerading as an ordinary seaman has attempted to show you is simplicity." Paddy did exactly what Percy attempted initially but with more nimble hands, counterpane on the bottom, sheet on top, the top folded back twelve inches and both sides to the middle. Holding it aloft he shook the linen, then placed it full length on the bunk, opening the folds and flattening the creases. A fluffed up pillow and a blanket folded at the foot completed the task. He grimaced. "I suppose we're lucky in one respect because if a functioning organ resided inside that bucko's ugly head it might be dangerous. Son, go forward the storekeeper's got a bucket of grease and a long handled brush. You've got winches and steering gear to grease. Another thing, the donkeyman lives here too, and it would be wise to forget past advice."

≈

Powered by steam and controlled by rods and chains, the *Colac's* steering gear passed from the bridge along both sides of the after well deck to the rudder post and relieving tackle on the poop. Greased pans carried the rod and chains, the relieving tackle rove with inch diameter wire, absorbing the stress of seas under the counter stern. The cramped steering arrangement caused endless problems tying up and letting go, access to the heads and accommodation.

"Is this how ships steer?" Sam asked, fascinated by the heavy rod and chain lying in the twelve inch wide greased pans, the distance from the poop to the bridge. The bosun commented he wanted more grease on the brush, more effort in the wrists.

"This class of ship does, which of course shows her age," Paddy said, his voice not so gruff. "She came down the slipway with her sisters built in Australia as a D class ship for the Australian Commonwealth Shipping Line.

When Australia knew little about shipbuilding on the scale demanded by the government's efforts to feed the war hungry of the United Kingdom. Rarely hear a complaint about it, though the occasional drunk thrown off the wheel has been known to use it in their defence."

"Drunks steer the ship?" Sam said in amazement.

"Drunks do a lot of things on ships, but on this ship don't get away with it."

"Are seamen allowed to drink onboard?"

"Holding back the tide might be easier than stopping a seaman from having a drink no matter where, even the confessional box if you ever found a seaman in one confessing a life of booze and conniving women."

Sam wondered if his efforts were to the bosun's satisfaction, supposing a curt nod and a grunt acknowledgement.

"Take your gear forward, Horace's got a something interesting for you. Got some advice, you better learn quickly because in Hobart your career at sea might come to a premature end."

≈

He found his way forward with growing confidence, not even flinching when a hook and monkey face slammed against the coamings, though still awed by the cavernous depths of the holds now being swept clean for loading. Percy informed him the captain taking him into his confidence, confirmed the loading would carry over until Monday, enrapturing his new conquest who craved for more of what jutted stallion-like between his legs.

Horace Firth guarded the bosun's store with a vengeance, his eyes firmly fixed on covetous intruders sent by the bosun for wads of waste, buckets, brooms, cordage, tools, spare runners and blocks. Every inch of space taken to hang, store or shelve gantlines, wire, chain, strops, slings, hooks, monkey faces, bottle screws, big hammers, crowbars, bosun's chairs, stages, shackles large and small, drums of grease, wire rope oil, red and white lead, tallow, soft soap, bags of rags, a shadow board of tools, boxes of scrapers and chipping hammers, rolls of hessian and a spare pilot ladder. In the middle of the store, clearance of about three feet all round, a vice on a pedestal for wire splicing.

Horace, an addicted hoarder and habitual scavenger, prowled the Sydney and Hobart waterfronts for anything he deemed essential for work at sea; baling wire, pallets, condemned slings, chain hooks, dunnage and threadbare canvas save-all's, all found a useful purpose in his store.

His dedicated maritime husbandry continued in the lower peak store, accessed by a small hatch forward of the collision bulkhead, shackled to a deckhead lug a single sheave block and gantline for hauling heavy gear from below. This store, smaller than the bosun's store due to the flare of the bow, even more restricted with tarpaulins old and new, runners, preventers, spans, old guys, insurance wire, tow wire, bales of rope, a spare mooring line, breast and backspring, coils of various diameter wire, gyn and heel blocks, guy pendants and save-all's. Nothing discarded, earmarked for future use somewhere in the storekeeper's frugal head.

The storekeeper begrudgingly cleared a small space in the lower peak and from a height of eight feet a small area of deck below visible, a target for the deck boy if he failed to make himself fast in a bosun's chair. He never minced his words, his South Shields accent so thick Sam could barely decipher his words: "Paddy's got the foremast to paint in Hobart and being the youngest you'll have the topmast. My advice, son, is you better be a quick learner or you're dead."

Sam wondered what the grumpy old storekeeper prattled on about, small of statue, a grimy cloth cap on his head, a deeply furrowed brow and a hedge of thick eyebrows shadowing a pair of unforgiving eyes. He pointed a finger at the gantline and shoved a bosun's chair at Sam. "Overhaul the lower peak gantline and make your chair fast with a double sheet bend."

Panic gripped him; what to do with an eighteen inch by ten inch by one inch thick piece of paint splattered hardwood with four holes endlessly rove with manila?

"First check your gantline and chair for broken strands or chaffing, and never go aloft until you do. That goes for lizards and blocks."

Sam choked. "Lizard?"

"A six foot length of manila spliced with a thimble and used to pass your gantline through when rigging chairs or stages."

It got worse. "Stage?"

"A long plank of hardwood with horns rigged with gantlines to paint the ship's side and forepart." Horace ignored the apprehension bordering on fear in the young boy's face.

"What's the topmast, Horace?"

With almost a leer, he beckoned Sam follow him on deck; he pointed up. "That exceptionally long wooden mast above the foremast table with a truck on top, or more specifically named the fore topmast. There you will be with a pot of paint under your chair and Paddy's eagle eye on you, and never forget Paddy can spot holidays from here to the truck."

"Holidays? Truck?"

"The truck is the cap on top of the mast. Percy's a good example of holidays, even when slapping on paint he misses more than he applies." Then he chuckled. "Don't think too much about it, lad. First trippers younger than you went aloft in North Atlantic gales a hundred and fifty feet off the deck because being small these boys could set and take in upper topgallants and royals. At least you'll be alongside. Sitting in comfort a mere hundred feet off the deck, a joy to behold conversing with the seagulls."

Horace took the chair from him, and with the tail of the lower peak gantline made the chair fast with a double sheet bend; he held the knot up. "Learn this important knot, your life will depend on it. A simple knot formed by passing the tail twice through the seized eye of the chair. Now you do it."

Sam successfully tied the knot.

"Well, that proves one thing, you learn quickly. Now you are relying on your own knot, not mine. Settle your rear around the chair and get comfortable. Hold both parts of the gantline with one hand and draw the tail up through the chair with the other, then over your head and under your legs. When you have done that take up the slack up and render it tight. Only then release your grip. Test it with a few bounces, then step over the coaming"

Awkwardly he managed to follow the instructions, then swung free over the hatch.

"To lower grip both parts of the gantline with one hand and render the tail through the half knot."

He felt jubilation flow through his veins as he lowered in a series of jerks, and then felt the reassuring touch of the steel deck beneath his feet. He looked up at Horace framed in the hatchway, the barest nod of acknowledgement for this outstanding feat of seamanship.

Euphoria turned to dread when Horace said in a calm voice: "Now do that by yourself a hundred feet off the deck."

"No way could I hold my own weight!"

"Let me tell you, a seaman can. Working aloft is an important part of your profession and you will learn always one hand for yourself and one for the ship. There is of course an alternative."

Hope surged.

"Some who reckon there's no bounce left in their bodies use a rope yarn to frap both parts, then make themselves fast. I've got nothing against that, plenty of rope yarn in the store."

"Would a seaman use a rope yarn?"

"It's your life, son, I'll say no more. Check and double check your gantline, knot, lizard and block. Always bend your own knots, a prime rule. Even if Paddy or me rigged your gear. Never forget that simple rule. Now do it again, this time over the hatch."

He would never forget this lesson.

≈

The *Colac* existed in a seemingly endless world in which it maintained itself with a life-force generated by the sweat and muscle of engineers, greasers, firemen and trimmers labouring deep beneath its waterline in dark and hellish heat. Its course upon an ever changing ocean, where its track vanished in an instance in a white wash of broken seas, guided by the hand of seamen. Officers who referred to a unique clock set in gimbals, with sextants measuring the angle of the sun and stars to find their minute place in the world. Who peered through azimuth mirrors at headlands and manoeuvred her through narrow channels marked with buoys and beacons.

Names Sam learned from childhood were without relevance. Walls were bulkheads, floors decks, railings bulwarks, ceilings deckheads, corridors alleyways, ladders companionways. Spliced wire became runners, backsprings, breasts, spans, pennants, preventers, kicking straps, strops and downhauls. Drawing stores peggying, scrubbing work clothes on the deck dhobying, soft soap washing paintwork soogying. Sam's mind reeled and as the *Colac* slowly sank to her marks and departure neared his indoctrination became even more daunting.

Cargo completed and hatches squared up by the wharf labourers, tarpaulins spread for battening, wedged by the carpenter. Locking bars and lashings completed the water tight integrity. Wilbur called Sam to his winch at No.2 port derrick.

"Flake the runner behind you as I run it off the barrel—and keep your feet out of bights—then unclamp the runner from the barrel. That small wire made up on the cleats behind you is called a topping lift and I want you to shackle it to the drum end and guide it on."

Sam followed his instructions with a sense of growing confidence, the topping lift taking the weight of the derrick. The derrick topped, the slack span lowering under the weight of its heavy chain and monkey face to the deck.

"Being the amidships derrick the chain is not as long as the yardarm, unshackle it from the monkey face and stow it in its box," Wilbur said, pointing at the heavy triangular plate shackled to the span and topping lift; when released he lowered the derrick into its crutch on the port bridge wing.

More orders: "Make the topping lift up on the cleats behind you after we run it off, then clamp the runner back on the barrel. We then shackle both guys to the runner and haul two blocks and make the tails up on their pennants. Our comrades on the starboard side will do the same, and as you can see the bucko on the monkey island landing the derricks, clamping and lashing them."

Though he stumbled over the confusion of gear on deck, tripped on ringbolts and lugs and burned his leg on a winch steam chest, his confidence grew. Unfolding before him the complexity of a ship and its survival at sea guaranteed by the skills of seamen. Paddy made his presence known, but only with his eyes and the occasional nod; a voice that could be heard from the focastle head to the poop, strangely silent.

Wilbur's answer simple. "Ships run smoothly and efficiently when left to seamen, and I mean that in the literal sense of the word, seamen. A bosun or mate shouting and pointing, blowing whistles and referring to a book on seamanship in their back pocket will achieve nothing. There is a British train of thought mind-dead seamen are no more than an extension of an officers will. It might work on a British ship, but try that on an Australian ship and all stops. Period."

Sam in his bumbling way felt himself being drawn into the team effort of squaring up, placing a wedge wrongly a gently reproach from the carpenter swinging his hammer. Covered in grease and grime he thought me might look like an AB, definitely not Percy who seemed immune from direct contact with greasy blocks and black oiled wire. Squared up, the after gang stripped and housed the gangway, the bosun leading his gang forward, the entire ship engulfed in choking, gritty black smoke as a tug nudged under the stern to secure a tow line on her swivel hook.

Forward Paddy and the chief mate seemed more interested in discussing some matter of mutual interest as the ship let go its last headline, Ben in the well deck throwing off the backspring with Sam on the handle of the focastle head reel.

He felt the slight vibration of the ship's main engine as the ship slowly swung to line-up with Blues Point on the north shore, the tug letting go and dropping astern. No one took any notice of the commencement of an epic voyage, as a matter of routine lashing canvas covers on reels and feeding the eyes of two mooring lines over the break, a single hatch board left off No.1 hatch to drop the lines on the cargo below.

A snarl for almost putting his foot in a bight from Paddy, having found his voice; it dragged his almost mesmerised attention from what soared between No.1 and No.2 hatches, the foremast topmast which must surely strike the towering dark grey structure of the Sydney Harbour Bridge.

An initiation to his new profession he did not look forward to.

6

THE DULL AND MONOTONOUS thump of her cast iron propeller as it turned at seventy-five revolutions a minute, a feather of steam fluttering abaft her all black funnel gave testament to the *Colac's* eleven knots with the assistance of the three knot East Australian Current.

Sam's first impression being called and stumbling on deck from the warm, dark and stuffy accommodation, he stepped into a world entirely of water. Night concealed the enormity of the ocean, falling instantly into an exhausted and dreamless sleep until a hand touched his shoulder and a muffled voice said: "6:30am."

Standing clear with nervous respect for the relieving tackle, he felt himself lifted with the slow rise and fall of the stern, to steady himself grasping dew wet rails; a fiery tinge on the port horizon, the loom of a light four points abaft the starboard beam. He saw a dark shape at a hinged arm bolted to the starboard rail, Uriah who earlier called him reading the clock face of the patent log streaming astern, committing the figure to memory.

He acknowledged Sam. "The light's Point Perpendicular, Jervis Bay. The last light we'll see until Cape Pillar."

Sam and his fellow day workers turned to at 7:00am, a mug of sweet tea sufficient to ward off hunger until breakfast at 8:00am. With no prompting he fell into his peggying role with ease, even after several attempts making the bosun's and donkeyman's bunks without a single fold out of place.

Breakfast amazed him, scrambled egg resembling a thick yellow jelly, fatty bacon and thick sausages, drawing stores from the steward with his store's box heavy. Scrubbing the messroom tables, mopping the deck and finishing his steering gear greasing, he turned to on deck at 10:30am.

Paddy classified ability or lack thereof in painting; gloss white for those with ability and those either through incompetence or lack of initiative, red lead and winch black. When painting the forepart of the bridge on stages Paddy made his presence from the deck well known to those he deemed suspect with a four inch paintbrush dipped in white gloss, his voice probing even the most insensitive of ears. This vocal talent no more apparent when he chaired a general meeting at 5:30pm, his voice commanding attention of all hands crammed in the firemen's messroom.

Percy, relieved by a day worker to record the minutes, droned the minutes of the last meeting, finding it difficult to decipher his own handwriting, shaking his head in bemusement with long pauses which brought a grumble from Paddy the ordinary seaman's status of village idiot in no danger. Wilbur persevered, suffering the cringing pain of Percy's stilted diction, of a mind younger ratings should learn early responsibility to their union, a first step, minute secretary.

Wilbur's delegates report noted a meeting with the chief steward resulted in a small improvement in the food and its preparation. Even so the chief steward proved to be a man of pint-and-pound whereas the union promoted sufficient without waste. What Wilbur said next caused Sam to sit perfectly upright in his chair and listen intently.

"Huddart Parker are not goodly benefactors of seamen as some think, especially those in our union with allegiances elsewhere. Their managerial policies originate from annual meetings of their rabid shareholders who abhor unionised seamen and continually grumble from their palatial mansions we seamen wallow in luxury and sup at the trough of plenty. It is obvious Huddart Parker and others are preparing to make their move to do battle with the union, that fact plainly evident with a new employment policy of not engaging seamen at the wharf gate, our current master an exception.

"We have made it union policy if you are picked up outside the wharf gate by the master or chief engineer you are thereby signed on. Other shipowners find this system fair but not Huddart Parker with an agenda to select their own seamen in the major ports. Isn't it their employer right to choose who will sign their ships articles, so say Huddart Parker? Selecting bulls and scabs and non unionists, that's what their agenda is. Engaging the compliant, the subservient and voiceless. It is we who go to sea in their rust buckets, and it will be us and our union who will declare employment policy."

Sam noticed a man pressed against the inboard bulkhead, dressed in a collarless and loose fitting grey flannel and stained shorts, his lean body and knotted muscles evidence of years of hard labour. His sour face embedded a permanent scowl, his gnarled fists a threat. Albert Waller lost few arguments among his own kind below, most settled with what continuously kneaded by his side and what growled out of his throat. He glared at Wilbur and even the chairman's withering retort of out of order failed to stop him from interrupting the delegate's report.

"Same old shit from you Militant Minority Movement mob and your Communist comrades bellowing the shipowners can't pick who the shipowners wants. We on the plates ain't saying it, no way. We are saying it is only right for the companies to pick who the companies want. The companies feed us and gives us jobs and good wages."

Wilbur remained calm; prior verbal confrontations with the fireman came close to being physical, the fireman's past not as well hidden like most of his brethren, a scab from 1927. As a result of that strike forced upon the union strike-breakers accepted into the union with full membership rights. "Shipowners feed seamen the minimum to exert the maximum, and even now in steam little has changed from the day of sail when men were habitually starved and driven. Saying the companies feed us, yes, companies do but with a humiliating system of pint and pound inherited from the starvation experts, British shipowners. Whoever advocates shipowners have the right to select seamen who are subservient to their corporate will and have no fealty to the union, a threat to unionised labour, is an imbecile or has his own hidden agenda." Wilbur drew a deep breath, willing himself to avoid confrontation. "There is a lot of concern within the union of the licensing of wharfies, fellow unionist who must show their government license to be eligible for a job. The Labor federal government to their credit have tried four times in the last five months in the senate to repeal licensing sections of the Transport Workers Act, thwarted each time by the conservative majority in the upper house. Speaking with our branch officials there's none without apprehension a dog collar could be riveted around our necks if we take widespread industrial action on any issue."

A murmur of dissent passed through the meeting; Albert with his close-cropped head close to the ear of one of his cohorts sniggered.

"How would those who promote shipowners having the right to pick their own carefully vetted seamen react to the union accepting the dog collar act? To my mind their reaction would be if the shipowner so decrees so be it, amen."

Albert muttered an expletive, a thought the commie bastard would one day be coming back to the ship in the dark and then see how much it would squeal from its big mouth with his fist rammed down it.

Wilbur continued the delegates report, his words enlivening the meeting before a throaty growl and a closed fist thumped on the table from Paddy demanded order. "Those among us who think the conservatives in parliament will standby the working class, the poor and the vulnerable, think again and think hard. Remember a New South Wales Labor government initiative to bring a small modicum of relief to the suffering of female victims of bereavement. Remember the vicious attacks and moral denigration. A pound a week to occasionally put a loaf of fresh bread on the table, spread it with butter and not suet.

"The rich, the United Australia Party, the self-righteous bible-bashers from their pulpits spewing lies that widows forced to spread rancid lard on stale crusts of bread, their malnourished children clothed in castoffs, this money tantamount to encouraging sloth and fornication. Widows so enriched from government coffers will no longer have to seek the blessing of God in His house to engage in the act of cohabiting, now able to drop their tattered underwear with gay abandon and engage in unspeakable carnal acts of depravity. So preach men carrying the banner of God, the arrogant buffoons who occupy the conservative benches of parliament. My God what a world we live in!"

Sam watched Percy with an amused on his face, the ordinary seaman's face twisted in agony as his confused brain tried to decipher let alone spell cohabiting. Wilbur eased his misery. "I'll write them up, bucko. Christ, we are faced with another failure of the education system, though when you think about it, spare the teachers a thought with nothing to work with."

After the meeting Sam saw the bosun and storekeeper leaning over the rail outside the bosun's cabin, the storekeeper smoking a pipe, the bosun a cigarette.

"Paddy, what's the Militant Minority Movement?"

Habitually he smoked his hand rolled cigarette to within an eighth of an inch from his nicotine encrusted fingers. "Thinking of joining them, son?"

"At the meeting the fireman mentioned them, that's all."

Paddy's fingers over many decades, layer upon layer, grew a thick and hard casing of black skin impervious to the smouldering heat of cigarette butts; no more than soggy ash he ground the remains of his cigarette in the deck and withdrew his tobacco pouch from his pocket to roll another. "Son, you are only young with a lot to learn. Become a Minority and your life will not be your own, which is not saying that is a bad thing if you're fighting for a fairer world. Being in the Minority you will be in the forefront of any militant action, similar if your sympathies lie with the comrades. Got some advice, those with big mouths make a lot of ruckus and can and do give the impression of militancy, intelligence and leadership. Mostly those blokes are all bluster and hot air and comes the time for blood and sacrifice, dodging police batons and the teeth of savage dogs, you can never find them. Son, learn your profession first, be a seaman and then a unionist because only when you know your job can you argue with skippers and mates for conditions and be taken seriously."

Lighting his newly rolled cigarette his old and craggy face disappeared in a cloud of blue smoke. "What're you doing standing around here? Get yourself up to the bridge for an hour on the wheel. Son, learn your profession. Go steer and box the compass!"

≈

In darkness except for the dim glow of the binnacle light and a faint chink of light filtering through a gap in the chartroom door drape, Sam bumped into an even darker shape by the wheelhouse door. "Bloody deck boys! Clumsy as well as stupid. I ain't the door, mate."

"What are you doing, Percy?"

"What's it look like I'm doing, looking out. Come 7:30pm I'm out of here. Be calling the eight to twelve, then the third mate at one bell."

"Eight to twelve? One bell?"

"Eight to twelve watch. Don't you know anything? We seamen strike one bell the last quarter hour of the watch. If Paddy's sent you to learn to steer, bad luck. Uriah's hopeless, wonder he don't get thrown off the wheel and yours truly begged to do the four hours."

A guffaw came from the wheel: "Well said there, bucko, but it could be said without fear of contradiction the deck boy would learn some interesting steering techniques from a brain dead ordinary seaman who sinks into a coma the moment it steps in the wheelhouse. Tell him the mate's threatened to put you on day work, but Paddy won't have any of it. Seeing you're a quartermaster of the highest order, you show the young lad how to steer and I'll finish your lookout. I'm certain what he learns from you will be a reference he can use to judge the sublime from the ridiculous. Sam, ask the mate can you relieve the wheel. You're in for a treat. Bucko, take the wheel. Steering southeast, the occasional half turn either side."

Pulling back the heavy chartroom drape, Sam received a curt nod for his request, the chief mate bent over the chartroom table writing in the log.

"What did I tell you? Uriah the cunning bastard's slunk off to the wing of the bridge because he's got no idea of teaching a deck boy." Percy squinted in the binnacle and applied three turns of starboard wheel to bring the ship back on course after falling off two degrees. "Then again Paddy always sends the first trippers up when he knows it's me on the wheel." Overshooting the course, Percy returned the wheel amidships, three turns to port to steady the head now fourteen degrees off course.

Sam felt a foreboding as he watched Percy all feet and arms grapple with the wheel; how could he keep a ship ploughing through the ocean at eleven knots on course? Percy returned the wheel amidships before the head started to swing, slowly edging back to five degrees off course. He stepped aside. "Near enough. Keep her on course, sailor."

"What course?" Sam's hands gripped the varnished spokes either side of the amidships spoke identified with a brass knob, staring with growing panic at the compass card now remarkably steady and the rudder indicator at zero.

"Whatever you're steering."

"What am I steering?"

"The course the ship's going."

"What is it? I don't know!"

"Don't you know nothing? Jesus!" Percy peered in the binnacle, the head now sixteen degrees to port off course. "Better put a few turns of starboard wheel on or the mate will throw you off the wheel like he threatens Uriah. What did that useless AB say before he shot through, southeast? Steer southeast."

Southeast? A large black triangular symbol! Starboard meant right! Two turns of starboard helm and when the head began to swing he released his grip and the wheel lay dead. The head's momentum slowed and he made a decision to apply a half turn to port; to his delight the head slowed even more, the compass in its gimbals finally dipping as if in acknowledgement of his prowess to steady on southeast.

The port door slid open and Uriah entered the wheelhouse to report a steady white light four points off the port bow, also to leave the bridge to call the watch. "There being the letter I in Wright, it's a wonder Percy didn't tell you to go back and dot it. Sorry to inflict such pain on you, but she seems to be heading in the general direction of Hobart. Remember less wheel the better. Watch your head but never chase it, and learn to read the sea. Also something you must remember she doesn't steer by telemotor so there's no compression in the wheel, and you have to manually return the wheel amidships. Of course the master seaman would have informed you of that."

Percy scoffed, other thoughts on his mind as he stared into space.

By a combination of head sea and wind, speed and set, the head held steady for a few minutes, then for no apparent reason fell off to port five degrees. "Percy, what am I doing wrong?" The head continued to swing, now ten degrees off course. Percy started to pant, on the verge of penetration of an exceptionally large, soft and warm receptacle.

Sam lost all sense of time as he wrestled with the wheel, the ship's head imbued with a wilful life-force of its own. Less wheel did work, then for no reason two turns failed to keep the ship on course. Seeking a logical explanation he asked Percy who jolted out of his daze and shrugged. "Might be the rudder's bent, or the bloke on the wheel's hopeless."

Mercifully the torture ended, the wheelhouse door sliding back, in the darkness a calm and reassuring voice: "You're chasing her and that's wrong. Also a recommendation for a good tongue lashing for Uriah for inflicting Percy on you. Paddy's not amused."

George Giann, first wheel eight to twelve, stood beside the binnacle; another dark shape put his head through the chartroom drape to give the mate the log reading before proceeding to the port wing, Raymond.

"You're unfortunate protégé is relieved, Percy, you fucking idiot," George said, indicating he take the turns off and counter with a full turn to starboard, the ship's head steadying before slowly returning on course. "For an old heap of shit she steers good. She should be steering with no more than half a wheel either side in this head sea, though in quarter seas she can act up. Then again if she sat on chocks in dry dock the bucko here would find it impossible to keep her on course. There's a rumour he cut the log on his last ship why we have the honour of his presence here."

A newfound confidence swept through Sam as the ship moved two degrees off course which he corrected immediately with a half turn of port wheel, releasing it as soon as the head steadied and rolled on the correct heading.

Percy emerged from his coma. "Gotta fail you, son, sorry. Not to worry, the dark's hid your shame, not even Paddy can see the wake at night. We're out of here."

"Percy, you're not done here!" George snarled.

He scratched an itch in his groin.

"The wheel is being relieved, bucko!"

Groin scratching activated brain activity. "Give him the course, son."

With relief Sam stepped away from the wheel with the ship only three degrees off course. "Steering southeast."

"Something else?" George close to the end of his patience wanted to take hold of Percy's throat.

"Yeah, son, tell cranky old George here how she's steering."

Sam swallowed the lump in his throat. "Half a turn either side."

George made himself comfortable against the chartroom bulkhead. "Not your fault, son. Steering southeast, half a wheel either side. Before you go I'll take a moment of your time, never steer alone by compass. The movement of the ship's head will indicate before the compass reacts and give you an edge in correcting. Your mentor wouldn't know that of course, other things on his mind originating from a brain the size of a peanut, in fact it might even be a peanut. When you're relieved give the new helmsman the course and what wheel she's taking, maybe even a permanent turn half turn if there are heavy seas on her quarter. You also tell him if she has wheel on or the wheel is amidships."

"Jesus, George, that's a bit advanced for a first tripper," Percy said. "Been watching him on deck and the lad's pretty dumb and useless."

"Percy, someone with a brain that can be salted and goes well with beer, I wouldn't put much credence in your observations. Sam, take another half hour and go out on the wing with Raymond and learn the duties of a lookout. Relieved of the wheel, give the course to the mate."

≈

"Some ships stand lookouts on the focastle head with no thought whatsoever for the wellbeing of the lookout wedged behind the windlass in fear for their lives, confronted by monstrous seas. Other ships use the crow's nest which offers a degree of safety though climbing a wet vertical ladder with the ship rolling its guts out might absolve that factor. Now the *Colac* has her lookouts on the wings of the bridge, a common practice if following a coastline the opposite side to the mates taking bearings." Raymond rested both hands on the dodger and looked ahead in a sweeping arc, then a glance behind. The light reported by Uriah a half hour earlier even fainter now two points fore the beam, a fishing boat.

Sam followed his gaze, ahead the only light penetrating the darkness the glow seeping around the edges of the foremast light, no stars or moon a heavy overcast a prelude of a weather change expected in Bass Strait. He looked aft, a dense cloud of smoke even darker than the night rising from the funnel, its direction changing with wind shifts, at times obscuring the mainmast light.

"From the wings we have under normal conditions about eleven miles of visibility, and if the other vessel is as slow as us about a half hour before we pass," Raymond said. "Lights of ships and other vessels are reported as steady white lights from ahead in points off the port or starboard bow to four points, then points fore the beam. From astern reported as points abaft the beam or fore the quarter. Simple and easy so the mate knows exactly where the light is in relation to the ship's position. Shore lights are reported flashing lights or looms."

"Looms?"

"Sweeps of light from a lighthouse beneath the horizon and yet to flash. Every light has a sequence of flashes which relates to that light so the mate on watch can determine the ship's position with accuracy. For instance the waters around Cape Otway on the Victorian mainland and King Island north of Tasmania in Bass Strait, a lot of water in between but mistake King Island for Cape Otway, which of lot of sailing ships four months out of England did, and alter course to the south to clear the landfall and disaster awaited on the shoals north of Tasmania. Hence, each light has its own distinctive sequence of flashes."

Sam stared ahead into the night, shivering in his cardigan, his mind reeling. He wished for a warm and high collared seaman's watchcoat like Raymond wore, but more so how could he possibly commit to memory the complexities needed to become a seaman?

"Without exception we all go through the pain of learning. Seamanship will come to you if you put your mind to it, observe and listen. There's probably even a slim chance for Percy if his excuse for a brain ever gets higher than his navel. Seamanship is a legacy handed down from men in sail reliant on their own inventiveness in ships that plied the world on the whim of wind, tide and current. Be proud of your profession, it is unique."

"Raymond, could I ever become a mate."

"Can't see why not. The third mate who's just relieved the mate came out the focastle. Of course you can, and there's not a man among us who would not say well done as long as you never forget your roots."

"Or the union?"

"Never forget your union. Without it we are nothing, vassals to shipowners. Forced to exist like our seamen comrades with different coloured skins. In conditions imposed upon them by their colonial masters who employ overseers in the guise of arrogant white officers to ruthlessly drive and beat them, toss bones and gristle from their sumptuous saloon tables. Paying pennies for endless hours of gruelling work. Accommodated akin to penned cattle and when finally broken of body, discarded like offal. Union protects us, give us dignity and a voice in the workplace. Union is touch one, touch all."

Touch one touch all, Sam mulled the words in his mind, the power of union. Workers with a united voice, respected and feared.

7

THE HEAVILY TIMBERED MASS of Mt Wellington dominated the toy-like houses clinging to its steep flanks, dissected by residential streets and commercial thoroughfares converging with rolling grasslands to the tannin stained waters of the Derwent estuary. Early winter cast a pall of cold air over the city and some even predicted early snow on the mountain.

Nature over the years blessed the farmers of the Derwent Valley with bumper apple crops, fruit destined to fill the cavernous chilled holds of magnificent British ships that during the season anchored in the estuary awaiting city berths. These vessels plied the world's trade routes with no equal, their speed unmatched to land Tasmanian produce in the United Kingdom and into the shopping baskets of the British housewife. Then the world sank into an abyss and the ships came no more.

This made the simple hardworking Derwent Valley orchardists look at their heavily laden trees with curiosity, wondering why the British no longer filled their fruit bowls with Tasmanian apples, the crispiest, juiciest fruit produced in the world. The farmers with sinking hearts, fears for their families, watched the luscious fruit ripen on the trees, then fall and rot on the ground. Again, why did the British no longer eat their apples?

The years rolled on and still the ships did not come, many of them rusting in British backwaters, others barely existing on tramp routes. The Derwent Valley continued to bloom season after season in riotous colour, in secluded valleys and rolling slopes, trees in perfect symmetry behind white painted fences. Winding lanes bordered with hawthorn and villages with a single pub.

Hobart went hungry amid plenty, some fortunate families surviving by running a few hens in the backyard, a vegetable patch, shuffling in line for a bowl of soup or stew, clothed in castoffs.

Those who fought against a failed system vocalised forcefully the absurdity of living in a fertile land, a land that could feed and clothe itself a hundred times over, starved amid abundance. Families torn apart with the breadwinner trekking the bush roads in search of non-existent work.

Why did governments with their legislative powers fail to curb greed and speculation, bring to heel the slick spruikers of prosperity? Expose the lies of wealth without foundations, for those who dared rewards beyond belief, champagne and caviar. Vaults overflowed with beautifully scripted shares, the currency of the speculating masses, now no more than a mountain of debt. Governments in good times built with millions of borrowed pounds, dollars and francs dams and bridges, railways and power stations, roads and schools, repayment with the powers of taxation.

Those with the courage to denounce a decayed system lambasted governments for not acting to alleviate the national suffering of the working class, repudiate debt to usuries and nationalise the banks. Knighthoods did not fill empty bellies or provide medicine for a sick child, but assured the ruling elite of prominence in a period marred by the blight caused by an even higher echelon.

≈

At the end of a long day, Sam for the first time working over the side on a stage with Wilbur, showered and wolfed his meal of boiled mutton and white sauce, boiled potatoes and cabbage, ashore in his first port.

Percy, his mop of rope-like hair slicked down with a mixture of dripping and rose oil, a concoction of the permanently drunk second cook guaranteed to attract females, looked a picture of sartorial splendour. Attired in his father's moth-eaten one size too large hand-me-down suit. Sam dressed for the cold;

warmed with a watchcoat loaned him by Uriah he felt like a seaman, a thought no girl could resist a young seaman ashore safe from the perils of the sea.

Uriah advised him on payday a marine outfitter in Hobart stocked such jackets favoured by Antarctic whalers provisioning in the port, and reasonably priced.

Percy boasted about a girl he gave delirious delight to in her mother's bed last trip, assured she would be waiting for him with her drawers in her hand. Sam might like to savour the ample fleshy delights of her body, his more discerning eye on her skinnier younger sister with fewer moles and eyes that could look you straight in the face. Percy voiced a theory, both girls from the valleys south of Hobart might indicate some inbreeding.

"Ever stuck your old fellow in a sheila, my son?"

Sam averted his eyes.

"No matter, Steph does it for you, grabs hold of it and feeds it in like a deck hose. Nothing to it, all over in few seconds not like them who can go at it for hours on end and get bored."

Sam thought the physical act of lovemaking should last more than a few seconds, but kept quiet in the presence of a supreme seducer.

Stephanie no longer lived at the address Percy walked her home from the Flying Angel Mission; the woman who answered the door, an older version of her progeny, said her eldest now worked as a cook on a trawler out of Launceston. Percy slowly digested the information, then asked her if the younger sibling might be available.

"Available?"

"Yeah, you know. Available."

"Patricia is thirteen."

Percy briefly wondered why her concern. "Jesus Christ, lady, let a sailor remind you, this is Tassie. Also I ain't superstitious."

The door slammed shut and Sam cringed.

Percy stared at the closed door as if mesmerised. "Ah well, not going to let that little setback spoil my day. Something else on my mind, there's a tattoo parlour close to the ship. I'm getting a naked sheila with an anchor up her arse tattooed on my back. What do you reckon, son?"

Sam shuddered, then a thought entered his mind; seamen and tattoos. His tattoo though would be a visual statement, certainly not an unclad female impaled on an anchor.

≈

With No.1 and No.2 hatches idle for a day, the bosun prepared to paint the foremast, rigging foremast and topmast with chairs and gantlines passed through lizards. From the paint locker gallon pots of paint in buckets, four inch brushes and cotton waste. Sam with Uriah climbed to the table, Uriah barely making mention of the occasion of the deck boy's feet leaving the deck for the first time except for advice one hand for himself and the other for the ship.

"I would probably recommend using a rope yarn to make yourself fast for the first time," Uriah said, adding with a noncommittal shrug: "Paddy and Horace have confidence in you, that goes for me as well. Look around you at this scenic wonder, but remember this is for real and not the forepeak with a few old mouldy tarps to cushion your fall."

Sam forced from his mind the feeling of being on a tiny platform in space, his only protection absurdly thin and rusted handrails.

"Do you feel deep in your mind you can do it this, Sam? Not a soul on the ship will hold anything against you, and I shouldn't be telling you this at this stage, but in the award deck boys are barred from going aloft."

He looked up the tapering topmast, the manila gantline his life would depend upon rove through the truck sheave with a dummy gantline. With both hands firmly gripping the handrails, he thought a swiftly moving bank of dark clouds driven by a brisk southerly wind would soon shroud the table in mist. "Uriah, if I said I couldn't what would Paddy think of me?"

"Now that is something to contemplate, especially Paddy being in sail. No doubt sent aloft to the skysails and royals doubling Cape Horn as a boy in howling gales. Wouldn't like to reflect about that, Sam. Paddy's of the old school where men whose lives were in constant peril instinctively supported each other, whether seaman or boy vital to the wellbeing of the ship. Things of course have changed in steam, but I doubt if Paddy has." Uriah handed him a rope yarn. "I never carry rope yarns on my belt like some old salts, but the odd rope yarn comes in handy at times. Look at this way, you're already more than half way up the mast so what is another forty feet?"

Sam looked at the rope yarn, the rogue's yarn of an old mooring line; he handed it back and shook his head.

"Thought so. Now our illustrious bucko is on the forepart, me the ladder fleet with a hook chair. We'll paint the table leaving you enough room to step around the foremast light painting as you go to access the ladder, your job aloft finished. Not complicated, a simple matter of working together. I will by that time be a few drops down the ladder so I'll leave the rungs unpainted. No second thoughts on the rope yarn? Some aren't as strong in the wrists as others."

"Uriah, I have to do it without the rope yarn."

"That you do, also I'm below you and won't be far from your gantline. So when I let you go keep that in mind. Let's do it, Sam."

Somewhat placated by Uriah's support, he settled his chair around his buttocks, took hold of the hauling part of the gantline and took a deep breath. With both heaving and his feet bouncing him clear of the topmast his rapid ascent gave him a muscle wrenching fear he would career headfirst into the truck, then a jarring halt only inches beneath the wooden cap rarely viewed so close and badly in need of paint.

His right hand with an iron clasp gripped the two parts of the gantline, a forceful tug of his left a signal for Uriah to let go. Quickly, his mind blank of his precarious position, this nothing more than a seaman going about his work, he hauled the trailing gantline between his feet through his chair, over his head and under both legs. Assured now of survival, he quickly rendered the slack until the half knot cinched tight beneath the double sheep bend securing chair.

With an expulsion of breath and a deep intake, he released his grip and fell two inches and bounced.

No time to reflect on his mastery of seamanship, Uriah bending a bucket to his gantline with a pot of brown paint, a four inch paintbrush and a wad of cotton waste. With newly learned expertise he applied paint in even strokes, dipping his brush lightly and tapping the excess against the pot. Demanded by the bosun no holidays and that his eyes like that of a hawk would miss nothing. The topmast would not be painted again for at least a couple of years and his skill applying the paint would assure the seasoned timber would remain sound in its exposed and harsh environment.

So easy it all came to him, the rendering of the gantline and his weight lowering him three feet at a time, the nutty tang of thick paint smarting his nostrils, working his paintbrush with skill. Any fear of heights now gone looking down at the miniature figures on deck, the sweeping panorama of the city, river and mountain backdrop. Aloft, trusted by the bosun to perform the task given him.

Now on the table he looked above him, the topmast glowing like a beacon. With pride in his heart he slowly rendered his gantline and the attached dummy through the truck sheave, then made the lighter signal halyard fast with a clove hitch to the still wet railing. Breathing the fresh salty air a growl below brought him back to reality. "Get on deck! A pot of black paint for the derrick heads and gyn blocks!"

≈

Working day and afternoon shifts it took seven days to discharge and load for Sydney, cargo hard to come by; hogsheads of cider, potatoes, onions, hardwood timber, fruit, barely half the ship's cargo capacity.

"Reason for rejoicing for a few local farmers and saw millers fortunate to have markets on the mainland, if not their efforts would be totally wasted, ploughed in the ground and Tassie hardwood left standing in the forest.

Tasmania has stagnated, in fact gone backwards these last few years," Wilbur remarked, standing by No.3 hatch to square up with two slings of timber on a truck to complete cargo. "An indictment to politicians and leaders of industry who without a single trace of remorse supported the system which toppled humanity over the precipice. The deep rich soil is still there, abundant rain and sunshine, the will, but the system denies we feed ourselves, or at least the majority of us. Tasmania is nothing but fields of weeds and tussock grass."

Uriah agreed. "There's a madman in Germany hailed a statesman supreme by envious world leaders having devised a system to give his country gainful employment. Put his country to work with picks and shovels, mattocks and hayforks. It doesn't matter where the army of singing, happy workers dig as long as the work is productive and there are newsreel cameras close by to record it for other happy workers to aspire to."

"True, as well as joyful workers being conscripted into Germany's peace loving armed forces. With swollen chests parading in their new uniforms or poking their perfect Aryan heads from the turrets of shiny new tanks and armoured vehicles rolling off production lines that months earlier were rusting relics of the Depression."

"With a price of course," Uriah added, watching as the last sling disappeared down No.3 hatch. "Unpalatable for some but a reason for rejoicing for conservatives entrenched in Canberra and their industrial mates. Suppression of the trade unions and the jailing of union officials as well as Communists."

"Hitler's tried and proven methods of crushing union dissention has a big following here in Australia," Wilbur said. "A particularly high profile and articulate one being Attorney General Menzies who seems to find Adolph's jackboots policies to his liking. Let this nation be aware, that man if he has his way will further bind this country to the apron strings of Great Britain. Subservient to knights and barons, earls and lords and their fancy dames."

8

PYRMONT AND ULTIMO MIGHT have been replicas of drab northern industrial England, and in many ways not difficult to understand when the city's forefathers from the greatest colonial power on earth industrialised the inner city because of proximity to rail and sea. Industrialists built the factories and the government the power stations to drive them. Workers beat and shaped metal in glowing forges and fabricated the machines of the industrial revolution. Industrialists contracted master builders to construct monotonous rows upon rows of tenements to house their workers, workers now able to step out their front door and walk through the factory gate on the opposite side of the street.

Pyrmont and industry coexisted, children playing hopscotch in the narrow, congested streets uncaring of the poisonous smoke as black as ink spewing from the power station's three chimneys. Then the world collapsed, wool an early victim of the Depression, a large employer in Pyrmont. With no buyers unsold hundreds of thousands of bales of the world's finest wool threatened to burst the masonry walls of twenty wool stores.

Occupying a large portion of the Pyrmont peninsula sprawled a sugar refinery, hissing steam and from multiple chimneys emitting smoke, sweetening the atmosphere with a permanent stench of molasses that clung to the walls of the grimy tenements and tiny cottages nearby.

A green sanctuary survived amid overwhelming industry, a small park that offered respite for families, where courting couples could sit on benches or the grass and in their minds escape their industrial world.

Loading in Darling Harbour for the last five days, sailing in two days, Sam walked the now familiar streets of Pyrmont. Hotels held not interest but the window of baker's shop did; cream filled lamingtons, Viennese shortbreads, macaroons, éclairs, iced rock cakes and sponges. With no money, having spent his pay in Hobart on a navy blue watchcoat, denim shirt and dungarees, money saved for his union book, he could only dream and press his nose against the window.

He remembered with a smile Percy posturing in the messroom too consumed preening himself to eat dinner of hogget as tough as boot leather and the chief steward's standby, broad beans. Percy donned his suit and plastered his hair with the second cook's blend of dripping and rose oil, guaranteed to give him a Latin look no girl could resist. According to Percy a tremulous young thing waited in Balmain with her bloomers bunched around her ankles, an offer to Sam he might like seconds.

He declined, content with his long walks from Darling Harbour to Pyrmont. Twilight softened the stark encroachment of surrounding industry, a park bench beneath a single lamp on a rusted steel pole, on the last three evenings a place where he rested his tired legs before returning to the ship. On the park bench sat the hunched figure of a girl wrapped in a woollen shawl. He thought she might be sixteen, possibly younger if a smile broke the seriousness etched in her face. She sat in the middle of the bench and made no effort to move closer to the edge and he wondered if she would mind if he sat beside her. Taking the initiative, he did and felt the briefest touch of their thighs.

She gave no hint of being aware of his presence, drawing her thin shawl even tighter around her shoulders and head, staring at her feet. He saw the tip of her nose, her bottom lip full and pink in the soft glow of the lamp now with greater intensity as the light faded.

She became aware of him across the street before he entered the park; tall and good looking, in fact she chastened herself to stop staring as he approached where she sat. Remaining in the centre of the bench she offered no invitation to sit down, but he did; still ignoring him, she finally relented and moved to the edge of the bench.

"Thank you," he said shyly, his hands clenched beneath his knees. "I've walked from Darling harbour. It's a long way. Going to be a cold night."

She nodded, thankful for the warmth of her mother's shawl, though the night air more acceptable than the rising damp, mould and leaking gas of the home she shared with her mother and two younger sisters. Unable to contain her curiosity she turned slightly to look at him out of the corner of her eye; a little older than her she thought. His hair, what she could see under his thick woollen beanie, dark brown and eyes that at times caught a glint of light. Smiling, his teeth were straight and white.

She broke her silence: "Yes it will be."

"Hobart is much colder than here. Then I suppose if you can see the southern lights at night that would be the reason."

"Southern lights?"

"The third mate on my ship said the lights are the Aurora Australis. A solar wind reacting with the Earth's magnetic field and reflecting off the Antarctic icecap."

Her mouth formed a perfect O. "Have you been there?"

"No, but I would like to. I am a seaman on the *Colac* and I don't think she would make it that far south. Nothing but mountainous seas and snow, and of course icebergs."

"I've never seen snow."

"Me either. Sometimes in the middle of winter the frost on the ground in Balranald could be near an inch thick."

"Balranald? That's a long way from the sea."

He wished he could see her full face. "My ship's berthed in Darling Harbour loading for Melbourne and Adelaide. We normally run to Tasmania, but there's no cargo."

"A lot of seamen live in Pyrmont."

"Does your dad have a job?"

She tensed, her eyes locked on her lace up boots, the right one with the sole and upper about to come apart at the seam. "My father is away in the country working."

"Lucky for him to have a job."

"We think he has though he doesn't send money home. We haven't seen him for a long time. There's just my mother and my two sisters." She continued to stare at her boots, allowing the shawl to fall around her shoulders.

Long light brown hair framed her face, her eyelashes incredibly long; he knew her eyes would be blue, would have to be blue to complete the perfect picture of classic beauty. "What's your name?"

She never replied, her breathing shallow as she thought of her father. Normally dashing and exuberant Wallis Knight came home from work one day and informed his family his job at the wool stores no longer existed. Not only him, but hundreds of other men who worked in the wool stores in Pyrmont; the United Kingdom and Europe could no longer afford to buy prime Australian wool even at prices at their lowest in history.

A not rare quirk in these troubling times he blamed his wife and family for his predicament. He drank heavily which quickly depleted the family's small reserve of money. Wine, dregs affordable for those existing on the dole, as if the potent and acerbic swill would anesthetise his brain and remove from his life four heavy and unwanted burdens.

One day she noticed a black swelling under her mother's left eye, too quickly dismissed as bumping into the laundry door in the dark; she knew different, remembering the raised voices.

A mother drew closer to her three daughters, her eldest fifteen, twelve and eight as if their love and dependency would shield her from a world collapsing around her. In her despondency she never abandoned her role as mother, drawing her daughters even closer about her.

Then one day the girls found their mother with her head cradled in her arms on the table, her body spent of grief; their father no longer lived with them, joining the army of unemployed moving like a broad and slow flowing river over the land.

"Emily," she said at last. "Emily Knight."

"My name is Sam, Sam Wright. Our names sound similar."

"Sam's a nice name. Yes, our names do."

"Are you at school?"

She shook her head. "I wanted to stay another year but mother needed me home for my sisters while she looked for work. Also I might find work, but what I did didn't pay well. Do you live in Balranald when not on your ship?"

He shook his head. "My home port is Sydney though I have no address here."

"Do you go home to visit your parents?"

"My mother died and I wouldn't call living with my father home."

"Why?"

"Many reasons, but since leaving home I have thoughts it may not have been entirely my father's fault. His dark moods, incapable of showing affection. We live with hopelessness as a way of life, a disease that causes men to lose hope and blame themselves for not being able to provide."

She looked at him quizzically.

"I don't really know. Talk on the ship and I am a good listener. Our union delegates should be elected to parliament to fix the Depression."

"Could seamen do that?"

"Yes, I think seamen could. I watch them on the ship without any fuss going about their job. Paddy our bosun never seems to give them orders, and you rarely see a mate on deck."

Darkness and lamplight gave old masonry a sombre look, the scars of industry hidden; she seemed in no hurry to leave. "The girls nice in Hobart?"

"Most of them looked nice, but none took any notice of me," he said, his words coming more easily and relaxed. "Wouldn't have done them any good anyway, me with no money to take them to the pictures or dance."

She smiled. "You could walk with a girl and hold hands and—"

He held his breath "What?"

She blushed. "Kiss."

"Don't know so much about that. Girls would probably compare me with an ogre or a troll living under a bridge."

The redness in her cheeks deepened; she shook her head.

Why it entered his mind he did not know, but he thought with his dinner of hogget and broad beans he ate well; probably much better than Emily and her family. Paddy, owing the chief cook a favour, loaned him to the galley to clean out the freezer and chill room prior to arrival in Sydney. The old cook, stout and jovial, a glowing nose fuelled by copious amounts of brandy, rewarded the hardworking boy; a sandwich of thickly sliced fresh bread packed with a half pound of the captain's bacon. Also a wink that at times joints of meat fell between the gaps in the duckboards in the darker reaches of the freezer.

"Emily, if I ask the chief cook for some meat and vegetables could your mum cook dinner?"

She looked at him wide-eyed, her bottom lip dropping; only momentarily as her face shed its surprise for an excited glow. She thought of their dinner tonight, bread spread lightly with dripping, the last scrapings of apricot jam; with no money for the gas meter the family at least saved precious tea and sugar. "Could you?"

"Not really sure, but the old chief cook gave me the captain's bacon the other day."

She clapped her hands, her shawl falling around her hips. "I will even make my sisters take a bath! Also find money for the gas meter!"

9

SAM'S EARLIER CONFIDENCE THE chief cook would give him a joint of meat for a planned dinner with Emily and her family waned. Collecting the morning kits he gathered his courage, wondering if the hung-over cook with a nose glowing like a beacon and breath that could peel paint would be sympathetic to the abject poor.

Sam remembered a haunch of shrivelled and fatty beef at the back of the freezer earmarked by the chief cook for regurgitation as stew, mulligatawny soup or breakfast curry and rice. Eluding the calculating eye of the chief steward who without hesitation would rename it rump steak for a Saturday night with most ashore and those onboard out of their minds with drink. A menu when confronted by the delegates proof of the company's overly generous providoring.

Theodore smiled even though it hurt; he liked the deck boy, a damn good worker, polite and obedient. "This little bit of fluff pretty, son?"

"It's not that, but she is kind of pretty," he said, then: "No, Theodore, she is beautiful."

"All of them are beautiful, son, some just more than others. Minxes the lot of them who when their claws get firmly fixed in a man's testicles make the toughest of us as weak as babies." Theodore thought he would soon need another jolt of brandy concealed under a flour sack in the bread making bin. "Unfortunately the chief steward sprung what you dug from under the duckboards at the back of the freezer. Grand Irish stew for the lads, cookie, he chortles. Spoil the lads. Fuck him! Fuck all chief stewards!"

Theodore's eyes rolled to the back of his head, swallowing forcefully to dislodge the thick coating of residue blocking his throat. Anyone game enough to lift the duckboards of his freezer deserved better than rotten meat.

The beef rump received a debatable pass as fit for human consumption, sliced into five, two pounds of potatoes, ten rashers of bacon, a two pound loaf of bread and half a cabbage. There came with the stores a warning, keep a keen eye out for large men in overcoats and hats pulled over their foreheads, denizens of the pillage squad and absolutely heartless, relentless persecutors of waterfront scavengers.

Sam showered and felt his cheeks; no need to shave today. Dressed and following Emily's directions, he felt a growing expectation of meeting her again, even more so a family dinner he carried in a canvas bag borrowed from Uriah. He saw her on the corner, taller than he remembered from yesterday with her long hair cascading around her shoulders; she smiled and waved, barely able to restrain herself from rushing to greet him.

"Have you been waiting long?"

"Only a minute or two." For over half an hour she waited, willing him to appear, certain he wouldn't.

"Took me forever to get clean under the shower. We renewed the steering gear relieving tackle wire as well as overhauling the blocks. Grease and oil so thick you could stand the brush up in."

She glanced down at what he held in his hand, then up into his eyes.

"Better than I expected, the cook's given us a feast. Think he likes me."

"He must be very generous." She tried hard to maintain the mature dignity of a young lady, clapping her hands in excitement.

"Old Theo looked like Father Christmas this morning with his big nose glowing, a good bloke but like most onboard he likes a drink. Bosun loaned me to him to clean out his freezer and chill room. Whew, some of the old stuff I found in there would make you sick, but not this."

"The bosun works you hard?" She started walking, more a skip, then without thinking reached for his free hand.

With the feel of her soft and warm hand in his, he took a deep breath to steady his voice. "Paddy's a good bloke. Nah, I'm just a complainer. Paddy reckons all seamen complain and their last job always better than their current." His nose tingled with a pungent odour hanging heavy in the twilight air, Emily informing him the sweet smell steadily growing stronger approaching the waterfront came from the sugar refinery.

"Mum reckons all we need to do when we crave a sweet is to sniff the air." She squeezed his hand.

At the bottom of the street the harbour disappeared behind a dark compilation of brickwork and chimneys, ducting and piping with feelers of escaping steam. "The smell doesn't bother you?"

"You get used to it. It's not unpleasant, molasses is nice. When there is a ship at the wharf discharging the noise is far worse than the smell."

Paddy mentioned the *Colac* once discharged bulk gypsum in Balmain, the noise at night so bad the only remedy a walk up the hill to the Bald Rock Hotel to beg the publican a session of numbing intoxicants in his back room. "Gear and grabs are noisy."

A long row of identical tenements ran parallel with the waterfront, the homes once owned by the sugar refinery, but now sold to investment speculators who collected weekly rents. There were no streetlights in the narrow street, a wall of darkness ahead. Or any lights, not even an illumination filtering through drawn curtains in tiny multi-paned windows. He could hear movement on the harbour, the occasional whistle and breaking wash of water on rocks, the foreshore obscured by a high rusted corrugated iron fence.

He thought of her walking alone at night. "Is it safe here?"

She paused outside the door of the second last tenement, the street abruptly ending at a high brick wall. "We come and go as we please and no one bothers us." The door pushed open, the lock broken and he followed her down a narrow hallway accessing two bedrooms to enter a windowless room, a combined eat-in kitchen and lounge room.

In the middle of the room an oblong table and four chairs, two other chairs against the wall. Fashionable when hung years ago fleur-de-lis wallpaper in pastel blue might have once added a sense of light, but now stained sepia and in places peeling. Dismal, a stump of a candle burning in a jam jar the only light in the room. Emily introduced her family sitting on a divan against the far wall. "Sam, Claire my mother, sisters Mary and Harriet," she said.

"Mrs Knight." Sam immediately recognised where Emily's beauty originated, the woman though without the effervescence, a weary smile on her wan face.

Mary and Harriet giggled and hung their heads, the taller of the two the first to find the confidence to speak: "I am Mary," she said. "How do you do?"

He placed his bag on the table. "I am doing just fine, thank you, Mary."

Not be outdone by her older sister, Harriet chirped: "I am Harriet, how do you do?"

The two girls jumped up from the divan and crowded around him, their faces beaming until a rebuke from Emily caused them to again lower their heads, extend their bottom lips. "Leave Sam alone, but you can thank him for our dinner."

Claire studied her eldest daughter closely, where her attention continually strayed, her daughter no longer a child but an attractive young woman who even in her shabby clothes and scuffed boots drew attention. Soon her life would take another path when she took that first step into womanhood, hoping she would make the right choice. She wondered if a seaman could offer escape, probably not. The boy far too young, a mind more focused on a young girl's body. Thoughtful, who brought their dinner. Food she would need to work hours of drudgery cleaning the homes of the affluent, ironing until midnight. To cook this bounty, in her purse a single shilling for the gas meter.

Sam felt himself caught up in the excitement of Emily and her sisters; he could also feel the mother's tension. Ashamed of their poorness? Here in this home he didn't need the *Colac's* delegates to condemn the insidious disease of poverty, but tonight forgotten with a family dinner.

Claire inserted her shilling in the gas meter, a sputtering whoosh of gas jets igniting, a moment for celebration, a smiling mother shutting the outside world from her mind and three girls reaching for each other to hug.

Sam observed as if from afar, a home without a breadwinner, a man's strength at the head of the table, the younger girls yet to fully understand their wretched plight and their lowly position in life. Understand that nothing changed through the eons, leaders and followers, generals and soldiers, kings and derelicts, rich and poor, smart and dumb, the hodgepodge of mankind. Great minds philosophised humanity climbed the evolutionary scale led by those who stood unique among them, and that war and plague were nature devised to maintain a balance—not God because God controlled with His own gene.

The delegates of the *Colac* were right; manipulation by the establishment using the pomp and regal splendour of monarchy, the spiel of statesmen, dictators, presidents, prime ministers, elected by ballot or gun, thuggery or deception promising the gullible prosperity, security and freedom. None of these exulted beings ever retired to their beds hungry or clothed their bodies in rags.

Emily took charge, first ordering her mother to remain seated and allow her children to prepare dinner, a meal fit for the obscenely wealthy. Mary received instructions to peel the potatoes, the peelings later washed and saved for soup. Sam received instructions to sit at the head of the table, a silent overseer. Harriet, allocated to chop cabbage, received a warning to be careful with the knife, also to slice the bread and not hack it. Two pots of water sat on the stove, a frying pan with dripping.

"Have you been at sea long?" Claire asked from her position of isolation.

"I have just completed my first trip."

"The food comes from the ship?"

"The chief cook."

Potatoes cut in quarters filled the larger pot, cabbage washed and drained in the sink the smaller, covered with lids and put on a low flame. Emily turned the frying pan jet on low also, ten minutes to heat for the steaks and lastly the bacon.

"Emily, there is more dripping in the ice chest," Claire said. "You might fry the bread in that."

Another frying pan came from under the sink, Emily acknowledging her mother with a thumb's up. "Fried bread and bacon for afters. Mother, it's a feast to behold!"

"There is also tea in the cupboard. That would be nice, a pot of tea."

Sam remembered the tough and sinewy meat served over the past few weeks, hoping this joint didn't originate from the same paddock, a scrawny steer a victim of old age. Quality never entered Emily's mind, worrying if the shilling's worth of gas would last, more confident as the potatoes split open and the cabbage reduced to the bottom of its pot, the steaks cooked and bacon starting to curl. Then followed fried bread, placed on a cloth to soak up excess fat. Emily's pan gravy turned thick and brown, stirred with four tablespoons of flour and cabbage water. The kettle boiled and the tea made.

Flickering jets, dying spurts, the pungent odour of unburned gas lingering in pipes. Sam would carry the memory for a long time, three girls dancing a jig of triumph.

Almost a ritual the serving, a team effort placing steaming potatoes and cabbage in equal portions, the steaks smothered in gravy, side plates of fried bread with two rashers of bacon. Sam received orders to sit at the head of the table, Claire the bottom and the three girls as close as possible to their guest.

The steak though dry came from a well fed beast, though a little on the tough side. Boiled potatoes fell apart in a burst of aromatic steam, the cabbage steamed soft, tangy gravy enriched with singed meat droppings, a meal cooked to perfection.

Claire maintained a reserve, but not so the three girls who made no attempt to hide the sated feeling of full stomachs in their happy table banter, their mouths slicked with grease as the last shreds of fried bread and bacon suffered the same fate as their wiped clean plates. Emily gave orders after she and Sam cleared away and rinsed the dishes under the tap, filling the sink with the last of the kettle, the two younger girls to wash up.

At the front door Emily wanted to walk with him to the top of the street, Sam declining at this late hour probably not safe. She scowled lividly. "Of course it's safe. I have a sailor to protect me."

"Walking back home I mean."

She moved closer to him, passing her tongue over her bottom lip, her eyes fixed on his. A dream would soon become a reality, kissing a girl, tasting her breath, the exquisite softness of her moist lips. She pressed lightly against him and offered her mouth, their touching sending an electric shock through his entire body. Then he tasted the sweetness of her slightly parted mouth, the soft cushions of her lips, his hands on her hips.

She drew away, a teasing smile on her face. "Mother said a girl should be wary of sailors. Girls in every port, all destined to suffer broken hearts."

"No, Emily," he said, this time gently rubbing his lips against hers, drawing her breath into his lungs.

"Tomorrow, Sam?"

Then for the first time in his life he experienced a sensation familiar to all seamen, the pain of separation. "We are shifting ship to bunker early in the morning and sailing in the afternoon."

A sharp intake of breath caught in her chest and she chastened herself for being an impressionable and immature girl. She would never see this boy again, he would sail away forever. Staring at her feet, she sniffed.

"Emily, can we write to each other?"

"Yes!"

10

ORT AND STARBOARD HEADLINES joined with a length of point line lowered through the forward leads to six feet above the water.

Wilbur bent a heaving line to the starboard breast wire passed through the Panama lead at the break of the focastle head, placing the two made-up parts on the bitts and pointing at Sam. "The breast is yours after the headlines and bights are run. Of course you'll get a baking if the sandbag flies over your head, but don't let that put you off."

Paddy, his normal irritable self, growled: "Even the dolt aft masquerading as a bucko couldn't miss alongside." He changed the subject, even more irked. "This river's a disgrace to Melbourne, everyone on the focastle make sure you scrub your hands when we finish tying up. It never gets better even with all the factories closed along it. We've just passed the worse part, the stink and the scum from the abattoirs up Maribyrnong Creek. Blood and guts and yellow streaks of fat a foot thick foul that waterway. The Yarra south of the city is a cesspit, but go north of Princess Bridge and there's platypus and fat perch, grassy banks shaded with weeping willows."

Sam watched the bloated carcass of a dog pass between the ship and wharf, the water almost black, stagnant and streaked with slimy residues. Along its muddy and eroded banks lined with decaying wharves lay the wretched remains of once proud sailing ships, bare of masts and seeing out the remainder of their days as coal hulks. Leaning at all angles red gum piles driven as if haphazardly along both banks, dredging moorings. A bucket dredge hauled itself on winch driven chains back and forth across the river, serviced by a fleet of mudhoppers, maintaining the river at a depth to keep at least a few feet of water under the keels of deep draft ships.

"Would you believe the locals from Yarraville and Newport fish in the bloody thing?" Paddy said, leaning over the apron and signalling behind him to slacken the headlines to the line boat now under the bow.

The *Colac* under the command of Captain Finch passed through the Goode Canal into Victoria Dock, a reclaimed marshland of twenty-one wharves once filled with ships from the United Kingdom and Europe loading the produce from the rich pastures of hinterland Victoria.

Closing on her berth the *Colac* cast a lonely figure, one of three vessels; a poorly maintained general cargo ship under the Greek flag, the other a three masted topsail schooner, *Alma Doepal,* registered in Hobart discharging timber and cases of jam.

Paddy signalled the headlines be taken to the windlass drum ends and the carpenter to heave. He made another comment: "Once a forest of masts and derricks so thick the mind boggled. Sometimes ships even double berthed. Now an old Greek I can smell from here and a bloody ketch."

The *Colac* with the assistance of a tug secured at the break of the focastle head, gently nudged alongside. Sam surprised himself as he threw the heaving line and the sandbag landed six feet ahead of two linesmen finished placing the eye of the forward backspring on a bollard. Not a great feat of seamanship with the ship alongside and the engine room telegraph about to be rung finished-with-engines, not even worthy of comment from the forward gang heading aft to swing the gear over the wharf.

≈

Sam walked to the city following the sprawling Victorian Railways West Melbourne marshalling yards, rolling stock continually on the move, controlled by amber, red and green lamps and semaphores, shunting locomotives shrouded in steam and smoke diverted to spurs to allow unimpeded passage to mainline engines. Electric trains painted a drab red silently wove their way along polished steel tracks, their right of way not disputed moving tens of thousands of passengers daily to their suburban destinations. He followed the river, its slow flowing waters through the city a little less polluted though still turgid and muddy. He climbed the bank under Princess Bridge bathed in the shadow of Flinders St Railway Station.

Here in the vibrant heart of the city he marvelled at its opulence; St Paul's Cathedral rose in grand magnificence on one corner, the Princess Bridge Hotel on the other, the city beyond a backdrop of glass and masonry. Ceaseless noise assaulted the ears, trams converging on the city, their warning bells ignored by vehicles turning in front of them. Trams departing the city through tree lined boulevards, St Kilda Rd and Wellington Pde. People rushed to catch them, grasping greasy handrails and swinging onboard, elated on surviving threats to their lives dodging cars and trucks and others in an equal frantic rush.

He turned west and let his feet take him without conscious thought of his destination, unafraid of getting lost because the river close by would eventually lead him back to the ship. He walked down Flinders St, on his left the grand French Renaissance of Flinders St Railway Station.

At first no more than a niggling at the back of his mind, a change came over the city, more dramatic as he neared the intersection of Flinders St and Spencer St. Buildings showing years of neglect, peeling paint and crumbling brickwork, pavement cracked and stained, gutters choked with rubbish.

The transformation no more evident than the movement of humanity all about him. Men in worn overcoats and sweat stained felt hats, men without smiles on their faces. Shuffling aimlessly, their hands thrust deep in pockets. Old before their time, standing outside the pubs, pubs with dark interiors and few customers. From within emitted a stale smell of must and fermented liquors, a tease for penniless men outside.

Desperate men gravitated to this part of the city looking for work. Willing to strain their backs likes beasts of burden to put a single meal on the table, money to pay a doctor to treat a child with rickets, an elder family member with rheumatoid arthritis.

Rejection became a way of life, downcast eyes and a hand held out in the hope it would feel the crowned head of a British monarch in silver, even copper. Visions of a new life bogged in bloodied mud, trenches dug from the rolling farmlands of Belgium and France, the ever present miasma of death, rats feeding on the corpses of mates. Those who survived with their minds and bodies intact lived with a single hope, a promise from those who sent them on lies and patriotism to the living hell of war, a democracy fit for heroes.

Sam felt an impelling need to be away from this place, heading up Spencer St, on his left occupying an entire city block a drab pile of grey masonry, the Victorian Railways administration building. As suddenly as it gripped him, the feeling of despair dissipated as he approached Spencer St Railway Station, the hub of country Victoria rail, a station that never slept. Multitudes of platforms lined with passenger trains, powerful locomotives throbbing with full heads of steam, spewing ash and clinker that no one seemed to mind brushing from their clothing like dandruff.

The gritty air buzzed with barely suppressed excitement as throngs shoved their way in a rush to catch trains, most weighed heavily with luggage. Family heads frantically herded small children caught in the melee of rushing people. Authoritative voices demanded access, weaving through the concourses uniformed porters with two and four wheeled barrows piled high with baggage, no one daring to impede their progress. Interstate trains scheduled for evening departures, mail and paper trains, serviced by upwards of ten joined barrows and trolleys with stuffed mail bags, bundled newspapers, magazines and packages.

Catering for the travelling public hot food and beverages served in a cavernous cafeteria, on the main concourse a pastry shop, confectioner, tobacconist and newsagent. Sam bought a cream lamington, a feeling of euphoria that the world promised a future other than that what existed no more than a city block away. Bumped continuously with grunted apologies mattered not to a young man entranced.

≈

Wilbur gave Sam a battered, dog-eared copy of *The People of the Abyss*, advice to read it and commit to memory though mankind advanced nothing changed or ever would until man rid himself of the canker of greed and power.

Wilbur in a reflective mood sat on the after bitts with a mug of strong black coffee. "Jack London in writing *The People of the Abyss* lived with the poor of London's East End at the turn of the century, amid indescribable degradation and disease, infant mortality and premature death, starvation and work broken bodies. London, the most richest and powerful city in the world. The centre of enormous wealth sucked from its Empire upon which the sun never set signified by streets of mansions, palaces, the rituals of monarchy. Jack London saw a different city, city where the working class dwelled in hovels and filth, slept in the streets and doorways even in midwinter. Begged and sold the bodies of their young, worked for a pittance which the rich took from them so their families could be fed swill."

Sam, even though distracted with something else on his mind, listened with fascination. "Who is Jack London?"

"A prolific working class writer who died young but never lost his origins. Who wrote without fear exposing the world for what it is, a cesspool of avarice overlorded by a power craving elite. The working class led by this privileged few like timid lambs, lulled how good their lives are by smooth tongued sycophants, fed lies and bribed. Read Jack London and forever rid your mind how fortunate we are to live in our democratic world, being benevolently guided from cradle to grave by the pompous beings we elect to govern us."

From beneath their feet through the teak planking of the poop seeped the sound of muffled shrieking and high pitched feminine laughter; Wilbur smiled. "Probably not one of them has ever read Jack London or even heard of him, or that he once wrote when the good Lord finished creating the rattlesnake, the toad and the vampire with the leftovers He made a scab. Happy souls, I shouldn't begrudge them their pleasure."

Sam remembered Hugh and Cliff's escorts; he couldn't remember their names, one especially nice and caring. "Saw them come onboard. Some of them could be my grandmother."

"Fortunately lust is blind. Victims of life lambasted from the pulpit, but then again if the self-righteous condemn with thunder and damnation there must be something good in there. Mature ladies with a preference for sweaty firemen and trimmers, not a blush among them sharing a narrow bunk with three others in the cabin. Having come to the rescue of their morals, I have some advice for a young lad, don't tempt fate."

"What do you mean?"

"What makes them objects of desire, or I should say lust, is those two little fold of exquisitely tender flesh between their legs. In that warm, moist and most heavenly place some awful things can incubate."

Sam's mouth dropped. "What?"

"God got it wrong pandering to his legions of wowsers and do-gooders with a carnal desire suppressant, giving the world syphilis and gonorrhoea, herpes and venereal warts, crabs and chancres. Then again He might have used leftovers after making scabs, who'd know."

Sam pushed the horrors of venereal disease from his mind, thoughts of a girl far away who since that night their lips first touched caused his mind to wander, even to the extent of bringing down the wrath of the bosun for daydreaming.

More and more he thought of Emily, and for the first time in his life wrote a letter.

11

A PERSISTENT COLD NAGGING him over the last week moderated, the kitchen staff subscribing to an old fashioned remedy in alleviating symptoms of a common ailment; three juicy lemons squeezed in hot water and four aspirins before bed. The kitchen practitioners never bothered to inquire if the homespun therapy might interfere with blood thinning medication, dilute the old man's already thin blood obvious on cold days how the weather caused him discomfit.

It took only a hint of sunshine in the autumn landscape of Mt Osmond to have the wheelchair veterans bundled in their blankets, beanies jammed on the few strings of hair remaining on their scabbed and liver spotted heads, to suffer the therapeutic values of outdoors air. Early Sunday morning showers cleared to blue skies, a fresh southerly wind and the promise of a fine day.

Paul checked to see if his patient's blanket fully covered his legs, for good measure tucking it even more tightly; one task remained before the initial force needed to gain traction in the gravel of the path, wipe the old man's nose with a tissue.

Wendy might be a little late, volunteering to man a party fund raising cake stall in the Rundle St Mall; an end to a momentous week, an emotional peak meeting the leader of the opposition, Mr Abbott. Paul thought she came close to swooning when she mentioned his name over the phone, shaking hands with a prime minister in waiting: 'Oh Paul, television doesn't do Tony justice. He exudes charisma, charm and above all authority. I felt privileged to be in the same room with him. How fortunate this country's going to be to have a prime minister of his calibre.'

She hinted of standing for pre-selection for Adelaide City Council, quick to affirm being elected a councillor not a first step for higher public office: 'Local government should attract candidates willing to accept the onerous burden of dealing with matters at their source, our cities and towns.'

Paul inquired why a young person studying law at university would want to undertake such encumbrances dealing with potholes, blocked drains, trees infringing neighbours fence lines, impounding dogs and collecting garbage.

'No! Much more! Council is about zonings, planning and infrastructure. Constructing and maintaining roads and parks, foreshores and protecting the amenities of residential and industrial interests. Elected representatives meeting in council, not always agreeing owing to political and local loyalties, but eventually solving the issues of the day.'

He thought their relationship should progress to another level, a small apartment. Privacy in either of their homes never taken for granted, a dampener in their minds in their most intimate moments of parental discovery.

Coming from the car park, Wendy waved, his girl not late. "We sold twenty dozen lamingtons, a dozen fruit cakes, heaps of donations, in all $395," she said excitedly now within hearing.

He accepted her political passion which at first he found obsessive, but as their relationship progressed her intensity began to make him think beyond briefly scanning newspapers and catching glimpses of news on television. With a growing political awareness he began to see yawning cracks in a flawed Labor federal government her acid vitriol continuously condemned.

Quite possibly he loved her even more when her face radiated like a small child promised a visit to a circus when she reminisced of her political heroes, her loathing for bumbling, socialist Labor. Where did her zealous commitment come from, he wondered? Definitely not her parents, mainstream suburbia who swung either way with the political tempo of the day.

He knew now, a man of small statue but immense courage and leadership, vision and statesmanship, who against great odds within his own party governed wisely and with great financial prudence. A role model for aspiring politicians of all persuasions, Australia's 25th prime minister, John Howard. That this diminutive and unassuming man could as an equal clasp the hands of foreign presidents and prime ministers, stand side by side with them, the Australian flag flown as an honoured partner in the international community.

Her bubbling effervescence suddenly turned sour, her lips a pursed slit as she flopped down on a park bench. "This crude and dreadful labouring type reeking of alcohol made an absolute nuisance of himself at our stall arguing in support of the socialists. I told him quite strongly we come into this world not owed a living. To sponge on the endeavours of others willing to exert and sacrifice themselves to succeed. Conservative governments of this country have encouraged individual Australians to climb the ladder of achievement by dedication to goals.

"Liberal ideology does not believe in handouts to those who shun work through choice, chicanery and outright fraud of the public system. An advocate of choice in the workplace, Work Choice legislation which allowed individual workers to negotiate directly with their employers without union interference, thrown out like rubbish by a Labor government."

The kitchen packed a picnic lunch hamper; sliced roast pork, freshly baked bread rolls, sachets of butter, sliced tomato, lettuce, beetroot, diced onions, boiled eggs, tub of mayonnaise, fruit cake, thickened cream and three cartons of chocolate milk.

"My, aren't we are lucky today? Clear blue skies and a fine lunch to enjoy outdoors," Paul said to the old man who might have been asleep, breathing deeply with his mouth wide open. "In addition we have the company of Wendy who you might remember, but probably don't. Who knows, she might be the lord mayor of Adelaide one day, premier of South Australia, then the ultimate political prize, prime minister. Old Union, we are indeed in exulted company."

Wendy blew Paul a kiss, for her dinner roll selecting two slices of pork, salad and mayonnaise.

Paul halved a slice of pork and wiggled it on the old man's lolling tongue to rouse him, then put it in his mouth. "Election is all the talk in the news, Wendy? Do you think the government will go its full term?"

Swallowing delicately to clear her throat she looked where she would take the next delicious bite. "Well, Ms Gillard has announced in her arrogance a September poll if you can believe anything that comes out of her mouth. Though would you call it any earlier with the polls showing a defeat of the magnitude of the carnage witnessed in New South Wales and Queensland elections? Long serving Labor governments utterly decimated and their reduced numbers barely able to fill shadow cabinet positions, able to caucus in a telephone booth, I don't think so."

"Do you think a similar rout could happen here in South Australia?"

"With a popular premier and no major issues, improbable. Then again we have capable and high profile candidates waiting in the wings and nothing is certain in politics."

The old man did remember her. He thought the young nurse weak and easily led, besotted by a rapacious harpy. What spilled from her painted mouth and pearl white teeth no different than that which oozed like thick syrup from the sanctimonious talking heads which tortured him in the evenings. Enforced enlightenment before the respite of bed and lights out. Clones of the establishment portrayed in high definition on a wide flat television set affixed to the wall.

Fawning young females attired in high fashion, not a mole, wart or pimple to mar perfection, their fingers crossed and in their prayers a young British prince might serve a year in the Australian military. Their male counterparts in immaculate suits, silk ties; honey-tongued gurus blessed with a faultless grasp of world and local affairs. Dazzling white teeth aimed at the cameras, eyes suitably downcast and sombre, reporting in grave tones the death of an Australian serviceman in Afghanistan, followed with a report lasting ten seconds of air time of a train crash in India claiming two hundred lives.

Another news segment, ten seconds, the monthly tally of dead in Iraq over one thousand, the country sinking into civil war.

The clones lowered their voices and raised their eyebrows, projecting inferred outrage a media hounded paedophile resided in a community with a high number of children. Even a merciful break couldn't ease the pain, the screen filled with a sweet young thing in skimpy underwear afflicted with leakage, its solution a thick sanitary pad. Sympathy for a large family in public housing who lost their meagre possessions and dog in a fire caused by an overturned kerosene heater, a furrowed brow of indignation the home without smoke alarms. Scripted for the masses, from the mouths of vain and egotistical marionettes. The old man showed his displeasure at being forced to ingest a nightly dose of news and current affairs, turning his back on the screen and staring at the wall.

Wendy's irritating voice gnawed at him. "September election aside the coalition is of the opinion the four independents will soon withhold their wavering support for the government. One for certain after the disgraceful back flip by the prime minister over his private member's bill for poker machine reform."

Paul broke off a piece of bread roll, spread it with butter and placed it in the old man's mouth. "Read in paper the government were left with little option when the opposition numbers and remaining independents would have defeated the legislation. I think Senator Wilkie's correct though, gambling addiction is causing misery in the community?"

"With respect, I cannot agree with that surmise, Paul. Certainly not the whole truth or we would have voted for the legislation. Gambling to excess does cause problems for some but the clubs, and I believe their executives responsible to the community at large, have mechanisms in place to deal with such issues. Heaven forbid, the club industry is the backbone of the community with employment, support for sporting bodies and localised groups. Clubs have proved beyond doubt their industry can self regulate."

Paul wiped the old man's chin. "The independents though are still staying solid with the government."

"Who will pay the ultimate price at the next election, heed my word. Take Mr Oakshott who resigned from the National Party and successfully stood as an independent for state parliament in New South Wales, now the federal member. The other two independents, Mr Katter and Mr Windsor, rural conservatives representing graziers, farmers, farm and mine workers, simple country folk. Independents? I think not. Against the wishes of their constituents the three have thrown their lot in with the socialists."

Paul inserted a straw in a carton of chocolate milk and the old man sucked thirstily. "As usual you make a damning point, Wendy."

"Mr Katter representing a North Queensland outback electorate I especially find difficult to understand." She spread thick cream on her slice of fruit cake, licked her lips and bit off a large portion.

"He probably secured something important for his electorate. Who would really know what wheeling and dealing goes on in back rooms in Canberra?"

"I sincerely hope you are referring to the Labor Party's shady goings on, Paul. Shonky deals thankfully exposed by our press who monitor and expose their every devious move. Mining and carbon taxes, broken promises from a dysfunctional government."

"I'm not so certain about the mining tax. It is our country, Wendy."

"Paul, it is another Labor tax on successful business. Shouldn't those who risk billions in investment dollars receive a just and fair return for their commitment to our country? Miners are already heavily taxed and burdened with disproportional royalties not to mention excessive wage demands from rapacious mining unions."

"Isn't it a tax on super profits only?"

"No matter what spin the government puts on it, it is a tax on success and risk capital."

"Makes one wonder what will happen when the minerals run out."

"Think of it as this, what if the coal and iron ore miners withdrew from all mining activity in Australia and invested their billions in Indonesia, South Africa and South America? Abandoned Australia because of its government's avaricious taxing policies not to mention repressive environmental constraints forced upon their industry by the Greens? Where would the government's budget bottom line be then? I'll tell you where it would be, on a par with some tin pot dustbowl in Africa. Miners will continue to drive our economy, of course if allowed by government and the pesky Greens to conduct their business as miners know best. You only have to watch their informative television ads how the environment thrives in their capable hands. Amazing when you consider the big holes these corporations dig."

He thought of a visit to Sydney a few years ago, a side trip to the Hunter Valley, remembering standing by the road and looking out over a grey, lifeless moonscape of manmade mountains. Deep holes and rubble that rendered the land sterile for miles before ending at a green strip on the horizon where cattle grazed and what he thought might be a vineyard. "I suppose we are fortunate for the money invested by foreign miners, guaranteeing an Australian lifestyle the envy of the world. Pity though there isn't more Australian capital involved."

"There is, Paul, though proportionate to our small population and business sector. Australia has to understand that."

The pain would only end when gravel crunched beneath his wheels and this woman said her goodbyes with pledges of eternal love. Then the ritual of beef bouillon in a mug with two dry biscuits, freedom of the lounge to play checkers or snakes and ladders, access to a small library and a rack of magazines. Mustered for dinner at 4:30pm, followed by an hour of news and current affairs. Instead of turning his back he should run, but limited mobility made him unsure on his feet, thankful to be able to use the bathroom without assistance. Able to shuffle with the aid of a walker to the large bank of windows offering a panoramic view of the Adelaide Hills, usually obscured in the mornings with dense fog rising from the valleys to shroud the grounds, dew dripping from bare branches.

Before he turned his back and faced the wall he saw the intensive face of a man fill the screen; protruding ears sprouted from the side of an odd shaped head, a face more suited for a man of the pugilistic arts and not politics. The interviewer, moulded in waxy plastic, her perfect teeth glittering and not a single mole to mar perfection, almost cooed her carefully scripted questions, and the old man thought if not for sitting in a chair with her perfect legs crossed she might have curtseyed to the leader of the federal opposition.

12

PADDY WITH GREAT RELUCTANCE tinged with a rare sadness advised the boy running up the last strand of his Board of Trade locking splice with the ease of an able seaman, to consider paying off. He inspected the splice, a guy pennant, turning it over in his hands with a smile on his craggy, unshaven face. "There is an old trick used by those of lesser skills whose thimble drops on the deck when released from the vice, a chisel. No need here as this is the work of a seaman."

Sam felt pride, with the aid of the bosun using a foot long length of heavily gouged railway line to cut the ends. He buried six strands tucked through three for the final tuck, ready to grease, worm and parcel and serve.

"Paddy, why do you want me to pay off?"

"Only a suggestion for your own good, something to think about. After four months and a change of articles except for a few of us you are now the longest serving seaman on the ship. I am suggesting in the learning of your profession, a change of ship and possibly another to get your deck boy's time in. Jobs are getting easier we are hearing so matters out of our control must be changing for the better."

"The *Colac* has taught me much."

"Other ships will also. Burton guys, heavy lift derricks, swinging derricks, luff tackles as opposed to spans, gear housed aloft. Tie-ups using catted anchor cable, lashing deck cargo, a seaman able to cope with any challenge. The *Colac's* got none of that."

Paddy waived the worming of the splice, with a keen eye watching as Sam lightly greased and parcelled the splice from the jaw to the last tuck with a narrow strip of burlap, frapping it with sail twine. With a hank of marline he wound four turns tight in the jaw, then threaded slack in the well worn grooves of his serving board; Paddy took the marline from Sam, hand-over-hand with each turn of the serving.

"You're a good deck boy and I'd rather have some of these Melbourne ABs I have to suffer make my bunk and empty the rosy and have you on deck or in the store," Paddy said, pleased how the boy served then slackened the last five turns, cut the marline and passed the end through to cinch the serving tight.

For three months the *Colac* tramped, coal from Newcastle to Fremantle, sailing south to Bunbury to load sleepers for the Victorian Railways in Geelong. Change of articles in Geelong and with the exception of the bosun, storekeeper and deck boy resulted in a mass exodus on deck. From Geelong to Thevenard, South Australia, salt for Sydney.

Sam wrote to Emily once a week, her replies in a delicate slightly backhand script precious and placed with his first discharge in a duck canvas wallet stitched seven to the inch under the discerning eye of the storekeeper.

Berthing in Balmain Sam showered and even shaved, then stood outside the galley with a dejected look on his face and empty canvas bag in hand; the chief cook's defences crumbled. The love struck boy received a shoulder of pork, potatoes, pumpkin, parsnips, carrots and loaf of bread.

"I'm starting to think you're married to this girl, son," Theodore said, wrapping a slab of butter in greaseproof paper to accompany a tin of blackcurrant jam. "Word of caution, watch the vultures on the gate. Make sure when you go through there are others getting the attention of the watchmen. Probably around change of gangs."

Emily knew of his ship's berthing, having visited the Huddart Parker Darling harbour wharf on numerous occasions, an excuse to herself no more than a visit to the city. Even though she kept his letters which said he missed her under her pillow, he may have forgotten her. Why wouldn't he? In other ports much prettier girls to choose, not a dowdy one in patched hand-me-down dresses.

Gate watchmen mainly ignored her, though some looked for a bump in her belly with ribald amusement, of a mind an easy waterfront mark dumped by a seaman lover. Then news from a more sympathetic watchman, the *Colac's* orders berthing in Balmain to discharge salt.

She waited at the top of a steep and narrow street leading from the main thoroughfare of Balmain to the wharves, dressed in her best dress with the seams intact. Below the *Colac* low in the water clearly visible in a cloud of black smoke billowing from her funnel, her eight derricks swung over the wharf and the rattle of winches and escaping steam.

Sam passed through the gate with a dozen wharf labourers with bags who dared two watchmen of advanced age to challenge them; what could a man get in the pub for salt scraped off the deck?

Both saw each other at the same time, Sam breaking into a run, both stopping abruptly no more than a few feet apart. Breathless, he dropped his bag and held out his arms.

"Emily, I hoped you would come."

"So you don't think me a brazen waterfront hussy," she teased, lifting on her toes to briefly press her lips against his.

"No, not Emily Knight."

"Suppose I have to believe you." She grabbed his hand, almost singing her words.

"Got our dinner from the chief cook."

"He must be a very generous man. Will you thank him for us?"

"That's not what the crowd thinks of him, then none of the cooks get anything good said about them. Abuse having to make do with what the chief steward orders on the cheap. Now there is a real mean man, company through and through."

"Sam, there's another for dinner," she said, a tremor in her voice. "Father."

"He's home from the country?"

"For a few days now."

"Your mother must be happy."

"Father hit her arguing over money. He wanted her ironing and cleaning money."

He glanced at her with a scowl. "Emily, I sail with hard men who would batter you for looking sidewise at them, but I am certain none would harm a woman."

"Said he spent all his money catching the train from Goulburn, and Mother should be grateful for him keeping the home together. I don't really know what he meant by that. We have nothing."

"Is he home now?"

She nodded. "We could smell beer on his breath, it makes him so angry."

He remembered his own father, reaching for her hand. Older now, a young man of the world; he squeezed her hand tightly, following the waterfront precinct to the ferry terminal.

≈

At the front door Sam hesitated. "Emily, if your father finds fault with dinner he can sit in the corner and sulk." He felt certain her father's bravado amounted to no more than ascendancy over the vulnerable, a man who carefully picked his mark; parasites who preyed upon the weak, their period of ascendency over others usually short.

Wallis Knight sprawled on the divan, his bleary eyes challenging anyone who dared glance in his direction. Sam calculated his size, near six feet, broad shoulders and stocky; if the man possessed heart he would be a formidable opponent. A man no doubt attractive to women, a full head of hair brushed casually to one side of his face, white teeth and a ready smile for those he targeted with his charm.

At forty the Adonis veneer of youth begun to yield to facial bloating and cheeks filigreed with broken capillaries, streaks of grey in his hair he obviously took great care of with brushing and pomades.

Sam sensed the uneasiness in the room, Mary and Harriet cross-legged huddled in an opposite corner playing a made-up game, mostly their eyes flitting from their meaningless moving of wooden blocks to the brooding presence of their father.

The slightest hint of a smile and narrowed eyes challenged Sam. "You got intentions with my daughter, son?" he said, a slur in his voice. "The mother tells me you're a seaman and by what I know of seamen around this waterfront there's not one of them you'd trust with a dried up old hag on crutches."

"What do you mean do I have intentions?" Sam's voice remained calm, a thought if some of his more aggressive shipmates stood in his place the challenge met and dealt with Wallis Knight spread on the floor.

"Don't worry about me crowding your game, sonny. Won't be around long enough," he mocked. "Nothing to keep me here. No swooning missus, no yelping kids rushing up the hall to greet Daddy. A man sends good money home and his family begrudge him a thanks. What you got in the bag, son?"

"The chief cook on my ship gave me dinner."

Prominent veins at the base of his neck pulsed as he made an effort to get up from the divan, the effort not worth it and slumping back. "You getting it off with the mother as well? Skewering the cold slag for some offal you stole?"

A faint protest came from Claire hunched over the table, tears welling in her eyes as she prayed her daughters never heard.

A full bladder would soon make it imperative a visit to the lavatory. "Let me tell you, sonny, this man don't take kindly to charity, especially from them bedding females in my family."

"Father, that's not true!" Emily cried, stricken. "Sam is a nice boy. We like each other and we don't think like that."

"Yeah, and I believe in fairies at the bottom of the garden," he snarled. "Word of warning to you, girlie, don't be a naive easy mark. Take it from a man who has trophied many a sweet young thing, the boy's got one thing on his mind, and if you don't know that by now your first full belly ain't far off."

Emily hung her head, clenching her hands in front of her, silent tears streaming down her cheeks.

"Dinner, you said, son?"

"The chief cook gave me a shoulder of pork and vegetables. Bread, butter and jam."

"What you mean is you stole it when he turned his back? Truth, son?"

Sam breathed softly through his nose, his eyes fixed on the smug man. "I would be careful how you choose your words."

"Well, what do you know, the boy's got spirit. Feel like trying it out on me, son?"

"I don't want to fight you." Paddy would have, Wilbur and Uriah without hesitation. What would fighting solve? Nothing, an easy victory for the older, stronger and more experienced man to boast about. Retreating from a physical confrontation in no way lessened a male ego, a mindset of not wanting to fight in this home.

"Your type never does. Good for sniffing around young skirts who think it's only to pee out of, but when it comes to being a man, you're all talk." He rose unsteadily from the divan and stretched. "Cook your bloody dinner, I don't care because I'm going where a man's appreciated. Where I'm wanted." He directed the last of his words at Claire with her head cradled in her arms on the table.

Sam felt a helpless observer, relieved to hear the front door slam.

"Oh, Sam, I'm so sorry," Emily said, at her mother's side caressing her shoulders. "It's the bad times that have changed him."

The only sound in the room the soft sobs of a distraught mother, her frightened daughters by her side, Sam at a loss what to do. Take Emily and her sisters in his arms and soothe them, sympathy for Claire. Meaningless words from a stranger, an intruder. At this moment in time in a dark and cold room bare of adornment he stood witness to a family breakdown, one of thousands throughout the land because of as Emily said, the bad times.

Their dinner eaten in silence, Sam noticed a meal put aside on a pot with a half inch of water in the bottom; for the head of the family when he returned.

Emily walked him to the end of the street, pausing in an alcove which hid them from view. She felt his arousal, hers as strong as his as a hand softly kneaded first one breast then the other. Words tumbled out of her mouth in a rush: "Sam, I love you!"

13

A DAY BEFORE SAILING Sam took Paddy's advice and paid off, his payoff calculated to last him a month ashore. He found cheap lodgings at the harbour end of George St, sharing a room with two others made more acceptable with ease of access to the wharves and Pyrmont.

With a sense of great loss he said goodbye to Paddy, a parting gift from a seemingly emotionless and sea-hardened man a deck knife and marline spike in a pigskin pouch. The honed razor sharp blade of the six inch knife and polished marline spike greased in pig fat, a residue deliberately left inside the sheaf for that purpose.

"A seaman without a knife is a seaman in name only," Paddy said in his normal growl, adding a less fiercely: "These are the tools of your profession, care for them."

He met Emily in the city. "I am rich and with my second discharge I am no longer a first tripper. Though I suppose the term first tripper ceases to exist on your second sailing."

Her narrowed eyes chastened. "Are you going to be one of those seamen who throw their money about as if the world may end before it is spent on beer and girls?"

"A girl on each arm would be nice."

She grabbed his arm and dragged him close. "If you did I would pull their hair out and shoo them off!"

"Really?"

She pouted. "Really."

"Emily, I have never seen a seaman lucky enough to have two girls in tow. I listened to the bosun talking about the South American nitrate ports where the sailors fought each other over girls. Mad drunk on pisco, using their deck knives to carve each other up. Then after months and months in hard ships at sea who could blame them for losing their minds?"

"What's pisco?"

"Something similar to brandy, distilled in Chile and Peru. Paddy kind of drooled when he said grapes grown in dry and rocky soil and watered with snowmelt from the Andes."

"Seamen fought over girls?"

"So he said, also there being no need because the girls in the cantinas were available for a few pesos, whatever pesos are worth."

She blushed. "Do you do that in port?"

"Emily, no! Wouldn't say no to a kiss from a special girl who lives in Pyrmont. Who has a pretty mother and two gorgeous little sisters."

The colour in her cheeks deepened. "Mother would like you calling her pretty."

"She is pretty, but her eldest daughter far surpasses her."

With a toss of her head, she bumped her thigh against his. "My father might be right about your intentions."

In the bright sunlight he noticed her best dress, shabby and worn and his heart went out to her. She didn't need to dress fashionably, in furs and satin, shiny lace up boots, her natural beauty enough to avert eyes from frayed hems, tatty lace and parted seams. "Emily, can I do something for you?"

"Ask and it is yours," she said. "What, Sam?"

"Would you think it wrong of me to want to buy you a gift?"

"Hmm, don't think so, but I couldn't return the good deed."

"Let's pretend it's Christmas or your birthday or some other special time. Let me buy you a new dress?"

She shook her head and tried to hold back the emotions that threatened to reduce her to tears.

"Emily, it's only a dress. Like me buying a pair of dungarees. Can I?"

She pulled a handkerchief from the sleeve of her dress and buried her nose in it and blew. "Sam, it wouldn't be proper."

"No more than a gift from a rich sailor. Well, wealthy for a week or two," he said, adding: "Of course the boardinghouse takes most of my payoff, and I have to put a stamp in my union book. That more important than anything, even your dress."

A lessoning of sniffles signalled weakened opposition to his offer, an impetus to press the issue. "Now if I bought you delicate things it might be construed as your father said having intentions, but not a simple dress."

She stuffed the handkerchief back up the sleeve of her dress, a coquettish smile on her face. "Sam Wright, what are your intentions?"

"Emily! I am buying my girl a dress, nothing more."

"Promise me not expensive."

The dress on sale cost thirteen shillings, Emily entranced by the pale blue material that swept the top of her boots, white lace accentuating her small bosom, a tiny white lace bow at the back. When she drifted on tiptoes out of the fitting booth he felt a constriction in his chest, unable to take his eyes off a girl transformed into a beautiful young woman.

The dress fitted snugly, hugging her small waist, the flare of her hips, the curvature of her bottom. Her smile, her hands caressing the satiny material, all that Sam needed to know this dress and this girl were one.

The gift troubled Claire and after tucking in her two youngest daughters sat with Emily on the divan. "Emily, what do you feel deep down for Sam?"

"I love Sam, Mother."

"Does he feel the same for you?"

"Sam loves me."

"Love for a boy doesn't always mean the same as it does for a girl. A word that can be used by some men to exploit a girl's weakness."

"What weakness, Mother?"

"One's instinctive defences against desire."

"Mother, Sam has made no advances to me."

"Sam is a wonderful and generous boy, and when I say boy I mean exactly that. Both of you are far too young to take steps reserved for older, more matured couples."

"Falling pregnant?" she murmured, her voice barely audible.

Claire took her in her arms, with a circular motion gently rubbing her back. "Pregnancy is one, making a lifelong commitment is another and discovering what you thought love as no more than a painful illusion. I have in this life three beautiful daughters, living, breathing evidence that all is not wrong and there is hope for the future."

Disgruntled, Wallis came home around 9:00pm, earlier than he would have liked, the last of his money gone. The barmaid serving in the back bar, the liquid motion of her ample bottom and the swell of her exceptionally large bosom the object of his attention. With little money his chances of success relied wholly on endless palaver, flattery and exuding the image of means in his pocket. Unable to fill the glass she held up questionably, he regrettably said goodnight.

To relieve the bulge in his trousers he would have to resort to parting the unenthusiastic thighs of his wife, ignore her pathetic bleating of his forceful entry. Pitiful moans his weight hurt her, his ramming, his response she should be grateful of his servicing her, a small price to pay for the pleasure his body gave her. When he released, whining his roar of pleasure would be heard by the children.

No matter, forcing apart her legs to gain entry, her complete submission beneath him satisfying in itself, a thought possibly his copious discharge might find a productive reception in her frigid sheaf. Her bad luck as this time he wouldn't be back. Let them fend for themselves, he didn't care, for far too long a burden upon him.

≈

Sam put a pound note in the Knights housekeeping jar, protests from Claire unheeded. Not generosity, he made it known clearly, seeing he took most of his meals with the family. He enjoyed shopping with Emily, the markets at closing time with vendors heavily marking down their leftover produce before the desperate came begging. He thought he would soon have to stand for a job, the prospect filling him with a melancholy that grew each day the thought of separation from Emily.

Rare quietness filled the house, Mary and Harriet at school and Claire in Chippendale cleaning and ironing, for her a long walk home. Dinner simmered on the stove, beef stew awaiting its dumplings.

"There has to be more to life than cleaning up the dregs of the wealthy," Sam said. "Your mother after work comes home exhausted, walking miles and miles."

Emily sifted flour, added water and salt and made her dumplings; washing her hands at the sink she sat beside him on the divan. "I left school to get a job, silly me because there weren't any but of course my sisters needed me at home." She settled against him as the divan took the full weight of their bodies; she felt his lower body press against her, her eyes clamped shut as she returned the pressure.

"Emily?" he whispered, trailing kisses down her face to the base of her neck.

Her emotions raced frantically out of control, wanting to take hold of him, place his hardness where she felt a searing heat between her legs. Without hesitation, she arched her lower body to allow him to push her dress around her upper thighs, exposing her cotton undergarment. Alarmed, she thought she may have wet herself, a warm dampness between her legs, uncaring as she felt him raise one leg and place it over his, drawing aside a leg of her underwear and slipping a finger inside her.

She let out a muffled cry, tightening her muscles around the intrusion, wishing it could reach deeper. Instead the hand now kneaded the soft lightly downed flesh of her mound, murmuring a weak protest as he removed his finger, slipping the buckle of his belt and unbuttoning his fly.

"Emily?"

She looked between their bodies, the exposed engorged head of his organ secreting a clear fluid, resisting the temptation to touch it, grasp it, in awe of its power. Instead she drew a deep breath, closed her eyes and turned on her back.

With one hand he eased the undergarment down her thighs, over her knees, her feet. Parting her legs, for the first time he gazed in wonder at her sheaf, her prominent mound crowned with a fuzz of down, two thick folds a clear division slightly parted to expose other lesser lips shielding an entry of moist and delicate pink flesh. His weight crushed her into the cushions and she felt him pressed against her entry, releasing her breath and relaxing her body to receive him.

The sound of shrill voices caused both a moment of panic, the front door opening and the voices more clear, Mary and Harriet arguing. Sam and Emily struggled upright, both making frantic adjustments to their clothing, regulating their breathing and sitting a body width apart.

Mary and Harriet far too young and innocent to know why their sister and Sam breathed heavily, flushed with looks of utter dejection on both their faces.

14

S O CLOSE TO FULFILLING a dream. A minor accident, the early release of two children from school, the younger suffering an abrasion in the playground to her knee and the headmaster authorising the older sibling to escort home.

For the first time he gazed upon and touched the wondrous secrets of girl. Now steeped in misery as he listened to the excited chatter of two children, one in gory terms relating a mutilating injury, the other peeved at having to act as nursemaid.

Next day he walked from his lodgings to the Adelaide Steamship Company wharf at Darling Harbour, the *Aldinga* alongside discharging general cargo from Queensland ports. Among the seamen standing outside the wharf gates a more knowledgeable of waterfront word-of-mouth reported jobs in her. Even elaborating, three ABs, one fireman, one trimmer. Those gathered began to doubt his information when no master or chief engineer appeared. The informant to boost his credibility proffered a theory the company with a long record of favouring scabs to union men would first scour their books for trustworthy men known to the company and whom their officers and engineers could rest easy dissent would be minimal if non-existent.

"Adelaide Steamship Company prefers bulls, those who at the flick of a mate's finger will drop to their knees. Their books overflow with scabs, let me tell you," Josh Atkinson said. He singled out Sam standing by himself. "Deck boy or bucko?"

"Deck boy."

"How much time?"

"Four months."

"Why did you pay off your last ship? Things aren't that easy. Didn't you consider it wise to get your time in, join the lofty ranks of buckos?"

Sam stared at him, irritated at his belligerent tone of voice. "No, I didn't consider it wise. On advice I paid off to gain a wider knowledge of seamanship, ships with different gear, tie ups and cargo."

Josh grinned and his whole face changed from a serious, piercing demeanour to that of a young man without a care in the world. Tall and thin, his sallow face reflected intelligence; coming off second best in an altercation a few years ago his broken nose reset with a slight bend. "Counsel from shipmates?"

"From a seaman, yes. Bosun of the *Colac*."

"Paddy Fenton, the old dog! Sailed with Paddy, knows how to run a job. A rare one with most of the bosuns I have suffered no more than a mate's messenger boy. Tough old bastard, not many I know would tackle him even though he is getting on."

"Are you standing for the *Aldinga*?"

"Loading for warmer climes as far north as Cairns, yes I am. There's also a sweet young thing in Cairns who pulls beer in a pub on the Barbary Coast who might remember me."

Sam warmed to Josh, misjudging him as arrogant and aloof. "What would she load in Queensland?"

"Sugar for Pyrmont."

The brick façade of the Adelaide Steamship Company's wharf and offices at No.6 Darling Harbour obscured from the roadway any view of ships berthed alongside twin wharves serviced by a single warehouse. The size of the warehouse occupied almost the entire wharfage set on bedrock with turpentine piles, cargo landed on narrow aprons immediately transferred by barrows for storage within the perpetual twilight depths. Massive Oregon beams with equally strong trusses and columns supported an iron roof ridged with a broad cap of sky lighting along its entire length.

Sam's earlier view of the *Aldinga* and her tall yellow and black funnel came from the iron railing at the top of the Argyle Cut. Even from this distance he could hear her winches rattling, their power sourced by steam through deck lines bracketed to the hatch coamings.

Built in Belfast in 1920 hard work scarred an aging workhorse and its many misjudged encounters with wharves, the black painted hull and its gaunt frames blistered with thick rust, plates buckled and dented. Bridge and amidships accommodation separated by a geared bunker hatch and port and starboard side pockets, accommodation for master, officers, wireless officer, engineers and catering. Single five ton union purchase gear set on the foremast and mainmast serviced four hatches. Aft below and above the steering flat, certified accommodation for seamen in four berth cabins.

A glance around the men growing agitated as time passed Sam made a mental note of their ages, himself the youngest, the closest to him around nineteen with a pasty face and permanently hunched shoulders; he thought possibly a steward.

Many began to have serious doubts about the validity of jobs on the *Aldinga*, the recipients of contemptuous stares from clerical staff and foremen stevedores impeded clear access to their offices.

"Maybe the old man and chief engineer's got hangovers," Josh quipped; no one bothered to add a dubious parentage comment, some giving up to head for the Melbourne Steamship Company and Huddart Parker wharf offices farther down the street. "I do know that an old faggot by the name of Marshall Langford is master, God bless his evil and black as midnight heart and his fondness for logging and excluding from the industry ABs and firemen on a fairly regular basis. Served his indentures licking the highly polished shoes of the upper crust officer elite in British India, returning the induction tenfold with his up the rears of Chinese and Lascar crews. Ah, then gracing us with his regal presence on the Aussie coast. His life blighted by loud-mouthed belligerents, cesspools of Bolshevik unionism, sea lawyers supreme."

Sam suddenly began to have second thoughts about the *Aldinga*.

"Don't take any notice of me," Josh said, throwing his arms in the air. "I'm well known to exaggerate the attributes of those who make my life a misery at sea, but when it comes to that old bastard I have a right to be carried away. Speaks with an aristocratic plum in its mouth and I know for certain the rat's birthplace is Fitzroy, seen it on the articles. A bloody Fitzroy slum though you wouldn't know it by what drips and hisses out of its mouth."

Captain Langford in achieving officer class cultured an acceptable British accent. Australian born his Anglo-Saxon bloodline contained the tiniest trace of colour attributable to a Moor washed ashore on the Cornish coast from the fleeing Spanish Armada, well hidden in family archives.

The man sauntering through the wharf gates wore four gold bars on his jacket cuffs, his hat piped with gold thread and leaf in which nestled Adelaide Steamship Company insignia. A razor thin nose divided a long sallow face from which beneath hedged brows two flint-like eyes took umbrage upon an inferior world. Members of the Federated Seamen's Union of Australasia proliferated in this flawed world, thick skulled cretins better suited to carting maggot blown, overflowing nightsoil pans on their shoulders if by some miracle a deity could get them to raise a sweat and give an honest day's work.

He swept the now animated group of men with a contemptuous uplift of his nose, a slight curl to his thin slit of a mouth. Over the years an odorous task for masters and chief engineers selecting uncertified ratings from the hotchpotch available on the Australian coast, schemers and incompetents offering their wretched endemic sloth for gainful employment. Who then besmirched the privilege of employment with their unionised and political dogma and work ethics drowned in a bog of cheap alcohol and tobacco.

Concluded instantly any chance of signing articles if a man in line sniffed, coughed, sneezed, limped, a vacant face and loose mouth symptoms of a wet brain prevalent amongst their kind. Even more damning, his glower of rejection if his delicate nostrils sensed the vapours of alcohol in the air.

Captain Langford viewed with disdain the motley dressed group of seamen, even though most would acknowledge their clothes were their best going ashore gear, the master certain one used his tie to wipe his nose. How different from loyal and hardworking Asian ratings whose limpid brown eyes filled with gratitude when offered employment in well-found ships under the command of diligent masters. Obedient and submissive, humbling themselves in the presence of their superiors, who hurried on deck to fulfil an order, who acknowledge their officers with total respect.

This lot would fill their bellies with booze prior to square up, shout and shake their fists while chanting Bolshevik slogans. Rabble, waterfront scrum indoctrinated by disciples from hell, the Industrial Workers of the World and the Federated Seamen's Union of Australasia. Cajoling, breathing their alcohol saturated fumes in his officers faces, threatening bodily harm if any dared step foot on their decks! Their decks! Retribution came with the authority vested in him by the Navigation Act, and when used to the fullest extent gave the greatest of pleasure.

Log them until not one penny remained in their account of wages. Instant dismissal, suspensions from the industry. Culling drunks and the mentally impaired, thugs and slackers, agitators and incompetents.

"Three ABs with their last discharges stamped VG stand out," Captain Langford snapped.

Nine men formed a ragged line, eyes averted except for two to avoid the master's accusing appraisal. Unfortunately to make his selection more luck than founded on company recommendation, none offered for selection with a newspaper folded under an arm, a flower in a lapel, feather in a hatband, a distinctive tie. A slender white finger selected three who at least could stand fully erect, though one cocky individual who seemed amused with proceedings might prove worthy of bridge ink in the future.

A satisfactory inspection of their last discharge completed the distasteful process, Captain Langford unchanged of an opinion of what offered for gainful employment in the lower ranks on a par with stragglers leftover from a cattle sale. "Shipping office 1400 hours. Turn to 0800 hours."

Selecting a fireman and trimmer far simpler, two men standing apart from the main group, both with newspapers folded under their arms; known to the chief engineer, of sober demeanour and a willingness to work.

Not worthy of mention in waterfront pubs, the selection of a deck boy presented the master with a minor dilemma, mentioned by the Sydney manager of a minor staff member wanting to get his son to sea, a boy with limited intelligence but suitable for deck duties. Captain Langford abhorred favours, of a mind beside nepotism those who could only advance on the dubious commendation of their peers deserved to remain on the bottom tiers of society. His mind made up, he called: "One deck boy with discharge."

Sam stepped forward. "I am a deck boy."

When would this uneducated rabble learn to address their superiors appropriately? A sharp yes sir, shoulders back, head up. "Last ship?"

"*Colac*. Four months with three VG's"

"It would be expected or your short tenure at sea would otherwise have been terminated by the shipping superintendent," Captain Langford said loftily. "Why a curtailed service with Huddart Parker?"

"The bosun thought it best I learn on other ships."

"In other words the man wanted rid of you."

Sam felt his stomach muscles knot. "The bosun and storekeeper taught me to splice wire and rope. Short splices, long splices, Liverpool and Board of Trade. I can make monkey fists, square sennits, manrope, ocean plaits and pineapple knots. I made a focastle head vent cover, and I know the difference between yardarm and amidships and can make myself fast aloft. Importantly, I know how to support on deck."

No doubt the union cadres were pleased with this one, their grasping tentacles well and truly implanted in this self-opinionated braggart, Captain Langford thought. He weighed his options of a boy who boasted the rudiments of seamanship and a dolt of a first tripper who might end up rove through a quarter block on his first square up. With a full overhaul of the gear northbound and load line survey on arrival in Brisbane he said begrudgingly: "Shipping office 1400 hours. Turn to 0800 hours."

Sam felt a rush of adrenalin flow through his body, receiving a grin from Josh who quipped: "Follow me mate, I know the way well."

≈

The *Colac* nurtured its share of malcontents, but nothing as aggressive as the anti-unionism on the *Aldinga* led by the bosun and two highly vocal ABs. Dissent raged among ships due to the union's federal executive's recommending acceptance of the Justice Dethridge Award handed down earlier in the year. The published acceptance in the Seamen's Journal, signed by the general secretary and federal executive, stated on the gain side seamen would receive an increase in wages of £1/5/0 a month, the offset a small reduction in overtime from 2/9 an hour to 2/6 in addition to the loss of deferred sailings and working cargo clauses. The union executive signatories noted in their statement penal clauses applied, though acceptable as punitive clauses were an integral part of arbitration and out of the influence of any single union.

Adding to rank and file anger and frustration Attorney General Menzies made it clear addressing parliament that if seamen did not accept the Dethridge Award in its entirety he would invoke the licensing provisions of the Transport Workers Act. Subsequently, every seaman licensed under the colloquial dog collar act.

The deck delegates having paid off the bosun called a special meeting at 10:00am. Kiernan Chapman, a Shetland Islander, lumbering and broad shouldered without a single hair on his large, misshapen head settled most of his arguments with his fists and boots. A permanent scowl, a bulbous nose infested with blackheads, black beady eyes that glared out upon the world with hostility and challenge.

Except for the muffled sound of winches a silence descended in the ABs messroom perched above the steering flat. "Call for the nomination of two delegates," Kiernan snarled, his eyes obscured so fiercely did his brow knit.

Sam watched Josh who rested back in his chair with hands folded behind his head; he seemed disinterested by the proceedings, the occasional glance at Garry Macintosh and Perry Marquand who joined with him. It came as no surprise the presence of a clique, support for the federal executive in recommending acceptance of the new award, that seamen should accept their lot in these difficult times. The outcome of election for delegates also held no surprises.

Silence.

Josh casually raised a forefinger at the back of his head. "Me, I volunteer. I nominate Gary."

"Seconder and those in favour?" Kiernan grunted.

Unanimous.

The bosun drummed a thick finger on a ledger bound with a leather spine on the messroom table.

No one recording the minutes, Josh looked directly at Sam.

Sam jolted upright, a lump caught in his throat. "No!"

"Give the meeting one reason why?" Josh said, enjoying himself. "We're willing to take a gamble on your writing prowess. A show of confidence in you, son."

Sam immediately regretted his first reaction, leaving his chair to sit in the vacant one beside the bosun, also on the table a notebook and pencil.

"Don't look so terrified," Josh added. "To alleviate your fears the delegates aren't going to throw you in the deep end recording union business. Take heart, your first meeting's only a couple of lines, election of delegates and minute secretary."

Sam relaxed, even more when Josh took him aside after the meeting. "Most of these blokes come from Newcastle which is well known in union circles a port with an abnormally high number of groupers."

"What is a grouper?"

"Members with a fair grasp of the English language and politics to the right and extreme right. Because the majority of the union leans to socialism and Labor policies, groupers use stopwork and shipboard meetings to further their cause. Usually these members in a disruptive way oppose union policy, spurious claims the union is jeopardising jobs because of excessive claims upon the shipowner, making our presence indefensible and subject to shipowners employing low wage Asians. Now with the Dethridge Award which has slashed our conditions and wages the groupers are supporting the federal executive who have accepted the award on the pretext of difficult financial times."

"Can't the union stop groupers from promoting their agenda?"

"Promoting their agenda, I like that, Sam. You're a good choice for minute secretary. Our many enemies refute it, but the Federated Seamen's Union of Australasia is the most democratic union in Australia, a union of diverse nationalities, creeds and above all, worldly views. I have a rule book which I will give you so you can read how the membership controls the union. How the union has united its members, and how through the strength of leadership and a strong rank and file have achieved dignity of labour, legitimacy and respect."

"Groupers oppose these gains?"

"If you mount a stump and demand the world share the bounty, among your working class audience will be those who will cut you down. Condemn you as a socialist and anti-monarchist. Australians dreading you will deface their precious flag, rip out that foreign bit in the top left hand corner. That you will refuse to stand stiff to attention with your hand covering your beating heart and sing for the long life of a British monarch. Cheer until hoarse for a visiting regal."

"Are you a member of the Militant Minority Movement?"

Josh's eyes widened. "Jesus, no. Those blokes are far too serious about the working class wresting the means of production and bringing down the capitalist system for me to be part of their crusade. Too disciplined, though I do share their views."

"Are these groupers dangerous for the union?"

"Not for only us, but all organised labour. I wouldn't exactly categorise groupers as scabs, but I reserve my opinion. Of the lowest of the low is the blackleg, the worker who will cross a picket line and bed down with the enemy. He has his excuses of course for abandoning his fellows, family, church, loyalty, politics, a long list of conscience cleansing lies to cover his ignominy, which of course he does not see as shame. Oh no, he will swagger the streets in proud formations with fellow blacklegs, arms swinging, head held high, led by police triple their number on horses armed with batons, to pass through the factory gate.

"Your average grouper differs slightly from the potential blackleg in that with his ceaseless verbiage he will have you thinking he is a union conscious man, a militant who has no more than a minor disagreement with the current course of action being undertaken by our union leadership. Scrape away the veneer and false comradeship and you will find a man who would crush the union in its present form. He is not a revolutionary who fights for a fairer share of what the working masses produce. He is a man who believes it is the right of the employer to be able to set wages and conditions with no input from the union.

"We who labour with our sweat are mere pawns in the grand scheme of things, fated to live a life of debt and exist on crumbs. We remain all our miserable lives chained to the system, dreading the rent man, the money lender, the butcher, the baker, the greengrocer. We have two men in government now who are far worse than that slimy maggot who gifted our overseas fleet to British shipowners, Stanley Bruce. Prime Minister Lyons and his attorney general stooge grovel at the feet of British royalty and lick the shoes and spats of those who spread their well fed rumps on British parliamentary leather."

"Why doesn't the union expel the groupers?"

"Because in our union groupers have a democratic right to voice their opinions. Even more so than the political parties in Canberra who must abide by party policy, though an old scoundrel called Billy Hughes who's worn quite a dent in parliamentary leather changed the concept of loyalty when he ratted on the Labor Party and crossed over to the Nationalists."

"I've heard a lot of talk about the 1927 strike and scabs, our members forced to sail with them."

"We've suffered some serious setbacks since 1875, but 1927 rates our lowest point, acceptance of the shipowners terms we sail with scabs who took strikebound ships to sea. Many of these scabs lived the horror of the going to sea in wartime, hailed rightly so as heroes. To my mind misguided fools in their false allegiance to the establishment. Some of them met their fate on stormy nights at sea, others thrown down hatches. Unfortunate, but when our members are in the minority we are treated with no less mercy. We still sail with them and most have covered their past well."

≈

The bosun stalked the deck bell to bell, his lumbering presence no more than an extension of the mate who like the master considered uncertified ranks a life form on a par with the most common of menial labourers. Additionally, their limited intelligence harboured a hatred for authority, imprinted in their psyche a vermin-like cunning and deviousness. Each morning on the four to eight watch at sea, 7:45am in port, the bosun received a long list of jobs and detailed instructions how to complete the work.

Kiernan accepted his lowly role, slow witted and devoid of self-worth. He communicated in a gravelly voice caused by a fireman's hobnailed stokehold boot ground into his throat when beaten to the deck with shovel.

The storekeeper became the recipient of the job list, issuing scrapers and chipping hammers, fish oil and wads, pots of red lead and topcoats. With a load line survey due this at times brought all the officers on deck to supervise, the apprentice with a notebook and pencil to record survey stamps on cargo gear for the gear register book. This important work failed to penetrate the thick bone protecting what remained of the bosun's alcohol befuddled brain, filter through the twisted gristle of his ears.

Sam enjoyed the work but not the order from the bosun to keep his feet firmly planted on deck, a day worker aloft sending down twofold quarter blocks. Sam's argument he painted the *Colac's* foretopmast failed, even prompting from Josh working three hours rare overtime watch below.

"Boys don't go aloft," Kiernan said, then with a leer: "That ain't my doing, son, it's the award. Me, I couldn't give a fuck if you fell."

"Boys and buckos belong aloft," day worker Henry Wood said; the old AB might well with the exception of the newly joined be the only man with a clean past in the ship. Of indeterminate years, probably in his late sixties, he sailed in the last of the Cape Horner's on the Australian grain trade, driven ruthlessly and even more hungrily in their twilight years.

Kiernan spat on the deck. "Fuck you aloft! Wire rope oil and don't waste any on deck. You do and the captain will make certain it comes out your wages."

Josh and Gary, four to eight watch below, passed a small strop around the heel of the port derrick at No.1 hatch, shackling it to a light wire rove through a snatch block shackled beneath the mast table. He took five turn on the drum end and signalled Henry on the winch to heave, slowly lifting the heel free of its gooseneck. He nodded to the bosun whose bumbling presence made the work more difficult, the derrick ready for the mate's inspection.

Kiernan stared dumbly at the derrick heel, as if mesmerised by the slight movement caused by a barely perceptible roll of the ship. Josh winked at Gary and Henry, then broke into laughter as he rotated his finger in his temple.

"Knock, knock, mate. Anyone home there, Kiernan? Time to run quickly and get sir to inspect this so we pack it with fresh grease. Make sure sir doesn't forget his little hammer."

The heel tap tested and greased, Josh eased off the turns on the drum end, the heel re-seated, tightened with a large nut and split pinned.

Kiernan came out of his self induced coma. "Come on, hurry up. Company's not paying overtime for slacking." Within hearing of the mate who showed his disinterest by sharing something amusing with the senior apprentice, an officer in the making who would be journeying to the United Kingdom for further study and sit for his second mates certificate.

Sam sat on the hatch with Josh and Gary knocked off for lunch, cleaning their hands in kerosene and cotton waste. Neither seemed eager to sample boiled mutton and white sauce, spongy carrots and jacketed boiled potatoes.

"So what do you think of the antics of our bosun, Sam?" Josh asked, weighing an option to make a sandwich of the boiled sheep with mustard pickles. "Some bit of work there. We would have this gear overhauled and in the register book without any fuss if that idiot did us all a favour and dropped dead. I think he might have a metal plate about the size of an engine room shovel in his head."

Sam thought of Paddy, the difference between the two bosuns, one a seaman and the other no more than the mate's extension, and a bungling one at that. Work on the *Aldinga* differed from the *Colac* and the technique of lifting derrick heels new knowledge gained; though Josh said on similar rigged ships the single sheave head block could be used by securing it to the heel and hauling on the span wire.

"This cretin masquerading as a bosun is leader of a clique, his type always has a close circle around him. Who can imbibe freely and be unconscious in their bunks come square up, survive a mate's head count. Not us, and I include old Henry. Dragged from our bunks. Instant dismissal. Loggings. Suspension. Never let yourself become part of a clique, Sam, especially one with suspect loyalties. You may be forgiven for not believing on this ship that we are a family of seamen with allegiance to the union and a single objective to improve our lives."

Gary decided on a sandwich, a final swipe of his hands with cotton waste and tossing the wad in a bucket of kerosene used to clean sheaves and bushes. "On some ships it might seem opportune, even safer to life and limb, to be part of a faction. I hate cliques, I bloody well do. Led by loud mouthed know-alls masquerading as militants and staunch delegates. Runners of tales to mates and can't get up the road quick enough on union business. I know what their union business is, getting out of throwing hatch boards in the tween decks or breaking out a jumbo. Oh yeah, there is union business, buying booze in the pub for an official. Sucks and dags!"

Even though hungry lunch could wait, Sam ingesting their every word, slowly grasping that conditions could only be won by leadership and rank and file participation. Understanding what working under an award meant. Sometimes that document written verbatim by a judge on orders from his manipulators in the boardroom or parliament. Symbols of the establishment attired in black silk sitting in judgement of seamen.

He remembered from the *Colac* listening to seamen who sailed the world in Australian Commonwealth Shipping Line ships, fully manned with Australian crews, interned German ships known as Black Germans, ex-British tramps, Australian built E and D class, five Bay class passenger ships, even wooden ships built in United States. Now gone, defunct by decree of an anti-working class bigot. Deliberately stripped of its assets before the final debacle, the gift of five passenger ships and two special purpose ships to their major competitors, British shipowners.

Ships that carried Australian produce for under £4 a ton to European and United Kingdom markets, with the ink still wet on the sale documents, a revised freight rate by jubilant and unbelieving British shipowners of £15 a ton. Financial ruin for Australian farmers though the nation could bask in pride of those involved in the travesty awarded regal honours, British board membership and the drawing of an upstart colonial child closer to blood kin.

Sam wondered how could this happen? Where were those who wrote the headlines and editorials? An Australia maritime presence with fifty-seven world trading ships, the Australian flag flying in the major ports of the world. Given away, the gift signed with a pen held in the hand of a prime minister who deserved not a dubbing on the shoulder by a British monarch, but vilification in the history books. From the press not even a whimper, a few frustrated threats from the union movement, then acceptance. Victory for the conservatives and a new breed hatching amid their festering ranks, even more voracious in their slavish devotion to all things British.

≈

Sam's homecoming after six weeks at sea that of a family head returning to the hearth. The *Aldinga* down to her marks with sugar berthed at the Colonial Sugar Refinery wharf in Pyrmont. Throwing open the front door Emily burst into tears as did her two sisters crowding behind her, all three trying to hug him in the doorway at once. Claire, more reserved, took him in her arms and hugged him tight. So quickly this fine young boy became part of their family, again a worry for a mother.

Claire became aware of a change in Emily, her rushing to the door on hearing the postman's whistle, her moods, eyes when Sam's name came up in conversation. 'Emily, I know and you know that you and Sam will soon venture further than a kiss and a hand touching your breasts.'

Emily avoided her mother's eyes. 'Mother, is that wrong?'

'As an anxious mother I say it is wrong, what most mothers would tell their daughters. Then in truth I cannot say it is wrong because the act of love between a man and a woman who love each other is as natural as the air we breathe. Emily, allowing your body to overrule your mind can change your life forever.'

'By having Sam's baby?'

'Yes.'

'Does it always happen when a boy and girl make love?'

'No. There are means.'

'Will you tell me?'

'Which makes my fears justified.'

'Mother, we love each other. Please, what means?'

'Lysol and a douche.'

'Lysol is bleach for killing germs!' Emily gaped at her mother in astonishment, a nightmare dawning in her mind. 'What is a douche?'

'Something we don't talk about.'

'Mother, I haven't got germs!'

'I know you haven't. Something very personal for a woman.'

'What?'

Claire sighed. 'When a man during the act of intercourse discharges he releases sperm, and for a woman to protect herself from pregnancy she must quickly flush her most private part.'

'Mother, what is a douche?'

'A woman's spray. Salt can be used but Lysol is best if you can afford it.'

'There has to be another way. Mother, that is awful!'

'Diaphragms cost money and most men refuse to use condoms.'

Emily unable to sleep and listening to the gentle snores of her sisters thought of how close she and Sam came to joining their bodies. Imagining what she saw between jutting his legs inside her, the wondrous feeling and the tightening of muscles and a warm secretion lost in an image of pulling a plug from a sink and releasing a gush of greasy washing-up water. How could a woman use a cleaning agent inside the most sensitive part of her body? She didn't have germs!

A mature young man sitting at the head of the table told his enthralled audience of his new ship, Brisbane, Townsville, Cairns, lightship to Townsville to load sugar for Sydney. Wharf labourers removing two middle slabs and landing over the opening a wooden bench called a piano on which a dozen slung bags of sugar landed, slit with a boot knife to cascade into the hatch. Mountains of raw sugar to the coamings, the pungent almost overpowering smell of molasses seeping through the accommodation.

Claire baked a meatloaf and vegetables, dessert stewed apples and custard.

"Couldn't compare her with the *Colac*, but she's a good working ship if a bit heavy on deck," he said with the knowledge of a seasoned seaman. "There's a seaman called Josh who's a radical, but he reckons not. Heard the bosun going off at him and calling him a Bolshevik Wobbly."

"Bolshevik Wobbly?" Emily repeated, unable to take her eyes off him.

"There are a lot of them on the coast, Industrial Workers of the World. Bolsheviks are Russian revolutionaries."

"Will you become one, Sam?" Mary inquired innocently, trying to edge her chair closer to his.

He shook his head. "Josh doesn't admit to being anything, but he is very radical. Top delegate, the mates keep their distance from him as do the Newcastle groupers."

Claire's brow creased. "Newcastle groupers?"

"We have a new award which is not being readily accepted by the majority of the membership even though the federal executive of the union recommend its adoption. Groupers, those who normally oppose union directives, are supporting the federal executive and saying we should accept the award."

"What is an award?" Emily asked, also moving her chair closer to his; she wanted so desperately to cover his hand with hers, knowing if she did her sisters with squirms and giggles would also. More than take his hand, to be alone with him, in his arms.

"An award is wages and conditions of employment. Under this award we have lost much."

"Shouldn't seamen like everyone else in these times be content with their terms of employment? At least seamen have a job," Claire said.

"Seamen don't see it that way, not when shipping companies are making big profits. Even though the executive of the union are recommending we accept the Dethridge Award there is talk among the rank and file of strike. Josh has a list of shipowners who have staggering amounts of profits. One if I remember rightly, BHP, Broken Hill Propriety, close to £700,000. So why shouldn't we share in these profits? Are times that bad? I don't think so. It is only the worker who is suffering."

An even more troubled Claire put an end to the conversation, rising from the table with orders for her daughters to wash the dishes. Her eldest on the threshold of womanhood and the young man who would take that step with her a radical.

≈

Seven days discharging alongside the sugar refinery the *Aldinga* cleaned out her hatches and squared up, her orders to shift ship to Balls Head for bunkers, sail 8:00pm for Port Alma, Queensland, salt for Sydney.

Balls Head nestled in a small cove west of Blues Point adjacent the north shore headland where two massive Moruya granite faced pylons anchored the soaring grey span of the Sydney Harbour Bridge. Since 1920 coal mined in the Lake Macquarie and Hunter region and transhipped by small colliers, Balls Head functioned as a major coal and bunkering facility.

The *Aldinga* with tugs secured on her port quarter and break of the focastle head, gently eased off the berth. Sam watched the bow swing slowly to port as the ship lined up with Blues Point, the forward tug engulfing the ship with black smoke and cinders. He might well have been alone on the focastle head, ignored by the badly hung-over bosun and two oafish day workers still drunk, Henry at the wheel, the chief mate in the eyes aloof from them all.

He thought of another bosun; not a man like Kiernan, an imbecile leading the insipid and weak. Kiernan did not take him aside and explain the importance of overhauling gear, safety drills, attaining a lifeboat ticket, lashings, load line surveys and ships stability. On the *Aldinga* barred from going aloft, driving a winch or attending a yardarm; he never held a tee or round spike in his hand, his pride in being able to splice ignored. His lot to make the bosun's bunk, scrape winch beds, chipping hammers, holystones and a soogee wad.

Resulting from an order from the mate based more on contemptuous sign language the forward gang lowered a headline to a lines boat, the ship's bow lined up with the loader head.

An endless chain of coal buckets, empty and metal against metal rattling, soon to be filled from the huge concrete bunker built in the side of a cliff which loomed above the berth.

The bosun slurred his orders to Sam making up the heaving lines and securing ratguards, with the ordinary seamen stand by with brooms, shovels and deck hoses, keep the amidships officers accommodation clean. Josh and Gary with plans to walk to Crows Nest and the pub offered no sympathy for the unhappy pair, Sam of a mind catching a ferry from the nearby ferry wharf and being with Emily a few hours before sailing.

"Deck boys and buckos, what do you expect?" Josh said. "Think yourself lucky the buffoon didn't add scrapers and chipping hammers, red lead for deckheads. Stuff the bosun. Make sure you keep our accommodation clean as well."

"The bosun said to square up the pockets," the ordinary seamen complained, scratching around the inflamed perimeters of a weeping pimple on his chin; thwarted from the steep walk to Waverton and a train to Hornsby, obsessed with a plump young girl whose father owned a bicycle shop adjacent the station.

"So? Single hatch boards shouldn't bother two strong young lads. Go to it. Make certain though the polished shoes of the mates and engineers are not fouled by coal dust."

"Fuck ABs!"

Sam gravitated to ordinary seaman Joel Linguard, easily excitable and prone to talking too fast, like himself eager to learn and of a union mind. Born and raised in Wickham, a working class suburb of inner Newcastle, in Sam's mind partly disproved Josh's theory of the heavy industrial city's propensity for breeding groupers.

He thought of last night, alone with Emily with her sisters asleep and Claire visiting a sick friend. His hand on her knee and moving up her leg stopped with her own. From him a silent and desperate plea, feeling the pressure between her legs ease, resistance gone. The exquisite sensation of her satiny inner thighs, the soft roll of downed flesh where her legs joined, between them a warm and moist opening he sought with his finger. She drew away, closing her legs, her face flushed and breathing forced.

"Emily?"

"Sam, my sisters—"

He drew a deep breath and stared at the floor, wondering when his suffering would end. When at last he raised his head, her stricken face mirrored the same anguish.

15

THE *ALDINGA* ROLLED IN an oily swell, her speed reduced to dead-slow-ahead on command of the Port Alma pilot cutter coming alongside. The small port south of Rockhampton lay at the mouth of a muddy tidal creek infested with mosquitoes and sandflies. Flat and featureless except for a hazy line of hills far to the west, spreading out from the old timber wharf horizon to horizon salt pans. Beside salt live cargoes also loaded at the wharf, the evidence thousands of cloven imprints moulded in red clay by what erupted from the bowels and bladders of fearful and disorientated animals.

With mooring lines still dripping water, swarms of biting insects descended, injecting their larvae under the first few layers of skin. It took only minutes for red welts to form, soon followed by weeping lesions of inflamed tissue. Extreme cases who sought medical attention received little sympathy, swabs of iodine or calcimine lotion, advice when the ship sailed and reached colder water their agony would end.

Thoughts of fresh white bread, tropical fruits and tender meats not bloodsucking parasites filled the minds of the fore and aft gangs making up heaving lines, stoppers, ratguards on moorings. All eyes on the agent boarding, a puzzled frown and shake of his head when asked by Henry securing the gangway net on the wharf apron about expected steward's stores.

Using ship's gear and grabs the stevedore foreman assured the ship would be loaded in around five days using day and afternoon shifts.

As if expecting a sneak attack from behind the chief steward habitually glanced over his shoulder, the nervous little man drawing hungrily on his hand rolled cigarette more paper than expensive tobacco. Hawkish faced, grey skinned and thinning hair, he watched with disdain the tying up, the gear swung over the wharf and runners shackled to grabs.

Magnus Barwick climbed the catering ranks slowly, bellboy in British liners, bedroom steward, pantry man, first class saloon steward, assistant chief steward. Aware like all of his brethren conditions were far superior on the Australian coast, as well as an infatuation with a comely widow, he jumped ship and placed his impeccable British credentials on the desk of Adelaide Steamship Company.

Magnus learned his profession meticulously where even on the famous liners victualled with only the finest of food and vintage wines, the crew suffered British Board of Trade pint and pound sustenance in their airless and windowless dormitories. His role in sustaining life at sea pertained to articles of agreement framed outside the *Aldinga's* messrooms, sustenance meticulously apportioned by regulation and dispensed by fluid measure and scales. Not a fraction of an ounce overweight or a pint exceeded by a single drop escaped his calculating eyes, hardened iron-like to the pleas of a trimmer or deck boy drawing stores.

He could without taxing his mind inform an inquirer how much apportionment of butter, tinned milk, sugar, tea, cheese, bread or bread substitute, beef, pork, mutton, ox tongue, sausage and mince in pounds and ounces per man per day. To the exact inch measurements of company issued towels and bedding, how many buckets issued for washing clothes, and if on water rationing how much per man per day minus the galley's whack.

Magnus became an object of derision with his purchase of hogget at a farm gate price giving rise to suspicion the feeble creatures might have succumbed to old age in the paddock. The gristly meat, also with a strong odour, so tough and rancid it defied chewing, solved with a hammer and fistfuls of curry and salt, added to soups and the bones minus every shred of meat to the stockpot.

Potatoes in Sydney purchased cheap, rejected at the markets by local greengrocers but pounced upon by those who victualled ships, classed as fit for seamen. Other vegetables were suspect as well, cabbages with sodden hearts, wilted carrots and apples destined for rabbit baits. The chief cook without a single trace of discomfiture, a hide as textured as the hogget that hung in his freezer, directed the aggrieved delegates to the chief steward, what came onboard out of his control.

The delegates called a special meeting after lunch.

"Sharpen your pencil well, Sam," Josh said, draping an arm around his shoulders. "Listen well as it will not be an easy meeting. Now what comes onboard labelled food fit for seamen normally affects us all, but on the *Aldinga* we are dealing with some who when asked by the mate or second engineer to jump their reply is how high, sir. The minutes will be important, and resolutions worded exactly as moved and seconded. Names as well. Remember, not only a union official will read these minutes when he stamps the minute book, but minute books can be used in court as evidence."

The bosun disagreed with the meeting as did four others, two on deck and two below. As standing chairman he opened the meeting with a ferocious scowl at the delegates, having quite enjoyed his lunch of curried hogget and rice, the highly spiced and salted juices sopped up with brick hard bread. Sam, recording the minutes in his notebook, noted the following: *Special meeting 12:30pm Port Alma. Chairman: Kiernan Chapman. Deck delegates: Josh Atkinson, Garry Macintosh. ER: Ross Gittern.*

"We have tried to get through the chief steward's thick company head since leaving Sydney but he refuses to be drawn into any admission the food is not fit for human consumption. The master ordered us out of his cabin and the mate snarled what we eat is close to bankrupting the company. Now the agent tells us we are not storing in Port Alma." With the ABs messroom crowded with all hands, Josh stood hard pressed against the bulkhead. "I've heard Henry say he's eaten some appalling meat on sailing ships, pit pony, mule, donkey, but the chief steward's hogget must surely beat it all. What potatoes ferment in the spud locker the spud barber peels with a piece of cheesecloth wrapped around his nose. Speaking with the chief cook all you get is a blank stare when you remark we use his bread to chip rust. There have been no green vegetables on the menu since Sydney and the rice is alive with weevils, according to the chief steward a source of protein."

The bosun jabbed a finger at the messroom clock. "Better keep this short, those of you who haven't got their day in are turning to at 1:00pm. Mate's got work over the side."

"The mate will wait until we finish union business about this arsehole chief steward feeding us shit. Kiernan, you can go and tell the mate to rig his own stages, get his own paint. Go fuck himself!"

Kiernan snorted, his mouth a purple slit of compressed flesh.

Henry interceded, his moderate voice a calming effect. He rarely offered an opinion, a man of few words. A forgiving man who never castigated the bucko mates and bully masters of his past who ruthlessly drove him, bashed him for breaking the order of silence on deck. Of belly robbing shipowners who made a mockery of human compassion, accommodating sailors worse than the pigs and fowls carried for meat and eggs, this fresh animal protein of course for the saloon table. "Mr Chairman, the delegates have a legitimate reason for petitioning the master with complaints in respect of victualling. In all truth I have eaten far worse, meat so rotten and flyblown we threw it overboard and ate the maggots. This is 1935, not the last century, chief stewards likened to morticians who fed us embalmed meat and biscuit you could chip the deck with, open focastles and voyages measured in hundred of days."

Josh grinned at Henry. "Well said, Henry, I couldn't put it better myself. As we have no union representative in Port Alma we will have to make contact with Brisbane in respect of this resolution to get their ruling. As the master is in conflict with our opinion the food is not fit for human consumption, I move we inform him at sailing time a dispute exists and the ship will not sail until resolved on a union and company level. Of course in the meantime if by some miracle fresh stores appear at the foot of the gangway we reassess our position."

"Second the motion," Henry said.

Sam scribbled the resolution, most of it legible only to himself.

"The minute secretary will read the resolution," the chairman grated, eyeballing Josh.

Sam read the resolution.

Much to everyone's surprise Henry's talkative spell continued. "Something I have learned over the years and that is when dealing with food and shipowners we seamen are not considered human, and subsequently improper to use the term human consumption."

The chairman banged his gnarled fists on the table. "Bullshit! Vacating the chair I am against the motion and I so vote! What do you fucking want, silver service and tucked in bed?"

"Put the resolution to the vote!" Josh pointed a damning finger at the chairman. "Now!"

The resolution carried; eighteen for, the bosun, two ABs and two firemen against.

Josh could almost feel the barbs of loathing from Kiernan, a thought he would now treat the bosun with a lot more caution, for certain watch his back. "We'll ring Brisbane this afternoon and put our case. Brisbane's a strong and militant branch. I harbour no doubts we will get a fair hearing and support."

≈

Captain Langford on his bridge waited patiently, attired in full uniform for departure from Port Alma, hot and uncomfortable in heavy blue serge. Soon his authority would come under pressure and he needed the full regalia of authority. Well prepared to perform his official duties, himself as well as the company, appreciative for the information from a responsible source the festering of dissent. The departing agent with the ship's papers and mail considered it a little unusual the master's choice of winter attire in tropical Port Alma, choking dust blowing from the hot hinterland adding to stinging salt grit stirred by a strong westerly wind.

Aware of only the mate and the bosun forward, the second mate and two ABs aft, he hesitated to ring standby, wondering when the delegates would make their appearance on the bridge, his thought answered as two deck and one engine room delegates stepped through the starboard wheelhouse door. Two bareheaded, the other black with coal grime wore a filthy cloth cap glued by sweat to his skull.

Josh stepped forward. "Captain, we are here to inform you—"

Captain Langford cut him short, a call to the third mate standing by the engine room telegraph. "Mr Hogarth, I ask for your full attention please as witness to the presence of the delegates on the bridge. Delegates, are you aware all hands have been ordered to their stations and that sea watches have been set?"

"The bosun mentioned something about fore and aft and if you look out the window you probably will see him on the focastle head with the mate, another couple aft," Josh said. "The three of them can stay all night for all we care. We are here to inform you the ship is in dispute and until resolved we are not obliged to sail."

Captain Langford pronounced each word carefully. "The Federated Seamen's Union of Australasia is refusing to perform their ordered duties to take this vessel to sea under the terms of the articles of agreement signed in the presence of a marine superintendent? A senior government official entrusted to ensure the clauses of the Navigation Act are adhered to by the signatories thereto attached?"

"If all that means are we refusing to sail, yes. Brisbane's been informed of our dispute and we have their support. We will continue to work normally on deck and below."

"Neither you or your union will decide on the sailing of this ship, or who will work or who will not." Captain Langford failed to disguise the contempt in his refined voice. "I as master of this ship entrusted by my company for its efficient and safe management will make that decision, and I am certain many of you will regret this irresponsible and uncalled for industrial action."

Josh maintained his calm demeanour with great difficulty. "Of that I beg to differ, Captain. Are you not going to ask us why we refuse to sail?"

Captain Langford tilted his head and looked down his nose. "That question will be asked of each individual when requested to obey a direct order to sail. Those who decline instant dismissal and logged, their discharges appropriately stamped. I would seriously advise you to reconsider your position and give me your answer immediately."

The engine room delegate pushed Josh aside and thrust his face close to the master's; he turned ashen. "If the chief steward with his gear packed doesn't slime down the gangway like the slug it is, or a truck of stores doesn't arrive in the next hour, you know full well what our answer will be! You want your answer immediately, you got it!" Ross ground the words between clenched teeth. "We are starving because we've been issued no fresh stores since Sydney and those were nothing more than shit you wouldn't feed coolies." A story circulated on the coast Ross a few years ago emerging from the fiddley at the end of his twelve to four watch in dark and stormy seas battered and threw his trimmer over the side, the unfortunate man a 1927 scab. "We never see anything of any good come onboard with this thing of a chief steward. We eat shit while you lot in the saloon feast and the chief steward fills his going ashore bag."

"Retract that nefarious statement!" Captain Langford remonstrated, blood returning to his face in a rush. "Mr Barwick is a trusted servant of the company! His honesty and dedication to his work is without question!"

"Ross is right, Captain," Josh said. "We have our suspicions your beloved company is not getting what it's paying for. Then again we may be wrong and what your chief steward substitutes for wholesome food is a boardroom decision. Also we see what ends up on the table in the saloon, and let me tell you a far cry from what crawls and congeals in the bottom of our kits."

"I order you in my presence to not make untrue assertions in respect of Mr Barwick and the saloon. Perceived disparagement in menus for officers and crew is a matter for your union and Adelaide Steamship Company. I will not enter into it or hear more of it."

"I stand amazed when mates and engineers side with the companies and oppose us gaining a common menu. Why? Don't we all work for ex-slavers, dope runners, pirates and swindlers? Captain, that's not why we are here. This ship is not sailing until we get an agreement on fresh stores."

"My company and Mr Barwick, myself included, are more than satisfied the food supplied and prepared is of highest quality, nutritious and adequate in quantity." Instantly dismissing and logging these recalcitrant individuals would be a pleasant task, for some with well documented belligerence suspension from the industry.

How fortunate to have among this obduracy dependable members among the crew with the backbone to ignore the dictates of fanatical unionism forced down their throats by their fellows. To have serving under his command men of the calibre of Bosun Chapman, ABs Hopwood and Thornton and firemen Umwell and Cuttance, who with the company's best interests at heart proved their fidelity. Forewarned of industrial disputation his and the company's contingency plans were coming to fruition.

"You shall inform your members to present themselves in an orderly fashion on the bridge where each shall be given a direct order to sail. Nays logged and instantly dismissed, their discharges stamped *Endorsement not Required*. Yeas will be placed on standby to sail awaiting the arrival of company replacements," Captain Langford said as if reading from a script.

The delegates knew the master could recite word for word the resolution to hold the ship, the company in Brisbane opening its thick ledger filled with the names of men with a misguided sense of industrial propriety. Days earlier Josh telephoned Brisbane from the stevedores office on the wharf and unable to get an official spoke with a fireman relieving in the office, Eliot Elliott. He advised even though the ship lay in an outport the union would support their dispute, but in couched terms to tread warily because of their isolation and to leave their options open.

With support from the union, pressure on the company from the charterer, the dispute over victualling long running, tugs, linesmen and pilot on standby, the delegates felt the odds of a favourable outcome in their favour.

Josh looked at his fellow delegates and lifted his shoulders with a deep intake of breath; the advice tread warily and leave your options open burned in his mind. Their options gone, he said resignedly: "Captain, you can put away your log book. Your bad discharges and stand down the welcoming committee for your Brisbane scabs. We are sailing under protest, but first we have a meeting to convene."

≈

The bosun knew when denied the chair, the bleak faces of the delegates, what accusations would follow as the special meeting came to an unruly order. Ross's smouldering presence seemed even more forbidding as he filled the doorway of the seamen's messroom and declared himself chairman. "Vacating the chair, we got fucking spies and scabs in our midst! Now that don't come as no surprise as in the past we've learned to live with coppers and scabs, women bashers and sucks, slime bags and mangy dogs. We got something to say but I'm leaving that for the deck delegates who've got a better grasp of the language than me."

Josh kept a steadfast eye on the bosun. "We have rescinded the motion of holding the ship, the decision taken on the bridge without a resolution granting us that authority. We apologise for that but it seemed the only action open to us. We have no stores on the wharf and I would assume the chief steward is gloating under that wet rock it calls home. The company has scabs on standby in Brisbane and has since the day we arrived. Do not take my motion as weakness, far from it because we'll take these bastards on again in Sydney. I move we sail at the conclusion of this meeting."

A rumble passed through the meeting, chairs grating on the deck as agitated men only kept their silence in respect of the delegate with the floor.

"It is obvious the captain and the company were informed of our resolution and made their arrangements to sack us. We go on the bridge and the old man's dressed like a Christmas tree with every bit of gold braid he could find perched on his big head and shoulders, loving every bit of it with his log book open and a busload of scabs arriving from Brisbane."

"We know who the prime rat is and I want his name in the minute book," Ross said, glaring at the bosun.

Sam writing the minutes in his notebook needed no prompting to add the bosun's name.

Kiernan took more interest picking at a broken fingernail, unperturbed stripped of the chair and Ross's accusation. He sucked noisily on the object of his attention, looked up and sniggered. "Read the minute book and you'll see there were members against the motion to hold the ship. We were never for holding the ship, so what are you going to do about it? Put my name in the fucking minute book. I don't give one fuck!"

"The resolution bound all hands to stick the ship up, the majority ruling." Josh wished with his fists to wipe the smug look off the bloated face of the bosun, hung-over but sober on orders he would need his senses at sailing time.

"The minute book's full of shit like that. Plus other stuff against the new award. You blokes like you shooting off your big mouths when we all know we've got it good."

"Comrades, you have noticed the bosun is not the chairman of this meeting, and I would move that such a role is never again the sole domain of a senior member of the crew," he said, then to Sam: "We know there are three on deck who stood by to sail, possibly two below who have not exposed themselves. Minute secretary, make sure you spell their names correctly. I will say it for the person who will top the list, standby fore and aft."

Strong words from the delegate in a struggle that would have the same conclusion as the many before it, company bills of fares written by conniving and falsifying chief stewards who on company letterhead paper could turn rabbit into ham and offal into filet mignon.

16

T HE FEELING OF EXPECTATION heightened as the *Aldinga* in the early afternoon swung and rolled her blunt bow to line up with North Head and enter Port Jackson. Today his kerosene soaked, grease ingrained hands would touch the satiny smooth skin of his girl, taste her moist lips and warm breath, feel the swell of her small breasts against his chest. Passing Pyrmont he hoped on the waterfront he might catch sight of her, a wave.

Emily waited outside the Balmain wharf gate, a small figure dressed in white, trying to keep her excitement in check, frantically waving a handkerchief to catch his attention. Similar with Mary and Harriet when he came through the front door, rushing to him, wrapping their arms around his waist. Claire more restrained, at arm's length, a kiss on the cheek.

Homecoming called for a feast, treats of chocolates and cream filled cakes.

Sam and Emily scoured the markets, produce at the close of the trading day marked down three quarters the retail price. Bruised even lower, carrying home the rewards of their negotiating skills in his new double stitched duck canvas bag with rope handles.

Sated with a dinner of grilled pork sausages and onion gravy, mashed potato and green peas, a final indulgence before bed, fresh cream filled chocolate cake. Emily ordered her sisters off the divan to give room for herself and Sam, the younger girls offered cushions; miffed the sulky pair tried to outstare their elder sibling from the floor.

Claire watched her family as she darned a pair of stockings for Mary. Sam the centre of attention, a part of her family, a boy growing into a strong and resourceful man. The girl sitting on the divan beside him, no, the young woman, still troubled her.

≈

Next evening Emily demanded her sisters remain home, that she and Sam should have time to themselves, a walk alone to the park, tears and tantrums failing to lessen her resolve. An hour in the park and slow footsteps home in darkness prolonging their time alone, hopes dashed entering the house the girls and Claire would be in bed. On the divan Sam nursed Emily in his lap. Watching Mary and Harriet sitting at his feet cross-legged on a threadbare rug he thought it must be hard on their bottoms, seemingly of no concern playing another makeup game which made no sense. Claire sitting in a chair found more stockings to mend.

"There is talk on the ship she might layup," he said.

Emily made herself more comfortable on his lap, an eye on her mother. "What's layup?"

"Paying the crew off. The ship has no future cargoes according to the company. That's what the talk is anyway."

"You will be out of work?"

"Yes. More ominous though is the talk of strike."

Claire rested her darning in her lap, frowning. "Why would seamen go on strike when jobs are hard to get?"

"Because a new award is not acceptable to the majority of the rank and file. There is a lot of dissention in the union. Those who say we should accept what we've got, those who say strike and to hell with the shipowners and government."

"Why the government? You work for shipowners not the government," Claire said, her interest roused.

"The government is involved in all award negotiations to maintain an impartial balance between labour and industry through the arbitration system.

On paper it seems a fair and just system, but it isn't. In the majority of cases arbitration favours industry."

"Industry provides jobs, strikes destroy families."

"If the system occasionally ruled in favour of the unions the movement might accept it as fair and unbiased. It doesn't, and the blame for this is the federal attorney general and his hatred of unions."

Claire, disturbed, wondered where all this radicalism came from in a boy so young.

"Hearing them talk onboard he is a powerful orator and can have an audience cheering themselves hoarse, wanting to carry him from the hall on their shoulders."

"Sam!" Claire exclaimed incredulously.

"That might be an exaggeration, but his aversion to unions no more obvious when he forced waterside workers to pay for a license to work on the wharves. We have been told there are plans he will do the same with seamen if the union rejects the Dethridge Award."

Emily again moved her bottom, taking his hand and placing it on her knee. Alone she would have positioned the hand higher, and what Mother would have thought of that boldness she didn't dare think about.

Claire put away her mending, troubled with many things; a daughter, disturbed about a boy, her own life in turmoil. "Being faithful to an employer, wouldn't that guarantee permanent employment and security? To my old fashioned mind loyalty has its own rewards."

"What I have seen at sea there are two loyalties, shipowner or union. I know which one I would prefer."

"What will you do if the ship pays off?"

"Hopefully join a new ship. We have a stopwork meeting tomorrow and there is talk of forming a strike committee which the officials are against."

"With so many men out of work such irrational behaviour is beyond me."

"Will you be an official one day, Sam?" Mary asked, pushing at Emily's legs to get closer to him.

"Not an official, but a delegate I hope. I would have to know the award by heart and learn to speak better, especially at meetings and fronting the captain and mate. Then of course you have to be elected."

"Sam will be a delegate one day, and the best," Emily said, asserting her seniority with a forceful foot pushing her sister away.

≈

Sitting at the back of the packed Sydney Town Hall Sam made a guess at the number of seamen in attendance, 500. At times the noise deafened, lulls with movement of officials on stage, more clamour when seamen in groups shouted down others in opposition, or condemned a speaker on his feet.

On the stage seated at a table five serious faced men seemed detached from the meeting, at times conferring among themselves, shuffling papers; three officials, chairman and minute secretary.

One rose to his feet and approached the edge of the stage; an imposing man formally dressed, a confident stance, a smile on his face. Jacob Johnson, general secretary, addressed the meeting in a strident voice, in no need of amplification. "Brothers, among you are members who quite vocally and voraciously oppose your federal executive's acceptance of the Dethridge Award. This is your right and there is not one person in this hall who would refute that. Your right for dissent! The right of every member of this great union of seamen. Among us are those who are saying the union has taken a step backwards accepting the Dethridge Award. I say, and your federal executive concurs in a single voice, wrong!"

A roar reverberated through the hall, groups on their feet trying to outshout each other. The chairman's chair fell to the floor as he bounded up and joined the general secretary. "Order! Order!"

Assisted by the cavernous acoustics of the hall, his voice penetrated the din, a semblance of order restored as the general secretary's voice penetrated the discord. "Yes, we have accepted a small reduction in overtime payments, but look closely at the final wage outcome and the amount is higher."

"You're a fucking magician then, mate!" The voice sounded like a foghorn, the fireman dressed in a flannel singlet, baggy shorts and stokehold boots, a giant of a man with a voice to match. "We're two quid worse off than we were ten fucking years ago!"

"Brother, your figure is wrong," Jacob said, unperturbed and completely at ease in the uproar around him; he even acknowledged his adversary with a half wave of his hand. "Accepting the Dethridge Award we have gained £1/5/0 a month, that fact irrefutable."

Bluey Parkinson, buoyed by those around him, shouted for an immediate strike. "Did I read that wrong we lost deferred sailings? Working cargo rates lowered? I ain't even close to the penal clauses yet! What about those fucking penal clauses?"

Jacob's verbal jousts with Bluey at stopwork meetings were legendry, the greaser unperturbed of his dress or sweaty odour, coming direct from the plates after a twenty-four hour gear turn. "We must never lose sight that in all awards there are penal clauses. Even though we condemn these insidious insertions, it is encumbrance we and our brother unions have to deal with when negotiating awards with industry and government. In a workers world, a world with full employment, we would be free to walk down gangways on a whim. No punitive clauses to force seamen back to work when in disputation, heavy fines and threats of jail for officials.

"Brothers we do not live in such a Utopia. We exist hand-to-mouth in a flawed world, a world that has cast out the working man to tramp the outback roads for illusionary work. Ships still rust in backwaters, idle for years. Seamen asked to make small sacrifices to maintain jobs in a climate of financial adversity, I say is that too much to ask? We might complain our overtime has been cut a few pennies, deferred sailings traded for an increase in the base monthly wage, but at least our mutterings are onboard a ship that is still sailing and has a full manning of our members."

The voice boomed even louder than Bluey's, the member an AB with a nose spreading like rising dough over his face, standing on a chair and shaking his fist. "Bullshit! Jacob, take a fucking bow, all the executive. We can read and read we did in the Journal what you lot came up with, accepting the fucking Dethridge Award. You can have it! Lyons and that fucking thing from Victoria, his attorney general and his dog collar threats!"

"Order! This is a final warning! Those who do not keep order will be ejected from the meeting!" the chairman threatened, his legs widespread and his voice rising almost to a shriek.

Sam wondered who would have the courage to eject the AB who though not having the best of it weathered ten rounds with the light heavyweight champion of Australia.

The general secretary displayed remarkable calm, confident and fluently able to mix it with anyone in the disintegrating meeting. "Brothers, your federal executive studied each clause of the award letter by letter, word by word presided on by Justice Dethridge. From the very onset of negotiations with shipowners we never paused in our intense scrutiny of what lay on the table before us. We negotiated with shipowners pleading ruinous financial times and historical low returns on investments. We understood, finally agreeing the way forward only achievable by compromise and lessening the financial impact on employers by small reductions in current conditions.

"We finally reached an agreement with the shipowners who have been open and sincere and presented the facts on the parlous state of shipping in Australia. So, brothers, do we continue negotiations wielding a big stick, bludgeon those on the opposite side of the table when the table is bare, nothing to gain except the laying up of more ships. So let me tell you from your federal executive, rejection of the Dethridge Award would result in our numbers decimated, queuing for the dole. In the event of a strike seamen following the same erroneous path as the waterside workers and miners."

The meeting erupted in uproar, in some places punches thrown. Groups tried to outshout each other, shoving and grappling. Unable to regain control of the meeting the chairman turned to his general secretary and with an apology closed the meeting.

≈

The *Aldinga* about to sail for Newcastle to load coal for Melbourne, a possible delay of a week before loading at the Dyke hydraulics, Sam asked Emily a question. The house in darkness and Emily in his arms on the divan, the family asleep, he held his breath waiting for her answer.

She half turned and slightly raised her lower body so he could bunch her light cotton dress around her waist and rest his hand on her satiny thigh. "Oh, Sam, if only I could. Mother would never let me. She would kill me!" His hand caused a tremor to pass through her, a yearning for him touch her more sensitive flesh. "If I could where would I stay?"

"I haven't thought about that. I suppose a hotel."

"Sam, isn't it correct only certain girls stay in hotels with men?" She teased. "Is that the girl you want me to be?"

"No! Anyway, your mother wouldn't let you. My idea stupid and farfetched and your mother would flay me for asking."

"What if I wanted to be that sort of girl," she breathed softly in his ear, aware of his arousal pressing against her; she took the initiative and with a subtle move of her hips caused his hand to slip between her legs.

"Emily, Emily." An edge of despair entered his voice.

She knew what her mother's answer would be, and for the first time in her life she planned to defy her.

≈

On foundations sunk deep in the river's mud to bedrock, twelve feet from landfill, sailing ship ballast of grey granite and sand from the Andes, rubble and red brick from the San Francisco earthquake, the circular brick plinths stood proud testament to the masons art. What sat bolted into their solid concrete cores were engineering masterpieces shipped from the United Kingdom to the

Carrington Dyke, cranes capable of slewing from shore to ship five ton coal wagons from their bogies.

The cranes in near perfect alignment followed the ballast rock lined Carrington foreshore, powered by hydraulics from the Grecian style pump house in the Carrington Basin. Also on the foreshore a marshalling yard ten tracks wide, on every track loaded and empty wagons and noisy, idling locomotives, a scene of bustling activity that never slept. The finest black coal in the world, chunks larger than a man's head heaped high on the wagons, won by miners deep underground in the coalfields of the Hunter Valley, hewn like black diamonds with glass-like facets.

The *Aldinga* not scheduled to load lay at the Timber Wharf, the wharf offering easy access to the waterfront suburb of Carrington, an even mix of industrial and residential development. Small workers cottages lined exceptionally wide streets following the southerly course of the river, their back entrances serviced by laneways for the removal of nightsoil. Eight hotels with a noisy, hard drinking cliental of wharf labourers, coal trimmers, painters and dockers, seamen, miners, tradesmen and railwaymen.

No single dwelling of substance stood out or made a lasting impression among an assortment of mainly timber and iron roofed homes, the occasional brick and tile giving the fleeting impression of affluence amongst working class poor. Homes were poorly maintained, front gardens weed choked, their neglect heightened by coal dust and grit in the air from a coal mine close to the Dyke, the smoke of shunting locomotives. Steam trams rumbled down the major streets of Carrington, small localised industries and the steelworks to the north adding to the pall.

Josh disappeared the moment the gangway hit the wharf, ignoring the bosun who wanted the draft figures and plimsoll painted, his destination no more than a few streets from the wharf. A call over his shoulder he would be back, intent on rekindling a dalliance of a few months previous.

Sam watched the departing figure, a similar but more frustrating thought in his mind; if only his girl waited across the railway tracks.

Running a gauntlet of suspicion and raised eyebrows, having to book into a hotel with a young girl. He didn't look eighteen, Emily most definitely no more than sixteen. His only chance of success if the hotel catered for casual waterfront liaisons, a reputation which would immediately brand his girl.

≈

Josh and Sam shared a stage over the name aft, their first drop five feet below the fishplate and a foot beneath ALDINGA. "The river's pretty murky," Josh said, making himself comfortable and hauling up a pot of black topside which hung beneath the stage on a lanyard. "Remember, one hand for yourself and one for the ship. That scum floating on the top must come from the monster upriver, the steelworks."

Sam painted from the fishplate to the top of the name, using inch brushes to cut in the white A and black infill. Confident, he moved about with ease, also having learned to inform his stage mate of such actions. "Josh, you find your girl?"

"This lucky scalyback sure as hell did. Dear Tess sitting alone at the kitchen table with a cup of tea munching a biscuit. Got quite a shock, of a mind she'd never see me again, but in no great rush to seek solace in the arms of another. Jesus, do you think I should take that as a compliment?"

"I asked my girl to come to Newcastle," Sam said, almost to himself.

"Speak up louder, mate. What's that about a girl?"

"My Emily. Asked her to come to Newcastle, but her mum wouldn't have let her."

Josh indicated to a drop beneath the name. "Of course her mum wouldn't. How old is she, bloody fourteen?"

"No, she's fifteen."

Together both threw off their turns from the outer horn, rendering the two remaining turns on the stage to lower. "From a seaman's point of view all mothers should be damned for eternity for protecting their innocent progeny from the clutches of debauched seafarers. Sam, your time will come."

"It's not that, Josh. We just want to be together." Almost a plea which brought a guffaw from his stage mate.

"Feel for you, mate, the agony of young love. We've all been there, some encounters more painful than others. What desirable creatures these girls are who capture our hearts and fire our lustful instincts. Soft and sweet to the touch, warm and clinging in all those secret little places these girls conceal from us in silk and satin. Oh my god, Tess, I need you!"

Dropping beneath the name the stage pivoted on the stern, making it less stable to paint MELBOURNE. Finished another drop took them to a few feet over rudder, above them gloss topside black glistened as did the high gloss white of the name and port of registry with a small portion of blue added to bring out the sheen. A job that could have been finished in half the time if not for a brutal head continuously glaring over the side, a demand for more haste, he wanted the job finished and the stage moved to another fleet.

"One day, Sam, you will reach the dizzy heights of bosun. What I have seen of you on deck that promotion assured. Some advice, never push, never cajole, and most certainly never keep sticking your head over the side and bellow like a bull about to be castrated for more haste. You'll get your job done, yeah, but at the pace of the seamen on the stage who hates your guts."

Sam followed Josh up the Jacob's ladder, hand over hand on the very edge of the rungs; climbing over the poop railing both made up their pot lanyards. "Sam, instead of being poisoned tonight how about you come with me to Tess's. She promised something palatable, can't remember what because my mind focused on far more interesting things than food. Not far, and if I crane my neck I reckon I could see her home from the ship."

"Thanks, Josh, that's nice. I think I'll just walk along the wharf. Maybe head up to the BHP wharf and have a look at their ships. I counted three."

"Most of the country might be scraping the bottom of the barrel to survive, but BHP blast furnaces continue to stain the sky red and drown Newcastle in a blanket of ash and cinder. Of course Novocastrians living around its skirts extremely thankful for small inconveniences to their health. Then again I suppose any ship at the BHP is a sign things might be improving for us all."

Sam only half heard, his thoughts elsewhere. Josh gripped his shoulder and shook it gently. "Come on, how about a home cooked meal, though you're going to have to earn it?"

"Earn it?" Both hauled in the stage and turned up the gantlines on the horns; a few minutes to 5:00pm and knock off.

"Agile enough to climb on wagons and select good sized chunks of coal for Tess's stove. Christ, there must be thousands of tons of it marshalled along the Dyke, but get sprung taking one cobble and the police will have you locked up in an instance for depleting the immense wealth of the local coal barons."

"Josh, I might be a distraction you don't need."

"No way. Time is on my side and you'll fall in love with Tess and her humble abode. Helping me fill a potato bag I got off the spud barber with coal should cover a meal."

Sam, about to enter the accommodation paused, then moved to the rail; he cleared the obstruction in his throat, narrowing his eyes to better focus the tiny figure standing on the gravel verge across the railway tracks. At this point shunters uncoupled coal trains to give access to the Timber Wharf from Carrington, a narrow boardwalk laid between the tracks. He rubbed his eyes; the girl in a large hat seemed lopsided, as if the bag she carried in her right hand weighed her down.

Emily!

Everything forgotten, his face splattered in black and white paint, he rushed for the gangway. Tears of joy streamed down her face as she collapsed in his arms, felt her legs lifted off the ground in his crushing embrace.

"Emily! Your mother let you?"

"She will reach for Father's strap hanging on the laundry door and may even use it. Then because it is you she may forgive me. My sisters, never," she said between sobs, her floppy hat fallen in the coal dust and gravel.

"How did you find your way to Carrington?"

"When I got off the train a porter directed me to Hunter St where he said trams ran regularly to Carrington. Then a nice lady who I am certain did not think of me in such terms, told me get off at the Carrington terminal if looking for a ship loading coal."

This tearful girl trembling in his arms away from home for the first time wholly dependent on him. Panic gripped him, where to stay? He would ask Josh. "Emily, wait here. Give me about twenty minutes—and don't talk to anyone."

She clung to him, then drew and away and nodded. Then a cheeky grin through the tears. "Sam, I must surely look that type of girl."

He never heard her, racing across the boardwalk and up the gangway, pausing at the top platform to wave before looking for Josh.

≈

Showered and dressed Sam bounded across the boardwalk, Josh breaking off his conversation with Emily to point at the closest coal wagon, indicating Sam climb aboard. With a lot of complaining and shifting of his right shoulder to ease apart the more jagged lumps of coal protruding from the bag, Sam followed Josh from the wharf verge to a wide tar sealed road fringed to the north with groves of lush mangroves. "Tess lives a couple of streets on the left. Now turn right and you'll end up in the United States. Those humpies you see through the scrub, that's Texas."

Unlike the major streets, sixty-six feet wide and gun barrel straight due north and south, Tess's street narrow with barely enough room for two vehicles to pass. The cottages both sides of the street were identical, wooden boxes with tiny multi-paned windows either side of the front door, separated by a dark cavity eighteen inches apart and sharing a common roof more rust than iron. Another joint feature, without exception all in an advanced state of decay, paint peeled and many exposing bare studs.

"Tess will owe me a favour for the paint I'm going to pinch for her. Poor girl's an orphan barely on the right side of forty, an only child of a coal trimmer dad who died like so many of his kind of pneumoconiosis, her mum something equally insidious as black lung, consumption."

"Josh, I think I should put Emily back on the train."

"You're worrying for nothing, Sam. We can only ask, and Tess's got plenty of room. These Carrington folk are the salt of the earth. People here don't even lock their doors or close their windows, except of course when the BHP on exceptionally dark nights lets it all go up the stacks at midnight. Walking back to the ship one time and I thought a fog of biblical proportions descended upon mankind."

Tess proved Josh's analogy of Carrington geniality correct, the buxom woman at the peak of her feminine allurement embracing a nervous Emily; sweeping her long blonde tresses from her florid face hinted of Scandinavian blood in her family's past. An amiable host with a sparkling eye never far from Josh sprawled with a glass of wine in a lounge chair; a cast iron pot of lamb stew and another of potatoes simmered on the coal fired stove. Tess's table might have come from the pages of a magazine illustrating rural America; an oval table set with a red and white check tablecloth, serviettes of a similar material, four white plates, wicker basket of bread, cutlery, two fluted tureens, four glasses and a cutglass decanter of claret already sampled by Josh.

For all her outgoing persona, Tess remained a product of working class Catholicism, never completely in adulthood shedding the puritan gene imbedded by past generations; with Josh these high morals did not apply, but it did for the young lass undoubtedly besotted by the deck boy of Josh's ship. Her eyes would stay firmly focused and her ears attuned on him, no adventurous forays in the bedroom she prepared for the girl. Assuredly, the boy would sleep on the lounge.

Tess thickened the stew with flour and strained the potatoes. "Only ever been to Sydney twice, didn't much like it. Too many people, too much of a rush."

"Sydney can be a challenge," Emily said shyly, taking hold of Sam's hand under the table. "Tess, thank you for allowing me to stay in your home."

"No problem, the company's welcomed." Then her smiling face turned serious as ladled stew in a tureen, potatoes topped with cubed butter in the other. "The fare's simple but wholesome, all we can ask for in these times. I ask only one thing of my guests, we offer grace."

Hands joined, Tess's grace amounted to a few words of thanks; though simple Sam felt Tess's deep conviction, her strong beliefs, and knew this woman would cause no harm to others, would never take and would always share what little life gave her. He glanced at Emily, still holding her hand and saw a light in her eyes, the briefest of smiles on her lips and knew she felt the same. He thought Claire would be relieved that her daughter in this home would be safe, but even so with this absolving thought he knew retribution from an anxious mother would be certain.

Josh filled their glasses from the decanter, topped his own and raised it. "To Tess. Sweet Tess who I am beginning to believe has a little bit of mother superior in her. Sam, I think I told you people don't lock their doors in Carrington, wrong. She's fitted one to Emily's bedroom."

Emily's face turned crimson; Tess came to her rescue. "Emily's not that sort of girl. Josh, you've embarrassed the girl."

With a grin he further toasted: "You're right. I'm a no good lecher. Thank you, Tess. From all of us, thank you."

Tess's dour face failed to hide her amusement. "There are no locks in my home. Emily, your bedroom is next to mine, dear."

"Which comes with a warning, Emily, these old tongue and groove walls are as thin as paper and our hostess has the ears of a wolf. Gotta love you, Tess," Josh said. "Something else, folks, Tess is one hell of a cook."

≈

Emily drew close to Tess, a child reared by middle-aged parents, a sheltered life. On leaving school she found employment in a large department store in Newcastle, but years later in a culling of her department, a board decision to cut costs and increase profits, she stood aside for a young widow with two children. Tess like so many living alone drifted into reclusive ways, her needs few and owning her home she managed to put away money from odd jobs, even surviving the worst of the Depression without an authoritative knock on the door.

Over the years she came close to committing herself to lasting relationships, for reasons she kept secret withdrawing before taking the final step. Names like spinster, wallflower, old maid, meaningless and no more than words. She never gave the gossips much to wag their tongues about, the comings and goings of suitors barely of interest because of the rarity.

Meeting Josh waiting for a tram at the Carrington terminal she knew instinctively the handsome young man a few years younger than her came down a ship's gangway at either the BHP or the hydraulics. As a young girl a possibly racial father warned her to be extremely cautious of Filipino seamen who came ashore imbued with foreign depravity and lust for young girls in their seductive brown eyes. Josh's green eyes were similar to hers so that made him acceptable; she brazenly returned his smile and made room for him to sit beside her.

When Josh sailed being a realistic person she thought she would never see him again and this made her sad, wondering if the emotion equated to falling in love. Probably and when his ship berthed at the BHP a few months later she knew for certain.

Emily's wealth amounted to small change leftover from her train ticket and Sam gave her a pound to spend on herself, another pound for the housekeeping jar when she returned home. With Tess as a guide she planned a window shopping spree in Hunter St, boasted by the locals as the longest main street in Australia, some said even the world. The many who imbibed even went as far as saying the most pubs in the world which might not have been an idle boast.

Waiting in the terminal tram shelter in Scott St at the east end of the city Tess commented: "You've a nice lad in Sam, Emily. Polite with good manners and no fancy airs."

"I know," she said, happy with the small parcels in her lap; some badly needed underwear and a special gift for Sam. It only cost a few shillings, a small silver anchor on a silver chain. She hoped he would like it as he wore no adornments, except of course his tattoo most of the time covered by his shirt.

Tess felt a motherly obligation to Emily, and though preoccupied with Josh the young girl's wellbeing came first in her mind. Without ever having parental responsibility she felt it her duty to warn Emily of the risks she faced surrendering to her bodily impulses. So young and naive, especially for a city girl.

Sam exclaimed it a miracle extracting Emily from the clutches of Tess, even having the home to themselves for an hour, Josh taking Tess to the Carrington Club Hotel for a beer before dinner. "Tess has an obsession I have animal desires for you."

She cuddled close to him on Tess's four cushioned lounge, thickly padded and comfortable. She nibbled his ear, in a cooing mood. "Have you?"

"Thwarted by your mother and sisters in the next room. Now Tess with an eagle eye and the alleged hearing of a wolf."

"Sam, I have something for you," she said, in her hand a small velvet pouch with drawstrings. "I hope you don't think me extravagant, but when I saw it I couldn't help myself."

He felt his emotions about to boil over, a child with a lump in his throat, unable to form words. At last he did draw a deep breath and swallow, again and again, his eyes welling with tears. Gently she passed the chain over his head, settling the anchor on his chest. Then she pressed her lips to the smooth and cool metal and whispered: "To keep the boy I will love forever safe. A beacon to guide him home to me."

"Emily, Emily, Emily! Oh my god, how I love you! It will never leave me as I will never leave you!"

≈

Josh on Friday night took Tess into Newcastle for dinner and a picture show, the home theirs at last. Their dinner simple, meat pies from the local baker's shop swamped in tomato sauce. A walk along dark Throsby Creek holding hands, stopping often to kiss and hold each other close.

On the lounge he took her in his arms and ran his tongue along her bottom lip, her mouth opening to accept his tongue. He cupped her right breast and gently kneaded it through her blouse, her response her eyes firmly shut and her breathing as forced as his. "Emily, can we?"

"Can we what?" She knew, rolling the right shoulder to intensify the pleasure of his hand. "Tess won't be home for hours."

"She's enforced strict rules where I am concerned."

"Yes, to keep me from a fate worse than death."

"What the hell is that?"

"I think it originates from Victorian times. Girls falling pregnant before matrimony."

"Emily, I know nothing about these things. There must be ways which makes it safe for girls."

"There are."

He drew away. "What?"

A mischievous smile flickered on her lips. "Lysol."

"What the hell is Lysol?"

She felt him slip the two top buttons of her blouse, then the third. "It does something inside a girl."

He gazed at the division of her breasts captured in her bra, first lifting one small laced cupped breast then the other. "Something what inside a girl?"

"When a boy finishes."

He tried to visualise what she said, baffled. He could think of that later as he fumbled with the ridiculously tiny metal hooks securing her bra, at last freeing them to feel her warm firm flesh roll in his hand.

She got to her feet and reached for both his hands, completely at ease with her exposed breasts.

He looked up in awe at the elongated pink nipples crowning the perfectly formed globes, his body rising under her will. She led him to her bedroom, unbuttoned his shirt and released his belt buckle, watched his dungarees fall around his ankles. Her wonder no less than his, a thought she dismissed instantly how could this enormous proof of his desire enter her, a warm wetness seeping between her legs telling her otherwise. Her clothes followed his and both lay side by side on Tess's narrow single bed, their bodies straining against each other.

He became the initiator, a hand on her shoulder gently turning her on her back, spreading her legs and lifting on top of her. She drew a deep breath in anticipation as she felt the engorged head press against her entry, even with his weight lifting her bottom and letting her muscles relax.

Many times he listened to the bawdy tales of conquest, of women writhing in the throes of orgasm begging for more of what impaled them and gave them spasms of rapturous joy.

Aware of women in various states of undress moving about the accommodation, he tried to imagine what their underwear and petticoats concealed. Most not young, sagging breasts and pudgy thighs, blotched faces with smeared makeup, but still mystical. So different from Emily, her skin like satin, her belly flat and firm, where her legs joined a prominent mound dusted with tiny ringlets of silken hair.

Slowly he entered her, both clutching each other's shoulders, a gasp of surprise at the ease of the joining of their bodies. Slow, slow, he wanted this exquisite sensation to last forever, muscles inside her sheaf nipping and contracting in an age old prelude to achieving their purpose. He felt it first in the pit of his stomach, unable to control the first rush, crying out as spasm after spasm flooded inside her.

Emily felt the warm wash of his ejaculation, thrust after thrust forcing his seed deeper inside her, each partial withdrawal smearing her swollen lips and pubic hairs, slicking her inner thighs.

She felt him stirring again, at first a gentle movement of his body still inside her. His slower movement gave greater intensity where his heat and hardness filled her, each stroke a throb of pleasure that gripped her from her toes to where his intrusion forced apart her sheaf, a cry of absolute pleasure as her orgasm gripped her.

Exhausted and without a thought for Tess's guardianship role Sam and Emily slept in each other's arms. He woke at 5:00am, his mental alarm clock not failing him. He did wonder as he dressed without waking Emily, Tess's reaction when she saw the lounge unslept on last night, unknown to him her fleeting thought their being in bed together no more than she anticipated.

Josh already dressed waited for him on the veranda, a brief nod before stepping into the dark and silent street.

Their last night together Emily buried her head in his chest and cried. She saw him only as a blur and what she did next filled him with anguish; as if a blessing she again kissed the anchor around his neck, her entreaty muffled: "Your beacon, Sam. It will guide you to me always."

Alone and stricken, she prayed that a child stirred in her body.

17

THE *ALDINGA* BERTHED AT Fishermans Bend in the Yarra River, a discharge partly out of the normal and not without nostalgia for Henry when an old rusted hulk came alongside under the tow of a tug. The gear at No.2 hatch swung outboard, the hulk's decks gutted to give greater access to her ribbed hull for the storage of bunker coal.

Of her three masts only one remained; two stumps and the stripped mainmast rigged with a swinging two and a half ton derrick, steam raised by a donkey boiler on her poop. Henry searched for a name on the tarred bow, a slapdash attempt to keep rust at a minimum, then the poop to no avail; for some reason the Melbourne Harbour Trust painted the number 7 on her stern, even that barely readable.

A sad end to a once greyhound of the sea, a Cape Horn veteran that confronted raging gales with contempt. With canvas and cordage, the sweat and muscle of men and boys, sailed the trade winds deep in the wastes of the world's oceans. Under full hamper buried her proud head in the awesome seas of the Roaring Forties, Screaming Fifties and the Howling Sixties. Henry wondered what rig, barque or ship, unknown with her masts mere stumps.

He rigged a Jacob's ladder over the side and with Sam boarded her. Stripped bare the focastle stunk of black mould which hung in festoons where once iron bunks lined the curvature of the bow; even the dividing bulkhead for the port and starboard watches gutted, the concrete deck strewn with anchor cable and old wire.

"Maybe twenty men would have slept and eaten here, bathed at the break in buckets of saltwater," Henry said reminiscently. "That's of course if she manned with a good working number of men, which towards the end of sail would be doubtful. With focastle accommodation she may have been other than British who liked to house their crews in deckhouses."

Sam wondered how ten men could cram in the focastle let along double that number, fascinated by the ship, his imagination running rife. The magic aura of sail and men aloft, hauling on braces, reefing, manning the capstans and winches to rousing sea shanties, seamen in the true sense of the word.

"Those were the days, lad," Henry said. "Forever hungry, wet and cold. Driven and bashed, logged for an utterance on deck. Worked eighteen hours a day. Bully masters and bucko mates maintaining their supreme authority over seamen. This breed even more savage with Yankee blood in them. Though any sign of weakness from the afterguard exploited to the full, seamen sometimes giving as good as the mates gave, knives, spikes, pins. What mattered to seamen after months at sea, beaten, driven and starved, liberty with cheap booze and even cheaper women. Also the possibility of getting even if a mate found himself in a dark alleyway."

"What did you eat, Henry?"

"Not much, some ships better than others. Mean, coal for the focastle bogeys measured in pounds on the steward's scales each morning, water as well, three buckets each watch less the galley's whack of one. Then the issue of stores to the peggies, pantiles, a couple of tins of milk and jam to last each focastle for a week. Of course unlike the officers we never got fresh bread, we got what came from barrels stored in the lower peak and under the steward's padlock. Pantiles baked brick hard, mouldy oats for skilly, dried peas for soup, embalmed pork and beef more fat and bone than meat. Experts starved us, the British Board of Trade, true authoritarians on a scale of rations designed to keep a man alive and extract the maximum of work. Medical science might note, we were a healthy lot and quite virile ashore if not lying drunk in the gutter."

"I'll never complain again, Henry."

"On the coast we still have far to go, a common menu for one, no more than a shipowners strategy to divide and suppress. We do have it a lot easier thanks to our union. Have you read of the Tolpuddle Martyrs?"

Sam shook his head.

"Gathering about him a group of likeminded men, one a close family member, a Methodist preacher in Tolpuddle in the United Kingdom made them swear an oath of allegiance to organise and fight against the exploitation of landlords and masters. The first trade union in the early 1800's, men bound together to better their lot in life. To give the working man dignity of labour and fair remuneration. Not much to ask the aristocratic elite who lived in splendour and luxury on their estates from those who existed in squalor and poverty.

"Wages cut at the whim of masters, farmers their share of their labours while the coffers of the regal gentry swelled to overflowing. For their audacity to question the system of master and servant, a more equitable distribution of wealth, the unionists who became known as the Tolpuddle Martyrs, were transported in irons to Australia. That, lad, is the history of the first union, the first voice raised by workers. Think hard about that. What has changed today?

"We still remain embattled with the few who control the wealth earned by the labour of the majority. The excuses are still the same, it is we who risk our wealth to create employment, we who give you jobs so that you can eat and clothe your families. You should be on your hands and knees in gratitude, not demanding more money and better conditions."

Sam wondered if standing on the deck of the old derelict triggered a past militancy, having never heard him speak so much.

Henry found a bollard with enough metal for him to sit. "Get yourself a copy of *The Ragged Trousered Philanthropists* and read it, let it seep into your soul. Get angry and search libraries for working class history and the brave few who stood against the onslaught of goons hired by industrialists to intimidate. Those that didn't yield, bashed, shot, lynched, garrotted, their homes burned to the ground. Use this knowledge to engage in the struggle those who have sold their hearts and minds to the enemy, a foe who without second thought will turn on them as quickly and rapaciously as it would those it intends to crush."

"Henry, seamen are militant. Though obvious there are a few exceptions on this ship."

"Unfortunately so. Blighted by those who would turn against their union without a single trace of remorse."

"Henry, are you a member of the Militant Minority Movement?"

"In my young and reckless years I proudly carried the little red book of the Industrial Workers of the World close to my heart. Joined in San Francisco, attended rallies while on the beach and did battle with thugs hired to smash a strikebound laundry. Now I'm old, but the struggle still lingers in my bones."

"Do you think the unions one day will win over industry?"

"Having a painful knowledge of the past, and being a believer the past is reflective of the future, we will win skirmishes, sometimes even battles, but never the war. The enemy has a compelling weapon the union movement is powerless to combat, the control of money. Money is the driving incentive, the carrot on the stick for the reluctant ass, and every worker is addicted. Control money and the world is yours."

Henry normally kept his own counsel, his solitary cocoon a personal choice, and Sam felt it a privilege to be in the company of a rare man, a Wobbly and survivor of the transition from sail to steam.

"We are lemmings led by the irresistible scent of money, mesmerised by engraved etchings of monarchs and presidents, why we toil and sacrifice our bodies. Occasionally there emerges from among humanity those blessed with vision and true compassion who expose the system for what it is, manipulation and control. These unique individuals offering solutions come from the union movement, the land, sometimes even from industry and commerce itself. By a strange quirk of human nature these rarities eventually get turned upon by the very people these saviours are attempting to lead from the mire. Moses led the Israelites on a long and perilous journey, but I am sorry to say we have no such person to take up the fight and lead us into true socialism."

"Like Jack Lang?"

"So bitter that particular battle against the moneyed class employers inserted in Friday pay packets a slip of paper stating vote for Jack Lang on Saturday and don't bother coming in for work on Monday. We dare to challenge the establishment and there is no bitterer enemy, fangs bared and claws extended. Cemeteries are filled with the fallen who demanded fair rights for all."

A belligerent head peered over the side, a growl his pocket watch indicated 1:00pm. Henry stretched off the bollard and looked at Sam. "Now that's one bad hombre who'd join the New Guard in a flash. Our very own home-grown brown shirts."

"New Guard?"

"Fascist thugs. Extreme rightwing zealots. Willing tools of employers to smash picket lines, intimidate, bash, burn and terrify."

Sam gaped at him in amazement. "Here in New South Wales?"

"Everywhere. A tool of the fascists let loose upon the land."

18

ARRIVAL IN SYDNEY THE delegates contacted the Sydney branch office of the union, convening a special meeting for 12:30pm. The Dethridge Award would be the only item of business on the agenda. With history as a painful guide, the crippling of the once powerful Waterside Workers Federation and their members forced to work under license, the federal executive continued to recommend acceptance of the contentious award.

"Comrades, I am a loyal and committed member of the union and shall never waiver from my oath of fealty, but I like far too many rank and file cannot accept the Dethridge Award," Josh addressed the meeting. "Against all my union principles and allegiance to our leadership, I have to reject the recommendations of the federal executive and prepare for a strike."

"Your opinion, not fucking mine and others on this ship. Try forcing that down our gullets and you'll get your comeuppance," Kiernan threatened, glowering from his table. "Our officials know best."

Josh expected no other reaction from the bosun. "As a principle of unity I would normally agree with recommendations coming from our federal executive, but not this time. There is a lot of talk damaging to the union our general secretary Jacob Johnson has sold out. I don't believe waterfront hearsay spread by those who muster against us, but the rumours persist."

Sam scribbling hurried notes found it difficult to keep his mind focused on the importance of the meeting. Even though his future hinged on the issue of the Dethridge judgement, Emily clouded his thoughts. The *Aldinga* with her hatches washed out, bilges and strum boxes cleaned and cover plates wrapped in fresh hessian, loaded general cargo for Adelaide with only one gang. With a near empty wharf warehouse and bond store the ship would be alongside for an indefinite period.

With Claire house cleaning in Glebe, Mary and Harriet at school, for Sam and Emily a rarity, the house to themselves. He wanted to eat the tearfully happy girl he carried to her mother's big bed, savour every part of her willing body, possess the warm living flesh she offered him with the same ardour. He tried hard to hold back the flood, failing in a cry of pleasure as he erupted inside her and collapsed on her sweaty flesh. Again and again until he shredded skin, Emily swollen and sore. An outburst from the bosun wrenched his mind to the present.

"Lies, fucking lies spewed out by the comrades, Minorities and Wobblies!" Kiernan, unshaven for a week and coming out of a brandy induced binge, looked haggard, almost Neanderthal. "We all know that!"

"Brewed, distilled or fermented in that vacant space between your ears!" Joss threw back at him. "We have the right under our rules to question our federal executive as we do branch officials, a right we exercise at shipboard and stopwork meetings. Christ, this award has put us back ten years, twenty years."

Kiernan lurched to his feet. "I move a vote of confidence in Jacob Johnson and the federal executive. I move acceptance of the Dethridge Award and I want it recorded in the fucking minute book."

"Have we a seconder for the motion?"

Four hands shot up.

"Obviously we have some with confidence in our federal secretary and acceptance of the Dethridge Award," Gary said from the chair. "Let's put it to the vote. Those for the motion raise their right hand."

The bosun's hand made it five.

"Those against the motion and I don't give a stuff what hand you raise."

Seventeen.

Gary pointed directly at Kiernan. "Declared lost. Now the chair calls for the resolution this meeting is about."

Josh found his feet. "I move this meeting fully endorses the formation of a strike committee to report to the federal executive the directives of the rank and file and the rejection in full of the Dethridge Award."

The resolution passed, five against.

Josh like a terrier with the scent of a cornered rat asked a question of the bosun: "Kiernan, you want to accept this award, that's your prerogative, but I am curious how would you feel working with a dog collar around your neck?"

"If wearing one gets rid of shit like you, I'd welcome it. You lot don't fucking get it, go on strike and it is a dog collar around your neck!"

≈

Sam felt certain he would miss Christmas even though cargo still only worked one day shift gang. Josh held a more positive view, the ship would not sail at all if the December 3rd stopwork meeting tomorrow declared a strike.

With emotions high and militancy at its peak a stable element within the union recommended caution, their reference Waterside Workers Federation members now employed under license. Union men with years of service on the wharves ostracised by foremen selecting labour at the wharf gates. Even overlooked for obnoxious cargoes like cement, soda ash and hides.

In an environment of despair and hopelessness industry and commerce wielded enormous power worldwide over the labour force, that power no more evident on Australian wharves and ships. Gradually, almost agonisingly, the Waterside Workers Federation clawed back some lesser conditions through board of references convened for rule breaches, but the victories few and far between. Now seamen faced the same fate forced upon it by an award written in the boardrooms of shipowners and stamped by the anti-union federal government.

Apologists abounded for the Justice Dethridge Award; constraints such as seamen's high wages and unsustainable conditions spelled disaster for the maritime industry, shipowners forced to layup tonnage, unable to build or purchase new ships. In a climate of extreme financial peaks and lows Australian shipowners provided accommodation far above world standards, food of a high quality, and wages and leave provisions exceeding Australia's trading partners. Under the Australian flag shipowners without exception provided a safe workplace, their ships in survey and maintained to the stringent recommendations of the classification societies.

For Christmas Sam put aside £10; £7 for gifts and £3 for Christmas fare. What to buy his girl? Dolls for Mary and Harriet? No, more practical to buy clothes, something for summer. Claire? Thinking about her gave him a warm feeling of acceptance. Because of respect for her position within the family and age he addressed her as Mrs Knight until one day she asked him to call her Claire. He did and it felt as natural as if he called her mother. Definitely perfume.

On stopwork meeting day, the messroom filled with the majority dressed for going ashore and eating breakfast, the bosun put his head through the door and ordered the overhaul of idle No.4 gear. "Essential work! Any of you fucking know-all sea lawyers reckon it's not, then get a union ruling on it!" Kiernan jeered.

Josh looked up from his curried beef and rice on a thick slice of toast. "Look at it this way, Kiernan, you and your gutless mates and this essential work bullshit you've pulled from your arse can go to hell. Stuff your No.4 gear!"

≈

The Sydney Town Hall, a garish mass of local sandstone, shared the corner of George St and Druitt St with St Andrews Cathedral. The plaza overflowed with a sea of men in hats, a small sprinkling of bare heads.

Sam joined Josh and Gary talking with Henry. "My count is a thousand and I have this distinct feeling it's a lynch mob," Josh said.

The men slowly passed through the huge ornate doors of the hall, even their large number swallowed by its immensity, taking their seats in rows and rows of wooden chairs on polished floorboards. Rising to the high vaulted ceiling a multitude of voices, hardly a country not represented. Men shook hands with old shipmates, embracing, amazed at faces thought long dead.

On stage behind a long table the federal executive of the Federated Seamen's Union of Australasia sat in pensive mood, sometimes talking with their heads close, the occasional laugh more forced than merriment. For the casual observer there seemed no sense of urgency, no trepidation at the endless multitude of men flowing into the hall.

Their seats fourteen back from the stage offered a wide panorama of the meeting, the stream of men entering the hall reduced to a trickle as the large clock on the wall read 9:15am. "All this because of one man," Josh observed. "Justice Dethridge and his award dictated word for word by the shipowners and given imprimatur by the workers worst enemy, Menzies. In this venue right now if graced by that man's illustrious presence we could pillory him instead of our officials. To get rid of him I would gladly help him up the gangway of one of his favoured British ships. Refreshed after a long voyage to London to supplicate himself at the feet of royalty and the preserved mummies in the House of Lords."

"Why would he when he is Australian?" Sam said.

"Is he? Yes, you're right, he is. Being born somewhere in Victoria should make him one, but you'd be hard put to know."

Chris Herbert left the table, the Sydney branch secretary advancing to the microphone at the edge of the stage; clearing his throat, he called for order. Nominations for chairman caused a ruckus in three clearly defined groups, three passenger ships in port; Huddart Parker's *Westralia* and two new motor ships under the house flags of Adelaide Steamship Company and Melbourne Steamship Company, *Manoora* and *Duntroon*.

With the numbers in their favour the *Westralia* prevailed over other names shouted, their nominee struggling to pass through a group refusing to give way in front of the stage. The clocked ticked over to 9:31am and the doors closed, the doorman recruiting six men to pass down the rows and count numbers.

The doorman, a long retired AB with a shrivelled leg he dragged behind him, struggled to the stage to inform the chairman who in turn gave the attendance figure of 1300 to the minute secretary.

The branch secretary experienced the first twinge of misgivings his signed support in the Journal of acceptance of the Dethridge Award. He needed no intuitive insights to sense the mood of the meeting, or any of the federal executive who looked out over a packed hall of volatile faces.

For two hours speaker after speaker voiced condemnation, not a single voice in support of the federal executive. Speakers took out their wrath on the federal executive who remained steadfast, stony faced, their collective thoughts on salvaging the meeting from its inevitable path of rejection.

Jacob Johnson felt as if over a thousand belligerent faces aimed directly at him, livid with rage. Voices louder than others shouted damnation at selling out the union to the shipowners, the general secretary no more than a stooge for the union bashers in government.

He refused to back down, his amplified voice reverberating throughout the hall a potent weapon. Even so he knew as did the disconsolate men behind him this meeting would be a precursor of industrial suicide leading the union down the same precipitous path as other unions now rendered impotent.

"Resolution! Resolution!"

The chairman gave vent to a hoarse shout of order immediately lost in wave after wave of dissonance; he indicated the general secretary stand aside and gripped the microphone with both hands. "Have we a resolution from the floor?"

In a controlled voice it came from a single piece of paper in a seaman's hand, an unexplainable lull in the meeting giving it foreboding clarity: "That this meeting of members of the Federated Seamen's Union of Australasia reject in its entirety and refuse to work under the clauses of the Dethridge Award. That this meeting issue a statement to shipowners and the federal executive of the Federated Seamen's Union of Australasia of the immediate resumption of a new award negotiation with shipowners."

"What about the rats in the union?" a bullish voice demanded in the silence that continued to hang like a heavy pall over the meeting. "Them on the stage who put their names to this award. We going to let them get away with selling us out?"

"Order! Order!" the chairman admonished. "There is a resolution from the floor! Seconder!"

Though some groups shook their heads and shouted condemnation, the majority of the meeting vocally seconded the resolution.

"Comrades, raise your right hand—"

Echoing from the pressed metal ceiling of the hall, the meeting on its feet, those who opposed the resolution their voices lost, came the roar: "Strike!" The chairman to legitimise the vote called for a show of hands of those against the resolution, small inconsequential islands swamped in a cauldron of vehemence.

≈

As the meeting poured from the Sydney Town Hall so began a nationwide refusal by seamen to work under the Dethridge Award, their right to terminate their employment giving their employers twenty-four hours notice. Returning to the *Aldinga* all hands gave their notice, or so the delegates assumed. Sam about to stuff his seabag with working clothes felt a hand on his shoulder.

"Not you, mate. Though, and this doesn't come as a surprise, you're going to have the company of five lowlifes who have decided to ignore the strike resolution. You know who these scabs are."

"No way am I going against the strike resolution. I am throwing my hand in."

"Not for the strike you aren't. Deck boys might sign articles but under the Navigation Act you don't count in the manning."

"Josh, I am a fully paid up member of the union. I put my hand up for the strike."

"You did. Think of it this way, you're a protected species."

"Sailing with scabs." Sam felt a leaden weight in the pit of his stomach.

"Yeah, no prizes for guessing. Sam, you will be subjected to their dubious company for the duration of the strike, for your sake let's hope it's a short one. Then we can get rid of them."

The bosun locked himself in his cabin and Josh pounding on his door received no response; he pressed his mouth to the brass door vent. "Hear this good you diseased dog, with a chisel I'm going to engrave your scab name an inch deep in the Argyle Cut sandstone!"

19

THE *ALDINGA'S* FUNNEL BLOOMED with eye smarting smoke, the steady scrape of shovels and slices below as two firemen in twelve hour gear turns maintained steam for the winches and domestic power. The crew's accommodation remained incongruously silent at 8:00am, no grumbles of stumbling men having overslept, others dragged from their bunks in a hung-over stupor.

The cooks prepared breakfast for the deck according to the instructions of the chief steward; four halved black puddings, four rashers of fatty bacon and four fried eggs. Sam, in a quandary, stood outside the messroom and watched the three men within laughing over something amusing. He preferred to go hungry than eat scab fare, scab rations even less than Board of Trade at its worst.

Kiernan glanced up from his plate, his yellowed teeth chewing a rubbery portion of black pudding, grease trickling down his chin; in a good mood, only two double shots of rum needed to rid the hangover from last night's binge. He beckoned Sam standing in the doorway. "Come and eat a hearty breakfast, lad. Got a job for you after we turn to, a run to the Admiral Nelson."

"For what?"

"Stores, son. One rum, one brandy. There'll be some change so you can shout yourself a cordial. See how generous your bosun is?"

"You can keep your soft drink and you can get your own booze. As a scab are you frightened to pass through the picket line?"

Kiernan's chair crashed to the floor as he lunged for the door, grasping Sam's shirtfront and lifting him off the deck. "I'll rip your fucking tongue out if you ever you say that word again! We're not blacklegs! We're men with our own minds, not dumb fucking crackers! Remember that when you come up for air in the bilges, under the winches, fish oiling the chain locker. Remember that when you're scraping officer and engineer shit off the wharf. For the next couple of days though you'll be over the bow painting the names, topside, boot topping and drafts. How the Brits do it, one man to a stage. We got a statement to make to them outside the gate."

Sam having risen early spoke with one of the seven men setting up the picket line and placards outside the gate. Returning to the ship he felt despondent, deserting his fellow unionists to work with blacklegs, though he supposed a consoling bear hug and a pat on the back enough for him to come to terms with his role in the strike.

At lunch Sam joined the picket line, hungry enough to make a sandwich of his two thin slices of pickled pork. He ignored his remaining share of the kit, a small boiled potato and half a parsnip; a depressing thought, not a delegate to take the chief steward to task, maybe even throw the snivelling weasel over the side. At the picket line, now eleven strong, he saw Josh and his day brightened; he remarked about the food.

"The chief steward has ascended to chief steward heaven. Fare fit for scabs, and it will get worse. Maybe tomorrow one slice of rancid pork and half a boiled potato, heaps of broad beans for regular bowel movements as decreed by the Board of Trade. There is of course what ends up in the officers rosy with a crust baked on it. Think yourself lucky you got an egg for breakfast. I see you and the others over the bow."

"Kiernan put us there deliberately to gloat at the picket. Josh, this is not right. I should be here with you, not working with scabs."

"You're here in body and spirit, Sam. Within you burns true sincerity no shipowner can extinguish. No scab bosun, master or mate able to force you to break your oath of fealty to the union. I know that, so work with the bastards and keep you peace because the union will prevail."

"The wharfies think I'm a scab."

"We know you're not and that's all that matters. You have a union book which is something Kiernan and his mates now don't have. The five of them have been expelled from the union."

"So when the strike ends all of them will be sacked? It won't be like 1927 when seamen were forced to sail with those who took their jobs?"

"Now that is a matter I would not like to speculate on. Those of us on strike say yes, march them down the gangway. Though what the terms of settlement will dictate when the strike ends, who knows."

"So while Kiernan and his fellow scabs carry on as normal seamen on strike to gain better conditions starve. How can that be, Josh?" Sam almost pleaded for a reason for something so obviously unfair.

"Blacklegs are a breed nurtured by a culture that wants its asset to have no common voice or an ethic of unity among its fellows. It wants a single mind it can work, mould with false promises of security and freedom of the workplace. In other words if you trade your blackleg soul to industry and abandoned your roots we will take you to our bosom and shower you with rewards. Security, money, a venerated member of the management team. Blacklegs acclaimed as industrial renegades and lauded by industry are marched under police escort, sometimes ten police to one scab, through the streets to the factory gate or wharf. Heads held high, arms swinging, the sparkle of pride in their eyes. Filthy vermin taking the jobs of striking union men. Scab, rat, blackleg, call them what you want, no more than gullible stooges to be discarded with the rubbish at the end of its useful life."

Thoroughly depressed, Sam dragged his feet returning to the ship as if a slow shuffle would stop the clock with ten minutes remaining before turning to. Already on the focastle head and standing by their stages rigged below the name, Cyrus Thornton and Xavier Hopwood. Smiles and cheery banter it's near turn to time made it even worse, turning his head and ignoring them.

He rigged his bosun's chair above the draft figures, a Jacob's ladder between his chair and Cyrus's stage. Earlier he ran a bowsing line, an old guy, from the bitts at the port break of the focastle head to the starboard side, hauling it tight with a handy billy. Normally he would have felt a thrill secure in his chair, staring down at the water between his feet. Lowering himself, three pots of paint, red boot topping, black topside and white on lanyards, drawing himself hard up against the bow on the bowsing line. Now nothing but a simmering hatred. He worked with scabs. He slept with scabs. He bathed with scabs. He ate with scabs. He also knew, and this tore at his innards, why the waterside workers turned their backs on him.

≈

The December 6th meeting near overwhelmed the capacity of the Sydney Town Hall, 1400 striking seamen. Men stood in the aisles, backs against the wall, their angry eyes steadfast on the officials on the stage. The chairman with no affiliation to the Militant Minority Movement or Industrial Workers of the World, loyal to the federal executive, tried hard to maintain order.

The meeting though supportive of the strike committee ebbed with a tide of expressed rage, frustration and lack of confidence in the federal executive. Even those who could project their voices the loudest failed to penetrate the din, their voices wafted away on wave after wave of shouting. Resolutions went unnoticed by the chairman; a large bloc of men, among them many dressed in passenger blues and baggy white caps, sent their spokesman to the front of the meeting to mount the stage. His resolution, the strike committee be empowered to mount a High Court challenge as to the validity of the Dethridge Award.

Ominously, silence descended on the meeting, then a roar of affirmation. Jacob Johnson bounded to his feet. "Brothers, a resolution with great merit, but untenable in the current situation with the union on strike. I concur we should take our case to the highest court in the land, but no court will hear pleas when the plaintiff is on strike."

The silence grew more portentous, the tension like a coiled spring on a hair-trigger release.

Jacob continued in a strong and even voice: "We cannot continue on the course you have committed the federal executive and the strike committees in the major ports to follow. We have an intolerable situation with those who oppose strike action are refusing to pay off their ships and join their fellow members manning picket lines outside wharf gates. Let me also elucidate at those same wharf gates it is business as usual for the shipowners. While we inflict upon ourselves debilitating financial pain and family stress the shipowners are manning their ships with volunteers. Their marine superintendents are bringing forward docking schedules and layups.

"Brothers, the shipowners are feeling no pain or finding it difficult to pay the butcher or baker. If we continue this strike we face the same fate as our wharf labouring brothers, gutted and hung out to dry. At this meeting we have heard you loud and clear, and yes we will initiate proceedings in the High Court which means from your federal executive a recommendation of an immediate return to work. Then let us go to the High Court!"

His voice filled with confidence gave no indication two days earlier a death threat came in the mail, the federal secretary now under a police protection order. As a gesture of contempt, a large proportion of the meeting turned its back on the stage, angry men forcing a passage through the doors.

≈

With the skill of a surgeon wielding a scalpel, the consummate politician made his carefully calculated move. While mass meetings of striking seamen met in Australian ports, Attorney General Menzies gazetted the ports of Sydney and Melbourne with the licensing provisions of the Transport Workers Act. Seamen in these two ports to be eligible for employment would be required to apply for a license, their dog collar. In summer parliamentary recess Menzies liaised continuously with the prime minister, raising dire concerns of an imminent collapse of a weak economy slowly recovering from the worst financial crisis in history.

Menzies needed no goading to vent his spleen on hardcore seamen forcing their union executive to spearhead an illegal and nationally damaging strike, even though ships with loyal and volunteer crews continued to trade. A union now held in the vice-like grip of extremists such as the Militant Minority Movement, Industrial Workers of the World and Communists. He remembered only too well another conservative who paid a dear price in losing his seat and the election for his unwavering courage in attacking workplace extremism, Prime Minister Stanley Bruce. A man who forced the Waterside Workers Federation to its knees, a union now no more than a few annoying whimpers caterwauling from the shadows of the Argyle Cut in Sydney and the Hungry Mile in Melbourne. Though, and this troubled him, aware now of a new leadership cadre emerging among the dog collared waterside labourers, an articulate Liverpudlian named Jim Healy who could well in the future become a person of interest.

Charismatic leaders emerging like mushrooms from the compost of unionism rarely escaped being stored in a corner of the attorney general's brilliant legal mind. Another well noted in Queensland, Eliot Elliott, a highly vocal slick tongued Communist indoctrinated by his Soviet masters to rouse the mindless rabble, sprouting his dogma from the stokehold plates.

Prime Minister Lyons agreed with his trusted colleague, the full force of the law both civil and industrial be brought down in a single decisive blow on the striking seamen and their union, the attorney general given absolute prime ministerial authority to use whatever means needed to end this national dispute.

Ships sailed with volunteer and loyal seamen escorted to the wharves by police, in one incident a single AB protected by twenty-five police armed with batons and six constables on skittish horses. Winches rattled with full heads of steam, gear swung over the side by seamen with suspect briefs, faces stored in bitter memories by the growing destitute outside the wharf gates.

Those manning the picket lines became aware of scabs by an increased police presence, both on foot and mounted; especially when changing articles.

Jeered and spat upon, those identified their names shouted with abuse and threats. Seventeen seamen, deck and below, the majority with naval discharges signed the *Aldinga's* articles of agreement, the ship fully manned. These men vindicated their return to sea service as heeding a patriotic call from industry and the government to end a senseless and destructive strike, a threat to their nation saved by the sacrifice of past heroes in arms.

Sam, chipping and red leading on the focastle head, knew when a scab passed through the picket line, a howling wail outside the gate. Chanting over and over: "Blackleg! Blackleg! Blackleg!"

Unable to close his ears to the tirade, stomach muscles knotted like wet rope and to hell with the bosun, he threw down his hammer and advanced to the rail. Swaggering with a confident gait along the wharf three figures with suitcases, protection no longer needed now in the bosom of the shipowner. What consumed him, gnawed at his innards, one man looked up and briefly touched the brim of his hat, a smile and a slight inclination of his head to acknowledge one his own.

"To hell with you! I am not a scab!" he cried, stricken. "I am union!"

≈

Menzies worked swiftly with a hallmark efficiency he would hone to perfection in coming years to crush organised dissent, his solution to the seamen's strike concluded as the strikers met to find a compromise in the Sydney Town Hall. Effective immediately seamen with homeports in Sydney and Melbourne would be required to apply for a license, this license offered to a marine superintendent on demand as a legal right to sign Australian articles of agreement.

Seamen currently serving on ships articles for the fee of one shilling could apply for a license and those otherwise indisposed and not offering for employment would have their future service rights assessed in regards to their legitimacy to be engaged on Australian vessels.

Within days of the Sydney Melbourne licensing provisions, the ports of Brisbane, Newcastle and Adelaide followed. Thousands of seamen refused, effectively excluded from the maritime industry. Those that did pay their shilling paused on the steps of the shipping office and ceremoniously burned it. Now thrown wide open the ledgers of the shipowners for whomsoever wished to walk up their gangways, seaman or otherwise.

It seemed to Sam the strike slowed the loading of the ship, he supposed feasible with a picket line of aggravated seamen blocking the wharf. More so the economy extracting itself from a deep abyss, cargoes still elusive. This no more evident throughout the loading with only one day gang working, possible it might be early New Year before the ship sailed with a full cargo. The company with this lengthy delay in mind, even with the ship's consumption of coal in port small, decided on Sunday with no labour to shift ship to Balls Head for bunkers.

Little did Sam know the instant dismissal of the mud pilot shifting ship back to Darling Harbour almost mindless with brandy, would be a rung in the ladder of seamanship learned well before his time.

≈

Christmas! Home! A ring to it that dissipated frustration and despair. A ship of gloating drunks, thieves, thugs and overbearing ex-naval men with a loathing of unionism. Emily gave her comfort and love, shared her family's hearth, a balm to rid his mind of those who continued to climb the gangways of strikebound ships and take the jobs of his comrades outside the gates.

Emily and her sisters begun to decorate the lounge room with crepe paper, tinsel, baubles, balloons and a small Christmas tree in one corner. Sitting around the table all agreed the huge expense of a turkey of no consequence, their Christmas dinner menu decided. Claire relaxed more now with permanent work three days a week, Emily called in to clean larger homes. With Sam's housekeeping money, the Knights home radiated with an air of affluence.

Some volunteers on deck quickly lost their urge to serve at sea after a few days, with their gear never seen again. Two replacements Sam decided to keep well clear of, one with a long scar running from his left eye to his mouth, both men surly and introvert, avoiding eye contact. Josh informed him from the picket line shipowners were liaising with government correctional officials to have those with claims to be seamen early released from prison. Ordered with Sam to swing the gear at No.1 hatch from wharf to outboard for a barge, he needed no further evidence of their bumbling incompetency, their briefs bogus.

A proud boast by the government only licensed seamen could now sign ships articles of agreement, ridding the industry of militants and Wobblies, Communists and malingers, drunks and standover men who convened under the banner of the Federated Seamen's Union of Australasia. The uncouth mobs shouting their slogans outside Australian wharf gates would now have to queue and pay one shilling for the right to work.

Sam could not shut out the voices filled with scorn for the union, derision for his fellow seamen outside the gate, the futility of striking. He wondered did any of them give thought to the single kit he now drew for each meal, barely enough to feed half of them. His continued requests for dry stores, cheese, fresh milk and bread ignored. One kit, the law of scabs, first in first served.

Linen and towels previously laundered weekly now scrubbed on the deck. No bath soap, even the mate refusing to give the storekeeper sandsoap for work clothes. Sam wondered why this didn't cause some disquiet, then after observing the two reluctant members elected spokesmen when Kiernan grunted he would not front the master on domestic issues, his answer became apparent.

ABs Abner Horthy and Norman Peck, expelled years ago from the union for theft, refused to confront the chief steward, instead vented a verbal barrage of contempt for the comrade bastards at the front gate who imprisoned them onboard and kept them from the pub and skewering the local slatterns. Sam also came under attack for his continued complaints about the quality and quantity of the food and nonissue of stores; a snot-nosed union brat with a big mouth it should learn to keep shut.

Sam retreated, Abner and Norman's status as delegates made even harder to bear when Abner boasted his last job a cook in a shearing shed near Dubbo.

On the day of yet another stopwork meeting Sam defied the bosun and took the morning off, little knowing he would attend a meeting of unimaginable numbers in the history of the Federated Seamen's Union of Australasia. 3000!

He listened in shock as the meeting descended into chaos, but not before a member from the floor demanded the stepping down of the general secretary, his replacement Joseph Keenan. The resolution passed in uproar, another member screaming at the top of his voice: "Jacob Johnson is a master scab!"

≈

Sailing now confirmed for early January acted as a balm for Sam, the excitement of Emily and her family with Christmas, the sense of coming home when he walked down the gangway each day calming the demons that burned within. Times when alone, a rare event with two infatuated young girls in the house vying for his attention, their lovemaking concluded far too quickly, ears preened for the slightest noise at the front door. In the aftermath he wondered the likelihood of Emily falling pregnant, and that he should use methods to protect her. He never did, in the heated frenzy of possessing her body logical reasoning and biological consequences forgotten.

Menzies thoroughly earned his upcoming Christmas and New Year break, to languish in the comfort and love of family. Even so never far from his mind, a promise made to his nation, to himself and his prime minister, the wrapping in a shroud of a Communist controlled union languishing in its death throes.

20

SUNDAY PROVED ANOTHER UNSEASONABLY warm day, perfect for airing advanced aged and creaking bones from stuffy indoors.

"Wendy, for want of a more apt term, I have come off the fence."

"No, darling, you have always supported me and the principles of the party. Welcome to the past, the present, and the future. The Liberal Party of Australia!"

"Acceptance comes with some relief because I thought membership of the Health Services Union might be a problem with the credentials committee."

"Of course not! Far from being the bogeyman of unions the Liberal Party encourages workers to be active in their unions. Voice their concerns about corruption and favouritism to the socialists. I don't mean leftwing unions who are red raggers. Many, many people belong to unions and are members of the Liberal Party, the same with people who vote Liberal. We are a diverse party advocating the entrepreneurial spirit and freedom of choice."

"Australia is almost divided equally in the middle, conservative and socialist. Though of course it is the number of seats won which equates to winning office. Unions play a large part keeping Labor in office."

"One of our most venerated coalition partners from the past, Senator Flo Bjelke-Petersen, openly admitted union membership."

"Courageous of her. Don't think Sir Joh would have admitted such an aberration. Member of a union, odd."

"Working the land and serving his state I don't think Sir Joh Bjelke-Petersen saw the need for association, though he may have supported the Farmers Federation. Lady Flo admitted union membership when the wives of striking southeast Queensland power workers stripped of their superannuation and long service leave and seniority entitlements pleaded with her to act on their behalf and have Sir Joh rescind his decision. She said to the women I have been a member of a clerical union for decades and I have never resorted to striking. Never have I put my personal interests above those of the people of Queensland. Neither has Sir Joh, so go back to your husbands and tell them to return to work."

"Could never understand a word that came out of Sir Joh's mouth, and plenty did when he got riled and cornered by a reporter."

"Because the man spoke directly from his heart. He made no bones about his humble country origins, or put on fancy airs with grand speeches. He is sadly missed, a beloved and exceptionally long serving Queensland premier."

"Enough of politics, let's eat." Another Sunday perfect for a picnic lunch, the kitchen staff overly generous for a likable young man with company, a hamper of ham, turkey and spicy forcemeat, salad, boiled eggs, bread rolls and apple juice.

She reached over to run her fingers lightly down his arm, a coy smile. "I am getting jealous, the catering staff paying extra special attention to my man."

"Have to admit I do seem to be a favourite with Rosalinda. Very therapeutic to extract old folk out of the wards and dormitories on days like this, and our kindly staff need no prompting to make it a culinary delight."

She acknowledged the presence of the old man in the wheelchair for the first time, no more than a cursory glance; a fleeting chill as his near closed eyes peered back, wondering what went through the fossil's mind, if indeed at his great age conscious thought existed.

Not to worry, the shrunken old cocoon probably no more than a hollow shell; how revolting nature allowed humans to grow so old and thoroughly useless. She made herself more comfortable on the park bench, the action momentarily exposing a bare knee. Paul caught the brief glimpse, wondering how long since his hand rested there before commencing its journey up her creamy inner thighs. Two weeks, mother playing lawn bowls and the house to themselves for a few hours.

She enjoyed the physical act of sexual intercourse though not particularly the messy after part, wet and sticky. Quite acceptable the contraction of highly sensitive vaginal muscles, gripping her partner's shoulder blades, a suppressed groan announcing her orgasm. The last to admit prudishness, only correct in refusing with a polite rebuttal to let Paul trail kisses any lower than her belly button.

He pleaded to no avail, his tongue barred access to her pubic mound and fleshy sheaf, his partner adamant the coupling of the male and female organs sufficient for their gratification. Anyway, her diaphragm would be smelly with their emissions and anti-spermicidal cream.

Certain the old man continued to stare at her, she coloured slightly, uncomfortable. "Paul, are you certain the old biddy is in a semi-vegetative state? I feel certain he is looking at me, or more accurately through me."

"Those old eyes don't see much these days, certainly what's inside his head far less."

"No, he is looking at me."

"Imagination, darling. He might be cross-eyed. Far as the medical staff is concerned he's no more than old husk fortunate to have some mobility. Hunger pangs stirring?"

"Starving!"

Both layered their bread rolls with turkey and ham, lettuce and tomato, sprinkling with sachets of pepper and salt; Paul cut his roughly in half, placing the smaller portion in the old man's bone thin hand, a gentle nudge and scowl to eat. "Progress for you in the field of medical science, Wendy, the old bloke eating by himself."

The old man dutifully chewed and swallowed.

"Still on the lookout for an apartment, nothing big, one bedroom," he said, drinking his juice thirstily, sharing it with the old man who sucked noisily. "Mother's not happy about it, suppose my board helps out in the house with things so expensive these days."

She showed her displeasure of his sharing the same straw as the old man with a tightening of her jaw. "Give her my love. I'm certain it's not the money, my gain her loss." She carried bottled water in her shoulder bag and would use her dampened handkerchief to wipe his mouth before she allowed him to kiss her again. "While I remember, pass on my thanks to the kitchen for their thoughtful little extras."

"I will. When I find what I am looking for it might be opportune to make an announcement, you think?"

"We shall, darling."

"Wendy, changing the subject and assured the party recognises a person's right to belong to a union, there has been some bad publicity with the Health Services Union of late. Makes one think of resigning."

"Referring of course to a corrupt official who catapulted into parliament as a reward for forcing his union into the Labor Party camp. Paul, there are good unions and there are bad unions, especially the unions controlled by the Communist Party. Yes, I think you should consider resigning."

"Though it is yet to be proved the man misused union funds, but the evidence stacked against him is pretty damning. The Communist Party, does it still exist in Australia? I would have thought with the collapse of the Soviet Union there wouldn't be much radicalism left in the union movement."

"It still festers, never you mind, of course in a diluted form. I have heard my grandfather's hushed voice recalling commencing his indentures as a boilermaker apprentice at the Williamstown Naval Dockyard in Melbourne. Union officials wore red ties and red feathers in the bands of their hats, entrenched on the job condemning and blacklisting and enforcing demarcation."

"As well if you were not a financial member of one of a basketful of unions you were out the front gate, right?"

"Yes! Grandfather also talks of the fifteen years it took to build a naval ship. Can you believe that? No wonder all our shipbuilding is in the hands of Asians."

Paul urged the old man to chew more quickly, alert for choking; worth reporting to the medical staff his old watery eyes definitely seemed transfixed on his beloved. Recognition of objects a good sign.

Her voice droned on and the old man chewed and continued to stare at her.

"Don't upset yourself, darling. The Communist threat is long gone and for that we have President Reagan to thank. Mr Gorbachev, tear down that wall! My heart pounded when he said those words!"

"We do and I do so hope those lobbying for him to be portrayed on their dollar bill are successful," she said, turning her head slightly to avoid the old watery eyes.

"He has an aircraft carrier named after him, pretty big one, too. Do you think there is some of President Reagan in Tony Abbott?"

"I do, yes."

"Solve the refugee problem?"

"He has promised to turn the boats back."

"John Howard's Pacific solution?"

"Nauru really isn't a solution because the boats still keep coming loaded with thousands and thousands of alleged refugees who have paid their hefty fees to people smugglers. I would be certain a small island can only take so many people, the ones of course who manage to arrive without sinking. What I cannot understand is how the Labor government and the Greens, the Greens who are actually running the country, can class spurious foreigners who have paid thousands of dollars to people smugglers, hardened Indonesian and Pakistani criminals, as legitimate refugees.

"The news is out there in the third world slums, come to Australia and the Labor government will give you a house, a mobile phone, and pay you thousands of dollars a month. Why queue outside of an Australian embassy and wait years to hopefully migrate when a short sea voyage to Christmas Island, a bogus distress call to the Australian navy if not actually sinking, for your escort to your new home courtesy of the Australian taxpayer."

"What could Mr Abbott do about the situation? It is a very difficult problem."

"Turn the seaworthy boats back to Indonesia."

"What about the sinking ones?"

"Pluck them out of the water and send them back to Indonesia."

"I have a lot of reservations and I honestly think most of these people are fleeing persecution."

"Don't be fooled. Many have relatives or contacts in Australia who have paid their boat ticket. There are of course children to tug the heartstrings of the bleeding hearts, even thrown overboard to attract media attention to their supposed suffering!"

"Read somewhere being a signatory to the United Nations Convention Status of Refugees we might be in contravention turning these people back, but I agree wholeheartedly something drastic has to done. We just can't keep on supporting these people."

"The facts are simple. If it is true these people are escaping persecution in their own country the moment their feet step on Indonesian or Malaysian soil freedom is theirs. Correct?"

"True. As Moslems, which obviously these people are, why would you want to settle in a predominantly Christian country? You're so right, Wendy, we should tow them back to Indonesia. Bravo Tony Abbott."

"Accolades indeed Tony Abbott. Undoubtedly a tower of strength who will emerge from the large shadows cast by Sir Robert and John Howard."

The last name stirred no memory, but Sir Robert, the name might have caused the old man to draw blood on his bony knees if any strength remained in his fingers. He knew well the name Sir Robert, following his name an alphabet, not in the least Knight of the Order of the Thistle and Constable of Dover Castle and Warden of the Cinque Ports which allowed him to dress in voluminous robes and chains around his neck and wear a big feathered hat.

An exceptionally long tenure in power achieved by gifted articulation and an acute political cunning to render his opposition impotent by accusation, true or false of no importance. He used a mortal schism within the Labor

Party to remain in power for decades, welcoming into the political spectrum ultraconservative Catholic cadres who broke ranks and formed their own party.

Paul leaned close to Wendy for her to dab his mouth with her dampened handkerchief, a quick peck now assured of being germ free. For the old man a blessing as it temporarily closed her mouth. What did this nurtured product of falsity in a world without foundations know of the true Australian identity? Did she believe Australia forged its national psyche with idealistic young farm boys marching proudly with flags flying from dusty country towns shouting cooee and come join us, signing up to fight for the glory of Empire? Sacrificial blood soaked foreign battlefields that erased entire generations, written in history books as a fledgling nation coming of age through loyalty to blood kin?

Dismissed as rebellious and common working class by scholarly scribes those who roused and led their fellow Australians on the home front in a continuous struggle for equality and freedom, who without fear exposed the avarice and ruthlessness of colonialism followed in later years by industrial bondage. From the martyrs of the goldfields of Victoria, miners deep underground in the hellish coal mines of New South Wales, the hungry miles of Australian waterfronts, the army of despair who tramped the outback roads, came the call over the decades for true equality, an end to class segregation based on birth and race. Australia to fly its own flag, sing its own national anthem.

With the arrival of the First, Second and Third Fleets, crammed in their leaky, vermin infested holds a wretched human cargo of British felons, a national psyche evolved with the inevitable dilution of criminal blood. A characterisation embroidered in flowery rhetoric in newspapers and periodicals, on stage and in films, the sporting field and the world stage. Australia a gregarious and robust society, a thriving population above class distinction and snobbery. Respectful of authority but with a mischievous spark never far from the surface. Never taken lightly, or courage doubted. A free spirit led but never pushed.

So this stupid young woman believed.

Not a country almost equally divided down the middle; the right side promised salvation, the left hell. Conservatives and radicals, the honest and dishonest, the hardworking and indolent. For its democratic needs the nation created two parties of not dissimilar policies, one on the extreme right and the other fearful of losing its base support leaning from the centre to the right.

New to him, nightly on the big flat television screen in the lounge the old man witnessed a disturbed leader of the federal opposition in deep and meaningful dialogue with young workers on the factory floor. Proof against union lies his party's agenda would destroy organised labour, confirmation of his affinity with workers in fluoro shirts and reflective stripes, white hard hats and safety glasses. In government he promised to protect and enhance the rights of these young workers, the need for union membership under planned progressive labour reforms relegated to the bleak days of the industrial revolution.

Workers singularly could negotiate directly with their employers on an amenable platform legislated by the government. New age personnel on the factory floor, construction site, farm, office, hospitality, commercial, waterfront and transport, able to shed the union canker which hobbled free enterprise. Greater flexibility of employment, an agreed hourly wage rate removing the gross impediment of unaffordable and job repressive penalty rates. With real labour reform workers would have a new status, renamed associates and sub-contractors, consultants and casual human resources, eliminating restrictive imposts on business such as annual and long service leave, insurance premiums and unfair dismissals.

What did catch his interest one evening, a union official who wanted to know when Australia would stop importing thousands of foreign workers on special work visas and indenture the hundreds of thousands of young unemployed? A pretentious reply came from a particularly newsworthy minister of the federal government, amazed that the unions didn't welcomed with open arms these productive and nation building newcomers from Afghanistan, India, Pakistan, China, Philippines, Ukraine, Russia and Eastern Europe. The union official, barely containing his anger, also wanted to know when patriotic flag waving

Australian industry with their green and gold kangaroo logos would stop relocating their businesses to China.

"Minister, you mightn't want to know it from your cosy eyrie in Canberra, but as predicted we are fast becoming the quarry and poor white trash of Asia. Be that on you head and your successors!"

21

T HE *ALDINGA* LOADED TO her marks prepared to sail, fully manned and her sailing board posted January 3rd. The same day striking seamen met throughout Australia, the highest figure in Sydney, members of a union tearing itself apart.

Kiernan turned his motley collection of men to with threats, fists and his boots. The ensuring fiasco proved the worthlessness of the forward gang at No. 1 hatch, the slabs placed by shore labour and the tarpaulins spread. Without exception no cognisance of port or starboard, fore and aft, backing up, standing clear of bights, inside turns, hauling on guys, landing derricks, runners and topping lifts flaked clear of obstacles.

Cheap liquor fuelled their bleary-eyed stumbling on deck, the bosun shouting himself hoarse to stand clear of Sam lowering No.1 port derrick, his frenzied orders to haul on guys to line up the derrick with the crutch not understood. "Fucking useless bastards!" he bellowed, spitting in faces, kicking, wrenched from his own stupor by the chaos on deck. In desperation he beseeched Sam now lowering No.1 starboard derrick: "Don't let me fucking down!"

Sam shrugged, uncaring if the derrick landed on the head of whoever happened to be standing under the crutch. He shouted back over the clatter and escaping steam of the winch: "Your scabs, not mine."

"Mind your fucking tongue!" Kiernan dropped into a crouch for attack, hindered from reaching his quarry by an AB caught in a tangle of guy cordage. Sam thought his name Chalky, or something similar; his last job a prison officer.

"I'll mind nothing." His aim for the crutch without the aid of the guys successful, the derrick landing with a reassuring thud. "Hang your head in shame, Kiernan!"

Kiernan's hand hovered at his belt, his sheaved deck knife and spike; retribution could wait, he needed this loud mouthed whelp more than any other to get the ship squared up. "Keep your peace! You've been warned!"

"Go terrorise someone you can standover. You come near me and I am telling you I'll smash your big head in with a sledge hammer!"

Kiernan fell back, a frenzy building within as he saw his forward gang sitting on the hatch rolling cigarettes, one producing a flask of brandy, another missing in the accommodation.

It mattered nothing to Sam being ostracised, with deep seated bitterness accepting his lot. The food on a par fed to derelicts in a soup kitchen no longer bothered him, though in this respect he held the enviable position of collecting the meagre stores and kits from the galley; first choice his. He even tempered his resentment of the chief steward profiting with Board of Trade victualling, food worthy of scabs.

He received no sympathy from a new chief cook, offered no moral support from the stewards, not even a consoling word for his lone plight. Didn't the boy realise catering jobs were under threat because of the strike, and if the shipowners could find willing and able men to man their ships then so be it, though a nuisance having to pass through noisy and aggressive picket lines.

Kiernan about to vent his rage on the brandy sharing AB leading the merriment on No.1 hatch almost forgot a message from the master. "Wright, when we finish this shit the captain wants you on the wheel."

Dropping a derrick on a blackleg's head might make for a good day, but mud pilot made the suffering of these dullards a little less disagreeable. Steering at sea he loved the feel of a ship beneath him, obeying his command, feet spread widely on the duckboards, the wheel gripped firmly in both hands. Anticipating breaking seas on the quarter passing by the bridge in a broken wash and applying appropriate wheel to counter the lift of the stern. Seas on the bow keeping a half turn on. Hard over and the rapid swing of the bow, easing the helm turn by turn, countering to steady on a new course. The master's helm orders loud and precise, Sam's response immediate, repeating the order in the same sharp voice.

The impact of the master's order slowly penetrated a plethora of emotions, and when it finally did he experienced a heart pounding sensation that he with his feet spread wide on duckboards and his hand gripping the wheel would steer his ship out of Sydney Harbour. Not a scab, but him.

The ship squared up and Sam on the bridge, all he received on this momentous occasion from the mate about to go forward no more than a glance. Ignored by the third mate standing to attention, even the apprentice who seemed more interested in picking his nose standing by the engine room telegraph. He might not have existed, he who would steer this engineering marvel with a full head of steam to sea, sweaty hands on varnished wooden spokes.

"Wheel amidships," Captain Langford ordered, stepping out the wheelhouse, his attention on the tug steaming slowly ahead with the ship's stern line trailing in the water.

Sam repeated the order loudly: "Wheel amidships."

Returning to the wheelhouse, a snapped order to the third mate: "Let go fore and aft and signal astern, sir."

"Let go fore and aft and signal astern, sir!" The third mate obeyed in an instance, the master's instructions relayed by telephone, then hauling down on the whistle lanyard rove through eyes above the starboard wheelhouse door; an explosion of steam on the forepart of the funnel, then a deep throated series of three whistles.

"Dead-slow-astern, sir."

"Dead-slow-astern, sir!" the apprentice repeated.

Hardly perceptible at first the warehouses either side began to pass the bridge wings, the tug threshing debris strewn water slowly swinging the ship free of the berth.

"Let go the tug, sir. Steady as you go." The master now stood with his back blocking Sam's view through the forward wheelhouse window.

"Steady as she goes." Sam breathed deeply and flexed his shoulders, the ship in his hands even though the master commanded. Cool and calm, a mind free of clutter, the task at hand in need of full concentration.

"Slow-ahead, sir."

"Slow-ahead, sir!"

Why did the master call the apprentice sir, Sam wondered, a half turn to port to correct a degree movement of the bow as the ship's speed increased under the influence of tide, wind and engine revolutions? Did the master expect him to rely with a sir? Kiernan grovelled to the mate and called him sir, sometimes beginning and ending sentences with the title.

Lifting on tiptoe he saw through the window the forward gang flaking mooring lines down No.1 hatch, a single hatch board removed and the tarpaulin folded back. The *Aldinga* should not be sailing, alongside for the duration of the strike, a strike against an unfair and biased award forced upon the union. Rid your mind of everything else except the task in hand, steer a true course like a seaman with the responsibility of the ship in his hands.

"Ten degrees starboard helm. Mr Hogarth, one short blast."

"One short blast, sir!"

"Ten degrees starboard helm," Sam repeated.

"Full-ahead, sir."

"Full-ahead, sir!" The apprentice repeated, iron bar stiff to attention.

"Wheel amidships."

"Wheel amidships."

The ship suddenly cast in deep shadow as the massive latticed steelwork of the Sydney Harbour Bridge towered above, though disconcerting to the man at the wheel the fore topmast lined up with the centre diamond would hit the decking. No more than an illusion because sailing ships passed under this bridge; a muted rumbling and flicking of lights as a train passed overhead.

"Do you see the channel ahead?"

"I see the channel clearly."

"On your port hand are green buoys with conical topmarks. Keep her steady in the middle of the channel."

"Keep her steady in the middle of the channel."

The ship in his hands, nerves no more, the vessel obeying his commands without hesitation. Though he found it annoying his vision impaired by the master's back, his attention on two yachts beating into a stiff north-easterly who would on their current course cross close ahead.

"Announce what are you intentions, Mr Hogarth," the master said with a slight note of annoyance in his voice. "If ignored give them another to wake the Sunday sailors up."

The third mate rushed out the wheelhouse and pulled down hard on the whistle lanyard, five deep throated emissions of steam.

The yachts lost wind, coming about to return to their berths in Double Bay.

The ship's bow rose for the first time on a low easterly swell, North Head looming as a sheer crumbling and severely eroded sandstone bluff filling the entire front windows of the bridge.

"Steer ninety degrees."

"Steer ninety degrees."

"Ring full-away, sir."

"Ring full-away, sir!" The apprentice rang a double ring, noting the time in his notebook: 4:55pm.

"Notify the chief engineer we are fully underway and commencement of passage 1700 hours. Steer 190 degrees."

"Steer 190 degrees." Out of the corner of his eye he saw the four to eight watchkeeper, he thought named Silas and an ex-navy steward, step over the stormstep and enter the wheelhouse through the portside door. He ignored him, releasing a half turn to port, the ship steady on course. "Steering 190 degrees and wheel amidships," he said, then stepped away from the wheel without another word.

Sam heard the raised voice of the irate mate on the wing of the bridge, catching his breath from his hurried departure from the focastle head. "With the exception of the bosun, and he is on his final warning, I want the forward gang sacked on arrival in Adelaide! I have never in all my seagoing life ever—"

Captain Langford's raised hand abruptly stopped the mate's tirade as Sam approached. "Steering 190 degrees, Captain."

"Steering 190 degrees. Thank you, Quartermaster."

His striking comrades manning the picket lines would be proud of him.

≈

Sam felt an old hand as the *Aldinga's* head slowly swung to line up with the outer harbour leads, the spokes still warm from the hands of the man he relieved, not a word spoken, a sullen nod; Sam heard him called Larry.

In his line of vision No.1 port derrick in a series of jolts lifted, the derrick head still clamped and lashed lifting the crutch with it. Even on the bridge Kiernan's furious voice rang in his ears.

Even louder if possible a near hysterical command from the focastle head, the mate standing by with the carpenter: "Stop what you are doing or attempting to do immediately! Leave the gear and hatches until we berth! Good God, man! Enough is enough!"

Sam shut it from his mind, the ship in the middle of the river with two spokes of starboard helm allowing the head to follow a wide sweeping bend, the spokes released and countered with two to port to steady on for the long reach to Osborne.

The outer Adelaide suburb from the height of the bridge presented a low profile of dusty streets bare of trees, scattered homes built of sandstone blocks and iron roofs. Wharves on the starboard side and lush mangroves on the opposite bank thriving in mudflats giving way to a flat coastal plain on which the city spread buttressed by the hazy Adelaide Hills. He overheard the master talking with the third mate discharge scheduled for completion in five days with afternoon gangs, lightship Whyalla to load iron ore for Newcastle, Sydney for orders.

He let his hands drop by his sides, the ship not responding to helm as it lost headway under dead-slow-astern, a tug lashed up to the starboard quarter warping the stern into a landlocked berth, head facing the river. There would be a picket line and he wondered if Kiernan's mob would be brave enough to venture ashore. Though none of them would be packing their bags, a wireless message with company instructions to rescind the notices of those dismissed, to persevere and engage in more intense onboard training.

Armed with knowledge of their worth to the company would in no way lessen their sense of immunity from discipline, making the task of the mate maintaining some semblance of order difficult if not impossible.

Sam walked along the wharf, a broad expanse of asphalt with two warehouses merging with a drab residential street, a dozen galvanised iron clad cottages with front gardens daring any living thing to grow in the barren industrial environment. Five men stood close to double railway lines dissecting the street, behind them a two storey pub. One approached Sam and challenged him.

"Are you off the *Aldinga*?"

"Deck boy, union number 7171," he replied, holding up both hands. "Who because of the Navigation Act is the only member of the Federated Seamen's Union of Australasia onboard. Fully manned on deck and below with scabs. I have no choice but to sail with them."

He thrust out his hand. "Morley Trevallyn. How are you coping?"

"Some days better than others. More importantly, how's the strike going? When we left Sydney the stopwork meeting wanted the head of Jacob Johnson."

"Jacob's gone. Strikes not going well, throughout the union talk the shipowners don't give a damn if we accept the award or not. Their ships are moving, fully manned, just like yours."

"We passed many of our ships."

"Scabs are coming out of the woodwork like rats sniffing an easy meal. Doing the rounds of the waterfront talk of scabs forming their own union subsidised by the shipowners. That's the rumour anyway."

"A shipowners union?"

"Their very own union, probably set it up in their basements. It's hard with this talk going around not to believe the union's finished, shipowners won't even negotiate with us. Menzies is framing legislation to garrotte the union, worse than the dog collar act, deporting our officials."

Thoroughly depressed, Sam walked the darkening streets of Port Adelaide. Deserted, shops and the hotels shut tight, though from some muffled laughter came from their back rooms. At the Black Diamond Corner a Greek fish and chip café, an oasis of light, the strong odour of hot fat a lure for the hungry and desperate.

Returning to the wharf, the picket line dispersed, he found a bollard to eat his soggy rock cod and chips laced with salt and saturated in malt vinegar. The hotel behind him held his attention, in total darkness, barely distinguishable from the adjacent warehouses. Not even a working street light, probably deliberate to allow a clandestine departure if the licensing police raided the premises. The *Aldinga* working cargo, the sounds of winches and working gear loud in the still night air, but his attention kept returning to the hotel. The thought of crushed bodies consuming warm and stale beer under the threat of a police raid, the publican getting richer thanks to the temperance wowsers who decreed 6:00pm closing. From the rear of the hotel, a back room with laneway access, the silhouette of a man no doubt a lookout.

Probably as far as the crew of the *Aldinga* got from the ship, filling their bellies with slops the publican drained from his waste trays, worthy of such clientele. He didn't want to go aboard; walk, he needed to walk in the cold night air, fill his lungs with pure clean air. Walk until his legs ached, no destination in mind. His turning point the city limits of Adelaide, turning and retracing his footsteps. The lighted clock at the Black Diamond Corner: 12:15am.

Bell tents rigged on all four hatches, hauled taut on their runners and lashed to the coamings, lay limpid in the still air, the afternoon gangs knocked off. Still audible a faint hiss of escaping steam from contracting flanges, reduced to water flushed in the morning. From the gangway he heard the revelry from aft, shouting and singing, women laughing and high pitched shrieks. Coming from three cabins sharing flagons of sherry and claret women with brassy voices in various states of undress gathered and conversed in giggles in the alleyway. Sam wondered about his cabin, relieved to find it in darkness; he needed a mug of tea.

At a messroom table smeared with vomit an AB snored with his head in his folded arms, a woman sitting beside him; Silas. About forty, he thought; unruly blonde hair, long faced, sallow complexion, her left eye puffed and slightly blackened. Once she would have drawn attention, the accruing years clearly evident in facial lines around her eyes and mouth, an almost sickly thin body spent of its young effervescence. She smiled and Sam thought it might be an invitation, a woman who still considered herself with the allure.

He made a pot of tea. "Would you like a cup of tea?"

"Anything stronger?"

Shaking his head, he searched for condensed milk, an empty tin with the spoon still inside dumped in the rosy. "Seems your boyfriend's the worse for wear."

She shrugged.

He found a stale half loaf of ship's baked bread in a locker, an open tin of jam by the sink. Scraping away furry mould, he made two sandwiches and handed one to her.

"Thanks," she said, obviously hungry as she quickly chewed and swallowed the crumbly bread and jam. Beneath their feet the party raged, interspersed with heavy thumps against the bulkheads.

"What's your name?"

"Sam," he said, then to vindicate his presence onboard. "Don't bundle me in with this mob of scabs. I am a member of the union."

"If so why aren't you on strike?"

"Deck boys are not part of the crew. Soon this is going to end and scabs will be got rid of. We stay united we will win."

"No, you won't," she said with certainty.

Her smugness and knowing smile annoyed him. "How can you say that? How would you know?"

"Around the port you hear things. The union won't win."

Annoyance turned to anger. "We will win and the bastards who stumble and fall over themselves in their incompetence and stupidity will be tossed down the gangway!"

"My husband used to talk like you, all this union stuff. Lot of good it did him when he lost his job to someone who worked for less and longer."

"From what I have witnessed in the workplace, I don't doubt that."

"Christ, I need a drink."

"As I don't consider myself part of this crew I don't share their booze. I don't even talk to them."

"Would you get me out of here? There's someone who frightens me."

"Silas?" Washing his cup in the sink, he turned and faced her. "Looking at the state of him he's no threat to anyone. What's your name?"

"Jacqueline. Not him, he passed out long ago. Someone else."

Kiernan crashed through the door in his soiled underwear, both front and back. He leered at Jacqueline, then narrowed his eyes when he saw Sam by the sink. Grasping his genitals he squeezed. "You're not fucking this slag, boy! That's work for a man!"

Sam kept his eyes firmly fixed on the unsteady figure now propped against a table. "Work for a man? How about work for a diseased scab?"

Kiernan straightened, further narrowing his eyes in an attempt to focus on his adversary; a dilemma confronted him, if he moved his feet and let go the table he would collapse on the deck.

Sam reached for the bread knife. "You've shit and pissed yourself, you no-good bastard! Come on, I think the odds are in my favour right now!"

Jacqueline stumbled from her chair and pressed against the bulkhead; she caught Sam's eye and shook her head. "Think of what you are about to do," she said between forced intakes of breath. "Is your life worth more than this miserable animal?"

He threw the knife in the sink and stepped around Kiernan whose eyes rolled to the back of his head; she reached for his hand and fell into him, her voice a hiss. "Get me out of here."

Chortling drunks courted drunken women, too sodden in alcohol to successfully sustain arousal, even with the objects of their desire in various stages of undress. The three who shared Sam's cabin caroused elsewhere, the cabin in darkness. Still holding hands he guided her to his lower bunk, slipping in beside her and drawing the bunk curtain.

Turning to him she pressed her lower body against his, teasing his lips with her tongue. "Your breath tastes as sweet as jam." Lifting on her hip she eased her underwear around her knees and hiked up her dress almost in one movement. Her well practiced fingers unbuttoned his fly and grasped his growing erection. She gently caressed the fleshy rim of his organ with the tips of her fingers, pleased as he fully hardened, murmuring: "Young boys secrete quickly as well as come."

No way in the world could he stop what coursed him, this woman who offered her body for his release. About to turn her on her back and enter her, she gripped him tightly.

"What?"

She released him and looked directly into his eyes. "You're young, you'll come too quick. Bring me to the edge."

Opening her blouse her small breasts lay flat against her bony ribcage, her nipples hard and prominent, in turn taking each in his mouth and suckling. She arched her back, muttering and breathing heavily, spreading her legs to open herself to him.

In dim light filtering through the bunk curtain he saw the thick patch of hair protecting her sheaf, a pronounced crease of puckered inner lips protected by two larger folds of flesh. With his fingers he parted the incredibly warm inner lips to expose the pink flesh inside, slicked and pungent. An odour of musk almost overpowering, hardening him even more as he lowered his head and forced his tongue inside her.

She let out a cry and bucked, clawing his hair, sobbing, trying to spread her legs even wider in the narrow bunk. "Now! Inside me!"

He wondered if he could before coming, feeling the first rush of ejaculation. With one plunge he succeeded, completely inside her before he erupted and cried out as spasm after spasm racked him.

She lay beneath him, clammy, gently rotating her hips, intermeshing their pubic hairs, heightening the sensation of his lessening spasms. Still hard and fully inside her, the crumpled sheet soaked beneath her, she wanted fulfilment. Her fingers played down his spine. "Deep inside me you're still big and hard," she moaned, lifting him with each gyration.

This time it would last longer as he began to match her rhythm, possessing her yielding flesh, ramming inside her, causing her to cry out as her orgasm engulfed her. Drained, an exhausted sleep overcame him.

The watchman called him at 7:00am and he struggled up, the bed in shambles and alone. Sometime during the early hours of the morning she must have slipped from the bed, dressed and gone ashore.

Staring up at the top bunk he felt relief mixed with guilt; failing to convince himself this is what a man did when a woman offered herself for his release and pleasure. Nature, no more than a physical act of nature. The lingering scent of Jacqueline's body, stale sweat and musk reminded him of his unfaithfulness to Emily, and his heart ached with remorse.

≈

The *Aldinga* finished cargo, the sailing board 4:00pm Whyalla. Forward orders though not definite, discharge Newcastle, sail Sydney to load general cargo for Fremantle.

An AB paid off and his replacement swaggered onboard without challenge, an ominous reflection of the strike on members of the union manning dwindling picket lines and their increasing disillusionment.

22

EMILY STIRRED AGAINST HIM, not yet a sense of urgency, but soon Mary and Harriet would be home from playing with friends in the park. At the moment both sapped of strength nothing mattered except languishing in the exotic aftermath their bodies created in the physical act of love. Claire would be home from work around 4:30pm.

Tomorrow their moments alone would be severely restricted with Emily starting work at Mark Foy's department store in Liverpool St. She leaped into his arms with the joyous news, not much of a job really and low paid, but money for the home. From hats, gloves and scarfs promotion possible with greater responsibilities in women's evening apparel.

"I have a real job, Sam!"

He rolled her on top of him and gently caressed her buttocks, wet and sticky. "We're going to have noisy company pretty soon."

"Mother knows. She has for awhile, suppose from Newcastle."

"What did she say?"

"We talked."

"Emily, I know nothing about girls. I never even knew that girls bleed every month."

"I'm due to in a few days."

"Are you certain you will?"

"Not always after we make love."

"You might not this month?"

"I will. I always know a few days in advance."

"We've never taken precautions."

"Do you want me to have your baby?" She raised her head and opened her mouth for him to kiss.

He pressed his lips to hers. "When I am AB."

"Would it matter if it happened now?"

Sam considered himself head of the family, the role undisputed by the abandonment of Claire and her daughters by a husband and father who sent no support home. "Emily, I am certain it would."

"Then I won't have your baby until you're an old AB. So there!"

≈

Two ABs paid off on in Sydney, replaced by men Sam thought were members of the union. When questioned he received stony glares to mind his own business and he better watch his back and sleep with one eye open. The replacements proved to be seamen, agreeable for Kiernan, but not Sam demoted from mud pilot to the forward gang.

Kiernan constantly derided him on deck, his orders bordering on threats, his communication in grunts; he wondered if the ire came from repentance when he passed through picket lines, especially from men he knew and previously sailed with. The bosun boasted the Federated Seamen's Union of Australasia no longer existed as a negotiating force, their pitiful pleas for a return to work ignored by the shipowners, soon to be replaced with another union, a democratic union unfettered by old socialist dogma.

Sam visited the picket line whenever time permitted, usually covered in foul smelling fish oil and wire rope oil; men who could only stare forlornly at their replacements working over the side chipping and scraping, listen to the constant rattle of steam winches working cargo. Worse, watching linesmen pass through the wharf gates, slip lines and the ship depart the berth.

The picket lines thinned even more as members increasingly grew disenchanted with the length of the struggle with no outcome in sight. An oddity of the industrial action, the number of wharves picketed increased, factories reopening and rusted chimney stacks issuing the first traces of smoke in a long time. Industry reawakening and the need for ships growing.

Though he normally avoided the messroom at times he found himself unable to remain totally isolated. Avoid an ordinary seaman who barely reached his shoulders who previously rode long odds hacks at bush race meetings. An AB who served in the Royal Navy and openly venerated a Nationalist prime minister. 'Lord Bruce of Melbourne served in the Royal Fusiliers, awarded the Military Cross and the Croix de Guerre. What more could a nation ask of its leader, as well as a man who brought the Bolshie unions to heel.'

His mate whose last job placed him at risk contacting hepatitis cleaning public lavatories agreed, stuffing his mouth with the last of the bread and cheese. 'A paragon of leadership who took no backchat from union bosses and their bleating sheep. Told them he did in no mean terms you go on strike you don't come back to work spreading your socialist diarrhoea. Good for him I say.'

'Sacrificed himself at the ballot box for his industrial principles.'

'Bloody disgrace! Just goes to prove Australian voters are blithering idiots letting themselves be led with nose rings by the unions.'

Another dolefully upturned an empty tea caddy, his last job watchman on a barge. 'Poor old Lord Bruce of Melbourne got the blame for giving away the Commonwealth Shipping Line, over fifty ships competing against the Brits. No contest really against the Old Dart, of course their seamen much more competent to sail ships deep sea. We all know of course where the blame squarely lies, at doors of the union fortresses. Seamen, cooks, stewards, we all know. Less work and more money, forty hours work a week, time off and leave, served what the officers eat and linen changed every week. Goodness me, how could we ever hope compete against the Brits?' He would have loved a cup of tea, the tea in someone's bag with two pounds of coffee to last the messroom a week. 'I say all those greed motivated union officials should have their heads impaled on pikes. Left to me the bastards would!'

≈

Sam asked Kiernan for the morning off to attend a stopwork meeting. The bosun, suffering a severe hangover akin to a hammer thumping against the thick walls of his skull, blinked to focus his blurred vision of what the deck boy thrust in his shaking hand.

"Why we fight. Here in black and white the reason we are striking issued by the Sydney strike committee. You should read it."

Kiernan found it impossible to read the small print, even the large headings in bold black letters; with trouble even standing erect, he prised open one mucus encrusted eyelid. "This is union. I don't want to read this shit. I'll wipe me arse with it."

"It's a true statement of the facts proving shipowners are making huge profits and forcing seamen to work under an award that has taken us back twenty years."

"Bullshit!"

"No, Kiernan, truth."

"Listen to me, you shut your fucking mouth or you'll get my fist down your throat and my boot in your guts. I got winch beds crawling with maggots, a foot thick with grease and rust. Reckon a few's been used by the wharfies as their personal shithouse."

"There's plenty onboard this ship perfect for that job. I have a right as a member of the union to attend tomorrow's stopwork meeting and as such I am asking for the morning off."

The bosun shoved his face close to Sam's and his putrid breath caused him to gag. "This is a union ship? You're telling me we are manned by union men? Where? For the life of me I can't see any union men about. Maybe these union blokes are hiding in the bilges, you think?"

"Me, you cretin!"

"So we've just found one, ain't we lucky."

"I'm going to that stopwork meeting and there's no way you are going to stop me. I'll see the mate."

A burst capillary filled his right eyeball with blood, his shaking limbs holding Sam enthralled maybe the man might be on the verge of a seizure. "Deck boys come under my responsibility and you go over my head you'll be crawling in winch beds the mate can eat his dinner off!"

"No!"

Kiernan's head throbbed; damn to hell this know-all sprat mouthing off about the union and the strike. Impossible to break his spirit, working him every debasing job he could think off, bilges, fish oiling the chain locker, wire rope oil, winch beds, sewing canvas in the lower peak with the ship pounding in a head sea, chipping and scraping deckheads on the weatherside. Snuffing its young life would be doing the industry a favour, his mind weighing options. Then rat cunning, a survival tool perfected over many years, filtered through the fog in his head. "I'll see the mate. Union boy, go to your fucking meeting!"

Time off could only be granted by the mate, the bosun consulted if he could spare the man, never the bosun's responsibility to grant the privilege. Kiernan swiped crusted vomit from his slack mouth, saw the mate on the foredeck talking with the foreman. He needed a stiff jolt, and with the mate otherwise occupied the time opportune. No need to speak with him on any matter, the day's jobs in his pocket.

≈

More than a thousand men gathered on the pavement outside the Sydney Town Hall, morose, silent, buses and trams disgorging more. Even catching sight of old shipmates barely raised a smile or an animated greeting, clouding their minds the union at a critical point and their futures now in jeopardy. Men started filing through the doors of the cavernous hall, shuffling between the tightly packed seating and sitting quietly.

The doorman tallied the numbers present with the assistance of his sectional counters, 1800. Sides were clearly apparent in large groups, others in clusters of five or six, electing their spokesmen.

The strike committee tried hard to reignite the earlier fighting spirit that fired the men with confidence, bounced them down gangways with raised fists. Committee members searched the very depths of their hearts for the inspirational words, imploring that light did shine at the end of a very dark tunnel, a force so powerful it would soon overcome the combined might of the shipowners, the massed strength of unionised seamen holding ranks. Contrary to groupers within the union negotiations were ongoing with shipowners, the union's case put strongly, the disputed clauses of the Dethridge Award addressed with vigour.

Counter argument crisscrossed the expanse of the hall, why would shipowners talk with the union when their ships sailed fully manned, crewed with volunteers? Even more damning, rumours of a new union under the imprimatur of the Commonwealth Steamship Owners Association, officials and members loyal company men who offered for employment during the strike. Leaders and seamen who did not dispute the necessity of licenses, a sterling piece of government legislation designed to weed out the belligerent and industrial saboteurs.

A low wail passed through the hall when a speaker asked for a denial of a rumour union members forced to sail with scabs when the strike ended. Joseph Keenan, speaking for the strike committee, held up his hands up for silence. He deftly avoided the question. "The Lyons government driven by the manic fervour of a certain anti-union dogmatist who is preparing legislation to deport our officials, which, brothers, will decimate the union executive. We have officials and prominent members of the union born in the United Kingdom, Europe and the United States. Jacob Johnson is an Australian but the *Daily Telegraph* spells his name the Swedish Johansson.

"The government with public sympathy on its side is confident it will triumph and forcefully march our officials up gangways of ships bound from these shores. Ridding the county of accursed socialism, in one fell swoop decapitating the Federated Seamen's Union of Australasia. Our officials are not traitors. Our officials served their country of adoption in war. Our officials are loyal to Australia."

Silence fell over the hall as Joseph held aloft a leaflet. "Why we fight! Why indeed referring to past profits of the major shipping companies. Adelaide Steamship Company a profit of £140,000. Huddart Parker £84,000. Burns Philip £212,000. Howard Smith £84,000. Melbourne Steamship Company £65,000. BHP in these hard financial times a mere £670,000. So what do these shipowners with bursting vaults seek, more and more profit by exploiting seamen. Using the arbitration system to remove seamen's hard won conditions. Deportation! Crippling fines and jail! Impose licensing provisions for a seaman to go to work and feed his family! This leaflet informs the public of the true facts, a story of deception, avarice and suppression."

"You and other officials have publicly declared acceptance of the Dethridge Award," a spokesman from a group directly in front of the stage declared.

"Your federal executive did negotiate on the premise of stability and avoiding direct action, to have the more controversial clauses of the award removed. Yes, I signed my name to a statement, and yes I wished to avoid the pain and hardship of strike on members and their families."

The spokesman persisted. "How can we fight a system when the captain can log us ten quid for refusing to work overtime at the new reduced rate? The delegates take the case to an official only to have the official lumbered with a hundred quid fine for advising them to tell the captain to jam his overtime up his arse. Joseph, can you afford that?"

"My job as a union official empowers me to be able to interpret the award, and if I advised the delegates that working overtime infringed on rest periods, meal breaks, unessential work, yes I would stand by a decision of support."

The exchange stirred the meeting, more voices added to the debate. Members rose in waves to their feet, others clambering on the stage to be heard. The vitality of previous meetings at the onset of the strike returned as the chairman struggled to maintain order, for him the odds in his favour with electronics.

Sam looked around for familiar faces, none. No matter, these men would remain steadfast with the union and would see the fight through to its conclusion. Even as the meeting spilled into the street he continued his search, then gave up as he headed for Liverpool St and Mark Foy's; his visit would need to be quick, he thought hurrying his step, back onboard to turn to at 1:00pm.

≈

Emily stood behind her glass topped counter, small and pale of face. He smiled proudly at his girl dressed in her best, a black dress that swept her lace up boots and a white blouse which almost completely concealed her breasts.

She looked about nervously to see if a department head patrolled the floor; just she and Sam and an elderly woman scowling at a hat display.

"Emily, are you well?"

"Sir should not be asking about the health of the salesgirl, but instead inquiring about a particular item of interest."

"Sir might do that later perhaps, but in the meantime he has no money only time to spend on a beautiful salesgirl."

"Sorry, sir, but we don't carry that line." She blushed, another quick glance to see if the elderly woman noticed the crimson tinge in her face.

If he could only lean over the counter and kiss her. "I have to run. I've taken the morning off for the meeting and I think I might be in trouble."

"For going to a meeting?"

"Trusting someone."

"What will happen?" Her hand fluttered to the base of her throat.

"Don't really know. I think though the bosun would like to see the end of me, appeasing any conscience he's got remaining, eliminating a blurry memory of when he too once belonged to a union. Everything might be fine, but I should have gone to the mate in the first place."

"Could you lose your job?"

"Worse for a deck boy. My first year is probationary."

A middle-aged woman swathed in a fox fur, the deceased creature's pointed head resting on her right breast with its glass eyes staring out at its departed world, placed both hands on Emily's counter. "Miss, I am seeking a birthday gift for a niece, a silk scarf perhaps? Have you an extensive array which might interest me," she said haughtily.

Emily bobbed, smiled at Sam who ignored the imperious glance from the woman; he blew a kiss, then almost ran from the store, his ship a long walk north along Sussex St.

≈

At the foot of the gangway Sam saw Kiernan's shaggy head hanging over the bulwark, fuelled with a lunch of overproof rum and a smirk on his blubbery lips.

"Captain's waiting for you in his cabin, matey," he slurred thickly. "Want me to hold you fucking little hand?"

Sam ignored him, turned forward and headed for the bridge; he expected ridicule from the bosun, the master a far different situation, realising his earlier concern warranted. He should feel nervous but he didn't, a sense of calm as if two delegates stood by his side to argue his case. He would defend himself though at a distinct disadvantage, the strength of one man against supreme authority.

Captain Langford in this instance did not particularly like the position he found himself in, imperative though he maintain strict discipline on his ship. Not a simple matter of terminating a hand found drunk and incapable in his bunk at sailing time, theft of ship's stores, insolence to an officer, disobeying a direct order. Matters dispensed with under the authority empowered to him by the Navigation Act.

The master harboured conflicting thoughts on dismissing a deck boy with obvious potential, a young man guided to a higher plain and losing the stigma of the focastle, could easily attain a more responsible calling. Proven in the past he would have this young man on his bridge in any circumstances, and to his mind the ablest hand on deck. He placated himself he acted purely within the guidelines of the Navigation Act, above all in the best interests of his owners who entrusted him to command their ship.

Captain Langford could draw upon precedents which allowed him flexibility in his deliberations, but then if he showed leniency based on immaturity the precedent he would set possibly used by conniving delegates against him in the future. Without a doubt, past uncomfortable experiences dealing with hardline recalcitrance entrenched in his mind. He would act firmly and without favour. Glancing up from his desk he said to the young man standing in his doorway. "Enter."

Sam stood in front of the desk, the master seemingly occupied with the open log book.

"Wright, I am the recipient of a report that you have been absent from your place of duty from 0800 hours to 1200 hours without permission from the chief officer. What have you to say in your defence of the matter?"

"I attended a stopwork meeting called by my union."

"Did you seek permission from the chief officer for this absence from your place of duty?"

"I spoke with the bosun who said he would inform the mate."

"Are you aware the bosun has no authority to grant time off?"

"The bosun didn't grant me time off, but said he would on my behalf request it from the mate."

"The bosun has informed the chief officer of no such request. Have you an explanation for this?"

"Captain, I trusted the bosun to ask the mate, and it would seem he failed to do so. Why he did so could be for many reasons which I don't think you would understand." He knew this would end badly, the cold severity in the master's face, the open log book. He hung his head and stared at his boots on the master's worn and threadbare rug.

"Under no circumstances will I question now or in the future the important responsibilities entrusted upon me by my owners, or allow myself to be influenced by a misunderstanding or conflicting statements whether true or false. It would be wrong for me to err in the fulfilment of my professional duties pandering to leniency in a case of deliberate disobedience."

"As a member of the Federated Seamen's Union of Australasia I wanted to attend my union's stopwork meeting. Hopefully hear the strike might be over, or close to a resumption of work." Sam's shoulders lifted as his chest filled with a deep sigh. "Nothing more than that."

"Unacceptable, hence my duty to inform you, Mr Wright, you are hereby given twenty-four hours notice of termination of employment and to present yourself before the shipping superintendent at 1400 hours tomorrow. Do you understand the gravity of what I have said?"

He nodded, another sigh.

"I have further deliberated and arrived at a decision recommending your discharge be stamped *VG* for ability, *VG* for boathand and *Endorsement not Required* for conduct."

A bad discharge!

"Captain, I only wanted four hours to attend a stopwork meeting of my union. I can make the time up. I can work all night. Please, not a bad discharge!"

"Regrettably for you that is the option I have chosen to deal with this particular incident." He thought a tea tray would cleanse the bad taste in his mouth, not from the matter at hand but from the cheap cigars the providor yesterday thought appropriate in seeking additional business.

"Not a bad discharge!"

"Wright, you are dismissed. This business is concluded and I have far more important business to attend to."

"Captain, you are excluding me from the industry! I will never be allowed to ship out again!"

"Wright, I am not privy to what the shipping superintendent will find appropriate in your case. He will make an informed decision I am sure. Be grateful there is no monetary penalty affixed to the dismissal and log entry."

≈

A terrible burden descended on his shoulders as he left the master's cabin, grasping the railings leading to the deck, the cold painted steel a touch soon to be gone from his life forever. Tomorrow the shipping master would intone sentence of life suspension from the industry, his probation period falling two months short of promotion to ordinary seaman.

To add to his misery assuming a responsible role in Emily's family others depended on him.

Kiernan waited on the foredeck for him, a leer on his unshaven face; he held up a long handled scraper and a bucket. "Company's paying you to 5:00pm."

Sam's despondency weighed heavy; an ordinary seaman could boast about a bad discharge, shafted by a scab bosun and a rabid cur of a skipper. A bucko, but not a deck boy.

23

SAM WITH HIS CANVAS bag in his hand and a seabag over his shoulder passed through the Adelaide Steamship Company picket line, a familiar sight to the men outside the gate. One called him over, inquiring why the downcast face.

The words spilled from him, consoled by a tall and unkempt young AB with a shock of flame red hair; about him an untamed wildness mirrored in his fiery eyes.

"So that righteous old anti-union pig Langford sacked you with a baddie for attending yesterday's stopwork meeting?"

Sam nodded miserably.

"You're a financial member of the union? Of course you are, or you wouldn't be attending the stopwork meeting. This could be discriminatory, but we won't go there yet. Though the deliberations of this judicious master mariner ensconced in his sanctimonious eyrie can be challenged."

Sam hung his head and shuffled his feet.

"What's your name?"

"Sam Wright."

"Master mariner Marshall Langford, I know him well. I think he might even be an extra master now. A fact the worst skippers on the coast are the ones who have knocked down more wharves and hit more buoys and beacons than any others in command. A perfect cover their incompetence is to become a complete bastard, and the *Aldinga's* skipper is probably on top of the list. It matters not he is in command of a garbage scow manned with festering scabs, the deck boy must be punished for his audacity attending a union meeting.

Sacked and a bad discharge, the penalty befitting the gross travesty usurping the master's authority."

He grinned and thrust out his hand. "Barney Collins. What we are dealing with here is a faithful servant to his owners, a paragon of industrial virtue who can only see in black and white and thick volumes of manuals issued by his overlords and acts of parliament. My analogy harsh you think? No, learned from painful past experiences sailing with these postulating potentates of superior intellect.

"Parading on rust buckets in gold and brass. Strutting wafer thin decks of grease ball ships held together with the prayers of the insurers. These advocates of hard work and sobriety, loyalty and sufferance, starvation and sacrifice, obedience and silence, do have one thing in common, a quest to rid the world of a pestilence called the Federated Seamen's Union of Australasia. Captain Langford though might have encountered an unforseen obstacle, his standing reference to the buoys he's sunk without a trace."

Sam looked at him, puzzled.

"Me."

"You would help me?"

"Why wouldn't I for a fellow unionist hard done by? Lesson one in this life never let the bastards get on the top of you, especially those who have sold their souls to the enemy."

"You mean shipowners."

"Them and others who make our lives a misery. What time do you front the shipping office?"

"I'm on my way there now, 2:00pm."

Barney looked around; eight men manned the picket line. "Our numbers dwindle but we're well represented today. This might be interesting, and I feel like upsetting a certain someone's belly after his lunch. For another good cause I can postpone a speaking tour of a few factories this afternoon, and there's plenty of time for the butchers we hound at closing time for meat none of them are game to turn into tomorrow's sausages."

Sam's face filled with hope, repeating: "You would help me?"

"We're on our way. The shipping master is a stickler for the Navigation Act, a hard man though fair. I have in the past seen him side with a wretched seaman threatened with penalties that hanging would have been a more pleasant alternative."

"Do you think there is a chance?"

"We might not be able to beat the system stacked against us, but there are ways of making a dent. The crucial point is to remain calm and never lose faith, think clearly. It also helps if you have right on your side. I read the ravings of the doomsayers predicting utter ruin if a carrier of night pans wins a halfpenny an hour rise in his wages, coming to the conclusion it is all a game. Them at the top who have the money, me on the bottom thrown a few quid so I can sink further into debt so committed for a life of drudgery.

"I accept my lowly place in the scheme of things, but what I cannot are those of us who climb out of the pile with a hand offered by those who decree us as nothing more than a replaceable human resource. Who become the overseers of the system and who instantly forget their roots. Seduced with gold bars on shoulder boards, titles and enforced respect from the lower orders. I would give respect if I found deference deserving, but I've never come across a skipper or a mate yet worthy. Of course I am biased which might account for my reluctance to give due where it is warranted. Come on, we can't keep the shipping master waiting."

"Barney, are you a member of the Militant Minority Movement?"

"The Minorities demand too much of their devotees as do the crazy Wobblies and the fiery comrades. No, I am just your normal hater of society carrying a more than noisy anarchist's banner. I've been hard done by and licked my wounds, but have seen far worst dispensed to my mates by those we begrudgingly share this world with."

"Thanks, Barney."

"No thanks needed. I like to keep in practice giving the system hell. Well deserved when only a few years ago we denizens of the focastle shared a well polished board with three holes for calls of nature, bathed in a bucket of seawater heated with a steam pipe. Survived on substitute food and worked at the whim of those we hated. Why shouldn't I give a serve to those who decree we are the lowest of the low labouring class? Who won't share their fine China and silverware, leather and brass, sheets and blankets, mats on the deck."

Sam struggling to climb the steep stairway of the Argyle Cut with his gear, Barney relieving him of his seabag, his tirade far from finished. "Seamen are exceptional creatures mostly referred to by shipowners as algae, the nadir of marine life. Lost souls drifting aimlessly from ship to ship, waterfront bar to waterfront bar, brothel to lockup, sleeping in gutters and open sewers with mangy dogs pissing on them. Adrift until an adhesive as powerful as the physics that rule the planet binds them together. You know what that glue is?"

Sam shook his head, breathing heavily, relief at sighting the grey arch of the Sydney Harbour Bridge ahead, the shipping office beneath the roadway obscured in its deep shadow.

"The Federated Seamen's Union of Australasia."

Entering the musty depth of the shipping office no seaman, even those in the euphoric grip of paying off, escaped the repressiveness of governmental authority. Shipping superintendents also known as shipping masters, senior public servants, dispensed maritime justice on a similar scale as did their courtroom counterparts. On occasions meted with a modicum of mercy, but rare for a wayward seaman to agree the dispensation impartial.

Barney thumped down both hands on the rosewood stained cedar counter which divided the shipping office. "We have important business with Mr Stuart."

The clerk knew Barney from many previous encounters. Nervously, he glanced behind him at a large wall clock, then at one of four closed doors. "Mr Stuart's at lunch."

"Got better hours than those he passes sentence on. No, I need to see him now, I really do."

"About signing on?" Interrupting Mr Stuart from his lunch not advisable for a lower ranked public servant.

"Now what would a staunch member of the Federated Seamen's Union of Australasia be doing signing on in the midst of a strike. Are you accusing me of being a blackleg? Do I look like one of those species of contemptible humanity that of recent times have been passing through this establishment with alarming regularity?" Barney said, shocked, a wink at Sam beside him.

"No! No!" His squeaky voice might have been a trigger for a door with a highly polished brass *Marine Superintendent* plate to open. In the doorway stood the imposing figure of a grey haired man in his late fifties, a permanent scowl on his heavily jowled face.

The shipping master knew Barney Collins well, all too many times arguing the finer points of legislation promulgated by the cream of the legal fraternity from another century for others of perceived high intelligence to decipher. His half eaten lunch of sardines and onion sandwiches would have to wait, ambling his ample frame from his inner sanctum to the counter. "Mr Collins, to what magnanimous turn of events do we owe this visit? Surely not to sign on a ship."

"You know me better than that, Mr Stuart. This deck boy, Sam Wright, is a victim of prolonged industrial action and a captain who should have arrived at a more understanding judgement other than rigid adherence to his onboard leave policy. Dismissed for attending a stopwork meeting of his union, a fully paid up member of the Federated Seamen's Union of Australasia exercising his right to attend his union's stopwork meeting."

The marine superintendent, informed by the *Aldinga's* master of the circumstances relating to the deck boy paying off and the recommended discharge, maintained neutral ground. "Mr Wright according to the log entry absented himself from his place of duty without the consent of the master and has been dealt with in a manner adjudged appropriate by the master."

"Sam Wright as a financial member of the union, sadly the only one on the *Aldinga*, would under union rules have no recourse but to attend a stopwork meeting. Arising from this is a side issue difficult to prove, the deck boy naively asking the bosun for time off. This of course is not in the bosun's limited realm of responsibility, but even so he should have acted in the boy's stead. He didn't."

Mr Stuart felt on solid ground, a lot firmer than some former debates with this hot-headed young man indoctrinated through and through with loathing for the system of stability and authority. He struck a telling blow. "The master is wholly within his rights to terminate the employment of a seaman absent from his place of duty without permission. No one has come forward from the ship to support a misunderstanding in the matter so I am at a loss to understand your logic, Mr Collins."

"The master of the *Aldinga* failed to take into consideration the deck boy being a member of the union signed an oath of fealty and as such to abide by decisions and directives of the union. Yesterday's stopwork meeting, I might add stopwork a misnomer, the union requested its members attend with high hopes the strike might end." Barney paused for breath; with both hands still planted on the counter he lifted on his toes to make himself higher than his adversary. "The lad with hopes of his industry returning to normal attended the stopwork meeting. Also, Mr Stuart, it might interest you to know he got shafted."

"I have no word from the ship of such," the shipping master countered. "Leave granted is at the discretion of the master and the master did not excuse Mr Wright from his place of duty between the hours recorded in the deck log."

Barney dismissed the rejoinder. "Stopwork meetings are not classified as leave. Attending stopwork meetings is a condition of membership of the Federated Seamen's Union of Australasia. The deck boy, a financial member, is entitled to attend a stopwork meeting if it does not impede with the sailing of the vessel."

"The fact remains, Mr Collins, and I will not alter my position, the boy from 0800 to 1200 hours did without permission absented himself from his duties."

"The penalty invoked for this petty misdemeanour effectively ending a young man's life at sea. I have a question, has the miscreant been logged?"

"No logging. Dismissal and *Endorsement not Required* for conduct."

"Effectively a life sentence, of which I am certain you well versed in draconian dismissals in the past, would agree. I know the captain of the *Aldinga*, Blackbeard showed his crew more mercy."

"Captain Langford acted as he ascertained the situation warranted, within the guidelines of the Navigation Act."

"So you are satisfied justice has been served?"

Mr Stuart allowed himself the briefest of smiles, on rock solid ground and about to close the argument successfully. "I am curious, Mr Collins, how many bad discharges have you incurred over the years?"

"Jesus!" Barney counted on his fingers, frowning in concentration as he used them all up. "I'm still shipping out! I've been blessed by the pope!"

"If the pope became aware of your misguided beliefs, Mr Collins, he would rather bless a dweller from Hades."

"Yeah, you're right. Well?"

"Well what, Mr Collins?"

"What are you going to do about this miscarriage of justice?"

"The master can make an amendment to the log entry and decide to stamp the discharge three *VGs*, which is his right. Captain Langford is a strict disciplinarian of note and I would not be overly confident he will alter his mind."

"I don't ask much in life, a reasonably able cook and a warm dry bunk, a forgiving mate and an occasional fling ashore. The *Aldinga's* a shit job and maybe the skipper's done Sam a favour sacking him, but not destroying him. *Bad* and *Endorsement not Required* I can laugh at, paper my mum's walls, but for a young lad it spells the end. I wouldn't like that on my conscience even if I saluted the funnel and house flag each morning. I wouldn't, I really wouldn't."

"Your final argument, Mr Collins?"

"I'm not arguing with you, Mr Stuart, I'm just passing the time of day. Nothing else to do except maybe hope we outnumber blacklegs passing through the picket line."

"Mr Collins, would you leave me in peace to finish my lunch if I issued the boy a license, in the knowledge how you and your quite noisy associates are vehemently opposed to them?"

He though the offer over, then with a suppressed shudder said: "An acceptable bribe, Mr Stuart. Though I sincerely hope it goes no further than here me abandoning my principles of industrial liberty and emancipation of seamen. My God, a young man on the threshold of his working life dog collared."

Triumph tasted even better than sardine and onion sandwiches. "I will have a word with Captain Langford, though whether he will change his mind in respect of the log entry and discharge I cannot offer a definite opinion. With a seaman's license and a cursory glance at his last discharge, the boy's future might be assured if he learns obedience and respect for authority."

"It might well be a memorable career. Correct, Sam or Samuel Wright?"

His eyes brimmed with tears, he said: "Sam."

"Mr Stuart, there is just one other thing. The date stamped on the dog collar. Would it be tomorrow's date?"

The shipping master's brow furrowed.

"It's called hedging your bet. Issued after the event."

"Ah yes, I would expect nothing else from you, Mr Collins, a man of little faith with authority. No wonder people like you treat their workplace as a battleground."

"Not far from the truth there, Mr Stuart. I haven't been out of the trenches since I walked up my first gangway. Thanks."

"For what?"

He shrugged, a lopsided grin. "Hearing me out."

"Under your verbal assault certain things have manage to slip my mind. Mr Wright, according to the ship you will be paying off late."

≈

Sam paid off at 4:00pm, the master with more pressing duties in the company's office, the second mate deputised in his stead. Mr Stuart's face softened, Sam's small payoff methodically counted and placed on his discharge. The discharge stamped *Endorsement not Required* did not matter now, the issue of a seaman's license passed over the counter far more important.

"Protect this document and no matter what your union says, the law is the law and until amended it will be your means of gaining employment at sea."

Sam noticed the date: February 20th, 1936. Tomorrow's date.

24

THE STRIKE ENTERED A period of stagnation after months of stalemate. From an impregnable fortress of strength, their ships fully manned and business as usual, shipowners were reluctant to negotiate with the Federated Seamen's Union of Australasia, once a formidable force recognised in the maritime industry reduced to a status of irrelevance.

An indication of the hopelessness of the union's struggle, volunteers could now walk unchallenged through wharf gates, picket lines reduced to a small number of extreme socialist left. The Federated Seamen's Union of Australasia, a union in name only. The despair of defeat at this later stage brightened briefly when the cooks struck in support of seamen, their immediate replacement well practiced in prison cuisine.

Owing to the strike jobs normally filled from traditional line-ups outside wharf gates became the responsibility of clerks in company offices. Progressives in the industry saw the arrangement as efficient and less demeaning, a view not held by some masters and chief engineers able to scrutinise seamen exposed in a line, senior officers with long memories.

≈

Sam walking with Emily along the Balmain foreshore saw Howard Smith's *Burwah* in dock at Cockatoo Island, a feature that stood out an exceptionally tall white and black funnel. Nothing about the old ship in her twenty-seventh year could compare her to the modern builds trading on the Australian coast, though from a distance she seemed exceptionally well maintained. Four hatches, straight stem, counter stern, a three island ship with well decks fore and aft of the amidships accommodation.

Cumbersome steam winches working four sets of five ton derricks rigged to the foremast and mainmast occupied almost all of the limited deck space of both mast houses. Awning spars on the focastle head evidence her crew lived forward; her age and her era no less obvious with two heads at the break of the focastle head, flexible steam hoses attached to the steam smothering gear to boil clothes, tiny box-like extension to the heads cubicles with showers.

"She'll be manned with scabs, but I can deal with that," he said, his eyes transfixed on the old ship. He would go to Howard Smith's office tomorrow.

Emily, dressed in her Sunday best, pressed her hip against his, her thoughts not on the ship but the old single bed Sam bought from a second-hand shop, placed in a corner of the kitchen. Now a true member of the Knight family. With the family asleep and in her flimsy nightgown, sneaking in beside him, impossible to sleep two people comfortably, that physical aspect never entering either of their minds.

≈

The clerk's eyes kept straying to the young girl busy at her typewriter, more interested in her than the young man opposite him across the counter. Sam passed his discharge and license under a thick glass partitioning panel. The licence received the most attention, the document new to the signing on of seamen.

Overhearing Sam inquiring about registering for a deck boy's position and seeing the clerk reaching under the counter for a ledger the girl paused in her typing. "Didn't the master of the *Burwah* who came in yesterday say something about a junior rating?"

"Yes, I know, but I still have to refer to the ledger to confirm if we have deck boys registered and known to us."

Sam held his breath.

The clerk ran his finger down a page. "Deck boys with only a year to serve come and go quickly. Yes, we have positions in the *Burwah*, a deck boy and a trimmer. She will when leaving dock be loading coal at Balls Head for Melbourne. Your last discharge though places me in a quandary. The stamp in character and conduct might cause the master grave concerns accepting you."

Sam stared unwaveringly at the clerk whose attempt to coax sparse stubble into a moustache would have to wait a few more years. "Please look at the date on my seaman's license and you will see it is the day following my payoff from the *Aldinga*. Also the issuing signature on the license is Mr Stuart who as marine superintendent ascertains there is no valid reason to suspend or terminate my employment at sea."

"Well versed in jurisprudence for a deck boy, aren't you," he muttered churlishly, scribbling on a slip of paper and pushing it under the glass panel. His parting words hammered home a grim reality and Sam felt an almost crippling despair for his comrades still manning the picket lines. "Even though the ship is secure in dock there is a strong union presence at the island ferry terminal threatening those going about their lawful duties. I can arrange police protection."

Sam tasted blood as he bit down on his lip. "The trimmer, yes! Me, no!"

≈

His first long distance impression of the *Burwah* proved wrong, an expanse of harbour concealing flaking paintwork and blisters of rust, buckled frames and general overall neglect. The *Burwah* sailed with a full crew of company men.

The ferry ride from Pyrmont should have added to the excitement of joining a new ship, the vessel well over her licensed number of passengers, boilermakers, crane drivers, fitters, riggers, labourers, painters and dockers, blacksmiths and shipwrights going to work. Shipbuilders who burned and welded steel, with giant steam hammers and hydraulic presses shaped plate and beams, who crawled in double bottoms and wing tanks. Sam felt as one with this vibrant workforce starting a new day, but not those now eating their Board of Trade breakfast without even a momentary thought about the five seamen manning the picket line.

Supported by militant dockyard unions, seamen maintained a presence by the timekeeper's office at the Cockatoo Island ferry terminal, begrudgingly tolerated by management who sympathised with the shipowners plight of dealing with an industrial scourge, but fearful of their own workforce striking in sympathy.

The *Burwah* looked even more decrepit as Sam walked along the concrete apron of the graving dock in which the ship lay under assault. He climbed the steep dockyard gangway to the poop deck, picking his way forward through a maze of electrical cables, air, gas and water hoses, bins overflowing with twisted piles of burned metal and pipes.

Two doors gave access to the partitioned crew accommodation, firemen on the port side, seamen on the starboard, identified with brass nameplates: *certified accommodation for seamen*. Both focastles shared a hawse pipe, double iron bunks both sides of a wooden table with two side benches. Attached to the after bulkhead a stores cupboard with a bench top and sink, above that a steam urn.

Eight men sat at the table eating breakfast of cold curry and rice leftover from dinner the previous day, a two pound loaf of bread on a cutting board reduced to shards and crumbs. Sam from the door watched as the men ate hungrily, one more forceful than his fellows, scraping the pot for the last shreds of stringy beef flavoured with fistfuls of powerful curry and salt. He lumbered up from the table, a giant of a man with a round, boyish face, a few strands of lank fair hair hanging in his eyes; he smiled apologetically, almost childish. "Sorry, you're a bit late for breakfast. No one told us we were getting anyone new."

"I've eaten."

"Sorry again. She doesn't always feed well, or enough, but we cope."

A few mumbles passed down the table, using crusts to polish their plates; Sam thought the pot might hold enough for half the men present, a single loaf of bread drawn for the day.

"My name's Sam Wright. I am the deck boy."

"The last deck boy, we all like him. He didn't much fancy work, but then many young boys have yet to learn how to give a good day to their employer. My name's Bert. I'm the storekeeper."

He offered his huge hand and normally Sam would have backed away, refusing to shake hands; he took the hand and felt its warm firmness, a comforting and assuring grip.

"Where's my bunk?"

Bert turned and pointed to a top bunk jammed against the hawse pipe. "Not the best in the focastle and quite annoying when at anchor, but when someone else pays off you can move. That's what we do."

A damp and mouldy straw mattress, kapok pillow, a holed army surplus blanket. Linen?

"Chief steward makes you sign for your linen."

The information led to another question. "Changed?"

"Oh no, clean linen is our responsibility. Chief steward says that's why the company is not making money to buy new ships and give us jobs because seamen keep knocking down his door demanding luxuries."

As expected; even so he felt an immediate fondness for the harmless storekeeper. "Bert, don't believe a single word of it. Howard Smith made a profit last year well in excess of £80,000. Every shipowner made a profit, but of course cry poormouth when seamen ask for fresh milk and an extra loaf of bread."

"Don't let the bosun hear you saying that," Bert said nervously, looking over Sam's shoulder and the open door; those at the table agreed with nods of their heads. "Our bosun doesn't take to that sort of talk."

"That might be interesting. Did you all join together?"

"We did in Adelaide when the seamen and firemen didn't want to sail and the company advertised in the papers. Plenty of blokes turned up, too."

"What is your brief? Discharges?"

"Haven't any of them or someone might have forgotten to give them to me. Worked on ketches running around the Spencer and St Vincent Gulfs, but all of them got laid up in bad times. No one wants to buy wheat and barley anymore."

"AB?"

"Captain didn't call us ABs, deckhands. Pretty hard work lumping bags of wheat on your back all day, though it never bothered me. Could work all day and night, and did."

"The bosun run a good job?"

"Not according to the first officer who gets really angry on deck and shouts which makes the bosun shout at us."

"Bosun out of the ketches?"

"Don't say much, but we think he might have been in jail. Only rumour, he came here from jail. Don't let him hear that though."

At the stroke of 8:00am Sam met the bosun, a short, broad shouldered brooding figure silhouetted in the doorway; with a brusque voice he ordered all hands on deck, a list of jobs in his hand. The bosun's head fascinated Sam, large with protruding ears, a flattened nose proof of a lifetime of battering opponents and receiving likewise punishment. The eyes, small and beady, mirrored a man who survived life with the tools of cunning and malice.

"Geordie Clarke," Bert whispered close to Sam's ear. "Watch your step with him. Wouldn't recommend turning your back on him either."

"Deck boy?" The voice came from deep down in his chest, guttural and threatening.

"I suppose it wouldn't be appropriate to ask for the delegates so I can show my financial union book?" Sam glared at him.

"Show me a union book and I'll throw you over the fucking side! To make that even sweeter, we're in the fucking dock! Funnel, the lot of you!"

Bert nudged Sam from behind, a conspiratorial smile on his face. "Which means you will have to come to the store for your gear. I got up early to get it ready."

"The mate said you've got most of your time in. You know how to rig a funnel?" the bosun said, his fierce eyes holding Sam's.

"I know how to rig a funnel." This criminal scab bosun would not intimidate him, nor would be back down.

"That's good because this fucking lot can't tie their fucking shoelaces. See the storekeeper and take these useless arseholes with you."

Bert with a rolling gait and humming a mindless tune under his breath led the way from the focastle to the foremast mast house store. A bomb might have detonated in the store, a mess of wire and cordage, on the deck blocks and shackles, spare spans and chain, slab and beam hooks, strops and slings, open drums of paint and grease, wire rope oil and brooms, buckets and mops; thrown on the deck gantlines, bosun's chairs, pot lanyards and a bundle of rope yarns. What caught Sam's eye a pedestal vice in the middle of the store, draped over it a pilot ladder.

"Bert, these gantlines and chairs shouldn't be on the deck," Sam chastened. "A seaman's life depends on cordage with all strands intact and free of paint, grease and solvents."

Bert pouted sulkily, then brightened when asked how many fleets on the funnel. "The first officer said five chairs and one hook chair."

Sam selected a gantline and bosun's chair from the top of the pile. "Lizards or blocks?"

Bert's face went blank.

"On the funnel are there blocks rove with dummies, or lugs for lizards?"

"My goodness, who would know that? We could ask the officers I suppose. What's a lizard?"

"Six feet, two inch manila rope with a thimble spliced in one end, whipping on the other." Stepping out of the store Sam almost bumped into the mate.

"Wright, I wish to speak with you. The rest of you proceed with your gear to the boat deck," the mate ordered in a clipped British accent. "Are you familiar with painting a funnel? Does it pose difficulties for you?"

"No."

"I hold serious safety concerns. These men haven't been aloft before."

"The last funnel I painted I did so with seamen who could make themselves fast quicker than you could blink an eye. Seamen."

"Wright, we will not enter into that discussion. The bosun has duties assisting the surveyor checking lifeboats and I need to know can I rely on your limited experience."

"Limited experience?"

"You are a deck boy."

Irony, Sam thought, a deck boy leading a gang of company seamen, seamen in name only on the articles of agreement, glib tongued confidence tricksters. Gathered around the base of the funnel cluttered with engine room skylights, ventilators and funnel stays, he could sense their apprehension.

The funnel with permanent blocks shackled beneath the lip and rove with dummies made a simple task of marrying the gantlines and overhauling. Chairs made fast, no anxieties with feet firmly planted on the teak deck deeply scored and splattered with pitch. The difficult part faced them when hauled to a foot beneath the block, how to make themselves fast. Could these men suspended high off the deck grasp their gantline then have the courage to shout below let go?

With more men the simplest method would be to haul them aloft and lower on command. This not being the case another option remained, the bundle of rope yarns in his hand.

"You're going to be hauled two blocks, which means you will be hanging close the block. There is an apron inside the funnel so I will assist making yourself fast after checking the blocks and shackles are not worn and rusted. Understand?"

All nodded but Sam thought none did. Climbing the ladder he edged around the narrow inner casing checking the blocks and shackles, then looked down at the first terrified face hauled aloft. "Now I am going to frap this rope yarn around both parts of your gantline. Then we will overhaul the tail through the chair, over your head, under the chair and feet, then cinch tight."

With chairs made fast the faces of fear smiled, even thankyous which Sam ignored. After organising Bert to send up the paint and brushes on pot lanyards bent to the tails of the gantlines, his fleet would be the ladder using the hook chair. Bert relished the responsibility, fumbling with paint pots, brushes, rags and a bucket of turpentine. He thought he should give Bert a tip to add an eggcup of blue paint to the drum of white for added gloss, but why should he?

Half way down the funnel he could hear them singing and joking, safe and secured aloft by a simple half knot taught by a deck boy. He ignored the banter and chortling; the mate might experience pride in his glowing newly painted funnel, he would not.

In early afternoon sunshine the funnel blazed with fresh white and black gloss paint, gantlines made up, paint and brushes forward by 2:15pm. To Sam's amazement he saw the mate talking with the bosun who when curtly dismissed shuffled to the men gathered outside the store and knocked them off.

≈

Next day he found himself in the store with Bert, the storekeeper dancing a little jog of excitement. "Can you splice?" the bosun asked, turning his men to down No.4 hatch with chipping hammers and scrapers, his voice scathing.

"Board of Trade and Liverpool, cut and long, short and back, reduced and wireless. Yes, I can splice."

"Don't be smart with me, son. Mate wants you in the store with dimwit. We need eight spare runners and two guy pendants. Mate's talking of a grab discharge."

Sam took the opportunity to inform the bosun he would be asking the mate for the next morning off.

"The meeting is meaningless because your union is no longer recognised by the shipowners. Get used to it, mate."

"That's not true! It is still the union of the industry and always will be!"

"Got news for you, union boy," he sneered. "There's a new union being formed right now, a union that will not condemn its members to endless and futile strikes. Who will negotiate with shipowners without an axe in both hands."

"Malicious waterfront rumour. Any union founded and financed by industry is a sham, and anyone who thinks otherwise is a fool."

"Then a lot of fools are flocking to join the new union, sick of being dictated to by the comrades."

"I don't believe that."

"Believe what you want, remain blinded and deaf to change. Your union ignored the fate of the wharfies and now we have licenses. The comrades and militants you obviously worship, there'll be no place for them in the new union. Every one of them will wither and die because no master or engineer will pick them up, and the new union won't accept their verbal shit. Now get to splicing."

"First I am going to ask the mate for time off to attend tomorrow's stopwork meeting."

The bosun sniggered, turned on his heel and sauntered off. "I'll ask him and it will give me great pleasure to turn you to in the morning."

Two runners spliced, frapped with rope yarns and identified with canvas tags, the chief mate rested on his haunches to study a splice; three and a half tucks, the last tucks buried under three strands. Rising to his feet he looked at a third set up in the vice.

"Quite neat and the jaw acceptable. So you told the bosun the truth. Can you really splice a long splice?"

"I never have, but I know how."

"That round spike you are using has a bent tip, probably used for freeing shackles I wouldn't doubt," he said, a rare smile on his serious face. "There's a ships chandler in Sussex St quite close to your union rooms and if you look in tomorrow morning and select a spike, round or T, it doesn't matter, you would be doing the ship a service. A serving mallet and serving board as well. The company will have issued an order number and the chandler will expect you. Make sure you don't miss lunch."

≈

From near chaos, the meeting lulled as articulate militants vindicated the struggle, praising the strength of resolve of the membership in not giving up the fight against the Dethridge Award, listened to by a dwindling membership sinking even deeper into a morass of hopelessness.

The number in attendance counted by the doorman totalled 500, seamen who came to hear the death knell of the strike, and those more defeatist, the end of their union. The meeting listened in silence as General Secretary Keenan spoke from the stage of the Sydney Town Hall, his voice composed: "The shipowners have now refused to negotiate with the union, their offices effectively closed to us, their phones off the hook. We have been through the arbitration system seeking to have final and meaningful discussions to bring to a conclusion our initiative to have contentious clauses in the Dethridge Award renegotiated. The court's response, shipowners will only negotiate with a union recognised by the shipowners and not a union refusing to man their ships, in other words a union on strike.

"That union, brothers, is in its early stages of formation under the auspices of a group of Melbourne chartered accountants headed by a secretary who has never stepped aboard a ship in his life. This mockery of a union will apply to the commonwealth and the states for registration to represent seamen. It will have waterfront offices in all the major ports. This pariah's name even denigrates the meaning of unionism, the Licensed Seamen's Association of Australia!"

The mention of license gave Sam a jolt; amongst his fellow seamen he might be one of a few issued with a license. Hardline and unwavering militants of the union like Elliott, Bird, Smith and Franklin refusing point blank to accept a license.

"We have exhausted all avenues open to the union to successfully conclude our industrial action against the Dethridge Award." Finally to a now deathly silent hall came the words all dreaded: "The shipowners have stated that on matters pertaining to domestic issues and not the Dethridge Award there exists the possibility of future dealings with the Federated Seamen's Union of Australasia. If the union agrees it will be on the premise their membership accept without prejudice or malice seamen currently signed on articles of agreement. It is therefore your federal executive's recommendation that as of today under the terms presented by the shipowners you shall offer for employment."

With those sombre words the strike ended in total defeat and humiliation. The shipowner with victory not only crushed the strike but funded the creation of a new union of seamen, a union favourable to cutting wages and conditions so allowing Australian shipowners to compete with foreign shipowners employing low paid Asian and subcontinent crews.

The genius stroke of the attorney general and his licensing provisions would be the lynchpin binding employee to employer. Culling the militant, the sloth, the drunk, the deranged, those unemployable in any other industry but the sea and protected by a code of brotherhood fostered by the Federated Seamen's Union of Australasia. Out of the ashes of utter rout there did emerge a gain for seamen, government regulation of normally itinerant seamen under the jurisdiction of the Bureau of Registered Seamen.

Shipowners took into account of the cost of the strike, 112 ships involved. Most ships sailed within days of the first opening salvo of the industrial action manned with company seamen, and of course incarcerated seamen only too willing to have their sentences repealed to serve the maritime industry in a time of crisis. Cargo moved to and from the wharves with little hindrance, and ships sailed on time. Ships underwent surveys and dockings, maintenance programs completed. Well noted by industrial officers not one ship delayed through domestic action. Shipowners could appraise with complete satisfaction their balance sheets, emerging from the strike unscathed.

Menzies received the appropriate accolades for his involvement in crushing the Communist Federated Seamen's Union of Australasia, a person of note quite friendly to industry, a man destined for greater achievements in Australian politics.

25

T HE *BURWAH* HIGH OUT of the water lightship from Melbourne rolled and pitched in heavy south-westerly swells. Massive mountains of cold green water born in the deeper reaches of the Southern Ocean, unleashing its turbulence on a treacherous coastline from Cape Otway to Cape Jervis, an historic graveyard for ships under sail.

The *Burwah's* grab discharge confirmed, sailing in ballast to load gypsum in Stenhouse Bay on the lower Yorke Peninsula, a broad expanse of mineral rich and grain growing land separating the South Australian gulfs of St Vincent and Spencer.

Fine off the starboard bow the first hint of land, a thin hazy line on the whitecap broken horizon. Hours later and more distinct on the port bow the landmass of Cape Willoughby, the eastern extremity of Kangaroo Island. The first land sighted to starboard slowly rose from the horizon to form the prominent headland of Cape Jervis. Within an hour the *Burwah* would end her torment at the mercy of the Southern Ocean and enter the calm of the twelve mile wide Backstairs Passage.

From a bearing taken on Kangaroo Island's North Cape, the ship altered course to 315 degrees, fifty miles steaming to Stenhouse Bay. Protected by the western extremity of Kangaroo Island, Cape Spencer at the tip of the Yorke Peninsula offered a partial lee never taken for granted by ships masters from the savagery of south-westerly storms generated in the Great Australian Bight.

Sam, splicing a backspring, overheard the mate talking to the bosun and Bert, the expressions on both their faces clear evidence none of what he said penetrated; Sam later took Bert aside and explained: "What the mate said is

Stenhouse Bay is open to the sea and we will be running breast wires with messengers through coirs on the wharf, the eyes turned up on our bitts."

"What's them?" Bert's chin glistened with saliva, in his mind struggling to form a picture.

"Coirs are used in unsafe or tidal ports. Coirs can be plaited mooring line seized with a thimble it takes a couple of men to lift. The idea is to run your breasts or backsprings through the thimble, back onboard and turn up on bitts. These moorings being strong and flexible better absorb the surge of the ship alongside. Though even with coirs if the movement alongside is causing your bights to sing it's time to get out quick."

"Can we do that?"

"Do what?"

"Use these coirs?"

Sam sighed. "These moorings are no more than a variation of our normal tie-ups. Letting go you simply slip the eyes off the bitts and stand well clear, which goes for all tie-ups and let goes."

"Being so complicated I reckon we should leave it to the officers who know better."

"Jesus Christ, Bert, don't ever say that! Navigation, yes. Seamanship, no. We are seamen, not the mates." About to mention scabs as imposters, he changed his mind, instead adding: "Don't worry, Bert, you'll have the second mate aft with you. He will tell you what tying up in Stenhouse Bay is about."

"You've been here before?"

"No, but I have sailed with those who reckon the place is a nightmare if the weather comes in from the Bight. With plenty of evidence on the beach to prove it."

Returning to his splice Sam experienced confusing thoughts. Why not condemn Bert as a scab? He wondered if sailing with company men over a period of time tempered his attitude. No, he hated them, and so he should.

These men every month lined up shoving and laughing and doing little jigs outside the saloon paid in small brown envelopes. Not his comrades with empty pockets and the scars of battle etched in their haggard faces.

Shipowners connived with authorities to have dangerous men like the bosun early released from prison to man their strikebound ships. Empty your prisons and give repentant seamen another chance at redemption. Isn't this what rehabilitation is all about? We have berths abandoned by those who refuse to work for exceptional remuneration and conditions akin to luxury. Led by rapacious leftwing elements inspired with a single ideology, to reduce the maritime industry to no more than a branch office of their insidious union.

≈

In unusually calm waters the *Burwah* dropped her port anchor two hundred feet off the berth, her dead-slow-ahead momentum halted to swing her stern until she lay starboard side parallel to the timber wharf. Along the top of a sheer cliff overshadowing the wharf cable operated tramcars on wooden rails moved stockpiles of gypsum to a fixed loading head. A loading schedule agreed between ship and shore, four shift ships. First and final pours No.2 hatch, No.3 hatch, No.1 hatch and No.4 hatch.

A line boat forward rowed by two gentlemen who attired in Sunday finery might have been on a leisurely outing on a placid river, both resting on their oars watching with disinterest as twenty feet of mooring line dropped in their boat. The carpenter paid out cable, a light southerly wind easing the ship closer to the wharf. A similar boat aft ran a stern line, the rowers less opulently dressed in work stained shirts and vests. The mooring lines fore and aft now took the weight and with only the slightest of compression of timber pilings the ship nudged alongside. These lines would hold the ship in position until the backsprings and coirs were run and made fast; slacked off their role not ended, these lines used to shift ship, also the last lines let go.

Sam assisted the carpenter as the forward and after gangs rolled back three tarpaulins at each hatch and lifted one derrick to remove the centre slabs. Lugs welded to the fishplate of the mast houses served an important purpose, the carpenter attaching lengths of signal halyard weighted with a shackle.

Handing Sam a piece of chalk and a slat of timber he ordered him to mark a line the full length of the inclinator.

"Son, you only do this on an even keel. Know what you're doing?"

"No."

The carpenter pointed to the loader head lowering into position, attached to the chute an eight foot length of black rubber hose a foot wide with two lengths of rope hanging from it. "The loader is centred over the middle of the hatch, but gypsum being greasy and reluctant to slide has this habit of holding up, slipping without notice to one side which means you got to trim using the ropes. Why the inclinators on the forward and after ends of the mast houses."

"Smart. Never loaded in Stenhouse Bay before, hear it can get nasty."

"It can and puts the master under a lot of pressure for a full load. We don't break watches, all hands on duty to shift ship with the watches trimming. Normally one bloke hour about, simple. Having said that I have doubts that introduction to ship's stability beyond this lot of cretins."

Sam observed the eight to twelve watchkeepers ordered by the bosun to standby both trimming ropes. With the belt yet to start up both stared moronically at the inclinator, under threat by the bosun not to leave their post until relieved by the twelve to four watch.

"See what I mean," the carpenter said resignedly. "Union blokes hour about, mug of coffee sitting on the hatch, all hands on standby to shift ship. This lot, the bosun's got the day workers painting deckheads between shifts."

A feather of steam threatened to activate the pressure relief valve abaft the funnel, the engine warmed through and ready for sea the moment the telegraph rang standby.

With darkness the wind fell away, the sea an oily calm. The master now confident of a full load still kept a cautious eye on the stable barometer, a more concerned one on the rusted skeletal ribs of past victims embedded on the beach. Probably not all casualties of Stenhouse Bay, some blown in from the Great Australian Bight. Loading completed around mid-morning, thankfully with no parted lines or injuries, his owners would be pleased.

The agent brought mail, also mail that missed the ship in Melbourne, Sam with two letters dated a week apart. In the seclusion of his bunk and able to read in the dim light filtering through a porthole, he opened the first. Suddenly his entire body filled with a feeling so intense he felt a tingle from his toes to the top of his head. His girl pregnant!

He stared at the deckhead, rusted rivets beaded with ship sweat only inches from his nose. Emily with a baby growing in her belly! Her body at last accepting his and now nothing could stop their entering a permanent relationship. Their lives joined together forever. With great care as if not to further crease the precious letter he replaced it in its envelope, then opened the other.

A barb of pain so sharp in his chest it penetrated to his spine. *Dearest Sam, please do not be angry with me I never shared with you the periods I missed, but I needed to be sure and this time I felt certain. . . .* The words spilled from a grief stricken girl, the joy of falling pregnant and keeping it a secret until her body assured her the following month. She miscarried at work.

He read her sorrow in every line, her perceived failure as a woman. For the first time in his life he felt the helplessness of a seaman far from home, of being unable because of distance to comfort a loved one. Offer strength and love.

So far away and helpless, unsuccessfully searching for solace that in four days with fair weather the ship would be in Sydney and he would have Emily in his arms. Try as he could he failed to stop the tears that flooded his eyes and streamed down his cheeks.

26

THE *BURWAH* ARRIVED EARLY morning at her Balmain berth, the hatches stripped and the gear set for grabs by 10:30am. Sam, concerned for Emily, asked the bosun for time off, his surly reply if he walked down the gangway one minute before 5:00pm he would recommend to the mate instant dismissal. His reply took the bosun by surprise, further strengthening his opinion of him, a weak bully. To hell with you!

He caught the ferry to Pyrmont, his heart heavy, wanting nothing more than to draw Emily's pain into his own body. His girl in the comfort of his embrace, reassured. The sound of running feet in the hallway, the door opening and Emily collapsing in his arms. Half carrying her into the kitchen, he eased her down on his bed.

Lying beside her he kissed the tears on her flushed cheeks, her nose, her lips, whispering his love. "It doesn't matter, Emily. Nothing does only you and me."

"Sam, I tried so hard to hold it back! Our baby, Sam."

"I know, I know."

"My head of department who I thought old and crabby understood. She brought me home and spoke with mother."

Anguished, he murmured in her hair: "It's over and you are not hurt, that's all I care about."

A tremor passed through her as she felt his hand rest on her hip, but instead of lifting her dress to caress her intimately he removed his hand.

"Sam, it's all right if you want to."

"Emily, the time might not be right."

In an act of desperation she took the initiative, scrambling from the bed and stepping out of her dress, only for a moment pausing before pulling down her underwear. She pressed against him, relaxing as he felt his hand slip between her legs. "I am still me," she whispered, turning on her back.

"What if I hurt you?"

"Please, you won't."

He held her sheaf in half his hand and wondered how nature made it possible for a child to enter the world from such a tiny portal. How it bled every month and the exquisite pleasure it gave him when he entered its clinging warmth, the lips that gripped him tightly in a caress as old as time. How it stripped him of his seed again and again, how he never tired of it, touching, possessing.

She helped him release his belt, tug down his dungarees, his erection brushing her hand and causing her to catch her breath. He entered her immediately, her hands raking his back and forcing him deeper inside her, with each thrust willing him to saturate her and rekindle a lost cycle of life.

She felt the warm wash of him inside her, her pleasure of no importance as her muscles pinched his pulsing organ. Exhausted he lay on top of her, sucking air into his labouring lungs, an occasional stab causing him to groan.

"This time, Sam, this time," she said, muscles contracting causing him to cry out. "Do you think so?"

"I think so," he said, labouring for breath.

"Why did it take so long? Then when it did happen it came away."

He recognised desperation in her voice, withdrawing and turning on his side. "Those things I know nothing about. What did your mother say?"

"She said she expected it."

"The miscarriage?"

"No, the pregnancy."

"Mothers when it comes to that are probably of the same mind with their daughters."

"I would talk to our daughter." Close to more tears she reached between them and took hold of him. "When I have a baby."

She made a pot of tea and glanced at the clock on the mantelpiece, almost time for her sisters to come rushing through the front door from school. Sam reached across the table and brushed hair from her eyes, her cheeks still flushed.

"Emily, we have all the time in the world. First we would need a home," he said, then suddenly burst out laughing, shaking his head. "I think some might say we need to grow up first."

"We could live here?" She poured two cups, adding milk from a small jug covered with lace doily edged with beads.

"I suppose we could give the old place a coat of paint, do some repairs. Lot of repairs by what I see. Then one day we can think of moving to our very own home."

"Our home sounds nice, Sam."

"With a brood of kids with runny noses."

"Yes, lot of kids. Not with runny noses though. With visits from Mother and my sisters. Sam, what if Father comes home?"

"Do you think he will?"

She sipped her tea. "Mother has heard nothing from him since he left, or sent money home. She thinks he might not come back."

"How does she feel about that?"

"Happy I think if he doesn't."

≈

Instead of instant dismissal the chief mate gave Sam the morning off to have his sea time counted at the shipping office.

Mr Stuart frowned studiously at the excited young man on the other side of the counter "I sincerely hope you have tallied your time allowing for those months of thirty days?"

"Yes."

Mr Stuart allowed himself a smile, though the slight crease of his lips might have been a reaction to spicy Italian sausage served on his breakfast plate. "Let us hope so because I have instructions from the master."

Sam tried but failed to overcome his exhilaration, barely able to stand still. "What instructions? Am I in trouble? The mate gave me time off."

"Which in due time will be revealed if you have not succumbed to the folly of counting your time in multiple of thirties."

Two days over!

Mr Stuart opened the *Burwah's* articles of agreement on the counter, dipping his pen in an inkpot and tapping excess fluid on its side. "Something that may be of interest to you as a member of the Federated Seamen's Union of Australasia, there is an AB joining the *Burwah* today and he has been engaged from the new seamen's bureau. A quite efficient method of engagement and hopefully indicative of change in the industry."

The statement caught his attention, even averting his unbelieving eyes from his name and above it written in copperplate script: *Endorsed to sail OS, Sydney 28/04/36.*

Ordinary seaman!

"The seamen's bureau is the new system of picking up men, right?"

"It certainly is, though still burdened with the cumbersome selection line-up. You might also find the AB to your liking. Quite vocal and who has serious issues pending over the licensing provisions of the award."

Could his day get any better? The strike ended and a union man joining!

"Mr Wright, it is my duty, and I must say in this instance pleasurable, to instruct you that now you are ordinary seamen your responsibilities at sea are similar to an AB with watchkeeping and attending yardarms. With responsibility comes maturity and strength of character which I hope you use to its full extent in your future years a sea. My congratulations, Mr Wright, ordinary seaman of the *Burwah*. You come highly recommended."

≈

Manfred Kaufman ignored the inviting open door of the Bald Rock Hotel and the pungent odour of malty ales and lagers as he hefted his seabag higher on his shoulder and headed down the steep hill to the wharf. Below the *Burwah* worked all hatches with grabs, a line of waiting trucks alternating between the cement and plaster works.

Normally Manfred would have stopped off at the hotel, breasted the bar and downed a few rums to poison any bug lingering in his belly, though debatable any adventurous microbe could live in an empty belly for the last long and bitter months manning picket lines.

Manfred enjoyed the challenge of a new ship, meeting old and new comrades, though not this time; he knew only too well what confronted him, an entire crew of company men. Or as he would describe them, loathsome creatures even a starving vulture would vomit from its guts.

He held no fears joining the *Burwah*, of being one man out. Mates, engineers and stewards who bedded down with scabs he could deal with in the knowledge these people did not traditionally believe in the unbreakable bond of unionism, and to his mind most would weasel out of paying their dues. Blacklegs he would bring to task the moment he stepped onboard. Unpleasant thoughts filled his mind, sharing the focastle, breathing the same putrid air, sharing a table and eating rotten blackleg food.

First he would thump his union book on the focastle table, followed by his little red book with IWW embossed in gold, inside a little less grand in black ink: *Industrial Workers of the World*. Over six feet tall his Germanic bloodline even more apparent with a large muscular frame and thinning almost transparent fair hair. Steel blue eyes viewed the world unwavering, a fearless mind supported by strength of character.

No lady friend ever thought Manfred handsome or suave. Charming, yes, affable when not on his stump berating the world. What people thought of his radical views mattered none, what did and what fired his manic zeal the rise of the working class in a corrupt and avaricious world to take their rightful place at the top of the human pile.

Manfred referred to the books of the great socialist thinkers, Georg Hegel, Karl Marx and Friedrich Engels. His keen intellect could regurgitate long passages from the vast library stored in his mind, and if this did not impress his capable fists backed him up, though in most cases to protect himself from the criminal goons society set upon him.

Hungry and broke, disconsolate in defeat, scores needed settling. He paused at the top of the gangway, first looking aft, then forward, passing an inquiring eye over the ship's gear. Sam, greasing wires of a grab landed on deck at No.2 hatch, watched him closely, in no doubt the man in his late thirties with a seabag resting on the deck and a livid scowl on his face the new AB.

Wiping his hands on a piece of cotton waste, Sam approached him, smiling at the reaction in his face, a look of contempt. He never gave him a chance at an opening salvo. "Federated Seamen's Union of Australasia 7171. I am the ordinary seaman promoted from deck boy and I supported my comrades in the strike. I am union and my name is Sam Wright."

Manfred removed one from his mental list. "Where's the bosun?"

"You will hear him before you see him. Bad bit of work."

"Is that so? The rest of them are scabs of course?"

"All bar me. The bosun when drunk boasts he got early release from prison to save the maritime industry from unionists like us."

Manfred received the information with a few nods to himself. "Then we shouldn't waste time sorting this ship out. Accommodation first."

He followed Sam forward and on entering the focastle threw his seabag on an unmade top bunk. He turned and in a cold and menacing voice ordered: "Go get the bosun and the crowd."

Sam found the bosun in the cabin amidships he shared with the carpenter, both well on the way to being drunk.

"What did you say?" the bosun slurred, starting to rise from his bunk but changing his mind to slump back.

"The new AB is calling a meeting." The words instilled a confidence not only of promotion, but the return of a union presence onboard the ship.

"We don't have Bolshie meetings on this ship! Go tell the bastard to see the idiot storekeeper for a bucket of oil and a brush for grab wires. Hear me? Fuck off!"

"Go tell him yourself. When I left the crowd were already heading for the focastle."

"I'll have the fucking bastard sacked!" Lurching up this time he managed to stagger to his feet, pushed past Sam and with head down and fists pumping lumbered forward.

Nervous men fidgeted with heads bowed at the focastle table, caught between two forbidding presences, one leaning with arms akimbo against the hawse pipe and the other blocking the doorway shoulders hunched ready to attack. "What the fuck is going on here? Who are you? You turn to right now or you get off the ship! Your choice!"

Manfred eased off the hawse pipe. "My choice is it? Oh, I wouldn't say that. Every one of you I would recommend every word I am about to say sink deep into your minds. Your days of taking the jobs of seamen on strike are over. Also I want you to know I joined this ship not from a shipowners ledger as you did, but from a seamen's bureau and that I do not have a license. I will not have a dog collar, and I am here to make your lives hell!"

The bosun tried to decipher what the shape obscured in the murky light of the focastle said, a survival instinct overcoming the torpor of liquor; his brow creased as he weighed options, at the moment in a position of strength with the support of the focastle.

"You who purport to be saviours of the maritime industry so vindicating your misguided principles are no more than expendable pawns. Names written in shipping company ledgers, erased when your use is no longer required. Though your egos might have soared when lauded for your loyalty and courage by some insignificant shipping clerk, you were never held in high esteem by those who do the bidding of the shipping moguls. Condemnation and ridicule is your fate. Shame and a place of infamy in the history of working class struggle. Progressive writers will continue to write about you for time immemorial, and never a single word will justify your crossing picket lines and taking the job of union men."

The bosun assessed his opponent, preparing for a full frontal attack; as large as himself and obviously strong, the determined face of a man who would not back down. To overcome this threat to his leadership he would need followers, and looking at the men with their heads almost on the table he started to have reservations.

"Whoever you are, you're full of fucking shit!

Manfred ignored the insult. "Without a twinge of scruples you slunk up the gangways of strikebound ships. Passed through picket lines, your thick hides threatened and spat on, abused and vilified. Know well one of your insidious breed did not join this ship today, and that soon a fireman or a greaser will join and bring the scabs in the adjoining focastle to heel. I am Manfred Kaufman, AB, member of the Federated Seamen's Union of Australasia. I am hereby the ship's delegate. Have any of you objections to my ascension to that position?"

The bosun opened his mouth, then clamped it shut. Sam saw Bert sweating with fear, the others too afraid to lift their heads.

"Declared and carried unanimously. I nominate and second and declare carried Sam Wright co-delegate."

A grin of pure pleasure filled Sam's face.

"First order of business is a warning if I hear any whimpers of a lackeys union representing seamen those responsible will answer to an official. This ship is Federated Seamen's Union of Australasia. A true union ship."

"Like fuck it is!" The bosun at last found his voice, still without the courage to enter the focastle and confront the threat head-on.

"Then what is this ship then?" Manfred inquired, his voice even and controlled, eyes transfixed on the bosun. "Explain to me in your own gibberish exactly what this ship is."

"Not being bludgeoned to go on strike! Hold ships up! Here we get good wages, accommodation, food, and no Bolshies like you ramming union shit down our throats. We've been done right by shipowners!"

"To work the same hours as Lascars, Burmese, Filipinos and Chinese on articles with no award hours, no overtime, crammed upwards of sixty in open focastles? Fed fish guts and a monthly sack of rice? Is that what you and those of similar mind aspire to?"

It took a few painful moments for the rebuttal to seep into the bosun's brain, Manfred concluding with a finger pointed directly at him: "Do not listen to this imbecile and what it subscribes to, what oozes like puss from its sodden brain. He does not subscribe to the belief conditions extracted from shipowners are achieved by union and unity, dedication and sacrifice, men driven to demand equality. Of standing strong and unyielding in the face of confrontation against those who would reduce your labours to the status of slavery. Shipowners who would send you to sea and benevolently provide you with a steel coffin, their munificence well insured of course. Who gorge at the trough of plenty while you quaff fare stamped fit for the consumption of seamen."

Manfred paused for his words to sink in, his conclusion taking Sam aback: "This is what you're going to do with the exception of the bosun. You are going to ask the mate to knock off a few hours early this afternoon and you are going to join the Federated Seamen's Union of Australasia. No excuses, no exceptions pleading your God doesn't allow union membership, politics or other lame excuses. There will be a show of books at a special meeting tomorrow morning and I better see union books on this table. Remember though and never forget, union membership does not absolve sins of the past and I do not welcome you, in fact I abhor you."

The bosun exploded, smashing his fist in the door, a sound of crunching bone. "Who the fuck do you think you are? We ain't doing anything you say and I want to know why you don't mention me joining your fucking union!"

"We survivors of the strike were forced by the settlement terms to admit those who took our jobs into the union. We feel bitterly against this unjust enforcement, but for our union to survive we must acquiesce to the terms of the victor."

"You purposely left me out! Why?" The bosun's broken hand throbbed, regretting his impulsive reaction; without supporters he needed two good fists to bring this Bolshie down.

Manfred again pointed at him, his eyes filled with scorn. "Thugs such as you are a special case to be dealt with accordingly by the union. We will see you rot in jail where you belong. Not one of you will ever join the union or walk up a gangway again. If by chance any of your more rat cunning mates manages to hide their felonious past we will find out, and when we do I would recommend avoiding midnight watchkeeping. Your names, your faces, your despicable past, will never be forgotten!"

"I'm going to the captain! He'll know how to deal with you!" The fight drained from the bosun's body, slumping in the doorway; he needed a drink badly. Then he whimpered: "What would you have done if someone came to you and said we'll cut three years off your sentence if you join a ship? What would you have fucking done?" His voice broke, reduced to a frightened plea.

"Exactly what you did, beat the system by joining it."

"See! Hear what he says? He would have done the same thing!"

Manfred seemed like an animal in ambush about to spring on a helpless prey. "One up on the system I would have given myself to the union. Every penny of my wages would have gone to the strike fund. I would have supported the picket lines. With my newfound freedom I would have stood at the wharf gates and shouted the loudest. I would have exposed the rotten to the core system! I would not have become a blackleg!"

The bosun's frenzied gaze begged the men at the table to support him, but not one head dared lift to look at him. Throbbing spasms of pain shot up his arm and he cringed, blubbering: "You're all the fucking same as me, every one of you. We are not this union thing the Bolshies want us to be. We are not ruled by bloody comrades who would bring the country to its knees."

"Bosun, I would seriously recommend you leave while you still have some trace of dignity left," Manfred said. "I would also advise you see the mate on your way aft."

Fascinated, Sam watched the interaction between the two men. Within him a new confidence if the Federated Seamen's Union of Australasia burgeoned with more men of the calibre of Manfred Kaufman the union would be invincible. It would rise from the mire of defeat to new heights, defiant and strengthened by lessons learned from the past.

Manfred turned his attention to the men at the table. "Hide your shame well because there are many empowered with a new drive to extract quite violently from our midst those who contributed to our defeat and brought us to our knees. We have been bruised by shipowners and government, but are survivors of the darkest period of our union's history. Among us have emerged men whose names will have the boldest print when written in the history of the union. Men who in the future will take us to the highest pinnacle, make us the envy of the union movement throughout the world." He threw back his head and sucked air between his teeth. "I sincerely hope you have listened well."

Heads still lowered, all muttered their timid acceptance.

"Then hide well your traitorous past."

Manfred met Sam's eyes. "Outside. The air in here stinks."

≈

Manfred ran his fingers through his thinning hair, drew two deep breaths and smiled at the chief mate and second mate at No.3 hatch, every so often glancing in his direction. "The mates and engineers may well parade their status of authority, but we remember well with unhealed wounds who supported us, only the cooks with the resolve to follow us down the gangway.

Then I suppose it is only fitting shipowners engage scabs cooks to cook for scabs. Now begins your apprenticeship to learn to be a delegate. Decipher the award and become the articulate means of liaison and communication for your comrades. Represent your union proudly and unflinchingly. Now with those grand words I am the first to admit unashamedly I am wrong many times in my judgements, but I am certain you have the makings of a fine delegate and a strong unionist, Sam Wright."

"Like you?"

Manfred chuckled. "Never like me. I have far too many imperfections in this scarred body. Be union, but be your own man."

"Will Geordie go?"

"By Geordie I assume you mean that slug now staring down the neck of an empty bottle. Put it this way with that man's attitude only a serial optimist would predict a long tenure at sea. Yes, he will."

Manfred's words proved prophetic, the bosun paying off the next day, his replacement engaged through the seamen's bureau.

≈

Manfred sat at the focastle table with Sam, nursing a mug of tea in both hands. "I know the new bosun well, a good seaman who saw the strike through to the end. I've spoken with him we need a storekeeper. Not traditionally a bucko's role, but from what I hear you are more than able."

"The strike made me mud pilot and possibly an AB before my time. In the store I spliced until my shoulders ached. Manfred, I wouldn't do that to Bert, I really couldn't. Also I am looking forward to standing a watch."

"Bert's a scab with an even greater liability; he's three quarters less than a full brain."

"What about you, Manfred?"

"Most definitely not. Mixing paints makes me lightheaded and I need my wits about me."

"Bert's a bit slow, but out of this entire crowd I am certain he doesn't realise the reality of his situation. I like him, and this is odd, if it ever comes to forgiving then he probably is the only one I could."

"Your call, but there is no way we're having a blackleg in the store and second to the bosun."

"What do we do?"

"Glad you said we. Give him something he's capable of doing, winch beds and bilges. Forget being on watch for awhile, I reckon you're destined to spend time in the store until we get a union man. Something else, that soft spot in your heart is going to be your undoing one day."

"Is compassion wrong?"

"Dear God, this world's going to eat you, Sam Wright!"

≈

Sam when he walked Emily home from Mark Foy's noticed a difference in the way people went about their daily business. Families that gathered in the parks were dressed more affluently, animated, money to spend. Newspapers still printed gloom sixteen percent of the workforce remained unemployed. Jobs were getting easier to find as money trickled from the financial institutions and government initiated major public works.

The despair and misery of thirty-three percent of the workforce idle now seemed a relic of the painful past, the eternal optimists predicting soon the figure would drop to a single digit. Australia's future assured with the finest wool and primary produce in the world, ingenuity in manufacturing, and the dedicated labours of hardworking Australian men and women.

27

SAM LEARNED FROM MANFRED a lesson how the strength of numbers tipped the scales of justice in an environment weighted heavily in the favour of industry and commerce. Regardless of two disastrous strikes over a period of ten years the Federated Seamen's Union of Australasia slowly rebuilt from the ruins.

A healing unguent eased the pressure of an ersatz union financed by the Commonwealth Steamship Owners Association, their attraction to company recruited seamen of suspect qualifications waning as the Federated Seamen's Union of Australasia offered a membership of skilled seamen.

Even so with a new direction the strike left a legacy of bitter discord among a large number of seamen, the casualties not only among the rank and file but the federal executive and branch officials. A barb ground in the hearts of those who remained united during the long strike, who suffered eviction and degrading poverty, a settlement clause company employees would retain their jobs, and if anathema to their religious beliefs, political views or abhorrence of organised labour, union membership not obligatory. Seamen who offered their services during the strike would not be intimidated or discriminated against, and those in senior positions such as bosuns, bosun's mates, lamp trimmers and donkeymen would retain their petty officer rank.

The union painfully steadied on a new course of conciliation with its broad and diverse membership, a reinvigorated federal executive and rank and file dedicated to gain higher wages and improved accommodation, leave and common menus.

The *Burwah* quickly thinned it ranks of volunteers, forced out by an increased union presence, unable to work with seamen who ignored them or in essential communication uttered contempt. Some feared for their lives, continuously exposed to an undercurrent of resentment and loathing. Even simple Bert, absent from the ship at sailing time with his gear, would never be forgiven, a marked man with a tainted past.

Sam now a watchkeeper spend considerable time watch below with storekeeper George Carney, learning macramé, ocean plaits, quoits, fancy knots and needlework that might have been stitched on a machine; George's last job saloon deck man on the *Westralia*, an old job he pined for. Sam's first ocean plait made from an old guy adorned the front doorstep of the Knights home, evidence of its outstanding workmanship stolen the first night.

He matured as delegate, confronting the master on numerous occasions, even once on Manfred's prompt, presenting the opening salvo to protect a drunk found asleep by the third mate on lookout. The miscreant faced instant dismissal and life suspension from the industry, the delegates only defence finding the master in a conciliatory mood, assurance the union would draw and quarter the man at a stopwork meeting.

The master did relent with a warning a reoccurrence would have the full punitive clauses of the Navigation Act brought down on the man's head, the logging would remain and not be rescinded on a month's good behaviour, the entry tempered with *Absent from place of assigned duty.*

Sam felt like a crusading saviour of a fellow seaman, the victory soured when the man missed the next square up, fully clothed and booted, unconscious and reeking of wine in his bunk. The crowd covered for him, Manfred though less forgiving who told him to pay off in the next port, his name forwarded to his homeport to front a stopwork meeting.

≈

With Sam head of the house changes came about the damp, landlord neglected and dingy tenement. With his heart pounding and his eyes seeing danger in every moving shadow as evidence of the prowling pilferage squad, his seabag weighed heavy with paint. The kitchen shone with a full gloss coat of white, the bedrooms and hallway a pale green blend of sidelight green and white gloss. Trims and doors pale grey, the merest suggestion of black topside mixed with white gloss. He experienced pride and satisfaction in his work, though unable to rid the anxiety the notorious waterfront police must surely see him staggering with his canvas bag in their precinct.

He gave up wondering about the reproductive cycle of Emily's body, a mother relieved not having the burden of a pregnant daughter. Claire in her heart thanked the presence of the boy who so openly loved her daughter, a joy to witness both in each other's company, holding hands, touching, a glow in both their eyes. Her sobbing on their parting obvious of her love.

Homecomings from three daughters greeted with wild handclaps, hugs and squeals, even normally reserved Claire joining in the excitement. A mother resigned to the fact of being a sole parent, at these special times emerged from her sombreness.

Sam would watch the sisters interact, Emily always the leader, her word usually final. Of the three girls the two younger were in obvious good health, but not Emily. Her skin though soft as satin and unblemished never shone with young health, and that worried him. A nagging cough she tried but failed to conceal, breathlessness and reaching for his arm climbing stairs. He tried hard to convince her to see a doctor who might prescribe a tonic or a high protein diet or whatever it took to make her well. The mention of a doctor would cause her to retreat within herself, spells of silence as though punishing him for making accusations concerning her health.

≈

With the *Burwah* close to sailing Sam paid off, Emily bedridden with bronchitis, Claire administering lemon juice and aspirin and piling the bed with additional blankets. The heavy dosage of vitamin C helped as did nursing a dish of hot water with a towel draped over her head.

Manfred took him aside. "The ship will miss you, Sam," he said, using both hands to grip his. "Fellow survivor, a young seaman who showed mettle far in advance of his years enduring scum now scuttling back to their holes in skirting boards. You never lost faith in your union and besides being a good, no, excellent seaman, it has been my privilege to stand with you as a delegate my equal. Your union can be proud of you."

He felt a tightening in his chest, words difficult to form. "Because of you and others of the same calling, Manfred."

"No way am I going to take praise for bringing out the very best in you. Union is inside you, a gene shared by those who do not cower before authority and industrial might. Men who can rise above their fellows in times of crisis, strength to bring to heel those who exploit and deem working class mere chattels to create wealth. Hurt one, hurt all."

"I'll miss the *Burwah*, Manfred. Well, the current *Burwah*, not the old."

"Young seaman need to change ships regularly. Some advice when you reach the top platform of the gangway check out your ship's gear, housed or cradled, burton or single guys, span or luff tackle, slabs or boards." Manfred suddenly went quiet, his eyes distant, then in an earnest voice said: "Sam, learn and learn well. Any seaman can get his hands greasy overhauling ships gear, but not many know the formulas for safety working loads and breaking strains of wire and cordage. Formulas for stranded wire, tonnages of cargo lashings either side must be the total weight of the cargo, loss of strength of wire when spliced. Learn and be able to debate it on equal terms with a mate, a mate who has to know and would get the surprise of his life if you did. Some of your comrades in the pub might argue this as blasphemy, but you might consider studying for your ticket."

"I don't think so, Manfred."

"Tell me why not? I thought every boy wanted to become a captain and get to steer the ship."

"I'm not saying it wouldn't be an achievement, but not for me. It takes a smart man to get his tickets, dedication of which at this time of my life I can't give. Also, I once opened a book on stability on the chartroom table and it might well have been in a foreign language."

"True, but never tell a mate he's smart. With a few exceptions most are hard to coexist with without putting them on pedestals as geniuses."

"Manfred, I hope we sail together again."

"Stay at sea long enough and we most certainly will. I move around a lot and I am of a mind the *Burwah* might be seeing the end of me shortly as well. As I said, Sam, it has been a privilege to have sailed with you."

≈

Captain Vance Styles stood six feet three inches and from that exceptional height gazed down imperiously at his fellow man with barely concealed contempt. The master achieved high rank through total commitment to his calling, indentured with the epitome of the British mercantile marine the British India Steam Navigation Company.

With total commitment to duty and exemplary scholarly application, he successfully gained his second and first officers certification. One gold bar on his shoulders became two, sufficient sea time to successfully pass his orals for foreign-going master. With promotion to master in British India agonisingly slow, he applied to BHP offering young British trained officers rapid promotion in their growing fleet of coastal vessels.

Captain Styles held views not uncommon among his brethren seamen with pale skins were habitual drunkards with an intelligence quotient about level with a trained primate. Lazy, noisy, foul mouthed, uncouth, unhygienic, incompetent and rabble-rousers united by a belligerent union of Communists and anarchists.

How he wished for a joyful crew of hardworking Asians eternally grateful for employment, faithful, loyal. Possibly sixty to seventy living in harmony together in their focastle accommodation, no nonsense of union dictated hours of duty. Today he would have the unpleasant task of picking up one AB and one ordinary seaman. Though he admitted, albeit reluctantly, the growing number of returning strike demoralised seamen under the strict supervision of his officers did fulfil complex survey tasks and gear overhaul, the number of company men thinning. He knew why, as did his officers, himself the distasteful recipient of increased visitations to his cabin by unionised thugs masquerading as delegates who trampled dirt on his rug.

He could feel it in his bones, the emergence of the bad old days when waterfront militants in grease stained clothing and stokehold boots stormed on his bridge disgorging from their mouths foul language of holding his ship alongside. He hoped the Lyons government, especially the brilliant Mr Menzies waiting in the wings for the call to supreme power, would purge the maritime industry of this trash by his licensing provisions.

The AB line consisted of thirty desperate and shabby men, hopeful Captain Styles would choose them. The ordinary seamen line, four.

The master's recognised a few familiar faces in the line, troublemakers from the past instantly rejected. One young man better dressed than the others caught his attention, standing upright and obviously not suffering delirium tremors; a close up smell determined the man not a frequenter of early opening pubs.

The choice of the junior rating; one with chronic acne, his face resembling a crushed pomegranate. Another with bad teeth, his mate continuously scratching his privates, the other badly in need of a haircut but tall and strong with an intelligent face. Intelligence of course debatable, any free thought the boy might have carried with him from the school gate soon knocked out of him by the scheming focastle mob.

Sam joined the *Iron Knob*.

≈

The *Iron Knob* discharged railway sleepers at Walsh Bay, the work arduous, slow and dangerous. Her pungent cargo oozed thick red sap from freshly cut jarrah from the forests of south-western Western Australia loaded in Bunbury and

Busselton, the only cargo available to avoid an eastbound passage to Whyalla in ballast. Optimistic estimates of discharge varied from ten days to a fortnight as disputes could extend unloading depending on the severity as union and stevedores argued danger money, gang sizes and allocation of men designated for more skilful work such as winch drivers and hatch men.

In 1922 the *Iron Knob* slid down a greased Adelaide slipway as the *Euwarra*, 3349 tons. Four hatches, eight derricks, officers, engineers and catering accommodated amidships, crew aft. The *Euwarra* represented a bargain for BHP as did the other E class vessels to various shipowners, predominantly Japanese expanding their deep sea fleet. The ships sold by the Stanley Bruce government in a bloodletting of destroying organised labour in Australia, sharing the top of the long list with the Waterside Workers Federation, the Federated Seamen's Union of Australasia.

Constructed in greenfield dockyards throughout the nation the D and E class ships previously traded worldwide, charging freight rates two thirds less than their foreign competitors, while putting Australia's balance of payments in the black and wide smiles on the faces of primary producers. Prime Minister Stanley Bruce further gifted five newly built passenger and two special purpose ships worth six million pounds to British shipowners for a quarter of a million pounds, his reward a lordship. Appreciative British shipowners now without a viable competitor in the Antipodes, reeling in stunned disbelief at colonial naivety bordering on gross idiocy, on signing the sale documents immediately tripled freight rates for Australian farmers.

From the wharf Sam gazed up at the ship, strongly built for her role with the Australian steelmaker; Manfred's advice came to mind, imprinting in his mind his new ship's gear.

The accommodation aft consisted of two messrooms, two bathrooms and sparsely furnish cabins, all hands housed in odorous cabins above and below the steering flat. Owing to union pressure original six berth cabins now accommodated four seamen, though poorly lighted and stuffy far superior to open focastles. Directed by a fireman to descend beneath the steering flat he found a cabin with an unmade top bunk and linen folded at its foot, the cramped confines steeped in perpetual twilight even with the door curtain drawn back.

Sam presented his union book to the delegate, Simon Coan, a young man with piercing grey eyes and a permanent scowl.

"How were you involved in the strike?" Simon poured himself a mug of tea from a large battered pot, Sam sitting opposite him at the messroom table.

"*Aldinga* and *Burwah* as deck boy with no option but to work through the strike as best I could. I got sacked for attending a stopwork meeting."

Simon raised his eyebrows. "So far that sounds very good."

"A bad discharge."

"Even better," Simon said, then with a smirk: "Now how did you as a deck boy overcome that quite substantial obstacle because obviously here you are still shipping out?"

"A seaman on the picket line who I think could talk his way out of a hanging took me to see the shipping master. I got a bad discharge, but I also got a license dated the day after."

"Take my advice, don't burn it, frame it. It saved you, though I wouldn't go around admitting I have one. There are so many of us refusing to submit to licensing the government's in a quandary and their scheme falling apart. Do you know the man who joined with you?" His amicable tone suddenly changed, that of an interrogator.

"No, I don't."

"He has a white card and freely admits on his last ship he took the job of a man on strike. No sense of guilt, even cocky when he knows we have to accept him."

"Suppose we will be seeing many white cards with blacklegs wanting a future in the industry."

"The coffers of the union will swell with blackleg dues, like those pieces of silver learned in bible class, but not one of them will ever be a union man when the time comes to stand firm. Every one of them one day will turn on the true believers and bring the union down."

"Do you know Manfred Kaufman?"

The anger in Simon's face turned to a smile, softening hard facial lines. "Manfred! A man who gives himself wholly to the cause and takes very few prisoners."

"He made the *Burwah's* scabs join the union. On joining called a meeting and laid down the law. The bosun paid off the next day and the rest soon followed."

"Manfred will round scabs up like sheep. Nothing daunts that man, though the loss of the strike hit him pretty hard. Then that goes for all of us who remained strong."

"The company got the bosun from jail."

"Would you expect anything else from those with a history of drug running, slaving, extortion and exploitation on a world scale? Against this formidable foe we are a union with three distinct divisions, rightwing, leftwing and blacklegs. The left on a permanent war footing lick their wounds and look to the future while the right seek solace with the conservatives and God. The blacklegs intent only on covering their past. Blacklegs are leaving in their droves, though for some of us not fast enough, remedies other than harassment hastening their departure."

"Isn't that against union policy?"

"Scabs are a protected species, so say the shipowners and agreed by the federal executive of the union. Another twist of the knife, another hand reaching in and wrenching out the hearts of those who stood firm. Got news for you, the white carder's your eight to twelve offsider."

≈

Bentley Reid at eighteen enlisted in the Royal Australian Navy and in the four years he served before discharged diagnosed with epilepsy his sea time amounted to ten days of exercises with a small New Zealand flotilla off the

New South Wales coast. Among his many and varied naval duties, after three weeks practical training, his discharge papers noted him an AB.

Newly married and living in a small cottage in Port Kembla, he became a statistic of the Depression, losing a clerical position made redundant by an increasingly struggling Wollongong City Council; an additional burden deepened the despair of inadequacy and unemployment, a three month old child. An advertisement in the *Daily Telegraph* inserted by Melbourne Steamship Company offered jobs in two of their ships berthed in Sydney, suitably certified ABs, greasers, firemen and trimmers need apply for immediate employment. Bentley's impeccable naval qualifications and a national crisis overriding his medical discharge, he joined the *Ellaroo*.

Having a common interest in watchkeeping Bentley gravitated to Sam, following him on deck after meals, an annoyance as he sipped a mug of tea on the poop bitts. Sam attempted to shut out the flat and monotonous voice, the same story over and over: 'Our country's recovery from economic devastation would have stalled if a core of nationalistic citizens remained uncommitted in the wings, observers of ships lying idle alongside wharves.'

Sam would stare at the residue of tea leaves in his mug and keep his peace. Lectured to by a gallant white knight who tethered his steed to the *Ellaroo's* gangway. Bentley tried to win acceptance amid open hostility, unfamiliarity with seamanship, even the basics principles of support, ensured his ears rang with vitriol.

Sam tried to emphasise with a man with a young family to support, but unlike the sympathy he felt for Bert he failed. Militants warned about men like Bentley Reid being a future problem for the union, their banding together to form splinter groups quashing militancy, direct action and political ties with the Labor Party. These groups dutifully attended stopwork meetings, a disruptive element preparing to put forward candidates for the next union elections.

≈

The *Iron Knob* sailed at 6:30pm light ship to Port Kembla to load plate and rolled steel joists for Melbourne, her berth not available until 6:00am. Squaring up Sam found the gear, chain and span, easy to work and well maintained. This Australian built workhorse proved the worth of older Australian dockyard workers recruited from all walks of life from a workforce decimated by world war.

The *Iron Knob,* with her bunkers and side pockets full could sail to Europe. Australian designed by the Cockatoo Naval Dockyard, classified a standard built ship, the E class traded worldwide.

Her triple expansion steam engine and iron propeller moved her through calm harbour waters at seven knots, under pilotage until the escarpment of North Head soared as a dark mass of crumbling sandstone on their port hand, rolling in a light easterly swell as she slowly swung on the crests to steer a southerly course for the shut-in forty mile passage. On the messroom blackboard in chalk, all hands ordered for 5:30am to berth. The ship's speed reduced from seven to four knots.

Sam's two hours at the wheel passed slowly, as did as the lights of Sydney's eastern suburbs still shining through the starboard wheelhouse windows; thoughts of home flitted in and out of his head, more so of Emily sick with another heavy cold and missing two days at work.

He sensed rather than saw the presence standing by the dimly lit binnacle, a jolt bringing him back to reality and irked the ship four degrees to starboard off course. A full turn to port held for a ten seconds, then released with a half turn of starboard, the ship creeping back on course of 180 degrees.

"Looking forward to getting home," Bentley said, rubbing his hands enthusiastically, returned to the bridge from his 9:40pm smoko with a pot of tea and two slices of buttered toast for the third mate. "Essie and tiny Millicent miss me so much. Essie said she almost took her first step the other day."

Sam stared straight ahead. "Steering 180 degrees. She's everywhere at this snail's pace."

"Steering 180 degrees. Sam, do you have friends in Port Kembla? Essie makes a great cottage pie."

Sam continued to ignore him, drawing aside the heavy drape blocking chartroom light from the wheelhouse. "Steering 180 degrees. Right to go below?"

The young third mate nodded; more interested in his mid-watch tea and toast, he intoned the master's standing orders: "No more than twenty minutes."

Sam paused about to step out the wheelhouse, turned and addressed the dark shape behind the wheel: "Next time you make tea and toast for a mate take ten minutes. Never in your own time, or let them go without."

≈

At midnight Sam made a small pot of tea and sat down at a table, his thoughts interrupted by an ebullient Bentley. "Do you think it will take long to load in Port Kembla? A lengthy stay might not be financially good for the company, but it would be perfect for me. I did say Essie makes a scrumptious cottage pie."

He should have gone straight to his bunk. "We will be in Port Kembla as long as it takes."

"Suppose you'd rather be in Sydney, correct?"

"At this very moment I don't care where I am as long as I have a job," he said, than as if an afterthought: "Secure and safe from those who thought it hilarious to hang over the rails and mock hungry picket lines."

Bentley's face turned ashen. "Melbourne Steamship Company advertised for seamen in Sydney because those in their employ refused to work under a new agreement, as such their jobs vacant. I personally felt my offer of service even though I lived in Port Kembla beneficial to Melbourne Steamship Company as well as the nation. Also after the strike I decided to ship out of Sydney with a wider choice of jobs."

Sam glared across the table. "Bentley, I would think long and hard of keeping those thoughts to myself."

"I am not afraid to speak my mind. I have nothing to hide or be ashamed of."

Sam choked, swallowing forcefully. "You may not think so in your naive ex-navy way, but others think differently and have been hurt badly by the strike. The word is out there people like you should hide their past well and do so quickly."

"Sam, you are a nice young man but what you have said indicates a lack of maturity. I have done no wrong, it is those who walked down the gangways the ones who should be condemned for abandoning their industry."

"Bentley, in all truth can you call yourself a seaman?"

"Of course."

"Earned by serving a year deck boy, two years ordinary seaman?"

He shook his head, hopes he and Sam would form a friendship, earlier euphoria recognising lights of the Illawarra Escarpment bringing him closer to his loved ones, gone.

≈

Bentley's absence in the crowded messroom went unnoticed, not uncommon as many liked to air their lungs from the stuffy accommodation when called. The bosun's voice caused an instant scraping of chairs on the deck, men rising from the tables. "Fore and aft. Tugs port side lashed up at the break of the focastle and quarter."

When swung facing out to sea for an inclement weather departure, six inch mooring lines warped the ship alongside; the tie-up two head wires and two stern wires, fore and aft backsprings, shackled to messengers passed through doubled twelve inch sisal coirs, the eyes hauled onboard and turned up on the bitts. Only a small window of manoeuvring remained entering the breakwater, the wharf no more than two ship's lengths from the open sea, the swing commenced with the bridge abeam of the eastern breakwater.

Sam bled the two warping winches butted hard up against the fore part of the accommodation bulkhead; a frequent, annoying occurrence when berthing a congregation of watch below firemen and trimmers gathered on the cramped poop, smoking and talking, oblivious to their obstructing seamen running mooring lines, bights and backspring. Unable to see Bentley, he called to the storekeeper: "Angus, you seen Bentley?"

"Maybe he went forward. The man's clueless."

"No, he let go aft leaving Sydney."

"If he's still in his bunk the second mate will have his name."

A shout came from under the stern from the line boat to slacken off the mooring line suspended a few feet above the water. Even with all thought occupied in this critical first stage of berthing, Sam felt a premonition, enough time for quickly enter the accommodation.

Bentley's bunk fully passed naval inspection, the counterpane tucked tightly and blanket perfectly folded at the foot. Rushing back on deck, Sam said to the second mate: "Bentley's missing. He's not in his bunk or the accommodation. His bunk hasn't been slept in!"

The order came from the bridge as the last wires turned up: lower the gangway for the BHP agent to board, shore leave denied. A full search of the ship found no trace of Bentley, leave further denied awaiting the arrival of the Port Kembla police.

Sam noticed an oddity, no sombreness or subdued voices, utterances of concern for a man supporting a young wife and child. Some even made light of the situation, Bentley might end up in New Zealand on the East Australian Current, in the offering a free overseas holiday.

Sam took an annoyed Simon aside. "What do you think happened?"

"How would I know what happened? Anyone who should know would be you, you were on watch with him. Anyway, who the hell cares?" Simon said. "A depressed blackleg decides to end it, that's got nothing to do with you, me, any of us."

Sam stared at him, bewildered by his dismissive attitude. "One of our own is missing."

"One of our own? Listen good, mate, I would revise that statement to one of them and not us."

"Simon, there is a wife and child involved."

"Evidence of blood in his veins, not puss. Could have fooled me."

"Bentley wouldn't jump over the side. We talked when we came off watch. He even invited me home for dinner."

"Would you have shared his table?"

"No."

"You're insinuating something, what?"

"We were in the messroom when we came off watch and he wanted to talk. He talked of cottage pie, hoping for a long stay in Port Kembla. He didn't talk like a man about to go over the side."

"Let me put you wise to a situation we seamen now sail under. With a scab involved in abnormal circumstance the police will immediately suspect every strike member of the union," Simon said scathingly. "We will have to prove our innocence. Even so our names will be entered in a police file for future reference if another scab on another ship decides to end it all."

"Or is helped." Sam watched Simon for a reaction, stunned when he laughed.

"Sam, I would seriously consider keeping that thought to myself. Remember you shared a conversation after watch and might have been the last to see him. You will be a person of interest to the coppers, your name mentioned in dispatches. Just think about that."

≈

Port Kembla police alerted fishing boats trawling in the area, information passed to Kiama the possibilities of a body washed up on local beaches, instigating searches even farther south due to a strong southerly set. Sombre matters needed immediate attention, the BHP agent in company with a clergyman to notify a young mother who lived in a small cottage in Jubilee St behind the Steelworks Hotel of a husband presumed lost at sea.

With the police onboard conferring with the master, the delegates called a meeting. Simon did not bother seeking nominations for chairman or minute secretary to record minutes, his words tumbling out: "Bentley Reid who joined in Sydney is missing. A deep six, there is no doubt of that and the law will have no hesitation aiming their inquiries in one direction, ours. My advice is say nothing. You saw nothing. You heard nothing. Of the man you know nothing, in fact for all the words ever spoken between Reid and this crowd might account to a few sentences, and that mostly abuse of which it would not be desirable to inform the police."

Sam looked at the inert expressions on the faces of those crowding the messroom; a trimmer even more disinterested than the rest, pulling a battered western paperback novel from his back pocket.

"You won't witness a mate or an engineer being given a hard time by the police, only us. Why? Because Reid happened to be a scab and since our return from the strike there has been a few mentally disturbed individuals ended it all. I suppose you could say a pattern has emerged which is interesting to those with police minds. A man jumped over the side, simple as that. You know nothing and accordingly you say nothing."

Sam again let his eyes pass over the meeting, studying faces, looking for some reaction to the loss of a life at sea. Nothing. How many others in the past met similar fates, volunteers of the 1927 strike, now the 1935 strike? With no convictions possibly even the police with their strikebreaking horses, dogs and batons held blacklegs in low esteem as well.

The meeting ended when the third mate asked for the bosun and delegates to present themselves on the bridge.

≈

BHP sent their agent and a Methodist minister to console the wife of the missing crew member of the *Iron Knob*, the woman of course not considered a widow. The final confirmation of widowhood would be a long time coming to the distraught woman, the Eastern Australian Current running south down the eastern seaboard at four knots.

Now late afternoon the company wanted their ship loaded, flattops on two tracks shunted the full length of the ship loaded with heavy plate and rolled steel joists, labour idle since the vessel tied up.

Singularly each member of the Federated Seamen's Union of Australasia presented themselves on the bridge for questioning by two detectives from Wollongong. The detectives seemed bored by it all, one in particular with a cramp in his right hand from taking notes of the questioning.

Both their minds recalled past bothersome altercations with seamen, well documented for their anti-social and aggressive disposition, this incidence with the ship only hours from its last port the missing man possibly in a state of mindless inebriation. This and foul play would be considered points of interest, an idiosyncrasy of seafaring types, alcohol and vengeance taken in an environment of ideal concealment. Retribution listed high in the line of questioning, the recent bitter and divisive strike which pitted seaman against seaman.

To a man when interviewed in response to sailing with a company volunteer, the stock answer came with a shrug and a few noncommittal words of union policy.

The last man questioned, a trimmer with a raging thirst and his mind set on the Steelworks Hotel, left the bridge much to the relief of the master who ordered commencement of cargo. The police preliminary report noted no firm conclusions as to the fate of AB Bentley Reid missing presumed lost at sea. The time last seen, established by the ordinary seaman, 12:20am.

Simon called another meeting amid rumblings men wanted to go ashore, the bosun chairman and the minute secretary taking minutes. "At this juncture there is no case to answer according to the police. None of us knew Reid and none of us before this sailed with him," he said, adding as if an afterthought: "He took his own miserable life so there's no need for me to begrudgingly welcome him into the union in a month's time."

One man knew, Sam thought with a sick feeling in his stomach. Maybe someone with thoughts of a barmaid in the Steelworks Hotel, sitting in this messroom griping about being late going ashore. Someone with a misguided sense of justice ridding the world of a canker upon organised labour. He needed to say something, anything. He rose to his feet. "Mr Chairman, I move we take the hat around."

Simon's smile sent a chill down Sam's back, his eyes pinpoints boring into his. "Mr Chairman, there is a motion from the ordinary seamen we have a whip-round for Reid's widow. Does anyone know how to deal with that?"

The bosun did. "The motion before the chair is we take up a collection for the supposed widow of Bentley Reid. I say supposed because who knows he might have swum ashore. Have I a seconder for the motion?"

The meeting fell into complete silence.

"Motion declared failed because of the lack of a seconder."

Sam remained on his feet, unable to disguise the resentment in his voice. "Are the delegates at least going to see his wife?"

"Are you volunteering, Sam?" Simon said, still staring at him, cold and menacing.

"Someone should."

"My questions to you are you volunteering?"

Sam looked away, unable to reply.

The bosun uttered the last words, his voice directed at the lowered head of the ordinary seaman: "Son, we are all victims here. Learn to live with it."

28

S AM WONDERED WHY HE stayed on the *Iron Knob*, the thankless work continually overhauling gear stressed to its survey limits on steel cargoes, the rigid industrial policies of the BHP hardly an inducement to remain. An unhappy ship, though he did get home with pig iron, the discharge usually three weeks.

He heard of another seaman reported missing in the Great Australian Bight, heavy weather and alone in the early hours of the twelve to four watch checking deck cargo lashings. The seaman, an ex-company man, initially raised suspicions though never delved deeply into.

There were times when he looked more closely at those passing through the *Iron Knob,* wondering how the strike affected them. Sullen and silent types able to vent their traumatisation with lethal revenge. Always though his mind returned to Simon whose moody face and cold grey eyes held many dark secrets. What did it matter now anyway? The police quickly closed the investigation, and it would be years before the authorities declared Bentley's wife a widow.

Resentment smouldered at stopwork meetings and on ships with volunteers granted full union membership. Simmering hatreds at times erupted violently at the union's capitulation to the shipowners and the Lyons government, epitomised by the gloating attorney general. Menzies, the all-powerful wreathed in glory, the man who neutered and dog collared two virulent enemies.

While the Federated Seamen's Union of Australasia rebuilt its nemesis moved on, inspired like so many ultra-conservatives by a new champion, a brilliant strategist on the European stage. The saviour of his nation, Adolph Hitler.

≈

Simon paid off and for Sam though he could not define it exactly, felt a relief. As a delegate Simon proved intelligent, forceful and articulate. He could with ease turn a meeting to his line of thought, convince the wavering, savvy enough to retreat when the moment called for caution.

Ezra Stein replaced Simon in Port Kembla, the ship loading steel for Geelong and Melbourne. Ezra, though abstaining from alcohol for years, boasted with pride his homeport's dubious reputation for drunks, madmen, anarchists and militants. Combatants of the BHP who considered their major employer who blotted out the sun, a scourge upon society.

Sam fell under Ezra's fatherly influence as did the deck boy, Gabriel O'Hara. Finishing work at noon on Saturday afternoon in Melbourne, Ezra took both aside. His large gangling frame seemed awkward in the close confines of the focastle store, an illusion to the lithe movements of his splicing wire and the roll of his shoulders, the flash and tap of his silk smooth round spike.

Sam thought him in his mid-fifties, a shaggy mop of black hair sprinkled with grey and a lean body which over the years defied the ravages of existing on the victualling of mercenary shipowners under a dozen different flags. He spoke fluent Swedish and Spanish, on the Swedish world roster for ten years shipping out of South American ports on both coasts. An avowed Communist, he made no apology for supporting a revolution to wipe from the face of the earth two mortal enemies, Prime Minister Lyons and Attorney General Menzies.

"What are you two boys planning to do on this fine Saturday afternoon?" he said, tossing a kerosene soaked wad to Sam who with Gabriel finished white leading survey identification stamped in spare overhauled quarter blocks. Even with their combined strength, the task of lifting the large blocks from the deck and shackling them to an inch thick iron bar welded to the deckhead caused an exertion of back and shoulder muscles.

Sam thought for certain write a letter home, reread three of Emily's he received the previous day.

"I'm heading for the Fitzroy Gardens to get splattered by spit."

Both Sam and Gabriel frowned.

"Sydney's got its Domain, Melbourne the Fitzroy Gardens. The enunciation of free and unfettered speech, raucous and ranting, lies and fantasies, quackery and villainy, salvation of the soul or eternal damnation. Snake oil salesmen offering cures for hair loss, cancer, heart failure, fatty livers, back spasms, consumption, colds and flu, epilepsy and all the rest that ails the human body for a shilling. Of course be informed these miraculous elixirs derive from ancient formulas confessed by Himalayan monks under torture and spirited out of the country by secret agents. The medical profession quake in their boots their public release, in dread their profession will become extinct. That's only on a Saturday.

"Now on Sunday out of the woodwork comes the Lord Almighty and women against the demon drink. The world's most ugliest women swaddled in black bed sheets, a mortal sin of debauchery to show even the hint of an ankle. Tambourines ring out and halleluiahs abound, the refrains of hymns to beckon those who have lost their way. Holy water runs like a flash flood to wash away sin and wickedness. Here is not dispensed cures for what ails the body, but the promise of eternal life resting at the feet of Jesus.

"On adjoining stumps the harpies add their shrill voices to the cacophony of the Lordly redeemers, the temperance mob. Their fingers wave accusingly in the face of their wretched victims whose nose aglow might not be from good health but the devil's wicked brew. These shrivelled up hags force our hotels to close at 6:00pm. Make it an offence for a public house to have a lavatory on its premises so forcing imbibers to empty their bursting bladders and loose bowels in the nearest back lanes."

"Could we come with you?" Sam asked, as excited as Gabriel.

"Only if you are desirous of being directed to a tortuous pathway of redemption, seeking a cure for cancer or to banish a craving for strong liquor.

You must remember though the cures both physical and spiritual are not without danger, one might burn a hole in your stomach, the other permanent damage to your eardrums."

"What about politics?"

"Sam, take your pick. There are rightwing fanatics who grovel to government, anarchists on the other stumps hell-bent on its destruction. Leftwing idealists who want to render capitalism defunct. Then there is a far left faction of the Labor Party condemning the Catholic Church and other anti-union zealots for eroding the party's working class principles written under a tree in Queensland. That mob is surely convinced an Italian pope runs the Labor Party."

"Does the United Australia Party have a stump?"

"Oh yes, that pestilence has a few stumps, the lowest of the lowest spat wearing hypocrites masquerading in various forms and speaking in many tongues. Coupled with the religious freaks and their abhorrence of unions only bested by their quaking fear of Old Nick and his pitch fork."

≈

Sam and Gabriel showered and dressed in scrubbed clean dungarees and denim shirts, their clothes paper thin from block sandsoap and deck scrubbers scouring the tough, hardwearing cotton fabric on the tiled bathroom deck. Outfitted for the cold Melbourne autumn afternoon, Sam wore his heavy woollen watchcoat.

The *Iron Knob* lay idle alongside a Yarra River wharf, her four hatches protected by bell tents hauled taut on runners, labour finished until Monday 8:00am. Silent, abaft her funnel a tiny feather of steam quickly lost in the chilly air, the only sign within this ship beat a warm, living heart.

Ezra waited at the top of the gangway, a shout for the two boys to hurry, a wharf watchman informing him a bus to the city would pass at 1:00pm.

The three crossed Princess Bridge, the city and its railway easement now separated by a sluggish and murky river from the vast parklands of its northern reaches.

Grey skies gradually succumbed to patches of watery blue, an occasional sun peeping out which seemed to liven the steps of the throngs of people heading for the Fitzroy Gardens. Groups of noisy young men vied to catch the attention of aloof young females attired in the height of fashion, feigning disinterest, but their glowing eyes telling another story.

Melbourne in the 1860's commissioned British civil engineer Clement Hodgkinson to design a series of inner city parks from open fields and mosquito infested marshland, recommending with Melbourne's cold climate the selection criteria be limited to exotic trees and shrubs, the exception being some outstanding natives species such as araucaria bidwilli, Port Jackson and Moreton Bay figs. In his grand plan mature English elm and oak would define pathways and avenues, their sturdy trunks and lush foliage giving strollers the impression of walking through green and leafy tunnels.

The yearly cycle of nature over the years enriched the soil, compost for raised garden plots of rhododendron and azalea, ferns and bromeliads, overpowering jasmine and wisteria festooned arbours for the weary to rest beneath. Silver birch and a wide variety of maples added to the northern hemisphere aspect of Hodgkinson's design, the cynical remarking those of British descent would be hard put to feel homesick whilst traversing Melbourne's prolific parks and gardens.

Speakers preferred the more exposed and wide sweeping lawn areas because it encouraged larger attendances to gather and hear their rhetoric; for some a more sinister reason, affording a better view of approaching authority and a clear escape route.

On sunny weekends there could be upwards of thirty speakers cajoling and tempting, lying and soul saving, tricking with offers of spurious schemes and miracle cures, enthralling the hundreds who made their afternoon destination the Fitzroy Gardens. The speakers begrudgingly gave each other space to create a personal perimeter for their respective audiences, a more intense penetration of their either damning or seductive avowals.

Ezra pointed at a man in a grubby suit he may have slept in, a not overly clean collarless white shirt buttoned to the throat, standing perfectly erect on a small stool. The man worked his gums and lips to activate saliva, his eyes aglow with fanaticism, a flat hand salute above a large head which supported a slicked down mat of black hair. "Last time I saw him a gang baying for blood chased him from the park."

"Does it get violent?" Gabriel asked, moving closer to Ezra.

"Word wise it can at times. That particular raving lunatic though comes in for a fair share of abuse."

The speaker paused to wipe his slicked chin, his glands though producing more than he could swallow which he rolled into a ball and spat.

"Have any of you with the exception of the larrikins I espy lurking in your number, any notion what a loaf of bread cost a German family in 1923?" the speaker in a falsetto voice demanded of his growing audience, a few supporters outnumbered by a large group armed with stones in their pockets.

"I dunno," one of the armed said, his hand in his pocket warming his missile. He turned to four of his mates who shrugged and shook their heads. "Go on, Adolph, tell us what a loaf of bread costs in Germany in 1923?"

The speaker accepted the name of his Fuehrer as a worthy accolade, though wary of the contributor remembering him from last week as one of the ruffians causing him to run for his life.

"Before the glorious ascension of the National Socialist German Workers Party, one loaf of bread in 1923 costs 200 billion marks! 200 billion marks!"

"What's a billion?" a father with two children playing between his legs inquired.

"One billion marks is a million marks multiplied by one thousand, my friend, and a loaf of bread costs 200 times that! A man would need a sturdy cart on iron axels to carry such money to pay the baker."

"What's that worth in real money, mate, our bloody fucking quids?" a ruffian asked, the recipient of hearty back slaps from his mates for his refined articulation.

Portentously a large crowd began to gather around the speaker, causing his acute senses to danger to come alert. "Almost nothing in our money, a few pennies."

"That's bullshit! No loaf of bread is worth what you're saying!" Among the crowd the Fitzroy push numbers swelled, many with hard liquor addling their brains. "I can get a loaf of bread from the baker for sixpence! Threepence if it's a few days old. Why don't the dumb Germans wait a week and get their bread cheaper?" This brought a roar of laugher from the push, now eighteen strong and their courage almost at full peak.

The speaker began to look for an escape route, women and children easily pushed aside in flight. "I lie, do I? I lie, you declare? Do you labour for your bread?"

"Ain't worked for years. Ain't any jobs I knows of," the man guffawed, exposing bare and nicotine stained gums.

"Then I would suggest forthwith you take immediate passage to Germany. Unlike the canker of Great Britain, America and decadent Europe there is no unemployment in Germany. In glorious Germany all have gainful employment and march proudly with heads held high to their workplaces. Toiling without recourse to discord at their lathes, hammering at their anvils, measuring and filing at their work benches, busy on the factory floor creating the means to make Germany strong. Crisscrossing the land new roads and bridges, an entire nation singing joyously in praise of their beloved Fuehrer and the dignity of work he has created."

Ezra's eyes narrowed. "Why do German workers sing joyously going to work?"

"Simple, my brother, because German workers are paid high wages. Offered by their benevolent employers and the state subsidised housing and low cost food and services. Women work with men for equal pay and have their young cared for in government crèches. The National Socialist German Workers

Party ensures each worker is treated equally and fairly and that workers and industrialists stride forward together with a single purpose, Germany."

"So these Utopian conditions were not won by German trade unions?" Ezra ground his teeth. "This workers paradise is a gift from the Fuehrer after he abolished trade unions and murdered their leaders?"

"The brother lies," the speaker said, then scoffed: "In the new Germany there is no need for unions. All German workers are happy and contented, secure in their employment and joyous in their service to their employer and the state."

"Earning hundreds of thousands of billions of marks each week?"

"Of course not, Chancellor Hitler abolished war reparations imposed by the warmongering British, French and United States Jewry. The Fuehrer with a single and contemptuous swipe of his hand removed a score and ten of zeros from the old Second Reich mark. The German working man and woman of the Third Reich can now afford their loaves of family bread and much, much more."

"So the need for a sturdy cart came to an end with Hitler's edict to repudiate Germany's war debt, its debt to humanity for the utter ruin it inflicted on Europe? Millions dead, gassed and maimed?" Ezra persisted.

"Be it known the world declared war on Germany! That it took the entire world to bring her to her knees! Manacled by reparations imposed by corrupt and avaricious Jewry!" the speaker shrieked, so enthralled by his invective he forgot his vulnerability to attack. "Glorious Germany will never again bow to the world under the leadership of Adolph Hitler! Beloved by his people!"

Ezra forced his way through the push debating in their alcoholic haze whether or not to prematurely end the tirade, the speaker definitely not on their list of toleration, a ranting imbecile good for baiting before drawing blood with a well-aimed stone.

Ezra now stood only a few feet from the speaker and level with him nose to nose. "So you are perpetrating the myth that this fascist dictator, this hysterical blabbering murderer of racial minorities, the disabled, political adversaries, union officials and Communists, has ordered his industrialists to force upon their joyous workers high wages, conditions dreamed of only in working class heaven? Is that what you are spewing in a torrent of lies to the gullible?"

The speaker puffed up his body to make himself appear larger than his adversary. Not wanting for courage against an enemy, he bleated: "Retract that statement! Adolph Hitler is the man of the century! Of vision! A man of the people! A man the government of Australia speak highly of and seek to emulate!"

"So what we see in newsreels of brown uniformed youth goosestepping with stiff arms are happy workers returning home from their lathes and anvils? I will tell you what those posturing brutes are, fascist thugs ordered by your Hitler to wipe Germany of organised labour, Jews and Communists and his besieged opponents!"

The speaker turned scarlet. "Fear mongering initiated by world Jewry with its vile roots embedded in London, Paris and New York!"

"Are we to believe that this decomposed fascist doctrine you pay allegiance to has no concentration camps filled with union officials, Communists, cripples, the insane, gypsies and of course a wide selection of Jewry?"

"Chancellor Hitler to right the wrongs suffered by his nation has been forced to incarcerate anti-German individuals and members of seditious organisations. His hand forced because Jews within his own country and overseas advocate the overthrow of the legitimate German government. Yes, he has jailed some criminal union officials and traitorous Communists, tried and convicted in the nation's courts of sedition and industrial sabotage."

"Hitler went to jail where he should have rotted for the rest of his life. Where he belonged living with vermin and his own shit in a bucket."

"Communist blackguard! The National Socialist German Workers Party and Chancellor Hitler Germany's glorious future! Adolph Hitler advocating world peace and prosperity through honest toil!"

"Quite a misnomer the socialist part," Ezra shouted back. "A worker goes on strike in Germany and he is never seen again. A man who practices his

Jewish faith has his shopfront splattered with paint, then stripped of his life's hard work and savings. That's your National Socialist German Workers Party, shining light and benefactor of the working class. Lies!"

The speaker descended into an apoplexy of rage, his forced breathing rattling in his chest; he looked to the heavens and slowly raised his shaking arm in a fascist salute. This brought a cheer from the push who readied for attack.

"You defame the name and glory of Germany! You slander the pure Aryan spirit which crushed the unjust and repressive yoke of surrender forced upon Germany! Germany forced to fight ruthless and merciless foes who threatened her sovereignty!"

Ezra with barely enough time to duck and retreat, felt the first stone whistle past his head, missing the speaker by a few inches who again showed his bravery by not yet retreating. "The Australian government recognises the Germany of Adolph Hitler! Applauds his grand achievements in leading the world out of the Depression by steadfast government initiatives and fiscal policies!"

Ezra felt the crush behind him and knew events would soon take another turn. "You refer of course to the Australian government of Lyons and Menzies. Two honourable gentlemen from the far right who revere Adolph's jackbooted policy of destroying organised labour, murdering union officials and sending strikers to concentration camps."

"Wash your fetid mouth with caustic! Prevaricator!" A second stone missed the speaker by a fraction of an inch, his safety now a real concern as he saw members of the push reaching down and scooping handfuls of quartz gravel for a shrapnel effect. Even though infused with the intense inner fire of the cause, last week he barely escaped a beating, this week with more of the hooligans present he thought retreat the more sensible part of valour and to regroup again next Saturday.

Ezra thought of a final retort at the fleeing figure, changed his mind and moved on, Sam and Gabriel following. Three nearby speakers promised God in varying forms; one vengeful and unforgiving for sinners and fornicators, another merciful if those present abstained from brewed, distilled and fermented liquors. The third, grossly obese with a mean and hawkish face, cajoled the crippled, the maimed, the diseased, demanding a substantial tithe for miracles. From his slick tongue flowed a litany of outlandish cures, for the crippled to throw down their crutches and the terminally ill to come forward and throw themselves at his sanctified feet.

The pastor's anger dissipated on the flight of the fascist pursued by his tormenters, may a thousand demons flay the hide from him. By proximity exposed to his ungodly ranting, though he did agree with some of the German chancellor's methods of dealing with God's lapses of concentration when creating man, filling his concentration camps with blacks and deviants.

≈

Sam and Gabriel thoroughly enjoyed their afternoon with Ezra, the company of a crusty seaman who overcame an ocean of booze to see the folly of his ways before his liver became a lifeless sponge. A man thrown out of more waterfront bars than he could remember, brothels and sly grog joints. Memories of various and extremely painful venereal diseases, broken bones, lost teeth and the humility of waking up in gutters with dogs urinating on him.

A mature lady in Sydney with strong views on the hazards of drink and hopelessly in love with Ezra, set his downhill and wasted life on a different tack. For this gentle female soul he gave up alcohol and the company of women of dubious morals and dressed more befitting a gentleman in the company of a lady of obvious breeding. Ezra survived the strike as a single man, his life's savings donated to the strike fund to help men supporting families. This brought home to him a disturbing fact, what would happen to him and others like him when he became too old to climb a gangway?

Seamen with no security of employment, aged and unable to work, a life of penury threatened their final years, their retirement fund their last payoff. The union raised the issue at times, but with the union under assault from different factions, the issue found itself buried in long list of future award proposals.

Ezra felt pleased with his encounter with fascism, buying his young companions dinner in The Princess Bridge Hotel on the corner of Flinders and Swanston Sts. As a bonus and full of youthful exuberance the pair of them would appreciate the beautiful painted curves of a young nymph named Chloe who occupied a wall in the main foyer. This brought a smile to his face when he recalled the outrage and moral indignation from the Methodist and Presbyterian wowsers prevalent in Melbourne who sneaked an outrageous peep of the magnificent body of the naked nineteen-year-old beauty, even worse she should titillate the drink sodden wretches who imbibed in sinful public houses.

29

EVEN WITH THE STRIKE ended eight months bitter divisions continued to split the Federated Seamen's Union of Australasia, making it vulnerable to highly disruptive and organised groups within the rank and file aligned to either the United Australia Party or the Labor Party infiltrated by the hierarchy of the Catholic Church. Holding varied views, one major point of internal dissention united them, hatred of officials with membership of the Communist Party of Australia.

The *Iron Knob* like most ships on the Australian coast did not escape the conflicts. For long periods the ship would be free of deck and engine room tensions, minor union matters resolved by the bosun or delegates without the need of meetings or union intervention. At general meetings the rules of debate were usually relaxed, within a set agenda an open forum, but not so when groupers joined.

Challenging, able to recite word for word union rules, the award clause by clause, quoting the Navigation Act, and writing their own minutes. Resolutions the ship correspond with federal office over matters personally raised at recent stopwork meetings and rulings sought from officials on contentious award clauses. Forever goading and rendering the delegates ineffective. Blinkered and dogmatic, grouper activity soon altered any balance of congeniality gained with other departments, especially officers and engineers.

Strong willed delegates with unwavering beliefs in solidarity took offence, some physically or with such damning articulation the usurpers kept a sullen peace.

Groupers made their presence known quickly. An incidence occurred in Newcastle discharging under the iron ore gantries when two well-known groupers joined and called a meeting to ascertain the ship's status of militancy and strict adherence to union policy. The deck delegates, hardened Port Kembla comrades, listened patiently to their militant spiel, then resigned and called for nominations. Sam observed with interest when the two men rejected their nominations, the most vocal of the pair declaring with two bad discharges earned in disputes supporting union policy a third would automatically suspend him for life. This of course exempted him from any future shipboard industrial action. His mate offered a less dramatic excuse; without the encumbrance of a delegate's responsibility he would maintain a vigilant observation on matters pertaining to the award, specifically non-observance by BHP so advising the delegates of breaches with recommended action.

Godfrey Finch rose from his chair and grasped the shoulders of the future observer and dragged him to his feet. "To what rightwing political pack do you and your martyred mate belong to? All you know is attack and undermine, gut the union and install your rightwing stooges? You're not a scab, your book is proof of that, but for me the slime you are is even more insidious because you and your cohorts are inside our union devouring it. This meeting is not looking for delegates blessed with oily tongues and the cunning of cornered rats, then again vermin craftiness not considered excess baggage for delegates taking on the BHP. I retract my resignation, but not my mate who is shaking his head. Have we another nomination or a volunteer, someone worthy of the union?"

Sam put his hand up.

Later, Godfrey took Sam aside. "What we have witnessed grows in strength because of frustration, a perceived lack of direction from our officials and a bitterness that still lingers. All of that giving momentum to the groupers who if possible would not belong to the union, any union for that matter. Those who support the rightwing of the Labor Party, even worse those who believe the conservatives are the best arbiters of industrial law, and of course the religious freaks. Personally I would have thought Jesus working as a carpenter in an oppressed country would have been an early union organiser so quashing the religious nuts loathing of organised labour. Unfortunately not so, and you should hear them bellow when their union dues are payable. I just tell them you don't pay, mate, you're over the side. Works wonders."

"Why don't we expel those who attack the union?"

"In simple words we are a democracy. We tell that to the world and the world calls us liars. Attrition will eventually rid us of them because in their small numbers the mass of the union leaning to the left will eventually overcome them. We have a lot of comrades and I would estimate one comrade the equal of ten whining groupers. Take heart, we have a new course being set by true unionists like Elliott, Smith, Bird and Franklin. Men who will not desert the cause or ever lose their direction in making the Federated Seamen's Union of Australasia a strong and feared organisation?"

Sam frowned. "Feared?"

"By the many who would destroy us and of course shipowners and governments of both persuasions."

"Thankfully not a government like Germany."

"Germany, now that's another matter entirely. We would have one hell of a fight on our hands there. Where that maniac is heading and the consequences for the rest of the world is frightening. Equally disturbing, how world leaders pay their respects to this arrogant and raving psychopath. Though not difficult to comprehend when he is exterminating union officials and crushing worker dissent. Wouldn't the federal government love his army of thugs to bash a few wharfies and seamen's heads?"

"Godfrey, we still live in hard times."

"We certainly do, and to my mind things aren't getting any better. For you who will meet a girl and have kids later in life, I can only wonder what the future holds. We live in a world of abundance and wealth, a world that can support and nurture humankind in full and plenty, but no, not for those who produce with their sweat and calloused hands the goods and services.

Humanity, except for the privileged elite, destined to toil their miserable lives away in horrible workplaces buried in debt."

"That's a bit sensational."

"For you time will tell. Now bring your mind back to the *Iron Knob*, without doubt a nasty workplace, and prepare yourself to do daily battle with BHP and their gold festooned industrial gurus masquerading as mates and engineers."

≈

Sam paid off the *Iron Knob* in Port Kembla and caught the 3:00pm train to Sydney. He felt the usual euphoria released from articles, signing off with a good payoff, money saved in the bank and not a single thought of how difficult it might be getting another job.

He felt a stirring within as he turned the corner and hurried his step. Emily in his mind, waiting at home, the long wait until the family slept soundly, the agony of touching but unable to release what surged through both their bodies. Claire and the girls vying for his attention, what his plans were while he tried not look where Emily's dress fell around her hips, her bottom, her breasts.

In one of her letters she apologised for giving notice at Mark Foy's, possibly ahead of an official termination when her poor health deteriorated over winter and her absences more frequent and longer. The doctor prescribed bronchodilators, but when this treatment failed to alleviate her symptoms he recommended an injection of epinephrine; this proved even worse than the disease with vomiting and diarrhoea, Claire having to nurse her daughter for a week. Her last letters cheerful as she recovered, her thoughts only of him, wishing him by her side.

A household celebration of his homecoming, dinner at the Greek's or Chinese, the girls usually opting for the Greek's fish and chips served on large willow pattern plates on red and white check oilcloth. In these happy times Claire wondered what the future held for her family, especially Sam and Emily. She continually worried about her eldest, her health deteriorating as she grew older, not the improvement the family doctor offered hope when she reached adolescence.

≈

Sam joined the *Kooliga* after two weeks ashore, one of only three ordinary seamen who stood for the job. From the wharf the ship made a picture no marine artist would clamour to capture; devoid of rake, fashion plates and fresh paint, smart bunting flying from taut halyards. A not so old workhorse scarred by encounters with wharves and unforgiving pylons, managed by frugal actuaries who counted every drop of paint, inch of rope, and pound of grease. The *Kooliga* discharged barley for Tooths and Tooheys breweries loaded in Wallaroo, South Australia. Normally a sense of company pride for most owners, their distinctive funnel colours freshly painted, but not so for parsimonious McIlwraith McEacharn, their *Kooliga's* stovepipe funnel rising forty feet from the amidships accommodation blackened and blistered by frequent internal fires. Both sides and a few feet forward of the funnel and almost the same height, like submarine periscopes, two cowled engine room ventilators.

When she came down her Scottish slipway ten years previous her cargo gear arrangement specified high ranging tidal ports, rigged with exceptionally long derricks set on equally proportioned foremast and mainmast and tapering topmasts. She cradled No.1 derricks on the focastle head, No.2 derricks housed to the foremast table, No.3 derricks landed aft of the amidships accommodation, and No.4 derricks crutched on the poop. Crew accommodated fore and aft; firemen, trimmers and greasers over the propeller, deck in the focastle head. Befitting a long shipowner tradition of cramming as many uncertified seamen as possible in the smallest, noisiest and weather sensitive areas of their ships, the *Kooilga* broke no new ground in comfort.

Offering meagre protection for northern hemisphere winters lookout cabs partially enclosed the bridge wings, a small wheelhouse and chartroom.

Hefting his seabag over his shoulder, he felt the reassuring thump of wood and metal bindings against the ship's side as he climbed the gangway. He would shake hands with the delegates and show his union book and ask the question now a way of life; any scabs in her?

30

1938

A MOTHER'S WISH CAME true when her daughter married a young AB, both far too young, but the enduring love she witnessed between her daughter and her chosen man proof their bond would survive the test of time. Emily chose a white dress that clung from her body in satiny folds, glistening in captured light as did the ecstatic glow in her eyes. Departing from tradition, Claire gave her daughter away, Sam's best man a chance encounter in the union rooms with Josh Atkinson between ships.

Emily modelled her gown in the kitchen, again against tradition with Sam in awe of the angelic presence of his bride-to-be who would only when she walked down the aisle look more beautiful. She exuded radiance absent for a long time from her life and Sam's heart went out to her, a silent wish that from this day on the Emily of old gave way to the new.

She smiled shyly and ran her hands down her sides before clasping them modestly in front of her. "Are you pleased with me, Sam?"

If his life depended on it words would not come, a jumble caught in his constricted chest.

"Sam?

Mary covered her mouth to muffle a giggle, tall and gangly and a mirror image of her mother. "Hope when you're married you get a bigger bed than your old one."

"Mary!" Claire chastened, putting a dampener on the high spirits. "Enough of this talk of beds! We have a wedding to plan."

Sam haggled with the publican of the Butcher's Arms Hotel in Harris St for a small wedding reception in the dining room after the hotel closed. The publican, sympathetic to the cause of seamen, agreed on a price for a family of five and seven guests at 12/6 a head; three course dinner, six bottles of fair quality house wine for the toasts and two rounds of drinks, after that a whip-round if thirsts so warranted.

He bickered, the price in excess of his budget; the publican's florid face laced with a filigree of purple veins and a scarlet nose creased in thought, a mental abacus calculating profit and loss. Only for seamen for whom he held only the greatest respect and with fervent hope his generosity circulated around the waterfront, he would include a wedding cake and three rounds of drinks, the last round exclusive of spirits.

Sam agreed, leaving him from his wedding budget enough for two nights in a hotel in seaside Manly and money for a double bed after moving the girls out of their bedroom into the kitchen, in effect changing places with him. The privilege of home ownership. Not quite, but a £200 deposit paid the rent man and owner, Julius Hymans, and the remaining £200 in three months came close.

Money saved that survived many temptations when a shopfront felt his nose pressed against it. Slowly accruing, Sam and Emily drawing even closer buying of her childhood home. This humble Pyrmont dwelling attached to other self-effacing family homes a starting point in life, something grander possibly across the bridge in years to come. It also gave a secured home for Emily's mother and sisters.

31

REPAIRING STORM DAMAGE TO forward hatch coamings in Storey and Keers Balmain ship repair facility, Sam joined the *Iron Warrior* in early September, the ship sailing to Newcastle to load steel for Geelong, Melbourne and Adelaide. If the ship remained on the steel run he could be home for Christmas, his first as a married man.

His head filled with thoughts of Christmas with his family, turkey with all the trimmings, plum pudding and custard, gifts under the Christmas tree. This Christmas would be bountiful, a feast of plenty, the years of impoverishment locked away in the dim past. Demand for steel and cement, timber and bricks, goods and services which translated to jobs gave a demoralised nation a glimmer of hope their world at last moved forward.

With new builds on the slipways seamen were as buoyant as the optimists who observed the first wisps of smoke issuing from long dormant factory chimneys.

As if some mystic hand passed over the nation the cogs of industry started to turn, money flowing into empty pockets. The socialist press editorialised why, the frenzied militarisation of a resurgence Germany, the United States, British Empire and France apprehensive, where before only accolades abounded of where Chancellor Hitler's expansive attentions focused.

Even if Germany raised the hackles of traditionalist with its pagan-like rallies and medieval streets filled with goosestepping Aryan youth, only the highest of tributes acclaimed its charismatic leader for not only overcoming crushing reparation demanded by its conquerors, but the worst financial crisis in history. A strong and united Germany, a bulwark against a new world threat, the Union of Soviet Socialist Republics.

Euphoric waves of platitudes continued to flow from the government benches of the Australian parliament, Germany's purge of organised labour with socialist allegiances, strengthening its military, and fortifying its borders against Russian aggression. Japan also came in for commendation from the government, a few on the opposition benches likeminded. Japan an emerging Asian giant with a fleet of modern ships sailing the world's trade routes.

Many in federal parliament found themselves in common agreement of the importance of both Germany and Japan in trade, and that their foreign policies enforced by military expeditions were of no concern to Australia. The press hailed it as a financial coup, the November sale of 300,000 tons of BHP pig-iron to feed the furnaces of Japanese steel mills, proof the world emerging from the Depression.

32

THE *IRON WARRIOR* BERTHED early afternoon at the ore jetty, a lazy swell from the northeast gently lifting the heavily laden ship on its straining, creaking coirs. In twenty-four hours her cargo of iron ore discharged and transferred by a complex system of conveyor belts and surge bins to the steelworks swaddled in a permanent haze of red dust, black smoke and glittering shards of fine particulates. Forward movements shift ship to a loading berth, washout and load steel for Adelaide, iron ore Whyalla for either Port Kembla or Newcastle. Sam's dream of Christmas home almost a reality.

Emily caught the midday train from Sydney to Wollongong, booking a room in the Crown Hotel close by the station. He eased her down on the double bed the moment he took her in his arms. Their mouths locked together, discarding their clothes on the floor, naked and both lost in their urge to devour each other's bodies, over far too quickly.

"When, Sam?"

He lifted his weight from her and rolled on his back. "Probably just over a week. We're shifting in the morning, then washout for the wharfies to start work on the afternoon shift. I'll be a bit late getting back to the hotel, our need to be on deck when the gear is set up for loading. Good news though, I reckon Christmas is certain."

"The hotel is expensive," she said distantly, something else on her mind.

"We can afford it."

"We could if I worked."

"There's no need for you to work, Emily. I am the provider. That's my role as head of the family."

"Quite a large family you inherited."

"Your mother seems settled into her role as a sole parent."

"She hears nothing from Father."

"Which bodes well for her future."

"She used to worry herself almost sick I would fall pregnant, but never raised it with either of us." she said forlornly. "There were times when I thought so, but no. Why, Sam?"

"Some people never have a baby, the way it is."

"Yes, but why?"

"We could see a doctor."

"For him to tell me I am not a woman?" Tears welled in her eyes. "That's what he would tell me. You are not a woman, Emily Wright! Your body is incapable of bearing a child."

"He would not. Emily, it might be me. We share each other, you and me. Do we need more than Emily and Sam?" He eased her on top of him, settling her between his legs, with both hands gripping the satiny cushions of her bottom. She drew a deep breath and guided him inside her.

Her eyes closed, she murmured a prayer.

≈

Berthed at No.6 wharf and lowering a deck hose down No.1 hatch, Sam jolted as the deep throated whistle of a ship startled him, the rust streaked bow of a ship high out of the water passing through the breakwaters. The ship secured two tugs alongside, her engines full-astern, swinging to head her bow out to sea and parallel with No.4 berth. Of the sixteen men forward thirteen were Lascars, a uniformed white officer and apprentice in the eyes, a white carpenter standing by the windlass.

The name on the port bow needed fresh paint and the general appearance of the ship evidence the British tramp's next cargo would not be taking her home, but still discernible: *Dalfram*.

≈

The first disgruntled comments concerned the heel block of No.2 amidships derrick, an object of penetrating scrutiny by the seasoned afternoon shift delegate. With the sharp point of his penknife he scraped away flaky paint and white lead residue, and to his delight saw beneath the block number and survey date chisel scoring where SWL 5T should have been stamped in the metal.

Concerned, the delegate informed the foreman he should as an urgent matter of safety check the chief officer's gear register book. What other gear aloft and on deck might have ambiguous survey markings? The foreman studied the chisel marks, he thought more a chipping hammer score and of the opinion three indents assuredly the number five, another two a little deeper T for tons.

A confrontation smouldering long before the commencement of the shift began to unfold, personality against personality, a recent old score to settle. Retribution for the sacking of a prominent member accused by the foreman of being drunk and incapable of performing his duties. The delegate would need to confer with his secretary about this series breach of safety, a recommendation all the gear be checked against the gear register book.

At 5:10pm with flattop railway wagons loaded with steel plate shunted alongside the ship, hooks lowered to the deck as proof the gear until proven otherwise unsafe to commence loading. The mate and the bosun calculated it would take all night to check survey markings against the gear register book, a time factor BHP industrial bluntly refused to accept.

Replacing the heel block with a new block did not alter the ultimatum all the gear be checked for current survey. BHP carrying many battle scars inflicted by the Waterside Workers Federation already set in motion notification to the arbitration commission that a dispute existed on the *Iron Warrior*, the company seeking an immediate order of resumption of work or face stand downs and heavy penalties. Their case against the federation damning, their entire fleet bound by strict safety regulations as set forth by the classification society, company ships manned by competent and long serving certified officers who followed without digression the safety guidelines inherent within the company.

Sam with the bosun, Dave Burrows, inspected the heel block at the centre of attention, a more troubling thought in his mind, Emily waiting for him in the hotel and hungry. "We know this gear's in survey. We overhauled it."

Dave shrugged. "The entire afternoon shift has a name for their foreman you wouldn't repeat a hundred yards from mixed company. This is not a heel block, this is payback."

"So we have to lower everything so the wharfies can inspect the survey markings?"

"If these blokes are aiming for a stoush, yeah. No way is this lot going to take the word of one of us aloft in a bosun's chair."

"Couldn't we haul their delegate aloft?"

The bosun grinned. "Yeah, we could that, then he'd want certificates for the gantline, chair, tail block and shackle."

"Could we talk with the delegate?"

"Only when all else fails and sound reasoning is no longer a bargaining factor. BHP won't be able to locate the wharfies branch secretary at this time of day, these blokes are going home. The ship's in dispute and that's that."

≈

Ted Roach, Port Kembla branch secretary of the Waterside Workers Federation, let the expected call from BHP industrial ring out. Not so the call a few minutes earlier from his delegate aware Ted never left the office until 6:00pm about a serious safety issue on the *Iron Warrior*. His men could take an early mark and stand again in the morning. Such disputes were a regular occurrence in the port and a night for it to simmer in the company indoctrinated minds of BHP industrial would not heighten its impact. With the least amount of bluster he would resolve it in the morning and his men could return to work assured of safety in their workplace.

The *Iron Warrior* represented a mere blip in the branch secretary's highly active mind, something far more important looming in the port; a message from Melbourne a ship would soon arrive in Port Kembla almost certainly chartered by Mitsui to load pig iron for Japan. An avowed member of the Communist Party, Ted held tenacious views on Japan's ruthless occupation of China, shipments of war materiel from the port banned.

China's suffering and genocide under Japanese militarism became an issue of extreme importance for the Port Kembla branch. Ted's powerful oration left no doubt where his and his members sympathies lay, resolutions bombarding the federal government to impose trade sanctions not only against Japan, but also Germany.

The mere mention of sanctions recommended by a fanatical Communist union against respected trading partners causing the government to unleash a barrage of condemnation. So the venomous snake with its back broken somehow found it could still inject its lethal venom upon the nation. It needed another hammer blow, a boot ground into its belly before lopping off its head.

Ted snubbed his nose at the government as he did the polluting behemoth he shared the narrow Illawarra coastal strip with, which daily coated his office desk with a fine red dust. Ridicule for the commercial and industrial chambers of commerce who sang the praises of unfettered industrialisation, requesting company executives visit the south coast hospitals to give cheer to maimed heavy industrial workers.

What he read on his gritty desk in the newspapers angered him, editorials no more than patronising accolades for BHP's coup in selling 300,000 tons of pig iron to Japan. Australian industry on the move! Australia trading its way to prosperity! Australia and Japan, their futures entwined!

He held no qualms what the genuflecting face of Japan, the false image it showed the world, would do with BHP's pig iron; bombs and tanks, surgical steel for bayonets used in a favourite military sport, impaling Chinese babies.

Ted in his methodical and seemingly laid-back style planned for the next day; settle the *Iron Warrior* dispute with the ship's delegates before breakfast, then as his men began collecting for the day's labour allocation convene a meeting to discuss the *Dalfram*. He wouldn't stop the labour call for the *Dalfram*, in fact he wanted his members to stand for the job and go about their normal duties. Not an easy task with the fully unionised port and a union run roster, a port that overwhelmingly supported sanctions against Japan and Germany. Port Kembla, a militant conclave with a single mind and purpose, to outsiders run with military precision and allegiance to the union and its strict code of conduct.

At 7:00am the *Iron Warrior's* delegates, bosun and branch secretary met on after deck, Ted seemingly more agitated than usual. He came straight to the point, could the bosun and delegates vouch for the safety and current survey of the ship's gear?

"Yes on all counts. On steel cargoes we never stop working on the gear. My blokes don't know what a paintbrush looks like," the bosun said.

"You would say the block in question is an oddity?"

"Someone careless with a chisel, chipping hammer, yes."

"We rarely have trouble on Australian ships, not like some we regularly get in the port."

Much hinged on the outcome of this informal meeting on deck, Sam puzzled why the branch secretary did not take the master to task and demand to see the ship's gear register book. "The ship's gear register book will prove it," he said.

"Of course it will, but I would rather take the word of the bosun and the delegates than from those who have traded their principles for a corporate pat on the head. Our lads get a little feisty when it comes to safety, usually with good cause. I'm telling my blokes we've got the word of the bosun and delegates and that's good enough for me as it will be for them." The four men shook hands.

"Probably unjustly because we reckon she's a rough feeder, but would you like some breakfast? Coffee?" Sam said.

"Thank you, but time is not on my side as my men tumble out of bed. I have another matter which assuredly is going to be worthy of some hysterical reportage of shareholder panic if my premonition proves correct."

≈

Ted's corralling of his members occurred in the laneway at the back of the pickup, a hurried count of the growing numbers enough for him to open the impromptu meeting with a broadside of policy.

"The *Dalfram* lying at No.4 this morning will be calling for labour to load pig iron for the Japanese steelmaker Mitsui. Being aware of this port's policy in respect of trade with fascist regimes, particularly Japan, BHP will swear on a dozen mother's lives the cargo is destined for Shanghai and not where the Melbourne branch has told me, Kobe. Our port policy is irretraceable, but we are dealing with a hardnosed industrialist and a government who believes Hideki Tojo and Adolph Hitler are worthy of sainthood. Comrades, we must and we will proceed with extreme caution.

"You all know me and that I am not blessed with an overly long fuse when it comes to dealing with shipowners and BHP. My first reaction, to hell with the *Dalfram,* a resolution without a second thought let her sink alongside. So I would put to you an alternative resolution that we give the *Dalfram* her gangs and go about our business as normal until we find out the truth where the ship is destined."

"If BHP says Shanghai how can we prove otherwise?" Barnaby Moore, one of Ted's port committee asked.

Ted's street fighter's instincts sensed an undercurrent of resentment among his members, almost to a man to immediately blacklist the *Dalfram*. "BHP well aware of port policy will not change its position on a Chinese port of discharge. The sailing board when the ship throws off her last lines will be Shanghai. The pilot leaving the bridge at Toothbrush Island will shake hands with the captain and wish him a safe voyage to China. You don't need to be a clairvoyant to know that, we are surrounded by rogues with a single driving force, greed.

"I will be boarding the ship with you this morning, but I won't be entering into meaningful discussion with the captain or his officers, me I'll be heading for the focastle to have a few words with the crowd. Also you up and coming classification surveyors who enjoyed an early mark on the *Iron Warrior* yesterday evening, I've spoken with the bosun and delegates and have their assurances their gear is safe and in survey. I believe them, and am recommending you do, too."

≈

While Ted disappeared in the focastle, his members proceeded to their allocated hatches; winch drivers kicked open drain cocks, men on deck setting up the gear, silently, sullenly. Preventers took the weight as guys paid out, yardarms lowered to plumb over railway flattops loaded with tubs of pig iron.

The serang, more intent on turning his men to with chipping hammers and pots of red lead, mumbled he did not speak English fluently enough to converse at length, and to conclude whatever business brought the agitated Port Kembla branch secretary of the Waterside Workers Federation into the crew's accommodation quickly.

"I need to know where your next port is," Ted said, unperturbed by the brusqueness of the serang, but it brought an amused smile to his otherwise serious face; the master would have served tea and muffins, ingratiating himself to a powerful and fearful entity who could with the flick of his finger bring to a halt cargo operations.

The gruff serang changed his mind about his grasp of English. "Kobe. Why you ask?"

"Of course it's bloody Kobe! This port has a policy of blacklisting ships loading for Japan."

"The master would have told you where the ship is loading. Why come to me?"

"Because like the loyal company servant he is he would have said Shanghai."

"Are you satisfied with my information?"

Ted stuck his hand out and the serang, who blended almost invisibly in the darkness of the focastle, took it with a perplexed scowl on his face. "Speaking to a truthful man, yes I am. Enjoy your stay in Port Kembla, it may be longer than you expect."

Emerging from the focastle, he paused at No.1 hatch for a tub of pig iron to cross the deck. At No.2 hatch two foremen stevedores were in discussion with the chief mate. Ted's presence onboard did not bode well. Of all three he asked two questions.

Destination of the cargo? Shanghai.

Mitsui charter? Yes.

He thought the information over for a moment, scratching itchy stubble on his chin. His members at No.1 and No.2 hatch could hear him clearly. "Comrades, your branch secretary has been informed the cargoes destination is Shanghai. Let me inform you I know otherwise, this pig iron is heading straight for the blast furnaces of Japan and then turned against our Chinese comrades. I am declaring the *Dalfram* black! Let its cargo of blood rot alongside!"

≈

With the *Dalfram's* cargo blacklisted recriminating communications passed between BHP head office in Melbourne and Canberra, Menzies immediately accusing the federal office of the Waterside Workers Federation of a serious breach of foreign policy protocol instigated by their rogue Port Kembla branch. The attorney general knew well the port's branch secretary, on his desk a thick dossier of the man and his close cohorts seditious activities spanning many years. A normally jovial man who delighted close associates and dinner companions with jaunty anecdotes and political banter, Menzies harboured an ingrained loathing of Communism, a festering disease spreading throughout the world. Contaminating everything it touched, a corrupting virulence that weaved its evil doctrines through the lower orders of society.

If left to him he would send Ted Roach and his Port Kembla Communist cell to Russia to cringe before their commissar masters, no doubt this lesser and inferior breed from the Antipodes herded in boxcars and sent to a gulag in Siberia. Ranting ingrates who supped on the nation's benevolence and bountifulness only to repay it with wilful disobedience.

According to the labour call the following day a dispute on the *Dalfram* did not exist, five day and five afternoon gangs called, also four day and four afternoon gangs for the *Iron Warrior*. Ted attended the morning pickup; amid a heavy silence he stood in the background like a prize fighter waiting for the bell.

With the port's labour roster in his shaking hand, the young clerk looked nervously at two burly foremen with livid scowls on their faces.

Ted broke the tense silence. "Tom, just do your job and call the *Iron Warrior*. I would seriously recommend you allocate labour to the *Iron Warrior* and leave the *Dalfram* to BHP and the federation."

One of the foremen broke away from his companion, hands on hips and feet spread wide. "No! You might have written the rules that govern this pickup, but I am telling you call the *Dalfram* first. Man by man, ten gangs. Those who refuse to offer for the *Dalfram* are suspended!"

The clerk dragged a large handkerchief from his hip pocket and wiped his sweat saturated brow. "I am calling five day and five afternoon gangs for the *Dalfram* . . ." His voice trailed away in a squeak as the men as one turned their backs on him; he looked helplessly at both foremen, then at the smug face of the branch secretary.

"Tom, let your stevedoring masters know that not one pig of iron will be loaded aboard the *Dalfram*, or any ship destined for Japan in Port Kembla, our small token of support for the oppressed people of China in their fight against Japanese atrocities and war crimes. Port Kembla pig iron is black! 300,000 tons of it!"

"Sprout your bullshit and strut your stuff, but let me tell you no one works in this port until the *Dalfram* is allocated full gangs," the foreman concluded, a surge of frustrated rage tightening his facial muscles. "So until you do, you're locked out!"

≈

The prime minister ordered his attorney general to bring this blatant abuse of union power to a swift conclusion. This single port dispute organised by notorious members of the Communist Party threatened serious diplomatic and trading ramifications for the government. Communists were dictating Australian foreign policy and trade in addition to embarrassment to an important trading partner.

Menzies needed no encouragement in dealing with the intransigent Waterside Workers Federation. As a matter of principle he would not initiate discussions with the Port Kembla branch which would elevate the status of its secretary, instead bringing to bear the full powers of his portfolio on the federal office of the union; moreover, the thought of travelling to Port Kembla made him queasy in the stomach.

He held no environmental angst against Port Kembla industries for the thick pall of pollution that environmentalists griped shortened the lives of those who lived beneath the Illawarra Escarpment. Even if true, the hypothesis extremely doubtful, a small price to pay for producing world quality steel. Making the nation self-sufficient in a vital commodity and adding substantially to Australia's balance of payments. Of course ignored by the militant unions who sucked the marrow from the bones of industrialised Australia and repaid their debt with schemes to crush entrepreneurial enterprise.

33

THE *IRON WARRIOR* LAY alongside with no labour, her four hatches strewn with hardwood dunnage bleeding red sap, a few hundred tons of steel plate on her ceilings loaded the day after the heel block altercation. Emily returned home, disappointed but an extended stay in the hotel unaffordable.

The *Dalfram* rode high out of the water, her derricks set for cargo and a long line of wagons loaded with tubs of pig iron shunted alongside. A few selected Lascars painted over the bow, name and draft numbers, the remainder with chipping hammers and scrapers scaling rust on the starboard foredeck. Ample time to do a thorough job with the dispute now in its seventh day, stalemated with no foreseeable solution even with threats from the government of deregistration, incarceration of officials and heavy fines.

With the exclusion of iron ore, limestone and manganese discharged by BHP ironworkers at No.2 jetty, the company diverted their ships and those on charter to Newcastle. The company continued to call the *Dalfram* daily, each man's refusal resulting in suspension. With no settlement in sight to the dispute and all labour in the port suspended, BHP made a decision to send the *Iron Warrior* to Newcastle to complete her steel cargo.

The Port Kembla waterfront seemed oddly at peace, even comfortable under its mantle of thick reddish-pollution, for an exceptionally long period safe from the Pacific Ocean swells which in bad weather rolled through the breakwaters. An illusion as undercurrents raged as the combatants prepared for a showdown. Ted's small office overflowed with members of the port committee and militants, volunteers preparing for a day of picketing the *Dalfram* wharf precincts with placards: NO SCRAP FOR JAPAN! NO PIG IRON FOR JAPAN! BHP STEEPED IN CHINESE BLOOD!

Ted controlled the port, not industry, the state government, the stevedoring companies who employed labour for a wide variety of shipping using the busy south coast port. He did so with determined willpower and fiery articulation against those who would exploit his members, as he reasoned his family of waterside workers. He imbued in his men an ethic of unity, and condemned those who employed labour with a single agenda, amassing profits while ignoring the safety and the welfare of his members. He continually warned of the United Australia Party and the Country Party supported by industry legislating even more harsher laws, both industrial and criminal, to neuter unions so destroying the workers only voice.

≈

The general secretary of the Waterside Workers Federation, Jim Healy, rang Port Kembla the moment he hung up on his call from Menzies in Melbourne, the exchange distasteful and a waste of time talking to an icon of the extreme right and union hater. Listening to his eloquent and patronising voice sickened him, a thought he should wash out his ear after putting down the receiver.

Of course the federal committee of management would have meaningful discussions with the Port Kembla branch, but as far as acquiescing to the demands of the attorney general of lifting the *Dalfram* ban immediately and the Port Kembla branch expelled from the federation for their audacity dictating Australian foreign policy, Menzies could languish in hell.

"Ted, we agree with your actions and that the *Dalfram* shipment of pig iron to Japan should be exposed for what it is, war profiteering. Now having said that, you might have let us know you planned to blacklist the *Dalfram*, allow the federal committee of management to decide what action should be taken."

"Would you have supported me, Jim?"

"No, I wouldn't have," he replied abruptly. "The *Dalfram* now involves the entire port with a lockout."

"We are coping. Are you against our action?"

"Ted, you know me better than that. It's just the way you've gone about it. You of all people know we have a federal governing body which binds our union. You might even say keeps us from committing industrial suicide, a repeat of what we did in the not too distant past, but more importantly giving us a resolute and powerful voice. Ted, with your unilateral standoff with the BHP and the government you stand alone."

"Like hell we stand alone, Jim. We've got the south coast unions mobilised and supporting our action. We've even got the messengers of God ordering their congregations to condemn BHP. Also, this just isn't me, this is the entire branch supporting our Chinese comrades."

"Which I don't doubt for a single minute, you're pretty persuasive when your tail's up. Put it this way, it's a federal policy issue imposed by the membership through resolutions which coordinates decisive action against trade with both Japan and Germany."

"Would you have convened a committee meeting to support our resolution to ban the *Dalfram* if I raised the matter prior our decision?"

"Aware of your branch members idle and broke on street corners, no. Look, that bastard Menzies has been in my ear for the last half hour about an outlaw mob of comrades in Port Kembla dictating Australian foreign policy and trade. I don't need to hear this bullshit from the number one baiter of organised labour. Ted, get your men together and fix this *Dalfram* issue with a resolution recommending a resumption of work."

"That an order, Jim?"

"No, it's bloody well not," the general secretary said resignedly. "Jesus, I know you too well to give you orders. I'll convene a federal committee of management meeting and hopefully gain support for your dispute, but I wouldn't hold out much hope of success. As you know we have those amongst us who don't see what's happening in Japan and Germany as any business of the union."

Ted smiled as he finished his conversation with his friend, putting his feet up on his cluttered desk, a pile of papers falling on the floor; this is going to be a long one, he thought. With bitter memories of disputes that started with a single ship and ended up with the entire port on strike fresh in his mind and the hardships on those involved, he hoped his members were strong enough for an ordeal far from ended.

Tomorrow he would organise a public meeting, draw more of the broader community into the conflict because this dispute did not follow the normal prototypes associated with waterfront militancy. His message simple, BHP pig iron in the hands of Japan ravaged China with the blood of the innocent.

≈

Ted's public meeting in the Church of England hall in Port Kembla overflowed into the street. Outside the port committee and members of the branch distributed pamphlets and held aloft placards condemning Japan, the federal government and BHP. The meeting supported by such diverse sections of the community, announced beforehand by the branch to the Port Kembla police, took the crown sergeant by surprise, a veteran of the force making a wise decision to keep his men off the street.

He stood fully erect with his chest outthrust, one fist pounding the other beating a rhythm in time with his blistering oration. Pausing only for his words to take full effect he recited the atrocities perpetrated by Japan upon China. He spared no sensitive ears the barbaric bayoneting of babies, rape and houses nailed shut with entire families inside burned alive.

With equal vitriol he attacked both sides of the federal parliament who ignored Japan's invasion and occupation of China, the last of his wrath saved for the federal attorney general. "We can understand Menzies supporting the board of BHP and lambasting Port Kembla waterside workers for refusing to load pig iron about to be marinated in Chinese blood. Menzies is what he is, no different than the gentlemen of BHP who signed the pig iron contact.

Supremely intelligent, you might even notice his nose slightly pinched as if aware of a faint odour in the air, the stench of people like you!

"Menzies drips venom in condemning Port Kembla waterside workers for refusing to load pig iron on the *Dalfram* for Japan. He threatens to jail officials. Incarcerate waterside workers for refusing to walk up the gangway of the *Dalfram*. Fine the federation into bankruptcy, deregistration and confiscate its assets. We have turned to the leader of the Labor Party for traditional support only to hear from John Curtain what might have dropped out of the mouth of the attorney general—if he occupied the treasury benches the Waterside Workers Federation, or any union, would not determine foreign policy and trade to his government.

"Well, that's the Labor Party for you, controlled by rightwing ideologues and armchair union supporters. Their policies simply watered down versions of the United Australia Party and Country Party. Brothers and sisters, comrades and friends of China, let me tell you the Waterside Workers Federation will forge a new foreign and trading policy for Australia. To hell with nations that wage war on others, who with their industrial and military might commit genocide and make sport of impaling infants on the points of bayonets. No Jap pig iron! No Jap scrap!"

Ted felt a rush of confidence course through his body as the meeting erupted into cheering, not only his members at the forefront and the most vocal, but the mainstream people in the hall and in the street. Owing to the size and volatility of the meeting and its unanimous support for the Port Kembla branch of the Waterside Workers Federation, the *Dalfram* dispute would spread from the pristine beaches and verdant bushland of the south coast, the federal government forced to reconsider planned reprisals against the union and listen to the common voice.

34

THE STOPWORK MEETING, ATTENDED by the entire Port Kembla branch, gave a rousing welcome to their secretary as he stretched to his feet to address them, a folk hero preaching to his flock. With the bans on the *Dalfram* now in its twelfth day the BHP continued to enact a daily ritual of calling labour for the *Dalfram*; the call ignored, the port's workforce in a state of permanent suspension.

Even though boosted by the huge response and press coverage of the public meeting, Ted failed to convince the federal committee of management the need to continue the *Dalfram* ban. "The federal committee of management has recommended the lifting of the ban on the *Dalfram*," he said; if his tone of voice held a note of disappointment it didn't show when he added: "The federal committee of management have recommended the branch stand for the *Dalfram* commencing with the afternoon shift today. My response to Sydney is this, Port Kembla is loyal to the last man to the federation, but the dispute on the *Dalfram* is our ban, our conscience, and for us to lift when the situation so warrants.

"Yesterday on page eleven of the *Daily Telegraph* Japanese soldiers razed an entire village and killed every living soul for the audacity of being a threat to their tanks and armoured vehicles. Ours is a struggle against corporate greed fuelling the military regime of a country so brutal and merciless there is no other horde, plague, pestilence or scourge upon the planet throughout history to reference it to. Comrades, I hereby request a resolution from the meeting the directive be received from the federal committee of management, but with a clear conscience and I would hope an overwhelming vote, decline the return to work recommendation."

The resolution came from a mass of voices, the entire meeting on its feet and shouting their support.

≈

Ted listened patiently to his federal secretary over the phone. "Menzies is threatening to reimpose the Transport Workers Act upon the federation. Like the bad old days when our members could only pass through a wharf gate after a goon checked to see if his dog collar fitted his neck nice and snug. We lost the dog collars, Ted, and we don't want them back."

"He's bluffing."

"Armed with an arbitration act written by socialite judges who move in the same stratified air as does government and industry, the man has no need to bluff. He also has a rightwing press baying on his side, supporting his every move against the federation receiving its orders from the Kremlin. The old clichés of freedom and democracy in peril waft from his mouth, the ink gets darker and people run to hide under beds. All the fatherly protector of his nation need do to have the masses in delirium is coiffure his hair, clear his throat and simper a single word that personify absolute evil, Communism.

"Paranoia flows unchecked into the homes of those who place Menzies by the side of God, not at God's feet, but as His equal. The man eulogises Australian jobs are at stake. Our reputation among our major trading partners in jeopardy. Are we going to allow avowed Communist union officials to dictate Australian foreign policy? Stand up, Australia! Applaud BHP who only wants to do what the company does best, manufacture and sell steel."

"I have good Australian vernacular to refute that."

"Abuse won't work, Ted. He thrives on it as it furthers his cause in highlighting the uncouth crassness of the labouring classes. We took years getting that dog collar off our necks, now it has surfaced as a threat which can only be ended by your lifting the ban on the *Dalfram*."

Ted barely managed to suppress the anger in his voice. "This is our dispute, Port Kembla and the south coast. We are taking on BHP and Menzies and we will win. Christ, Jim, I've got blokes who wouldn't be seen dead in my company giving me the thumbs up, clergy coming up to me on the street and shaking my hand, old ladies with baskets of cream cakes to sell to fund the dispute. We will prevail. I feel that. I know that. My members and the south coast community know that."

The line fell silent for a few seconds, only the breathing of the man on the other end audible. "Maybe so, maybe so. We are a formidable union because our strength is our unity. From Sydney to Fremantle, Hobart to Darwin. We are one union, Ted, not a single branch taking on the world. Be patient, there will come a time soon when our entire resources focus on supporting our comrades in China, but not now. Lift your ban, Ted."

This time the Port Kembla branch secretary went silent, then exploded: "Witnessing Chinese babies skewed on the bayonets of monsters? To hell with you, Jim!"

≈

The *Iron Warrior* loaded with iron ore passed dead-slow through the Port Kembla breakwaters, on her starboard hand the *Dalfram* still high out of the water, glistening with fresh boot topping and topside paint. Midway through December the *Dalfram's* ban remained, her pig iron rusting in tubs on flattops coated in an undisturbed mantle of grit and soot from the steelworks.

"The wharfies are still holding strong," Sam, running the breast wire from its reel, remarked to the bosun. "Financially there couldn't be much long grass around their homes."

"Ted he will have plenty of salt and pepper to season it, the man's a legend on the south coast and I reckon his members would follow him over a cliff," Dave said, backing up Sam flaking the breast wire. "By what we are hearing from our officials he has a battle on his hands with his federal office wanting the ban lifted. So far he's prevailed. I'll be going up the road later and I might get to see him, for certain the port committee. Might be the need for some extra troops on the picket line. You're welcomed to come."

With the ship discharging at the ore jetty and sailing the next day lightship to Whyalla, Christmas in thirteen days, Sam's mind centred on one thing only, paying off.

"Sorry, Dave. For me the shipping office at 2:00pm and the 5:00pm train home. Be interesting to find out how much pressure Port Kembla is under. Strange though why other branches haven't come out in support."

"Ted runs a closed port on the south coast, Jim Healy the rest of the country. Though many do not believe it, and most certainly the Sydney press barons, wharfies and seamen do practice democracy and freedom of dissent. Sorry to see you go, Sam, but I suppose I shouldn't wish an extended stay on anyone with what we are burdened with."

"You give them hell, Dave."

"It would be comforting to one day knock your men off a bit earlier for doing a good job. It never fails to amaze me what goes through the minds of those who wear with pride shiny gold bars on their shoulders, slipping and sliding in iron ore and black oil, grease and grime, because in the final count we are just numbers in a ledger."

"Tell that to a young apprentice swooning in a mirror with his first gold bar on his shoulders. The rule is simple, divide and conquer, create an elite amidships and cram the masses in the focastle head or on top of the steering flat."

Dave gave Sam the key to his beachside bedsitter inherited from his father in Stanwell Park, belittled by the bosun as on par with a humpy, but to stay as long as he wanted.

"Sam, you're close to Port Kembla and the wharfies need our support. There's a regular bus and train service from Stanwell Park."

"Dave, I'll make my presence known. Thanks for the home."

"Home? Jesus, I wouldn't dare call it that. It's a fishing shack my old man threw up with a few mates years ago. I needed a bulldozer to remove the beer bottles. I never use it, amazed the southerly busters haven't blown it away. For emergencies there is a hammer and nails under the sink. Take my place on the picket line, that's your rent."

"Sea air might be the cure for what ails my girl."

"If she's chesty, probably not. I think the medical recommendation is a dry and warm climate. Then again I wouldn't swap a dump in Stanwell Park for Lightning Ridge or someplace the back of Bourke. As I said stay as long as you like, forever if you want."

Sam didn't realise how prophetic the bosun's words.

≈

Jim Healy and Ted Roach met with Menzies in the attorney general's Sydney office, the two officials of little faith the *Dalfram* dispute would be resolved. Both men could almost script the meeting word for word, Menzies opening foray an immediate resumption of work followed by a judgement handed down by the arbitration court enforcing strict adherence to no bans or limitations associated with Australian trade and foreign policy.

The harangue would not end there, threatening the Transport Workers Act and awarding substantial damages to BHP for *Dalfram* demurrage and lost production. Old threats would also surface such as prosecution through the crimes act for officials and individuals, heavy fines and jail.

Menzies did not feel comfortable in the company of hardnosed union men; in fact his skin crawled having to offer such types the comfort of soft, squeaky and highly polished leather in his office, let alone forced to make an effort to treat them amiably. He represented the people of Australia, his trusted government returned to parliament with a vote of confidence. Honoured for his achievements by Prime Minister Lyons with a high post in cabinet.

Who did rambunctious men like Healy and Roach represent? Menial labourers drawn to the wharves like moths to a light on grandiose promises of a workers' paradise. The Healy's and the Roach's and their ilk could stand on stumps waving their clenched fists and promise a state where all were equal and each worth according to his needs.

Worthless invective dredged from the darkest depths of the industrial revolution. It caused bile to stir in his stomach this insidious breed of rabble rousers took for granted their freedom of dissent, a wish to pack them off to their beloved Soviet Union where dissenters disappeared off the face of the earth or ended their wretched days behind barbed wire in the frozen wastes of Siberia.

The meeting ended as it started, the warring parties despising each other behind beaming smiles and forced handshakes. With no agreement to lift the ban on the *Dalfram,* the final worlds were the attorney general's: "The government will reconsider its position, and at this juncture in the continuing hope of a swift settlement will not impose clauses of the Transport Workers Act against the Waterside Workers Federation."

"Believe him?" Ted said as both men stood on the busy city pavement jostled by Christmas shoppers.

The federal secretary's glum face answered his question.

Two days later without notification, the government imposed the licensing provisions of the Transport Workers Act; for the second time since its formation members of the Waterside Workers Federation would need to apply for a license to work on Australian wharves.

Ted summed it up in a few simple words: "What did you expect from a back-stabbing bastard? Now we really have a dispute on our hands."

35

THE MAWS OF TAPPED blast furnaces erupted molten rivers of raw iron one third the surface temperature of the sun, poured white hot into moulds and stockpiled. Four mountains of pig iron in a huge concrete pen serviced by an overhead crane; shunted railway wagons loading.

The midnight shift crane driver, a member of the Federated Ironworkers Union, studied his work sheet; 500 tons destination *Nellor* White Bay. The name *Nellor* puzzled him, though not White Bay, familiar with Sydney. He thought long and hard, a niggling of conscience he should show loyalty to his employer of three years, BHP having absorbed the shares of Australia Iron and Steel who first poured steel in Port Kembla in 1928. As a unionist he felt an obligation to support those who manned the *Dalfram* picket line, essential he speak with the shunter who would assign the train to the mainline. If a foreman challenged him he could easily as a matter of safety be recommending the shunter and other railwaymen remain clear of his crane with the night particularly dark and an even heavier pall of soot and cinders in the air like snowflakes.

"All I've got on my clipboard is this lot, 500 tons of it, is destined for White Bay, mate," the shunter said, removing his floppy felt hat and shaking a residue of grit from it before jamming it back on his head with a grimace.

"The *Nellor* is a ship, right?"

"White Bay, yeah would be."

"What kind of ship?"

"How would I know? The boys in Sydney would know, not me. I'm Wollongong and Port Kembla. Why the interest?"

"Just a thought maybe this pig iron in different circumstances might have gone to another ship berthed in Port Kembla."

"You mean the one stuck up by the wharfies?"

He nodded.

"Christ, those blokes are always on strike, but what I hear what those bloody Japs are doing to women and kids I reckon someone's got to make a show."

"Could you pass it along to your mates in Sydney it might be worthwhile finding out where the *Nellor* is loading for?"

≈

With a faint smudge of light in the east starkly outlining the taller city buildings and the arch of the Sydney Harbour Bridge, the Port Kembla train idled, a hollow drumming release every few seconds of steam between its leading wheels in the White Bay marshalling yard; a glance at his pocket watch the driver hoped a shunter would soon dispatch them a switch line and uncouple his locomotive. Weariness weighed heavy on him and his fireman, thoughts only of signing off after returning their engine to the roundhouse.

Pig iron took last preference in the marshalling yard, of more importance refrigerated rolling stock of frozen lamb and beef shunted alongside the Blue Funnel Line's *Nellor* which towered over the wharf, even more so her blue funnel topped with black.

The driver leaned out of his cabin and saw a stocky man with bandy legs hurrying along the tracks; both men knew each other and waved at the same time.

"Meat holding us up, Nobby?"

"Meat's always got preference, Ernest, but that's not going to matter to you and your pig iron. It's going back to where it came from."

Ernest's chin dropped. "What you saying there, Nobby? I hear you right?"

"Heard me right. It's on the black, just got word from the union. Seems you folk down the south coast aren't too bothered about sleep and are active no matter the hour."

Ernest wiped his blackened, grimy face with a scarf of cheesecloth draped around his neck. "Got some explaining to do there, Nobby."

"Nothing to explain seems your pig iron is the *Dalfram's* cargo and someone got the bright idea of sending it north to be loaded in the *Nellor*. She's not going to Japan, but close enough to make a lot of union folk suspicious of where it will eventually end up."

"Shunters supporting the wharfies?" Ernest's brow creased. "That's a new one."

"We're all union, mate. You're back to the roundhouse until arrangements are made to send this lot back."

≈

Old weatherboards warped and splintered, rusted roofing iron, a full frontal veranda facing the sea and leaning north against the prevailing winter storms. Sam estimated the interior about 600 square feet; a double bed, wardrobe, table and four chairs, ice chest, electric stove, cupboard, sink, and a three piece lounge. Tacked on the back as if an afterthought next to a water tank on four posts an outhouse with a single laundry tub, electric water heater, shower and a pan lavatory; a short handled shovel on a hook behind the door, its use obvious.

One of a dozen similar dwellings ignored by council planning authorities, connected to the power grid by poles held upright by their sagging wires. Sam and Emily thought bliss, able to stroll hand-in-hand along a unspoiled beach with the Illawarra Escarpment a verdant backdrop, the heat of summer dispersed by moisture laden north-easterly winds.

Even the perpetual long red cloud overhead that stretched from Port Kembla to Sydney failed to dampen the joyous feeling of freedom from city concrete and masonry. At night sizzling sausages and fried eggs, onions and potato fritters cooked to perfection on an iron plate set on top of a circle of large stones, fired with driftwood. Beer and wine on the veranda, lulled by a balmy sea breeze.

"Emily, I've heard seamen say there is no bad beer, only better beer. Slightly warm beer though is in another category. Wish Dave's ice chest didn't melt ice so fast," Sam said, his feet propped on the veranda railing, both he and Emily comfortable in canvas deckchairs. Tomorrow she planned to catch the train to Wollongong for the last of her Christmas shopping.

Sam would accompany her, but instead of the shops in Crown St he would catch the bus to Port Kembla. The Federated Seamen's Union of Australasia in support of the Waterside Workers Federation sent delegates to the daily port committee meetings to receive briefings and updates of the *Dalfram* dispute.

The picket line at No.4 jetty revelled in the festive season, happy, jocular, supremely confident of seeing the British tramp sail with her hatches empty. Their positive attitude and high spirits seemed incongruous with the government inflicting the first wound, imposing the Transport Workers Act on the union. As if savouring the taste of drawn blood the government completely out of character went quiet, especially its major spokesman.

Seven days before Christmas the peace ended, BHP inflicting a mortal blow that even staggered indomitable Ted Roach.

The chairman of the board of directors announced the company would from midnight be terminating 4000 employees; ironworkers, tradesmen and labourers, the Port Kembla steelworks effectively operated by staff. BHP's briefly worded statement made it clear the company could not function efficiently and in the best interests of its shareholders with untenable restrictions placed upon its operations by the Waterside Workers Federation.

The announcement and its dire consequences for the south coast economy stunned the community, breadwinners jobless, families existing from pay packet to pay packet facing destitution.

One week before Christmas.

Ted with his port committee stood before BHP's main gate and vented his spleen and called for the nationalisation of the steel industry. That the executive curs who cowered in their brick fortresses within the steelworks come out and show themselves. Explain to the wives of sacked ironworkers why there would be no Christmas fare on their tables. Presents under family Christmas trees. A Christmas of debt and foreclosure. With both hands he gripped the iron bars of the closed main gate, the uniformed watchmen behind retreating in fear as a wave of ironworkers pressed behind him.

His voice thundered: "You can close your gates and bar your workers entry from their workplace! Starve ironworkers women and children, but you cannot with your corporate greed and arrogance, contempt and ruthlessness, crush their spirit! Damn the lot of you to hell! Your steel makes weapons to annihilate the innocent, BHP engraved in the shell casings! We are one! We are workers! Above all we are union! You shall not destroy us!"

Reporters mingling with angry workers estimated the crowd at over two thousand outside the main gate, editors trimming that figure to half to temper the support and lessen the success of the union organisation.

A dread of reality swept over the crowd as each man thought of his individual circumstances, even the more radical held in check from storming the main gate. Some thought of highly paid directors and wealthy shareholders, a world far removed from those who shortened their lives for small recompense. The season to celebrate the joyous birth of their saviour, plans for the New Year gone.

36

T HE PRESS LIKENED THE boycott of the *Dalfram* to a methodically planned scheme initiated by the Communist Party of Australia, their goal to undermine Australian foreign policy and bring the government into disrepute.

With the *Dalfram* impasse close to being broken, the attorney general's aura of tireless strength grew in magnitude, a mainstay with a profound knowledge of world events, an awesome presence counselling his prime minister on matters national and international. Lies compounded by the socialist press concerning the Japanese foray into China, Japan with force of arms protecting her exposed borders and home waters. Threatened by belligerent neighbours to the west and north festering with Communism. Stalin's Russia and Mao Zedong's guerrilla forces fighting a civil war against the valiant General Chiang Kai-shek's Kuomintang.

No nation could deny Japan's sovereign right to expunge this threat at its source, and if that meant armed Japanese incursion on foreign soil the democracies accepted the decree of her esteemed emperor. What pretext did an unruly mob of labourers led by a petty despot puffed up like a peacock with his own self-importance have to threaten the corporate policies of BHP and the foreign polices of government? From his grubby little waterfront offices dictate trade policy? Jeopardise a huge export contract and create a balance of payment crisis?

The *Dalfram* ban entered a lull over the Christmas and New Year, the ship peacefully resting alongside her berth, gently rising and falling on the slight seas passing between the breakwaters. Menzies requested a meeting in

Wollongong of the Combined Unions Committee, seventeen unions affected by the dispute, for January 11th.

The *Dalfram* again became news.

≈

"Emily, it's going to shake the Wollongong establishment to its foundations," Sam said, helping Emily with the gap between the carriage and the platform, disembarking the train from Stanwell Park for the meeting in the Wollongong Town Hall. "The government couldn't have sent a better person to stir the pot of the suspended and destitute. Though what I hear of him he is well equipped with witty retorts and light repartee to fend off hecklers."

"Do you think he will be nervous with all these people? I would be terrified."

"I don't think so. He and others of his calling make a career of lies and deception, broken promises and delusions of grandeur, in the process developing a hide an axe wouldn't get through. He probably floats through this mundane world a superior being and us mere minnows."

She pressed close to him, gripping his arm as she struggled for breath climbing the steep steps from the station to Crown St. Humanity on the move filled the street from kerb to kerb, a slow moving river of people. From the west came coal miners who walked off the job, north and south men who worked in industry and on the land. Ironworkers, the number far in excess of two thousand and growing, wives with children in hand, infants in prams. Corrimal St, Crown St, Kembla St, Burelli St, a living mass of people and placards, Sam and Emily caught in the flow, heading in the one direction, the Wollongong Town Hall.

"Ted Roach has mobilised the south coast, Emily. Wharfies, miners, seamen, railwaymen, ironworkers, tradesmen, wives and children. He's got an army to throw at Menzies."

"I hope it doesn't turn violent."

"Too smart for that. He's got his troops better disciplined than to play into the hands of the press moguls. I could have got inside as a delegate of the union, but I would rather be here with my girl beside me. Get her a placard to wave in the face of some big nasty fascist policeman."

"Like Emmeline Pankhurst?"

"My very own suffragette, yes. Menzies called this meeting on his terms, now the unions are showing theirs. Just look at this crowd! Feel the energy! An army to show him the south coast support the Chinese people. Not pig iron soaked in their blood."

≈

Ted never left anything to chance, his organisational skills on a par with a veteran general on the field of battle. Menzies would be travelling from Sydney by car, and at a strategic position ten miles north of Wollongong would be a member of his port committee, a man with a reputation around town of a fondness for reckless racing his motorbike. By the side of the road his man would wait patiently, his motor idling until he caught sight of the attorney general's motorcade, then with great haste and disregard to personal safety, point his powerful machine south.

Ted and his port committee worked tirelessly to rouse the sea of people outside the Wollongong Town Hall, those who spilled into the side streets. Cheering, placards waving, baiting the large police contingent.

The roar of thousands of voices sounded from the north in Crown St, the crowd jamming the street parting to give a man on a motorbike access. The rider did slow his machine in respect for the sanctity of life, his leather helmeted head and goggles obscuring a conscientious man set on achieving his objective. "The bastard's gone to the pub for lunch!"

Menzies prior meeting itinerary included lunch in the Wollongong Hotel with the lord mayor and business leaders. Ted, aware of the schedule, took full advantage. "So we wait! Our lord mayor weighted down by his mayoral chains and flowing robes supping with a pack of bludgers in expensive suits and ties and polished footwear. Parasites who wallow in luxury behind their locked gates while you starve. Cutting your wages and conditions to the bone to maximise profits. Who regally decree you wait while hovering waiters serve them filet mignon. Those who support selling pig iron to Japan so it can be turned into the tools of war to kill women and children."

He paused to let his words take effect, pleased with a wave of anger passing through the crowd, even more satisfied as he saw large family groups with excited children holding high their placards: NO DOG COLLAR ACT!

"Comrades, brothers and sisters, while you swelter in the sun these sycophants stick their snouts in the trough to widen even more their overfed girths, of course paid by you. Quaff vintage wines and smoke cigars." He felt it in the air, emitting from the throats of thousands of people, a power about to be unleashed. Make it a long and hearty lunch, mate, because you're going to need all your strength and articulation to combat this storm of worker power unleashed.

≈

With only the black highly waxed roof visible the limousine passed at walking pace through a crowd begrudgingly parting to allow it access to the kerb and a nervous welcoming group in front of the Wollongong Town Hall. The driver averted his eyes from pure and unleashed hatred that glared through his windshield, globules of spittle sliding down gleaming glass. Those pressed by the crush of the crowd banged their fists on the panels, kicked at the tyres and shouted their rage; the driver waited for an order from the back seat to drive on, but it never came which made him think his important passenger a brave man.

As if a giant hand cleaved a pathway, the crowd fell back, stumbling, some falling, forced to retreat by a group of ten burly men with determined faces, an unspoken but grim command allow us unimpeded passage or suffer the consequences; Menzies bodyguard, the port committee, to man members of the Communist Party of Australia.

From the footpath Ted watched his committee bustle the attorney general and his anxious party through ornate double doors, begrudgingly impressed by the smiling countenance of the big man, not a trace of fear as he threw back his broad shoulders and stared the belligerents in the face. In fact he thought he relished the fury generated by the crowd, a rage so thick it electrified the air. A thought occurred to him did common working class hurling loathing and abuse at him accord him a sense of supreme power over lesser mortals? No matter, brimming with triumph he said to himself: "Seems even the local coppers dislike you, Bob, so we've provided you with a bodyguard."

Except for a long denunciation of damage to the national economy and Australia's trading credibility caused by the *Dalfram* ban as well as other trade union acts of irresponsibility, the meeting achieved nothing. For the union officials sitting around the large oaken table normally used for aldermanic squabbles it appeared the attorney general's attitude to the proceedings aloof and distant, the normally ebullient man not his usual dynamic self.

His secretary issued a vague statement the government would review its foreign policy and trade with Japan. Menzies added an aside he would liaise with cabinet to have the Transport Workers Act revoked on an immediate lifting of the ban on the *Dalfram*, not a single official present putting any credence in his words.

Sitting across from the attorney general Ted wondered if the continuous chanting, at times a crescendo of cheering as militants addressed the crowd, which seeped through old and the thick masonry might have found a chink in the man's armour. Maybe not, his detachment from the proceedings either from a position of power or he considered those with whom he shared the table of little consequence in the ultimate outcome heavily in the favour of industry and legislators.

Menzies at times met the eye of the Port Kembla branch secretary, proof of his iron self-control allowing himself a condescending smile. He regarded himself as a man of vision held in high regard on the world stage, how different from Mr Roach continuously smiling at him; a self-opinionated, blood and guts, them and us, storm the ramparts, trade union leader of little importance. Mr Roach's politics and loyalties, like that of his general secretary, were well known and documented by the government and he felt certain their permanent demise imminent, as well as leading their legion of malcontents to a freshly dug grave.

The attorney general shook the obligatory hands, a thank you for your participation and a smile not unlike the one used when taking the proffered hand of a child in a kindergarten.

Ted with no hesitation took his hand and shook it vigorously. "Mr Attorney General, you might have missed it in your busy schedule, but the only license taken out when you invoked your Transport Workers Act on the federation got burned in front of the Port Kembla Customs House. In the meantime your bodyguard awaits your pleasure, sir."

Menzies never replied, whisked away by his secretary and an assistant to their waiting car, its access by the kerb only cleared by the presence of ten men who held back the crush of people. Only then did the attorney general seem flustered, his eyes darting furtively, finally focusing on a woman who stared him full in the face.

"Go home, Pig Iron Bob!" Gwendoline Croft cried bitterly.

≈

The toll on south coast workers and their families mounted with each day the ban on the *Dalfram* remained, now entering its third month. The Port Kembla steelworks with staff labour continued to produce pig iron and steel though in greatly reduced quantities, the main gate still firmly padlocked to 4000 sacked ironworkers.

The *Dalfram* remained at her berth, a permanent fixture in the port and her cargo railed south to other markets, some to ports north of Sydney for eventual shipment to Japan. With shared agreements between shipping conglomerates, transhipping cargoes throughout Asia no more than a matter of logistics using hub ports like Singapore and Hong Kong.

While the federal government talked of reassessing foreign policy and trade with Japan, 70,000 tons of scrap metal circumvented Waterside Workers Federation bans, loaded into ships destined for Japan, the cargo worked by union labour. In Townsville concentrates loaded for Japan without a single hour lost to dispute, again by members of the Waterside Workers Federation.

The federal committee of management finally put an end to the *Dalfram* dispute and ordered the branch lift the ban. Ted and his port committee now isolated never hesitated obeying, convening a meeting to recommend a return to work.

When put to the vote, the motion only a formality, one hundred raised their hands to continue the ban, fifty-four to return to work. The result came as no surprises to Ted, his final words on the matter: "No matter how you voted, and I thank those who still support the ban, it is over. Comrades, put it this way, the mothers of Chinese babies can thank you for a brief respite from their brutal oppressors. You have shown the true spirit of unionism. You are men I am proud to say are union."

Next day under protest the port committee, ten Communists, led five gangs up the gangway of the *Dalfram*, shunted to the ship still warm pig iron produced by loyal servants of the BHP.

≈

Not long after the end of the *Dalfram* dispute Menzies fortunes soared with the death of Prime Minister Lyons, elected leader of the United Australia Party and subsequently twelfth prime minister of Australia. His election to the highest office in the land did not augur well with his party's junior coalition partner, the Country Party and its leader Earl Page. Page held severe reservations about the new prime minister's loyalty to his diseased leader as well as his reluctance to serve his country in 1914. With belligerent rumblings in Europe, he questioned Menzies qualifications to lead a nation once again under threat.

Menzies finest moment came when notified of the United Kingdom's declaration of war against Germany, without hesitation committing his nation's armed forces to the contagion about to engulf the entire world. He officially visited London, another pinnacle of achievement admitted to the War Council by Prime Minister Churchill. He even took a side trip to Ireland as a big brother with a comforting message for a less mature and worldly sibling, to convince the Irish leader, Eamon de Valera, the folly of neutrality.

Menzies clung to power only by the votes of two conservative independents, his leadership of the United Australia Party continually under threat from disgruntled fellow members. The leader of the opposition, John Curtain, did nothing to advance the government's stability by refusing a request for an all-party national government during hostilities.

Menzies tenuous grip on the prime ministership became even more difficult with increased internal dissatisfaction with his leadership, only resolved with his shock resignation.

In this leadership crisis the two independents members played a key and historic role, withdrawing their support for the government now led by Country Party leader, Arthur Fadden. On October 7th 1941 John Curtain became prime minister, his Labor Party forming government.

Curtain's new government called for the nation to make sacrifices, to link hands and work together for a single purpose, and in doing so forgo claims upon industry and commerce for the duration of hostilities.

The Federated Seamen's Union of Australasia ridiculed the proposal, arguing their members lived war twenty-four hours a day, their slow and antiquated ships prime enemy targets. A second argument, shipowners amassing wartime profits heightened the union's demand for modern accommodation, common menus, improved working conditions, higher wages and war bonuses.

37

1949

D URING THE WAR YEARS when the time came for Sam to join a ship Emily withdrew into herself; with his bags packed in the hallway his last view of her curled on the bed, trembling even though she wrapped herself in a thick woollen shawl. Hesitating to make his departure final, he gently caressed her, teased her hair, kissed her wet cheeks. Even his supreme confidence of surviving the war failed to overcame her dread of losing him. Her fears became a crippling terror in June 1942 with the sinking of the *Iron Chieftain* off Sydney with the loss of twelve men. Then the following day 240 miles south rounding Gabo Island, the *Iron Crown* torpedoed, her toll thirty-eight men. More losses of seamen followed the year after with the sinking of the *Iron Knight,* thirty-six of her fifty man crew lost. Ore ships, aptly known as death ships by their crews, sank in minutes.

Emily became bedridden, refusing to eat or even talk to her mother. She wanted to die, death more acceptable than living with the constant fear of Sam at sea. He felt her pain as if his own, unable to convince her that the Directorate of Manpower governed his service at sea. Also if he refused to join a ship he faced the distinct possibility of induction into the army.

Shipmates became war casualties, their ships and lives ended by submarines, aircraft, mines, raiders and surface ships.

He survived the turbulent and fearful years, and he and his fellow seamen could stand equal among those who bore arms. The strength and courage of seamen no more apparent than those who suffered and survived the Murmansk convoys loaded with tanks, guns, munitions, aircraft and food to supply the Red Army. Slow ships in mountainous seas with a life expectancy in high latitude northern waters of only minutes.

When the war ended and the final count became known 35,000 British seamen sacrificed their lives in the sinking of over 2500 ships totalling more than eleven million tons. 5000 seamen became prisoners-of-war. These horrendous statistics seemed of barely reportable interest to the press, carnage on famous battlefields and gallant tank crews levelling villages to rubble, daring air aces and courageous bomber crews, sea battles between capital ships where the glory of war lay.

Shipowners profited even with losses of ships, war generated revenues not enough to satisfy disgruntled shareholders or rid them of their beliefs seamen were avaricious and opportunist. Manipulated by Communist union officials holding shipowners to ransom for conditions and wages that in a peacetime economy would have resulted in bankruptcy.

One particularly virulent agitator, the federal secretary of the Seamen's Union of Australia, Communist Eliot Elliott. Seamen fully supported their union officials and ignored the loyalist dogma of total sacrifice on the home front at their stopwork and shipboard meetings, waterfront pubs and wherever seamen gathered. Their arguments to their detractors, seamen went to sea in coffins, who when watch below slept in their narrow bunks fully dressed in their lifejackets, who lived every second afloat as a reprieve from death. Why deny them decent accommodation and food, leave and wages?

For the many who condemned seamen their militancy and outright refusal to sail under conditions relics of the last century, none would ever hear the bone chilling sound of the continuous ringing of bells to abandon ship. Men, women, boys surfacing in a sea of blazing oil. Weeks, sometime months, slowly dying under a merciless sun in lifeboats. Prisoners crammed in the stifling holds of commerce raiders, their horror in complete darkness compounded when the raiders opened fire on a new victim. Would the target fire back and send the raider to the bottom of the ocean?

The Seamen's Union of Australia, a new name and peacetime goals to achieve gains in accommodation, increased leave and wages, tread cautiously with the hierarchy and many factions of the Labor Party, the relationship fragile.

Prime Minister Curtain, a man plagued with poor health, finally succumbed to the enormous burdens placed upon him during hostilities, his death close to war's end. Benjamin Chifley, an ex-engine driver from Bathurst, stepped into the breach, his union background falsely insulating organised labour their demands would receive a sympathetic ear.

Wartime rationing eased as Australia entered into a new politically aligned world, nations forming alliances with past enemies as a new scourge flushed with victory threatened world peace. World leaders defined two distinct worlds; the Free World and a grim Eastern Europe formed when the Red Army raised the hammer and sickle over the smouldering ruins of Berlin, the Communist Bloc.

A causality of war saw the erosion of a special relationship between an old colonial master and her former colony, the United Kingdom's cheap larder and supplier of warm winter wool. Some cynics remarked, cannon fodder.

As prime minister Menzies argued with Winston Churchill about British command of Australian forces, a forerunner to the most decisive decision ever made by an Australian leader, the Labor government's demand for the withdrawal of Middle East forces to defend the homeland from impending Japanese invasion.

The debacle of Singapore with gut wrenching reality showed the vulnerability of lightly defended Australia. Apologists for British failures in Asia became silent with the bombing of mainland Australia, and the new prime minister bereft of colonial baggage, looked to a new saviour, the United States of America.

Australia became a base for the might of America to defeat Japan, Australian forces fighting by their side. Many internal issues raised awkward questions for the Labor government, one an historic opposition to conscription.

The government argued for full mobilisation on the grounds hundreds of thousands of United States marines deployed in the Pacific and now based in Australia were conscripts. Another problem no less serious confronted the government, out of control militancy by the maritime unions disrupting the war effort with demands for exorbitant wages and bonuses in a time of national crisis.

The Seamen's Union of Australia thrived on condemnation from its enemies, the rightwing of the community it treated with contempt. With an incorruptible leadership, seamen exchanged sweat rags for suits and ties to stand equal before the most biased of arbitration judges. Judges supported by king's councillors, briefed by shipowners to drain union funds with court costs inevitably awarded in their favour.

Sam and Emily thought of their future and contemplated moving from Pyrmont to Stanwell Park on a more permanent basis, even buying out Dave. Restore the home, even add another room. Dave put a dampener on their plans when he informed him not to press the issue of ownership of the beach home, but never elaborated.

≈

He hurt her as he did so often. He quickly withdrew and rolled on his side to face her.

"Sam, I'm sorry," she murmured, on the verge of tears.

"It's all right, it's me. I shouldn't have been so forceful."

"I want you to be." A note of desperation entered her voice, a lone tear about to streak down her cheek.

"Maybe you're close to your period?"

"No! It's not that. It's me. It's always me." She buried her head in his chest, gritting her teeth and forcing her words. "I want you so much. Even more when you are gone and I can't sleep thinking of you. The war made it even worse, trying to ignore newspapers headlines and not listen to the wireless."

"I always came home to my girl. Never hailed a dead hero. I count myself one of the lucky ones with so many seamen who didn't make it. Their families will grieve for a long, long time."

"Sam, what is wrong with me? Am I old and dry and useless?"

"Of course you're not. It's just something that happens from time to time." Then he laughed and she scowled at him questionably. "Only a sudden flash of thought about the debauched storekeeper on the *Barossa* who mixed, no, stirred lovingly, this blackened pot over a fire for hours. Creating a silky smooth concoction of white lead and tallow for whitening down stays. He gathered bits and pieces of scrap timber laying around the wharves for his fire and stirred and stirred. Another equally depraved sailor remarked about the awful smell, but it would make a good starter. We heard he added lemon essence and used it to lubricate the captain's tiger." This time he burst out laughing. "Not a real tiger, wouldn't that be something trying to get it off with a tiger. A tiger is the old man's steward."

"Sam, that's awful."

"Got to admit that stuff made your hands smooth as silk, though white lead infects cuts. The lemon essence, we never got a report on that."

Her eyes widened in shock. "Would you use it to make love to me?"

He kissed the tip of her nose. "Not on my sweet girl I wouldn't. We'll have a talk with a chemist, he might know from experience what's best."

Her eyes widened even more, her mouth a perfect O.

≈

Even with hopes dashed of Stanwell Park ownership, their second home became an important part of Sam and Emily's life, the tiny beach house theirs to use whenever an opportune time arose; Dave who now shipped out of Melbourne abandoning it, uncaring if the southerly busters at last prevailed. Walking along the beach were moments both cherished, Sam at times distracted by the growing number of ships passing or close inshore to anchor off Port Kembla, many of them new on the coast.

At the end of the beach a high drift of sand piled against an eroded sandstone outcrop became their personal bower. "Emily, I would love to live here permanently. Maybe a house a few streets back from the beach. Old Marty a few doors up reckons he saw a few council blokes hanging around the other day."

"Doing what?"

"Didn't know, looked official though. Living here you could learn to drive, visits to your mum, gossiping with your sisters. We might stretch the finances and buy one of those new Holdens coming off the assembly line."

"With you home I could live here, Sam."

"It's hard for me, too. Away for so long, but that's all I know as a seaman, Emily."

She stared out to sea, hunching her shoulders with her arms crossed. "Mary's pregnant."

"Not over engrossed in her choice of husband."

"Like you he served his country in the war."

"I suppose for me I'm no great lover of the naval officer class, any officer class for that matter. Though I have to admit he looked good when he and Mary came down the aisle. Near got blinded by the gold hanging off his shoulders which kind of detracted from your beautiful sister."

"Mary's having a baby," she said in a distant voice.

"Which means you will be the most gorgeous aunty in the world."

"Though never a mother. Oh, Sam, I want so much to give you a baby. I am so useless, always sick. Clumsy and useless, dried up and barren."

"You are none of those things. You are my Emily and we don't need another to make our lives any more contented or happier or loving than it is now. You, me, that's all we need in this world."

Both fell into silence, the sand beneath them enough warmth to ward off the sea chill and dampness of approaching night, almost time to walk back along the beach to their home. Emily to prepare a salad while Sam scavenged for wood to fire up the rock fireplace to grill sausages. A bottle of red wine on the veranda, a dark but not empty sea speckled with the lights of passing ships and fishing boats.

About to get up Sam leaned forward and creased his brow in concentration; a ship low in the water heading north and close inshore. Australian, long and sleek and new. River class, thirteen ships planned for the Australian Shipping Board, the government shipping line. Five hatches, twelve derricks, a double set of gear and jumbo at No.2 hatch. In the fading light Sam barely made out her funnel colours, black with two yellow bands.

He heard only acclaim for the River class, double berth accommodation, messrooms for crew and petty officers, laundry, drying rooms and showers. Simple gear quickly adapted to a single swinging derrick. Squaring up five hatches and tween decks simplified by landing beams in a set position in the coamings and using scooters, vice-like windup single wheeled devices with two lugs to fit under the top flange of the beams. The River class, wartime designed and built in a period of scarcity, hailed by the maritime industry as an indication of future ships on the Australian coast.

"Not sure from this far off, but with an exceptionally large name it might be the *River Fitzroy* which I once saw in Whyalla. She's got gun turrets on the wings of her bridge. She is a beautiful ship."

She smiled, shivering now and pressing close to him for warmth. "Ships are beautiful?"

"Some you can't take your eyes off, others make you shudder and thank God you're not on them. Ships are hardworking and unforgiving of those who take them for granted. The same as the environment ships exist in, a world that ruthlessly overcomes those who flaunt its dangers and foolishly succumb to its placid moods which hide a darker presence."

"I'm cold and hungry, Sam."

Getting to his feet he drew her up with him, pressing against her slender body, enclosing her in his arms. The ship now a smudge in sea mist if Newcastle bound berthed under the steelworks gantries in the early hours of the morning.

"Sam, it will be all right."

The image of the ship lingered in his mind, seamen called in darkness, wedges spilling on the deck and the sound of winches. Making up tarpaulins, gear lifted, slab hatches removed on a single swinging derrick. Scooters rolling beams aft and clamped.

Distracted, he replied: "What will be all right, Emily?"

"Tonight."

"Tonight?"

"If you want to make love."

He chuckled. "White lead and tallow?"

"That's awful! No, just you and me and nothing else."

Emily passed through phases, days when she found it difficult to breathe, every few breaths forced to inhale deeply. She found it impossible to gain weight even though she made certain she ate nutritious food. The bane of her life her periods which sent her into joyous raptures of conceiving, no more than a late or missed period.

Deciding not to set the fire outside Emily's salad sufficed on slabs of fresh bread plastered with butter, a bottle of red wine between them on the table. Their eyes fixed on each other glowed.

"The sea makes you strong, Sam. Or is it the cooks?"

He almost choked on his sandwich; he reached for his glass and drank deeply. "The word I would use is we survive at sea with Board of Trade cooks."

"Possibly you could teach the cooks how to cook?" she said, the trace of a smile on her lips. "You cook well."

"That which I don't burn to a cinder."

Watching him across the table a pleasurable tingling between her legs intensified. She didn't need that lecherous storekeeper's horrible white lead and tallow, even what chemists dispensed in jars. She needed only the touch of her man, thoughts of her own body giving itself up for possession. The sensation of feeling him climax, each spasm causing her to tighten her inner muscles and draw more of him inside her.

Stanwell Park and its relaxed lifestyle agreed with Emily more than it did Sydney with its wintry inversion layer of coal smoke from domestic fires. War irrevocably changed old British traditions inherent in Sydney's narrow streets and colonial masonry, a city fast losing its rich maritime past, new and bigger hotels replacing old corner pubs.

Not only Sydney, the phenomenon endemic across the nation. Great white fleets of passenger liners with thousands of migrants crammed in steerage. Refugees, the displaced and stateless. Swarthy faces that tested the White Australia Policy, even that racist selection criterion relaxed with Australia embracing the world. These people came from countries still in darkness when the sun shone on the eastern seaboard of Australia, bringing with them old European ideals, strange and pungent foods, strict family values and loud voices in alien tongues.

Amid this massive resettlement came the announcement from Canberra of a scheme so bold and complex it would dwarf any major public works ever undertaken in Australia. A project so immense its critics and conservative doomsayers could only judge it's feasibility on a similar scheme in the United States, the Tennessee Valley Authority.

The Snowy Mountains Scheme made front-page headlines, grainy photographs of mountains ranges covered in snow, springtime rivers raging through heavily timbered valleys, editorials writers overwhelmed with engineering jargon and visions never before known in Australia.

In an address to the nation Prime Minister Chifley spoke of the scheme as the greatest engineering challenge ever faced by Australia, but Australian tenacity and ingenuity, a skilled labour force drawn from all corners of the world, the nation would prevail. The scheme would turn the wild and snow-melt fed alpine rivers flowing wastefully into Bass Strait westwards to irrigate the dry and fertile plains of New South Wales, Victoria and South Australia.

Two major rivers flowing west, the Murray and Murrumbidgee, would have guaranteed flows of catchment water dammed high in the Australian Alps, its release generating cheap electricity for a post-war industrial boom. As could be expected, a remnant from the days of colonial rivalry and pigheadedness, the three states involved in the scheme could only agree that scarce water resources needed to be managed, and that Australian rivers were reduced in summer and long dry spells to no more than strings of waterholes.

New South Wales, claiming sovereign rights to the Australian Alps, 3000 square miles of mostly inaccessible wilderness, wanted water for irrigation, its preferred option controlling the upper Murrumbidgee catchment in the Alps to maintain water levels along the entire river.

Victoria argued for hydroelectricity and higher summer river levels in the Murray River to sustain waterborne transport to its railheads. South Australia, the final recipient, guaranteed the dry state an assured water supply.

With an acute manpower shortage in Australia the federal government looked to Europe for its major workforce to labour in near impossible conditions, engaging a New Zealand engineer as chairman to build the scheme, William Hudson.

In the parliament the opposition led by a resurgence Menzies berated the government for its delusions of grandeur. Its irresponsible commitment of untold millions of pounds based on two rivers flowing westwards with bank-to-bank water. A web of irrigation channels creating thousands of square miles of arable land, released water in the Australian Alps generating electricity to drive new Australian industries. Construction of dams, roads, bridges and new towns, even relocating towns.

Chifley stood firm against the baying members opposite him in the parliament, the United Australia Party and Country Party now a coalition of city and rural conservatives, the Liberal Party. The scheme called for the construction of sixteen major dams, its centrepiece the damming of the Snowy and Eucumbene Rivers in the heart of the Australian Alps and their waters diverted through power stations westward to the rivers Murray and Murrumbidgee.

Tunnelling ninety miles through the granite hearts of heavily forested mountains, a fall of 2500 feet to the western plains through a fifty mile network of viaducts, pipes and channels. Generating hydroelectric power in seven power stations. Over 1000 miles of roads and tracks clinging to the sides of precipitous mountains. Guaranteeing water to the New South Wales and Victorian hinterland, South Australia its future growth assured.

Fortunately a peace offering more geographic than dispute settling resolved state rivalries between New South Wales and Victoria, the siting of the schemes headquarters midway between both states capital cities, Cooma in New South Wales.

Some close to Menzies confided the leader of the opposition thought the scheme grand in its scope and befitting a modern post-war Australia, but far beyond the reach of Australian engineering expertise, and not least, treasury's means to pay for it.

The prime minister tried another ploy to alleviate scepticism, the vulnerability of state owned thermal power stations close to the coast in the event of another war, fortress Australian Alps power output sufficient to maintain emergency supplies. In this train of thought the Labor caucus differed little from those across the political divide with fears of a new world conflict looming. The proposed scheme made for boisterous debate in the federal and state parliaments, the enormous magnitude of the project far beyond the industrialised capabilities of Australia.

Reliant on heavy manufacturing and engineering expertise from the United Kingdom, this brash act of irresponsibility imperilled traditional British Empire ties. Menzies espoused stirring words, generating bold newsprint; state rights set in stone at federation undermined by this blatant grasp of federal power. Did the federal government have the legislative powers to regulate and control state lands? State controlled water? It did not! Socialism from a government of leftwing ideologues with loyalties to a belligerent foreign power, its rightwing controlled by the Vatican. An act of unashamed capriciousness from a desperate and incompetent government shielding the parlous state of the economy and continued rationing by advocating a pipedream and total ruin.

The government shunned the detractors as it set a date for commencement of the scheme, 17th of October, 1949, and press released its official name: Snowy Mountains Hydro Electric Scheme.

Many saw it as a victory for progress, the beginning of a new era of nation building, some also as an end to reliance on the United Kingdom. Sweet victory for the government only soured by a turn of events both it and the union movement would live to regret.

The Labor government turned its back on those who advocated and lived by its working class origins, proud of its history, its reforms, and show a new face, a government no more than an extension of industry and commerce.

With growing talk of a federal election, the Seamen's Union of Australia though supportive of Labor kept the party at a distance. Not wholly distrustful but with growing concerns the suspect credentials of its powerful rightwing faction with allegiance to the Catholic Church. Rank and file party members promising true Labor principles stood for municipal councils, state and federal parliaments; drawn from union leaders, solicitors, teachers, businessmen, tradesmen, labourers, the magnetic lure of power.

Humbleness and self-sacrifice, fighting for the oppressed soon vanished in the sumptuousness of parliament. The articulate servant of the people grew even more verbose, learning the art of evasion and ambiguity, slander and character assassination, lies and false promises. Crusaders who once heralded the cause of the working man and women, promises to fight the establishment to the last drawn breath, now complained about the bitterly cold winters of Canberra.

Unions supportive of Labor both financially and with their membership available for electioneering, knew only too well what the election of a conservative government with debts to business, attached to its rump a wagging tail of wealthy farmers and squatters, would mean to working class Australia.

Over and over the message echoed from stopwork meetings, the Liberal Party's number one policy, the destruction of the union movement using the Crimes Act and arbitration rewritten by industry and commerce.

Menzies placed close to the top of his agenda on achieving power reforms to the Crimes Act. As pundits of law and order observed, a broad-axe to reshape the industrial landscape of Australia.

Coal drove Australian steelmaking and manufacturing, rail and power generation, bunkered ships and piped gas to feed and warm the nation, and when at the end of June, 1949, 27,000 coal miners in New South Wales and Victoria went on strike the nation ground to a halt.

Menzies quickly came to the fore with a public denunciation of the strike, outraged by the dictatorial demands from the miners Communist union leaders, to place in peril the Australian economy. A thirty-five hour week! Thirty shillings a week rise in wages! Unheard of long service leave! Claims guaranteed to send mine owners bankrupt and bring the nation to its knees.

The outpourings continued, even more chilling when newsreel cameras captured a shabbily dressed old woman pushing a pram with scrapings of coal scavenged from railway tracks. Even more frightening, images of stone-faced Soviet troops goosestepping twenty abreast and a thousand long in Red Square. Newspaper exposed conspiracies, the miners union infiltrated by Soviet cadres planning the erosion of democratic government in Australia and installing a Communist regime.

Chifley needed no goading from his opposite number in parliament to act decisively, though his trepidation of Communism less dramatic with a leftwing faction to contend with. It took the government only forty-eight hours to pass legislation that made it an indictable offence to offer credit to striking miners families, the object of starving them into submission with the doors of the corner shop, butcher, baker and milk for babies closed.

The eighth day of the strike, the credit embargo failing, the government ordered the union to transfer all funds to the industrial registrar, effectively shutting down the organisation. Still not enough to bludgeon the miners into compliance the state used its judicial powers in subjugating its subjects into submission, jailing officials.

The normally slowly cranking legal system with almost manic speed handed down convictions. Sentences of six months, one of one year, to two miners officials with fines designed to bankrupt.

Menzies, though miffed the government decided against invoking the Immigration Act to deport British and Irish officials, begrudgingly applauded the government's initiatives to bring the miners to heel and restore stability to the nation.

Sam attended stopwork and special meetings called in support of the Miners Federation and felt a growing disillusionment with a government of the people who chose not to negotiate but to use the heavy hand of oppression. Money poured from ships and union funds, seamen travelling to the Hunter Valley coalfields to man picket lines.

While in Cessnock and camped outside a mine gate in tents, pouring rain and bitterly cold, Sam heard that the government were in agreement with the anti-Communist Australian Workers Union to recruit a new workforce for the open cut and underground mines, the union to be granted full coverage of the mining industry. Another wedge to splinter the union movement, the Australian Railways Union guarantee of no bans against coal mined by the Australian Workers Union. The rumour proved false, a brilliant stratagem to implant fear and bring into play a contest of strength between unions who espoused leftwing ideology and open warfare and the moderate unions which placed the wellbeing of the country first.

Sam's cynicism grew even more when the government ignored their traditional supporters. Miners in the coalfields and their families who stood in the rain on election days and handed out Labor how-to-votes, who walked the streets of electorates stuffing letterboxes.

Still the miners refused to submit and the government played its final hand in the standoff; what all governments do when their subjects rise up in defiance, mobilise the army. Soldiers lacking the skills and training to work underground, would instead man the open cut mines where staff would train them to operate heavy machinery. Proof conveniently ignored by the government and mine owners the expertise and mental attitude required by specialist miners to hew coal underground. Also disregarded were the dangers working underground and the high death rate of miners, chronic health problems suffered in later life, and that remuneration and working conditions fell far short of the risks involved.

In convoys winding along the narrow and rutted roads of the Hunter Valley canvas covered army trucks with troops numbering over two thousand commenced arriving at the mine gates, welcomed by staff as saviours of industry. This decisive action by the government sounded the death knell of the miners struggle, demoralised, dispossessed, voting for a return to work. For their audacity baulking the system the miners union ceased to exist, bankrupted, its leaders jailed, the government declaring victory and a return to sound management. Lessons painfully learned by the union movement, no organisation could consider itself above the state.

Chifley rode a groundswell of acclamation for his decisive leadership in crushing the Communist inspired strike, Menzies again peeved not him but a socialist prime minister lanced a puss filled carbuncle and put on notice unions who preached the doctrines of Communism their fate guaranteed.

A political party of the people without a single trace of repentance turned upon its faithful with a viciousness as soul destroying as those who made no pretence of their loathing of organised labour. Sam in a leaking tent, his belly rumbling, pondered the question how could a Labor politician ever look a unionist in the face again, shake his hand and call him brother. Attend stopwork meetings and conferences and give fraternal addresses of lifelong unity.

Sam thought about joining the Communist Party that night under mildewed canvas shared with four other seamen, grateful of the communal body warmth warding off the chill of the night. Members of the Communist Party he knew were wholly devoted to the socialist cause, even more so than the Militant Minority Movement.

Did he have the time when ashore between ships to give up a large portion of his life to endless meetings, organising at factory gates, distributing socialist literature? Did he wish to sacrifice time with Emily to campaign against conservatism, a member of a party hounded and feared and with little chance of winning a seat in parliament, federal or state?

Also he pondered did he have the discipline to follow without dissent the unwavering and unforgiving party line demanded by membership of the Communist Party? Never veering from the cause or the doctrines of Karl Marx and Frederick Engels? On deeper reflection, though he prided himself on his militancy to his union, at this time in his life he didn't.

38

S AM JOINED THE *RIVER Murchison* in Woolloomooloo discharging gypsum loaded in Ceduna, South Australia, a welcomed diversion from her normal black and tan trading under BHP charter. He came onboard at 2:00pm, met by three men standing by the gangway.

"Frank Ahearn," the bosun introduced himself, a tall and gangly man who seemed to lean permanently to one side as if the touch of a finger would cause him to topple; ordinary seaman on the sailing ship *Passat,* if not for the medical virtuosity of her master he would have lost his left foot hanging by sinews and broken bones crushed in heavy seas doubling Cape Horn. "Graham Brown, Darren Kelly. Darren's on watch with you and one of the delegates."

Sam shook their hands.

Darren ran a cursory eye over Sam's union book; handing it back he swiped a thick tangle of hair out of his eyes. "You'll find the ship has an active crowd who work hard for the union, the minute book proof of their commitment." He led Sam down a long starboard outboard alleyway with rows of portholes ending at No.4 hatch. "Our cabin is two up from the messroom. Port side is the below crowd, usually a bit quieter, but then with this accommodation no one's complaining."

Sam felt the warmth exuding from the engine room casing which divided the port and starboard accommodation, aware of a sickly-sweet odour of fuel oil. As his eyes grew accustomed to the artificial light of the narrow inboard alleyway, he could feel the vibration of a generator beneath his feet, a steady hum in his ears. Deck boys cabin, messroom, smaller PO's messroom and ABs cabins. Below accessed by a steep companionway, bathroom, laundry and drying room.

Darren flicked the tip of his nose. "You'll get used to the smell. Beats squaring up bunker hatches and pockets at midnight, though I suppose the demise of coal burning ships is having a disastrous toll on firemen and trimmers. Even the term fireman dates you, boiler attendants."

"Obsolete bunker space for cargo, half the firemen and no trimmers. Shipowners win again."

"Our committee of management will make certain some if not all of the benefits of modern technology are channelled to the membership." Darren's unkempt hair like a curtain over his face almost concealed his cheeky grin.

"Without a doubt, though all we ever hear from shipowners is doom and gloom and tough economic times. To my mind the same old echo over and over."

"Our ships are never without cargoes, the River class on long term charters with BHP. New ships coming on coast almost every month, the future looks good."

"For the coast, but we are still effectively denied deep sea trade by the overseas conference headed by British shipowners. Something the union has to get its teeth into."

"Breaking those bastards grip on our foreign trade is a high priority. What have we got, a passenger ship on the Kiwi run. Fiji with sugar. Couple of passenger and cargo ships trading to New Guinea and Canada. The rest of the world, nothing. Our presence deep sea ceased the day a Nationalist government gifted the last remnants of the Commonwealth Line to British shipowners in 1926." Darren drew aside a door curtain for Sam to enter a cabin.

Twin portholes with olive green curtains bathed the cabin in soft dappled light; two bunks fitted with varnished bunk boards, separating them a four drawer dresser. Both bunks made with white sheets, a light blue and white woollen counterpane, two pillows and a blanket folded at the foot. An adjustable light at the head of the bunk, for privacy a curtain. On the deck painted pale green a mat which abutted the dresser and a narrow, two door wardrobe.

"Granted we are slowly winning the battle for better accommodation, this still needs to be improved on, albeit single berth. Given time and continued militancy we will succeed," Darren said, sitting on his bunk.

"What I know of Elliott he's not the most patient of men. When you think of the past and the challenges ahead, we're fortunate he's our federal secretary."

"True. Drive a car?"

Sam nodded. "I don't own one, but why?"

"Talk of an election before the end of the year and the utter bullshit being tossed around by the Liberals and Country Party supported by the rightwing press."

"I read we would be on the move again courtesy of the Liberals promising to abolish petrol rationing. Also safe in our beds with Menzies vow to destroy the Communist Party. The gullible will be conned and swallow lies as gospel. There has to be sound reasoning behind Chifley's policy of maintaining petrol rationing, a country without oil and dependent on overseas supplies." A swipe brushed aside his hair. "The miners' strike and the army used as strike breakers in the coalfields made me change my mind about Labor. Sickened watching soldiers march with their slouch hats cocked proudly on their big heads through the mine gates. We have a couple of comrades onboard, the bosun and Graham. The pair of them can make our meetings lively."

"Party members do stir the pot. It's just a pity we can get them elected to parliament."

"Comrades would make the parliament accountable."

"The Labor Party burdened with factions is a gift to manipulators like Menzies." Sam sat on his bunk, sinking in the soft foam mattress; he felt the presence of the engine room against his back, a slight vibration.

"Left, right, centre, fascist, and of course the Catholic Church. I see the church faction as being the future problem, splitting the party."

"What amazes me with the conservative camp is the Country Party. Supported aggressively by rednecks and hayseeds who labour under the delusion a party of land aristocracy will fight for their cause in a coalition of city based liberals."

Darren agreed. "Work from dawn to dust seven days a week for keep and a pittance, who cringe when the word union is mentioned. I think the flies and the heat of the bush must have sapped their brains. Or maybe an unhealthy love for their squatter bosses."

"More like an unhealthy love for their squatter bosses. We live in a world where the sole traveller is fair game for the establishment. Only when we band together does the employer and the state take notice, bend and sometimes break."

"On the picket line in the coalfields during the miners strike a Labor senator addressed us, a union man with a paid-up little red book. Not far from the truth when he said you will never beat the state. The state will always win."

$$\approx$$

Sam fell easily into the smooth routine of the ship, so new the builder's construction numbers still visible beneath her paintwork. Her forward orders were Newcastle to load coal for the Victorian Railways in Geelong, light ship Whyalla iron ore for either Port Kembla or Newcastle.

On sailing day, the *River Murchison's* cargo discharged in seven days, Sam experienced a five hatch square up with a difference. The storekeeper needed to give no orders, his after gang going about their duties with barely a word spoken, backing each other up and gravitating to where required.

The two deck boys kicked opened steam cocks on winch chests, removed clusters from the hatch and readied bags of wedges before standing by guys.

The outboard drum ends of the winches at No.4 and No.5 hatches, similar as No.1 and No.2 hatches, were in direct alignment so that spans with their topping lifts rove through deck leads were interchangeable. This allowed a single derrick to be plumbed the full length of the hatch operated by the winch of the adjacent hatch.

A shelter deck ship with a tonnage space forward of the steering flat her tween deck beams rolled aft and permanently clamped, single hatch boards stowed in racks against the ship's sides. On deck four hook slabs, three tarpaulins, bottom on the wood and two tucked, derricks lowered into cradles.

Seamless, seamen like their forebears in sail who could go to a pin rail in the darkest of nights and know which pin to pull, what buntline, brace or sheet to slacken or haul on. Another trait, backing up, a mind picture always present of where a block or a hook may swing, a floated beam or slab.

It took an hour and a half to square up No.4 and No.5 hatches, only No.3 hatch remaining, the forward gang scootering beams and setting up the gear. The storekeeper's gang stripped the gangway and prepared the pilot ladder at the break of the bridge on the starboard side, spare men sent to the boat deck to lash oil drums.

With three quarters of an hour before sailing, 11:15pm, the ship singled up, Sam sat with Darren on No.4 hatch with a mug of coffee freshly brewed by one of the deck boys. "So simple and so easy," he said.

Darren sipped his coffee and shrugged. "It's still span and chain which could be improved on. Ratchet gear, even clamps and wire made up on elephant pads would be a more efficient arrangement. Take the American Victories, a forest of gear set on ratchet winches. Those Yanks even cross the Atlantic with their gear flying. With us we have to lower our gear shifting ship from Geelong to Melbourne."

"I have seen the Victories in heavy seas with it all flying and rolling on their beam ends. An incredible sight. Though with ratchet gear you would lose the swinging derrick, an arrangement I really am impressed with."

"Swinging gear works well on a full square up. Though in Whyalla you need only lift one derrick, pull back your tarps and remove the middle section, sometimes the after section at No.2 hatch."

"Being able to simply swap topping lifts between winches to me is well thought out and practical when I think of all the horrific leads I've come across in my time. Inside turns, riding turns, leads that make no sense."

"Ships coming down the slipways in Brisbane, Newcastle and Whyalla are catching up with the rest of the world, though when compared with what British and Scandinavian yards are turning out, sleek and fast and forests of gear, we still have a long way to go. Big crowds to work them though as opposed to our scale of manning."

"Big crowds of low wage Chinese and Lascars, Arabs and Senegalese, not white crews. Wouldn't our shipowners love to get away with that."

"If Menzies wins the next election Australian shipowners will be banging on his door the next morning and ordering bags of rice from their provedores. The coast will be thrown open to all comers, to hell with cabotage."

≈

The *River Murchison* lay at King's Wharf waiting for a berth under the electric cranes in the Carrington Basin, chartered to load coal for Fremantle. The middle of November, Sam planned for Christmas. Light ship across the Great Australian Bight to Whyalla, back east around mid-December. Like most Christmas plans made at sea successful outcomes rare, failures the norm received with resigned acceptance. Going home for the weekend, Emily came down with influenza, and on the recommendation of the family doctor, Sam paid off.

≈

The federal election called for December 10th became a battle between two political parties of widely opposing views of the future direction of Australia. The Labor Party exuded confidence it would retain office, a record of strength dealing with union recalcitrance, the economy stable and goods and services slowly returning to normal from wartime austerity. Memories of war faded as industry completed it transition from war to peace, returned men and women fully assimilated into society.

Confidence though would not be enough to stop the juggernaut of the Liberal Party with its grandstanding and charismatic leader. From the conservatives poured accusations and fanciful fabrications, reassuring fireside chats to alleviate fears of a world on the brink of another war. Witnessed on cinema screens, bold newspaper headlines, shrill voices on the wireless, the Soviet Union's sucking tentacles encircling the globe, a cancer penetrating ever niche of society.

Could Australia saved from defeat in war by courageous men and women survive three more years of Labor incompetence and socialism? So headlined and editorialised the major city newspapers.

Exposures in the press became a daily event, seedy backroom deals with senior Labor figures and Communist union officials, the pledging of union funds for election purposes. Unity tickets, union officials and academics subservient to the Soviet Union promised senior roles in a re-elected Labor government. Truth played no role, accusations Labor would reintroduce unconstitutional legislation to nationalise the banking system.

Control every penny earned and saved by hardworking families. Allow Communists free reign. An open mind only need look to the United States, a stronghold of democratic freedom under attack from within by Stalinist cells, a portent of Australia stagnated under a Labor socialist government. Allowing Communism free reign throughout the nation, financed by the Soviet Union. Shunning allies threatened by hundreds of divisions of battle hardened Red Army forces poised on their borders. Nuclear missiles aimed at all the major cities of the Free World.

The United States led the cause of freedom in removing from its society the abhorrent disease of socialism. Ruthlessly exposing and humiliating sympathisers, incarcerating, deporting and blacklisting an artistic elite a threat to the state on the testimony of patriots. On sworn evidence of informers leftwing sympathisers were exposed and removed from public office, corporations, colleges, media and the film industry, some even hounded into suicide for subscribing to a shared society and a fairer distribution of wealth.

Australia under a conservative government would follow a similar path, an election promise as solid as granite. The grand man of the British Empire dominated the political stage as if already anointed to lead Australia into a new and prosperous future. Australia's security would be inviolable under a coalition government with old traditions unchanged.

Without question the coalition would maintain its bond with the British Empire, honoured to have as its head of state the British monarch. Retain the sacred symbol of the nation's birth in the flag, a banner under which the cream of the nation's youth fought and died in two world wars.

Menzies confidence soared with each week of electioneering, revelling in town hall meetings, humiliating hecklers with his lightning wit and fiery ripostes. His honeyed voice wafted over the airwaves, from the ceilings of packed auditoriums, reassuring, and caring; to those mesmerised by the melodious voice there instilled within a sense of paternal protection. This man would see the nation right. Strengthen ties with allies and rid the nation of the Communist peril.

Crowds begged for more, cheered themselves hoarse and stamped their feet and would have carried the orator on their shoulders through the streets.

Labor strategists still remained quietly confident of victory even with the wave of conservative sentiment rampant. A belief people, mainly working class, would remain faithful to a government who led them in war, a government stepping guardedly in an uncertain post-war era. Cautious yes, but a government of progress and vision with the commencement of government sponsored major engineering projects.

Chifley's stable economy would remain within budget estimates and keep interest rates low, inflation in check, and housing affordability within reach of the majority of Australians. Unfortunately the rationing of petrol would remain in place for the foreseeable future. With the nation wholly reliant on imports, rationing would be a matter of ongoing reviews by the government unwilling to permit a large proportion of sparse foreign reserves spent on foreign oil procurements.

The leader of the opposition held no such qualms, under a conservative government Australia would have freedom of movement. History would record the coalition guiding the nation from the last vestiges of wartime austerity with the abolition of petrol rationing.

≈

Emily recovered slowly, Stanwell Park and Sam by her side a curative. On the veranda sitting on an old lounge bought second-hand he nursed her on his lap. The warmth of his body gave her strength, turning her cheek for him to kiss, afraid she would pass on her germs; an offer refused, kissing her full on the lips and moving a hand to gently caress a silky thigh. Later in bed, a slow and gentle joining of their bodies.

Summer and balmy north-easterly winds, steaks and sausages outdoors, walking along the beach and watching the flickering lights of passing ships.

"Emily, do you want to come to Sydney with me tomorrow on the early train? I have the stopwork meeting, then the Eddie Ward rally in Randwick in the evening. We can throw open the windows and air the place out. Catch up with your mum and sisters."

"I feel better here, Sam. Not this time. Do you mind?"

"No, if you feel that way. Your mother would have been pleased to see you, how quickly you have recovered. Obvious how you drag me into bed and all that hollowing."

She pursed her lips. "I don't! Though I don't mind you carrying me to bed."

"The election rally should be something worth attending, by what I hear the member for East Sydney somewhat of a firebrand and an arch enemy of Menzies."

"When you come home we'll have a baked chicken dinner with all the trimmings, our early Christmas."

≈

The Sydney stopwork meeting always attracted a large attendance, noisy, verbal, and at times fiery and abusive. It also acted as a magnet for a collection of colourful characters with exceptionally loud voices and outlandish philosophies. Above all it highlighted the success of the small union, clear evidence of a family-like bond between officials and rank and file.

Seamen knew their officials no matter the port having in the past sailed with them, drank in the same waterfront pubs and engaged in verbal stoushes. This close kinship made the union strong, the true meaning of hurt one, hurt all. Shipowners and governments of both persuasions were forced to deal this power, an unexplainable metamorphous where a man could throw down his shovel on the stokehold plates and swap his flannels and sweat rag and stand before a judge and argue points of industrial law.

The monthly federal office report elucidated union business; visiting delegations, officials, disputes, award, committee of management, finances, branch reports, and new ships for the Australian Shipping Board and BHP. Grouping the lengthy report in segments, the chairman after reading his noted headings sought questions from the floor, on some points elaboration from the federal secretary. Clinical, efficient, formulating future policy, but above all giving the sense to each member present, to every seaman who carried a union book, of personal involvement.

The post-war Australian maritime industry boomed. Passenger ships booked to capacity serviced the states, New Zealand and Canada. Announcements of fleet expansions by the major shipping companies gave the union even greater bargaining power on manning committees and award negotiations. The union using the argument of a skilled labour base were able to exploit the formulae of man-per-ton crewing ratios, negotiate new wage scales, food, protective clothing, leave and improved accommodation.

The Seamen's Union of Australia with old wounds healed grew steadily in strength, a rallying cry for the union, the threat of a Labor government defeat and the emergence of an old combatant.

The absence of dry humour that Eliot normally wove into his federal office report confirmed the seriousness of the final item of the report. His pensive face looked out over the meeting, recognising many old shipmates, resilient men who in the desperate times remained steadfast, showed true mettle when all seemed lost. Also sprinkled among the meeting those he recognised as groupers, men with rightwing political affiliations. Such men plagued the Labor Party as well, entrenched in important positions within the party hierarchy with an expanding power base to change the course of politics. Unusually quiet, the reason he thought this normally disruptive element also troubled by the prospect of a conservative government.

He addressed the meeting in an even and controlled voice: "Comrades, we are witnessing a federal election without precedent in Australian politics. Vast amounts of money are pouring into the coffers of the Liberal Party from overseas sources. Money from extreme rightwing groups, religious zealots and anti-Communist extremists in the United States and Britain who see a perceived working class Labor government in Australia as a threat to their mercenary agenda to crush organised labour, silence the voice of labour, and banish worker representation in parliament. The union is affiliated to both the Labor Party and the Communist Party, both these parties proportionate to their role in the political sphere receiving electoral funding from the union.

"In this election with war a nonissue, austerity a relic of the past, a new world is promised by the Liberals and their lackeys the Country Party. Grand promises of jobs and freedom from the threat of Communism which when you delve deeper means the removal from the constitution of the freedom of association as deemed by Menzies. Put it this way, it's acceptable to join the boy scouts but not the Communist Party.

"You will be free to worship the past glories of the United Australia Party, the archconservative Stanley Bruce and that ex-Labor rat supreme, Billy Hughes. Free to join their party, induct your wife or girlfriend on a cake stall to bolster party funds, stand on street corners handing out pamphlets demanding the jailing of Communist union officials, leftwing journalists and academics.

Under a Menzies government do the opposite wearing a red tie and you'll end up in jail. Police will smash down your door. Speak your progressive views on a street corner and you will languish in jail for five to ten years. Freedom under Menzies. This is why this election is so important.

"Comrades, all that any rational thinking person has to do is wonder why those of the extreme right and the religious fanatics are supporting the Menzies camp, all this money to win an Australian election that will have no earth shattering consequences or bearing on world events. The red bogey of course, the fear of a workers state, fear of the means of production in the hands of the workers. Fanciful delusions from the mind of one who aspires to attain the pinnacle of power.

"The seer parading on the world stage who predicated the fall and surrender of the Soviet Union within months of Hitler's invasion. Who predicated conquered France would rally and repel the German invaders. Though the real Hitler when finally exposed as a maniac not exactly to his liking, but then my assumption might be wrong. Also misjudging the man thinking that on his mantelpiece there is a framed congratulatory telegram from Tojo for sending Japan the *Dalfram's* pig iron to return as bombs on Darwin.

"When you leave this meeting and are out and about ask the benumbed to whom the *Daily Telegraph* is their only source of dubious enlightenment, on whose side did the conservatives campaigned when Chifley attempted to nationalise the banking industry? When Chifley wanted a centralised bank for low interest home loans and the setting of rates. Rates affordable to average Australians not gouged for maximum profit for financial institutions in London and New York. An Australian bank with an Australian governor to bring the bloodsucking leeches of the banking industry to heel."

Debate on the federal election extended the meeting after midday, the chairman calling for an extension of time. Speaker after speaker denounced pro-Liberal articles in the pages of the *Daily Telegraph*, *Daily Mirror* and *Sydney Morning Herald*. The publishers of these widely read newspapers used their boldest print and fear mongering editorials to inform their readership, most who ate their sandwiches wrapped in yesterday's edition, of an ever increasing Russian nuclear arsenal aimed at the West. To instil even more fear and uncertainty, full page reports of the Red Army's brutal suppression of the Soviet Union's satellite states.

Union officials were fair game if their politics leaned to the left, rumours of misappropriated union funds, unions in the building industry engaged in thuggery against hapless construction companies. Drunken binges, slush funds, foul mouthed hooligans marching six abreast in city streets with banners and placards calling for industrial anarchy. As a public service the portentous newspaper publishers gathered about them a manipulative stable of hack correspondents and bitter and ingratiated columnists.

Still contentious with diehard Labor voters the recent miners strike and the use of troops to force the miners back to work. Also the lacklustre response, some said apathetic, of Chifley to dispute the fanciful oratory that only a conservative government could guarantee a managed economy and prosperity. Where were the practical men with callused hands, steeped in old Labor values, shouting from stumps the virtues of a working class government? Against the magnetism of the honey-tongued guru wooing audiences in halls throughout the land, on the airwaves, podiums draped in flags, ex-servicemen putting their hands up to again serve their country, not on the battlefield, but in the parliament.

A question raised at the stopwork meeting asked about the leftwing faction of the Labor Party's fraternal links with the Communist Party, camaraderie worthy of press attention.

Eliot replied laconically: "It doesn't exist. Labor has an identical policy as do the Liberals in regards to the Communist Party. Why do you think Chifley sent troops into the mines, jailed officials and bankrupted the miners union?" He paused, stepped back and reached for a glass of water on the table; refreshed, a wry smile crossed his face.

"Changing the subject somewhat, as nomadic well-read and philosophical men of the world who move freely through high and low society, poking your inquisitive noses in other people's business which is not always appropriate, you will without a doubt come across belligerence towards our union. Envy of conditions won through struggle that almost broke the back and spirit of the union. Your union survived because of its officials and a rock solid core of members.

"We are a union treated with respect because you, the rank and file, continue to be influenced by what some might call middle management and officials with membership of the Communist Party of Australia. Let me conclude for those who shift uneasily in their chairs or hang their heads and shake it, those who will leave this meeting and breast the bar and condemn the politics of your leaders. Not the Communist Party of the USSR. The Communist Party of Australia! Never forget that!"

Sam's next meeting commenced at 7:00pm, a reply to the leader of the opposition's policy speech broadcast to the nation from the Melbourne Town Hall.

≈

Sam heard many anecdotes about Edward Ward, known as Eddie. An unpredictable man with a union background referred to by analysts as the only true Laborite in the federal parliament. Ward's working class conscience and union roots made his choice simple when he switched allegiance to the Labor premier of New South Wales, Jack Lang, when the federal party turned on him with the ferocity of a cage of starving ferrets with the scent of blood in their twitching nostrils.

In the darkest days of the early 1930's Jack Lang rose above those of his party who accepted as fait accompli poverty and financial despair to rebuke the governor of the Bank of England's plan to keep Australia's honourable name sacrosanct, British loans with interest now due paid in full. This meant slashing pensions already below subsistence level, cutting government salaries, increasing taxes, reductions in bank interest, sacking entire government departments, cancelling government expenditure on roads, bridges, ports, airports, transport and utilities.

From Lang came a refusal so loud it reverberated throughout the state. Of large frame and equal intellect he would not allow his state to fall into utter ruin and its population, starving and clad in rags, turned out of their homes while Sir Otto Niemeyer's bank grew fat. The premier stated in his bullhorn voice to hell with bankers, the debts incurred by his predecessors repaid with interest at a time of his choosing or when the world financial crises caused by the avaricious and cavalier lending policies of the banking fraternity returned the world to sanity. Five years, ten years, twenty years, time mattered not. Not a single penny!

Federal Labor reeled, appalled, humiliated before their British peers. Gentlemen of honour did not repudiate their debts! Though the federal government could not interfere with Lang's right as premier to conduct the state's financial affairs legislated by the New South Wales parliament, it could not allow the loss of the nation's financial credibility to an act of socialist lunacy.

The federal government would repay the debts of New South Wales, deducting the amounts paid to the various foreign financial institutions, predominantly the Bank of England, from future state grants.

The Labor Party imploded. Ward, a forceful advocate of the Lang proposal, voiced his resentment and dismay at Prime Minister Scullin's sleight-of-hand, resigning from the party and joining Lang Labor. He would remain by Lang's side and faithful to the Lang Plan until 1936, re-joining the ranks of federal Labor.

Even so the fire never turned to ash in his belly as he fought for those he represented in parliament; the dispossessed destroyed by the banks, the schemers who sucked dry the life savings of their victims, the system of greed and freewheeling capitalism that plunged the world into chaos. He suffered no misgivings attacking his own in the party room, the rightwing he claimed were closet Liberals. Others as parasites who used a party of the people to achieve their political goals more easily than the organisation of their first choice, the Liberal Party.

The spirited member for East Sydney's anger against his fellow man reached its peak when he vented his extensive vocabulary of scorn across the political divide at the robust figure of the member for Kooyong. Menzies, well known for his many sojourns overseas prior to his standing down as prime minister, would be greeted on his return to parliament with a flamboyant bow from the waist by the member. 'Welcome home, sir, we sincerely hope you passed on our kind regards to the royal family.' A toothy grin that followed might well have been a cat about to lick whipped cream.

Menzies gave back as good as he received from the bespectacled and smugly smiling socialist agitator, a disgrace to parliament. Stern of face, posturing in pure disdain, his eyes filled with scorn, he would tilt his face and dismiss his tormentor with a slight curl of his lips.

Ward harboured no mercy in his heart for the leader of the opposition, and when asked what he thought of the man outside the thrust and parry of parliamentary debate, he quipped: 'The man's got the scowl of Mussolini, the demeanour of Hitler, and the figure of Goring. Need I say more?'

≈

Sam caught a tram to Randwick and easily found the Mechanics Institute Hall by the animated crowd milling on the footpath waiting their turn to file through the doors. Anywhere, especially on home turf, Ward could draw a crowd both for and against his radical views. Aggressive interjection never bothered the street fighter mentality of the man, in fact he thrived on those who attempted to debase his views of an unfair, lopsided world.

Fists shook and shouts of Bolshevik and comrade, or whatever name nurtured in the minds of those who believed the crumbs that fell from the tables of the rich were just rewards for the working man and woman. Abuse fired him to a fever pitch of grandstand oratory, but never threatened an inner calmness and the old adage that the man with sight in the world of blind is king.

For those who attacked him, attempted to shout him down, deride and refute his spoken word, he felt empathy. Not rightwing fodder fair game for Liberal Party strategists, but minds under a continuous barrage of ultra-conservativeness in a society divided into two distinct worlds. Simple people wanting nothing more than to go about their daily lives undisturbed, but slammed between the eyes with posters outside newsagents: SOVIET THREAT REVEALED. SUSPECTED SPY RING. CHINESE REDS MASS ON BORDER.

For the many that feared living in a world of disputed borders and political upheavals, a calming voice from a man who would be their prime minister crackled over the ether, from their mantelpiece a saviour welcomed in their humble homes. Dread not those who would destroy your places of worship, force you to labour against your will and confiscate your life's savings to build monuments to Marx and Engels, Lenin and Stalin. Together we will go forward and meet this challenge head on, and with our mighty allies finally wipe from the face of the earth this fetid contagion called Communism.

Sam tall enough could see over the heads of those he shared the back wall with, tried to close his ears to the buzzing din of hundreds of competing voices, coughing and shuffling feet on bare boards.

The meeting followed normal procedures, the chairman president of the member's branch, minute secretary a federal electoral council member, and the member sitting sprawled on a chair on stage seemingly disinterested in the proceedings.

To Sam Ward when at last he rose to his feet and stood before the microphone seemed smaller than he imagined; then he supposed the man's aura greatly exaggerated his stature. A trim bespectacled figure in a grey business suit of better days; more the retiring school teacher type than a tough and fearless advocate for equality.

Ward held in his right hand a sheaf of clipped papers which he slowly raised above his head. "Those with an interest in the future direction of this country would have listened to this a few days ago. Delivered in a rich and captivating, reassuring, even fatherly style to an audience of the faithful hanging with bated breath upon every word. It made you feel your future in the hands of this benevolent sage safe from all the perils this bad, bad world of ours threatens. Jobs for all assured, reduced taxes, money accruing in the bank, low interest loans, no petrol rationing, home affordability within the reach of even the lowest of incomes. Favourable reviews of pensions, and a healthy crimsoned cheeked population with the finest medical care in the world.

"Cast your vote for Labor at your peril! Higher taxes! Repossession! Eviction! Petrol rationing! Rampant inflation! Unleashed union power! Nationalisation of banks and industry! Communist Party infiltration into every facet of society! With his audience of true blue liberals on the verge of apoplexy, Old Bob delivered the Liberal Party's policy speech for a three year term in government. You heard it on your wirelesses, read it in your newspapers, listened to it being talked about in the pub, and of course you are now hearing it from the Red-loving ratbag from East Sydney."

The meeting stirred, some favourable acknowledgments, others opposing but changing their minds to rise to their feet and attack. Later, let the leftwing extremist who lived high on the public purse rouse the meeting to fever pitch, making it all the more easier to tap into suppressed outrage and aim it directly at the target.

Ward held the papers higher. "A fine document this is. Written by the hand of the great man himself, wartime prime minister, the shortest on record I might add, assuredly the most travelled. The good old royalist hasn't lost his touch when he talks of our country, not his, our country going forward together. We will follow a path together, not always an easy grade, in places rocky and treacherous, and we will together build a great nation brick by brick, nail by nail. Never fear, a gentle but firm hand will always be there to steady you if you stumble. I shall be your staff and your eyes, your assured footfall."

Feet that previously shuffled on the floor now stamped, scattered hand clapping, heads nodding approval, obvious now to the organisers of the meeting the member's supporters outnumbered those against.

"The future of Liberal Australia is outlined in clear terms. The banks are safe to conduct business as usual. There will be no expansion of public ownership because such policies are the negative pathways to socialism and the extinguishment of the free spirit which beats in the hearts of entrepreneurs. Now Mr Chifley's hand on the tiller, if not stuck firmly in your pocket, guaranteed to bring the nation to its knees, on a par with the suffering masses in the cold and grey Soviet Bloc countries. Mr Menzies is a prophet of conservatism, a man of immense achievement and profound knowledge, especially when it relates to royalty and the British Empire.

"Socialism we are told in simpering terms creates nothing, suffocates ingenuity and the entrepreneurial spirit. So sharing what the majority produces is wrong and amassing great wealth by the few is right. You could say there are few snake-oil and bridge salesmen thriving in the socialist countries. How will bold Mr Menzies rid the country of this scourge that threatens to destroy our way of life? He tells us in his policy speech he will present a bill to dissolve the Communist Party of Australia. This paragon of free speech and association will make members of the Communist Party ineligible to apply for a job with the government, barred in holding an official position in a union, unable to work in a defence industry, and to top it off, all the party's assets disposed of.

"Red fear mongering. It is not the Reds we should be terrified of, but Menzies and his Country Party hicks and the rabid fanatics who support them. Those who dwell in the shadows of religious righteousness, the far rightwing, the wealth and power of this country who hover over Menzies shoulder as he writes legislation to make it illegal to associate. Illegal because of political beliefs to work for the government or in defence, stand for election or be a union official. In one brilliant stroke wipe out three quarters of the union officials who now hold elected office. Is that an outcome that makes Liberals smile or what? You might say Labor would not be overly disappointed by such a purge and not be far from the truth, but Labor has no intention of outlawing any group or association because it has different views to its policies."

Sam felt the man's aura, his magnetism drawing his audience into his line of thought, not all agreeing but caught up in a flow of raw energy. His words filled the hall with one motive, to neutralise the outpourings of another, lay bare the facts as he saw them. The member for East Sydney would receive no foreign money to fund retaining his seat in parliament, telegrams of support from extreme rightwing factions mustering their forces to expose and destroy their fellow countrymen on the information of informers, sexual deviants and religious zealots.

Ward recognised in the Liberal Party a central body that held extreme views on matters relating to socialist ideology, their power base the support of high finance, industry and commerce. Another sector equally as important, highly intelligent and intuitive, those who harnessed the power of the workforce and skimmed the cream before distribution to shareholders. An elite upper management with one enemy, an irritation like a buzzing fly, the union movement.

"The Liberal and Country Party in its palaver to snare your vote on December 10th will try and convince you their vision is your freedom to worship and choose your place of employment. Study and build strong family relationships because, and the scrap metal and pig iron dealer just might have let a bit of elusive truth slip here, a stable life and education is the key to the future. Granted all that is good and worth attaining, but in the conservatives ideal world unions do not exist. The workers have no voice.

"The workers are mere dispensable tools of industry, work until you're no longer capable, given a cheap watch and shown the gate with your last pay envelope in your pocket. You worked all your life and because Menzies gutted the unions fighting to achieve financial security in retirement, that pay envelope has to last you until you die. No strength of numbers to support you. You obeyed without question, and in fear of your job snapped to attention in the presence of your superiors.

"Listen closely to Menzies speech and a shiver passes down your spine. As a clairvoyant our saviour preaches Labor's inevitable decent into socialism will sever our bonds with the United Kingdom who buys our butter, cheese, meat, wool, fruit and raw materials. She will no longer afford us preferential treatment like paying the lowest market price and shutting us out of shipping conferences, but look to Europe in the post-war future.

"Who knows how the dear old girl strapped for cash after a war will face the future? So what, don't we have an enviable position in Asia to sell our goods at fair market price? We as an independent nation have no reliance on the northern hemisphere for our existence. We should not be afraid of the United Kingdom weaning us. Our sights should be set firmly on an emerging Asia, forget the age-old British traditions and pomp, rid ourselves of British cannon fodder mentality. Bow our heads to those who by birth deem themselves superior to us mere humans. We are Australians! We should bow to no one!"

Australia's unquestioning acceptance of a British monarch as its head of state were sensitive areas the member normally steered well clear of at meetings where other more important issues needed raising. He caused enough ruckuses trying to convince fiercely independent Australian workers the need to unionise and become committed, rally to the cause of the betterment of the working class.

He knew in rare lapses when he stepped over an invisible line in respect of Australia's ties to the United Kingdom, wondering as he often did why a young nation not yet half a century old with a vibrant population and the riches of a vast untapped continent remained tethered to the British Empire. He could have argued all the old country wanted of Australia at the bottom of the globe some 12,000 miles distance, an ideal location to empty their overflowing jails, but he kept his peace.

"Read carefully the policy speech of the Liberal Party presented by a beloved and portly pastor to his country flock. Our industries will only succeed with the full and unfettered cooperation of capital, employer and employee. Sounds wonderful, the nation working together as a happy and contented team. Well, I've got news for the Liberal Party, tell that rubbish to a union official threatened with jail for negotiating a penny an hour rise in wages, a miner fighting for fifteen minutes bath time to wash the grime from his body, another union official arguing the rights of a maimed worker thrown out the gate.

"You preach a one-way street, Mr Menzies, where the union movement and the working class, the major portion of society, have no rights. A world where if a union dares strike its punishment are huge court imposed fines and compensation. Court costs with the intent of bankrupting. Assets frozen, confiscated, officials jailed or deported. In Mr Menzies free world I never see BHP and their compatriots being penalised for locking workers out, breaking award conditions to increase production. Forcing workers to work excessive overtime, compelling them to work in an unsafe and unhealthy environment without proper protection.

"In Menzies promised world, happy workers march off to work every day singing and laughing. Why shouldn't the workers be joyful? Their job is secure and the boss is paying them according to their worth. Employer, employee, capital and industry, working as a team for the benefit of the nation. Tell that claptrap to the thousands of workers walking through the main gates of the Port Kembla and Newcastle steelworks, factories and construction sites. You might see the occasional smile on the face of an ironworker, thankful for a delegate who opposed a foreman's arrogance, empowered by management to hound and drive for greater production.

"Menzies prattles on about class warfare as a tactic of the unions to intimidate industry and advance their claims. The man doesn't believe class exists in Australia. Well, I still see first and second class carriages on our trains leaving Central Station. Ships bringing migrants from Europe to Australia with a few thousand crammed in steerage. During the wars fleets of troopships departing Australia crammed with thousands of troops in the holds while their officers enjoyed staterooms. Does the chairman of BHP sit down on a slab of warm steel without washing his hands and eat a mutton sandwich and boil a billy of black tea on the job?

"The mansions of the upper class along the harbour foreshore, I don't think many of them collect our garbage and sweep our gutters. Private schools for the rich, for the rest of us government schools good and bad. Dress circle and front stalls, saloon and public bars. Australia a classless society? I would believe good old patriotic Bob flying the hammer and sickle outside his Toorak mansion before I would believe Australia is a classless society."

From the body of the meeting a few courageous hecklers tried to interject, their voices drowned out by the cheers and footwear threatening to splinter worn floorboards. A group of extreme religious right with their frontline speaker standing on his chair demanded a right of reply over the din, when ignored by the chair reaching in his pocket for a crucifix for God to strike the heathen dead.

Others tried but failed to say their piece, on their feet the meeting either cheering or looking for an easy target to vent their frustration. Time to end the meeting and let them spill their blood outside. Ward's voice boomed out over the hall, these his final words: "I thought it might be appropriate to mention in his policy speech Menzies in that brilliant legal mind of his failed to find a fitting quote from an Aussie scribe or statesman on freedom, let alone a beloved Pom to end with. Abraham Lincoln would you believe. Then again I suppose you would use old Abe who liberated slaves when you're gushing and prancing on a platform of freedom. Then again when politicians are spinning pure bunkum to win office, freedom and equality are mere words." Finished, he crumpled the papers in his hands and threw them into the audience.

Sam crushed against the wall felt his heart go out to the man on the stage; his face downcast as he drew a few deep breathes and flexed his shoulders. From this distance he seemed alone, vulnerable, though assuredly with the man's known strengths and his lifelong commitment to exposing political bigots it might have been a ruse to put his opponents off guard. The politician suffered no fools nor did he associate with those in his party whose slick grasp of the English language saw them noticed by the party hierarchy only to show their true loyalties the moment the doors of parliament closed behind them.

≈

In the few remaining weeks of the campaign Ward's evangelistic voice reverberated off the walls and ceilings of town halls, church halls and mechanic institutes, a plea to remain loyal to the cause. As an aside, conjure a miracle and convert the crusaders of the right to the left.

Menzies towered to unassailable heights in the final weeks of campaigning, in Sydney addressing a meeting of 4000 faithful. Like a conquering emperor parading before his adoring subjects, his chest outthrust, his mesmerising baritone voice boomed: 'We are going to declare war on the Communists this government has allowed to thrive in our midst! On our home ground and on our own terms we are going to thrash the Reds!'

Mothers in the audience wept with relief for sons of military age called upon to repel the heathen hordes of the Soviet Union and China advancing in their millions southwards. When their tears abated, thankful mothers wrung their handkerchiefs and dabbed their puffy eyes to see more clearly their saviour in a double breasted pinstripe suit.

The nation spurned Labor, a government resting on its past achievements. Labor campaigned it fostered no love for the Communist movement, rogue unions and unions dictating policy to the government, proof when it broke the miners strike. Labor jailed Communists. Labor fined Communist unions into bankruptcy.

The new prime minister could afford a smile of satisfaction, fifty-five Liberal seats won in the lower house, his coalition partner nineteen seats.

Seventy-four seats! Forty-seven Labor!

Labor retreated to the opposition benches to lick its wounds, its many factions already planning revolt, lesions that would remain open and festering for a long, long time.

39

THE WARNING FROM THE branch secretary at the Port Kembla stopwork meeting drove home the message Prime Minister Menzies would not wallow in the congratulatory aftermath of victory, ordering his legal advisors to draft the Australian Communist Party Dissolution Bill 1950, a core election promise.

Sam, chairing the meeting, saw in the faces of those present tight-lipped resignation to the inevitable. The branch secretary's voice, almost a monotone, listed singularly the major points of the bill. Now with a decisive mandate from the Australian people Menzies loathing of Communism surged to new heights, driven by a belief his nation faced being consumed by not only international Communism, but also from within by traitorous cells fuelled by organised labour.

While the branch secretary spoke Sam read a summary of the bill attached to the federal office report. The Communist Party of Australia declared illegal and absolved, its property seized and disposed of. Unions affiliated to the Communist Party of Australia deregistered and their assets confiscated and disposed of. Officials contravening this disbandment would face jail terms of not less than five years. Any declared person suspected of being a Communist banned from holding an official position in a union or in government employment.

Disbelief filled Sam's face as the printed words sunk into his mind. This legislation did not come from everyday Australians elected to federal parliament. It originated in the warped and scheming minds of extreme rightwing despots enforcing a system of control and manipulation far more restrictive and draconian than the socialist system these groups sought to destroy. Did a newly elected member of the Country Party from Bourke, another from Parkes or Albury, help compose of this neo-fascist doctrine? Did their constituents support this blatant suppression of human rights?

Disbelief turned to anger as he read on. Any person declared a Communist would have the onus of proving the accusation false. Didn't the Westminster system place the onus on the state to prove guilt, those accused of transgressions against society innocent until proven guilty? He could stomach no more as the branch secretary resumed his seat.

Sam cleared his throat, carefully choosing his words. "I have only read part of this document from federal office, but what I have makes me wonder do I live in Australia or am I in pre-war Germany worshiping at the feet of Adolph Hitler? The Liberal government is about to plunge Australia into an era of fear and repression. Make it a patriotic act for neighbour to spy on neighbour, to lie and slander, falsely accuse without fear of recrimination. When your eyes pass over this document one word is prominent, the word declare. The government can declare you a Communist on an anonymous phone call, the declared guilty as accused until the declared can prove otherwise. The government can declare you because your leftwing political beliefs condemn you as a Communist.

"Being declared means most of the officials in our union, probably all in the Waterside Workers Federation, will be banned from holding office. Do these elected officials pose a threat to our national security because of their political beliefs and militant stance in award negotiations with employers? To Menzies and his pack of yapping lapdogs these officials are because of their annoying habit of impeding the amassing of mega profits on the broken backs of workers for their industrial and commercial mates.

"Think hard about that word declare on the lips of Menzies. After hounding the Communists he might want to declare the leftwing of the Labor Party a threat to security. Or me who is not a Communist but could boast without exaggeration I have possibly a hundred good mates who are. I am declared because of association." He drew a deep breath and glanced at the branch secretary, a silent apology for not vacating the chair. "Comrades, I speak from the chair and out of turn, but if we as a union and all unions allied to the progressive cause do not fight this retrogressive legislation the trade unions of Australia will be relegated to history."

≈

"Do you feel up to it?" Emily nestled in his arms on a new extremely comfortable and soft outdoor sofa, the view of the ocean beyond the veranda marred by a further sagging of the roof on its posts, Sam confident without major repairs the next southerly buster would see its demise.

"Sam, I wish I could," she said.

"Even for someone fit I am told the terrain is hard. Very hilly from what I hear."

"Orange, odd name or a town."

"Named after some obscure European regal personage. I don't think there are many oranges grown there, lot of cherries and apples because of the higher elevation. Being Country Party heartland it will be the troops over the top stuffing letterboxes, staking a claim on street corners to preach salvation to the hayseeds."

"Why so far away? Why not closer to home?"

"The south coast unions are well organised, wharfies, dockers, miners, ironworkers and us. The bush is a totally different matter where the locals in their droves vote Country Party or Liberal, and on election day handing out Labor how-to-votes is a pretty lonely occupation. Labor branches are a rarity which makes me think city Labor might have given up on the bush. Common knowledge most farmers do it tough making a decent living off the land, but why set your dogs on a union organiser who wants nothing more for his members than a fair deal?"

Emily settled closer to him on the sofa, the pungent smell of the new waxy material pleasing to the nose; the setting needed something else; a pot of coffee and a wicker basket of cubed cheddar cheese and salted crackers.

"Wages in the bush are about half that of the city and what amazes you about this disparity is how the rednecks bolt on hearing the mention of award conditions and wages. Bragging in the pub the local Country Party member, probably their old boss, touched the brim of his hat in passing. Held in the highest esteem, a dedicated man of the bush called to serve his country in the public forum, squirming with feverish excitement as his revered prime minister rises to his feet with his hand over his heart to announce the demise of civil liberties."

"While you are away I might go home." Suddenly she sat up, her eyes alight. "Mother is seeing this nice man so Mary says. Though he seems more interested in something more permanent than Mother. I suppose when hurt once you want to avoid it in the future."

"What about your father? Hear anything?"

"No. Well and truly over."

"She should divorce him and make a new life for herself."

"Fourteen, fifteen years, it still doesn't count as a reason for divorce."

"So you can be separated all those years, probably shacked up with another woman with four or five kids, and it isn't cause for divorce?"

"According to Mary who has been given advice, separation has to be agreed to by both parties and where my father is, who knows. Even so her life is much better without him."

"Laws made by men to serve men. We really do live in a man's world."

"Harriet's still talking of marriage. I think he's an engineer with the roads."

"Yes, I am aware of her excited babbling. Did you know Mary's husband is a Liberal?"

"How do you know that?"

"Saw him shudder and grind his teeth when I casually mentioned over a few drinks, maybe a few too many on my part, that every member of the parliamentary Liberal Party and their rump should be castrated and put out in the paddock with their only benefit to society producing fertilizer."

She giggled. "Which made Mary almost choke as well. Yes, I think you are right, but it doesn't detract he is a good man, father and provider."

"Not my type. Then again the officer class has never curried much favour with me."

She and Sam would finish their coffee and nibbles, nothing to think about for dinner, salad and cold meat. A stroll along the beach in the fading light, holding hands and scampering as the surging wash of breaking waves threatened to rise above their knees. Their hips touching, bumping, hands fleetingly touching familiar curves. Sometimes making love in the sand dunes.

These were the good days, the days Emily remembered with a glow in her cheeks, not the others when she lay in bed and fought for breath. She and Sam discussed her health with the Stanwell Park doctor, his advice never varying that although a seaside environment provided health benefits, a drier climate would certainly assist with her medication and lessen the frequency of the asthmatic attacks. Both talked of leaving this idyllic environment where most of his leaves were spent though it could never be theirs permanently or Dave's, the dozen or so ramshackle dwelling along the beach described by authorities as illegal structures with a decision pending on their removal. At night in the middle of winter with a raging southerly gale rattling the iron on the roof, the thunder and roar of the ocean so close it seemed it would engulf the home, under a thick quilt and woollen blanket, the heat of Sam's body, she wanted nothing else in the entire world.

At home in Pyrmont and during the long periods of Sam's absence she kept in close contact with her family. Mary's two little girls adorable, doted upon by a beloved aunty though tinged with longing.

≈

A bus with forty-four seamen and three vigilant officers, waterside workers, painters and dockers, builders labourers, ironworkers, and miners drove into Orange early morning, their first stop after a midnight departure from

Wollongong the Royal Arms Hotel with accommodation for two nights booked. The publican, probably the only person in the mid-size western town who sympathised with the union cause, greeted the invasion as not only a windfall but a respite from those who normally breasted his bar championing the noble cause of rural conservatism.

He kept his peace as good business principle warranted, though sometimes the veneer wore thin which probably resulted in his establishment being the least favoured in a town of big drinkers. Assured of shelter, fine country fare and refreshments, groups of four commandeered prominent street corners with boxes of literature and pamphlets, banners and placards. Selected groups stuffed letterboxes, the town in military style dissected in grids, those of a persuasive nature to liaise with the radio station and newspaper, Sam allocated a busy corner in the middle of town with three old shipmates, Calvin Catchpole, Darcy O'Rourke and Kevin Brannigan.

The Orange regional manager of the Australian Broadcasting Commission showed reluctance to give the visiting delegation airtime, a suggested fifteen minutes which might stretch to twenty minutes on their high rating morning Country Hour broadcast. When official diplomacy failed, two particularly persuasive delegates from the painters and dockers needed no encouragement to have a word with the unenthusiastic broadcaster, a credit to their self-control keeping their voices fairly moderate when learning the man held the venerated position of president of the Orange branch of the Country Party.

The good people of farming stock who tilled the earth and lived far from the cities should not be fearful, their presence in town not an invasion, but seen as their city brothers on a mission of enlightenment, the painters and dockers argued. Did not history record farmers and unionists among the first to answer the call when the cry for help came from the threatened shores of the United Kingdom?

Another truth, farmers and unionists, kindred spirits with grit and fortitude, built this great nation of fire, flood and drought. Some advice, a few of their larger and less amiable comrades, no, brothers, were incensed at this undemocratic denial of free speech, of course forced upon him by his fascist superiors in Sydney, and might like to escort him safely home.

Outside the building and in view through his large office window he saw a group of men of an obvious heavy labouring nature, possibly with other more furtive occupations as a sideline, gathered on the footpath. More because of his professional commitment to journalistic ethics than fear for his physical being, he agreed to airtime. In doing so he wondered how Murdoch Fyffe, venerated host of the Country Hour, would deal with the distasteful segment, no doubt with his usual rapier-like dismissal of lesser species.

The manager as he did each morning browsed through a copy of the *Central Western Daily* on his desk, wishing for the nerve of its editor who ignored the union delegation even though informed days in advance by the police. Its entire front page a photograph and text of a prize Hereford bull recently sold for a record price at the Albury cattle sales.

Tomorrow's front page might carry a photograph of the new model John Deere tractor driven by a buxom young lass suitably attired in a wide brimmed hat and jodhpurs. Why bother the paper's readers with news of irritating city unionist and their Communist cronies beating their drums and chanting their slogans, gone soon enough never to return. He agreed with conditions; no officials, one rank and file member. Not tomorrow, the program already formatted, but the following day, their final day in Orange if the police allowed them to remain in town. He thought of his Country Hour host, a disturbing image of puffy feminine lips, the sneer and cultured voice, hoping the man would show mercy on air so not to distress his flock of female listeners.

≈

Easily the busiest intersection in town, late afternoon and the town bustling with townsfolk and people from the outlying areas of Glenroi, Narrama and Calare. Sam, Calvin, Darcy and Kevin threw themselves into their roles of endangered minorities, comrades and unionists, the Bank of New South Wales occupying most of the corner festooned with banners: VOTE NO CPA 1950 BILL! FREEDOM OF ASSOCIATION! UNIONS FOR FREE SPEECH!

Sam wondered when the police would make an appearance, the sun setting low over the town and their box of leaflets near empty. Those that took the material did so courteously, a puzzled glance at the banners and placards; Sam thought their presence should at least ignite a spark of curiosity, nothing but perplexity. About to pack up for the day he saw a smirk of pure pleasure fill Darcy's face, three policemen hurrying down the street.

"Only three of the bastards, couldn't be any easier," Darcy sneered, flexing his shoulders.

"There's a lot more police than that in Orange, and get that deranged look off your face. Remember, we are here peacefully to convert the unconvertible."

"Reckon a few roughed up coppers might stir things," Darcy persisted.

"Darcy, we have been on the road since midnight and I for one do not at this time of day need a confrontation. Or a bed in a police cell. Think of the cold beer waiting in the pub. You're a guest, you can drink all night."

"Might I remind you we are here on union business. Anyway, the sergeant's an old blimp and his two constables by the looks of it just out of copper academy. How about we convert them? Some good natured banter spliced with the odd quote from Lenin?"

"As well as keep the peace, Darcy. We are here in Orange representing the trade union movement. Be proud of that."

"On a street corner obstructing pedestrian traffic preaching the gospel according to Joseph Stalin? Yeah, I'll keep the peace, but will that fat bastard?"

The sergeant's large stomach constrained in a tight corset heaved with the exertion of the last few hours enforcing council bylaws in respect of loitering, defacing public buildings, impeding public access, littering, and one incidence of offensive and abusive language. So far he needed only two constables, a relieved thought overall the Communists fairly well behaved except for that one case, the foul mouthed hooligan given a warning and his name taken.

Their behaviour boded well for the rest of their stay, hopefully controlled by their leaders.

"You are hereby issued a first warning that displaying any form of advertisement, commercial, political, theatrical, sale or promotion, is an offence and punishable with fines, repeated offences with prison terms. I am ordering you to remove your paraphernalia immediately, and this public thoroughfare be left unobstructed or be charged with loitering."

"Get fucked, you great heap of fascist shit!" Darcy growled, crouched with his clenched fists close to his body.

Sam hoped the sergeant's hearing might have diminished with age, tired and only able to reply with a hackneyed response: "We have the right as citizen in a democratic society to associate freely and express our opinions. Sergeant, we have impeded no one or forced our pamphlets upon people, and we apologise to the Bank of New South Wales if we blocked out their afternoon sun with our banners."

An expected reply, storing in his mind for later retrieval an image of a small, pugnacious man making faces at him. "As a New South Wales police officer I am well aware of what your rights are. Also of the legal ramifications of illegally obstructing a public footpath and defacing public and private buildings." He removed a notebook and pencil from his lapel pocket. "Name?"

"Sam Wright. Why are you taking my name?"

"Procedure. Reference of a prior warning if future charges are laid."

"Charges against the proletariat for exercising their right to rectify a wrong? Has the law changed in the last few months with this fascist government making it a crime to peacefully protest a wrong in a public street? You do know those bastards in Canberra are rewriting the Crimes Act?"

"Mr Wright, I will not enter into political dialogue with you on a public thoroughfare, and if your discordant attitude continues we will further discuss this matter at the police station."

"Do that, mate, and you'll have to arrest the whole fucking lot of us! This busload and twenty more that will descend on your shithole of a town!" Darcy bellowed, advancing closer to the sergeant though keeping a wary eye on the two constables.

"Stand back, Darcy. We are not going to play into their hands. No violence, we do as the sergeant instructs. We comply, that's what we do for peace and for our union who sent us here to do a job." Sam eyeballed him, waving a flat hand across his chest.

The sergeant thought of ending a long day by soaking his weary feet in a dish of warm salted water. He should have acted earlier, though many would say the infringements petty, upholding law and order in Orange would remain invariable. Even though the south coast unions were given permission by the shire clerk to address the public and present their literature in a polite and unobtrusive manner, he held reservations now confirmed within their midst troublemakers.

Sam wanted only to retreat, for him and his comrades a long day over. Even so the largest crowd of the day gathered around them, people converging from everywhere, and he knew despairingly why. The sergeant and the constables carried batons on their belts and the crowd hungered for them to be drawn.

"We are going, Sergeant," Sam said wearily. "It has been a long day."

Tomorrow their banners and placards would hang from the same bank and the sergeant might have to march down the Mitchell Highway with more than two constables wielding their polished lignum vitae weaponry. A tried and trusted tool of supremacy, close kin to the cat-o'-nine-tails and gallows in cowering or eliminating those who dared rise against the state.

Sam and his tired group walked slowly in the direction of the Royal Mail Hotel, knowing their presence may not have changed any minds but possibly sparked a reaction in the form of an aroused curiosity to seek further knowledge.

≈

Sam's group the next day lost their corner to another group, theirs the hard slog of letterboxing, allocated a large grid on the outskirts of town. Wide and dusty streets filled with functional mail and parcel depositories, the array a neighbourly challenge to be more creative than the common store-bought tin or wooden variety. Nailed, wired, jammed, screwed, cemented, attached to posts, fences and gates. Milk cans painted post office red, cement pipes embedded in masonry, stuffed with leaflets, not a single one missed.

For the footsore a hazard other than exhaustion made distribution a danger, territorial dogs guarding the perimeters of their owners properties. Attacks came from various breeds, the most prominent and vicious blue heelers. Prone to rage induced frenzied leaps and frantic body contortions over or under fences. Head-on assaults, slathering red gums exposing lethal white fangs awash with phlegm. Darcy carried an ironbark fence paling which put a premature end to one foray, the dog in mid-air with a single intent, to rip its victim's throat out.

Sam thought he might have killed the dog, the lifeless animal flat on its broad muscular back with blood oozing from its unhinged jaws. "That's one supporter for the cause of freedom of association we've lost if that's the dog's master I see rushing down the street."

"Fuck him!" Darcy raised his weapon over his head and charged, his bloodlust only slightly less than his canine victim thankfully stirring in the dust. The dog's owner in his late sixties recognised the insanity in Darcy's eyes, saw his faithful bitch give a few twitches, and thought retreat his best option.

The last attack of the day came when thoughts were on pints of cold frothy beer in the Royal Mail Hotel's public bar. The blue heeler came squirming under the bottom rail of the picket fence, a well-worn tunnel dug for the purpose of attack, it too in a slathering fit of wrath. Free of the fence it paused momentarily to select a victim, then charged at Darcy and fell over in a cloud of dust. In the dog's demented mind three good legs were not an impediment in protecting its territory.

Its ungainly gait and continuous tripping, it legs uncoordinated, brought sympathetic smiles to fatigued faces, a call for Darcy to at least give the poor handicapped creature a fighting chance and throw down his weapon.

"Give the poor old bloke a break, Darcy," Sam said, watching the unfortunate dog roll in another dust cloud.

"How about I put a tag around its crazy neck that says I voted for Bob?" Darcy said, resting on his fence picket with a smile on his dusty face.

"No, a clown in the May Day parade more apt," Sam said, stuffing a leaflet in the dog owner's letterbox, his last for the day.

≈

Seated around six dinner tables in the Royal Mail Hotel's dining room, their last night in Orange, a selection process took place, Sam surprised when a protégé of Ted Roach's from Port Kembla called his name from two tables away. "9:00am at the ABC studios and the bus is leaving at 10:00am so make it count. You're up against what we think is an upper-class twit, a remittance man sent to the colonies from some inbred aristocratic family in England. We might be wrong, but listening to him yesterday almost ruined a successful day on the hustings with the heavies in blue distracted with the local Aborigines having a punch-up to rival their brothers in Taree."

≈

The national broadcaster's studio overpowered its victims in a futuristic mind numbing world of electronics, grey painted panels alight with flickering gauges, teasing the nose with a barely detectable odour of overheated bakelite. Intimidation by modern technology, Sam thought sitting uneasily on a straight backed chair at a cluttered desk with a large microphone. He also wondered how normal everyday people trapped in here could sound so at ease and fluent of speech.

What humbled him, held him in an almost trance-like state, the prodigious power of the microphone, a device so powerful that in the hands of maniacs and fanatics, evangelists and politicians, it reshaped the world. Its electronic waves could penetrate every home in the country, mesmerise, enthral, despair, bring joy and arouse. The spoken word and music saturating the ether, people from hundreds of miles away pausing in their daily chores to listen and be enlightened.

Murdoch Fyffe with hooded eyes studied Sam across the desk. He would give the Communist fifth columnist free reign to stammer and stumble over the basic principles of speech and make a fool of himself, waste the precious opportunity granted him to pollute minds. He passed a thick tongue over his sensuous lips, silent seconds like hours. Sam thought he heard classical music in the background.

He fidgeted nervously; others before him who sat in this uncomfortable chair rose to the occasion, a wish that Darcy or someone else sat captive. An uncertain finger to adjust the angle of the microphone brought a silent rebuke from the man opposite, Sam beginning to hate him. Lips too full for a man, red and pouting.

Skin almost albino, a first thought if touched fingers would come way clammy. Thin almost transparent hair combed flat on a small waxy skull. Detractors of aristocracy might say the result of the family keeping the bloodline in the family. Sam thought he might have misjudged him until at last he spoke.

Pompous, overbearing and patronising; he might have been talking to an illiterate, dim-witted farmhand with cow dung clinging to his boots. "I have a series of prepared questions which I shall ask you over the period of the interview," he said in a deep and cultured voice without meeting Sam's eyes, twirling a pencil through his fingers. "I shall not advance any personal views or deviate from the subject matter, but may ask for brief elaboration on ambiguous points. Do you understand? Also do not touch the microphone."

Sam's nervousness vanished in an instance: "Yes. Yes, I do."

"This broadcast is live but I have at my disposal a pause mechanism which can if warranted shut you off air. Use of profanities will conclude this interview without further notice. Vulgarities and asides considered libellous, licentious or injurious to third parties, will also result in termination. Do you understand?"

Sam nodded, suppressing mounting frustration as the pasty faced broadcaster lectured him like an errant child, his sophisticated voice an irritant that made his skin crawl. Then the entire aplomb of the man opposite ascended another notch, his voice edged with cordiality as he welcomed listeners back to the Country Hour, then morbidity as with barely disguised abhorrence he introduced his guest.

"Our guest this morning is Mr Wright a member of a visiting group of south coast trade unionists to Orange comprised of officials and rank and file concerned over the proposed introduction of legislation in federal parliament to abolish the Communist Party of Australia. Mr Wright, as spokesman for the delegation why is the union movement committing considerable resources and membership funds to bring their case to a small rural community? Saturating it with highly biased anti-government literature when the government as champions of self-determination are faced with the threat of Communism at home and abroad?"

Sam stared at the cold metal of the live microphone, for a few moments almost overwhelmed by the thought his voice would enter the homes of thousands of people. To his surprise his voice sounded relaxed and assured. "We feel legislation to declare illegal a political party, any political party, and ban its members from holding official positions in unions and working for government, is legislation not only to suppress freedom of association but to destroy the trade union movement."

Did a sneer on the lips of the man opposite mean a finger hovered over the pause button? Sam continued: "Recent history is still fresh in people's minds, Hitler, Mussolini, Franco, Tojo. Their ruthless suppression of racial minorities, trade unions and Communists."

Fyffe interrupted. "In your list of dictators one is pointedly missing, Joseph Stalin."

"Yes, some could probably say without fear of contradiction Stalin. You could also infer he led Russia to victory against Hitler in the same mould as Churchill and Roosevelt. That twenty million Russian died in the fight against fascism."

"Mr Wright, are you a member of the Communist Party?"

The microphone's aura vanished, Sam's thoughts clear and concise. "No, I am not a member of the Communist Party, but I would like your listeners to fully understand the implications your question raised because if Mr Menzies in his quest to save this country from the perceived scourge of Communism that query would have declared me. Facing five years of imprisonment. My assets seized and sold. My employment in a government job terminated. Unable to stand for election in my union. Ostracized, financially ruined, a criminal conviction. All because I belonged to a declared political party. A party falsely declared by the government as a threat to national security."

Sam watched the man opposite closely, if his hand moved to a lighted panel of dials and toggle switches; instead he stared at him in contempt.

"By an act of parliament I can be declared a Communist on the word of a wife beater, a drunk, pervert, child molester, the dregs of society that make an art form of avoiding work, scum who live by robbing and cheating. Fine upstanding citizens according to the government in their frenetic crusade to rid the country of their phobia, Communism."

"Mr Wright, are you a recruitment agent for the Communist Party?"

"I don't think the Communist Party employs recruitment agents. Am I still on air?"

Fyffe rolled his eyes. "Why wouldn't you be on the air, Mr Wright? Have you your countries confused? Please elaborate on the large union presence in Orange supporting Communism."

"We are not only supporting the right to be a Communist and freedom of association, but the survival of the union movement which the government hopes will be decimated with the removal of officials and the banning of others of similar political calling from standing for election. We feel as responsible trade unionists we have an obligation to inform not only our members but the community of the threat to the Westminster system of government if the Communist Party of Australia Dissolution Bill 1950 becomes law. Where the onus is on a declared person to prove he is not a Communist with the removal from the constitution that basic human right of being innocent until proven guilty."

Fyffe leaned closer to his microphone, a hungry predator sizing up an easy meal; tetchily, he pushed aside his prepared questions. "Presumption of innocence, yes. I could bore you with the Latin terminology ei incumbit probatio qui dicit, but for the common everyday folk who gave a substantial mandate to a government which promised on assuming office to purge the country of Communism why should it come under attack by vested interests such as the trade union movement? Surely all of you who have travelled such a long distance must agree the government with its legislative powers is protecting Australia from a foreign and alien incursion? I remind you, a pledge he compassionately promised campaigning for election."

"Yes, Mr Menzies promised if elected he would ban the Communist Party, but would the people have voted for him if the truth came out what declaring meant? If the press and the wireless gave the union movement the same biased coverage it did the government, I think the people would have voted differently. Declaring someone a Communist by an accusing finger, an anonymous phone call, an unsigned letter, word-of-mouth, and no right of appeal. This makes a mockery of the constitution, presumption of guilt until proven innocent."

"Do you dispute the fact, the trade union movement for whom you lobby, that there is a broad Soviet Union influence supporting Communist infiltrated unions and the Communist Party of Australia?"

Taking heart Fyffe's fingers seemed more interested in the pencil than the pause button, he replied: "So the government would have you believe. It is a fact to succeed in having contentious legislation passed into law you first have to demonise the cause, the government congratulated on its efforts. Unions with Communist officials and the Communist Party of Australia threaten no one. Once a few years ago the party might have mustered 20,000 members Australia wide, now barely more than a few thousand. It owes no allegiance to any foreign government, the Australian government using a tactic perfected by German propagandists to stir the population into a furore of nationalist fervour. We are now seeing the converted putting their hands up, groupers in unions and the Labor Party driven by a religious fervour expounded by an extreme and ultra rightwing prophet, Bartholomew Santamaria under the auspices of Archbishop Daniel Mannix."

"You make serious allegations the government would rely on informers, shirkers and persons of low morals to expose Communists in the community, but how can a climate of anonymous information exist when high profile Communists now hold office in unions and are well known in the community? My only disputation is if government legislation is successful these Communists will be driven underground to continue their subversive work."

Sam went on the attack, heartened by the pencil tapping on the deck. "Subversive activities? Is leading a union and gaining through negotiation conditions and higher wages a subversive activity? Union officials, especially Communist officials, are fair game for conservatives protecting the interests of their mates in industry and commerce."

"A point of view hardly supported by mainstream Australian workers, especially those of the land who believe in the ethic those who risk capital to succeed in business should be rewarded. Who subscribe to loyalty and that hard work is reward to one's self."

"No! We will become a nation of informers. People afraid to speak their minds. People spying on people, a nation rushing to the far right politically and becoming a corrupt and self-righteous society."

Sam wondered if the curled lip and the slightly raised left cheek indicated scorn, or the Country Hour host might have a particle of food caught in his teeth. Whatever the facial expression, the interview came to an abrupt end.

"You have been listening to a point of view not necessarily shared by the Australian Broadcasting Commission, a visiting delegation of trade unionists and members of the Communist Party of Australia concerned with proposed legislation to combat the rising threat of international and home-grown Communism. Prime Minister Menzies is proposing to introduce legislation into the parliament which would make it illegal to be a member of a declared organisation, albeit the Communist Party of Australia and those named as Communists from holding responsible office in trade unions and government employment."

Fyffe's normally pure white cheeks flushed with a cherry redness, a signal to his sound engineer visible through a clear glass panel. "This is Murdoch Fyffe and this is the Country Hour broadcast from Orange. A recent arrival to these fair shores last week, Dr Bruhn of the Mayo Clinic in Rochester, Minnesota, met with medical specialists in Sydney and in his busy schedule visited hospital facilities in western New South Wales. I deemed it a pleasure to be able to speak with Dr Bruhn on recent advancements in cancer treatment in the United States." Fyffe swivelled in his chair and turned his back on Sam.

"Are we still talking?"

"Talk all you want, and not a bit of good will it do you," he said, rubbing his hands together vigorously before clapping them nosily, his wet lips creased in a smile of pure malevolence. "My advice to you and your ilk, you are living on borrowed time. Enjoy your long leash while you can."

40

THE UNION MOVEMENT MOBILISED to fight the Communist Party of Australia Dissolution Bill 1950, even unions centrist and rightwing. To counterbalance this negative and at times volatile reaction the government called upon the nation to remain calm and read their newspapers for factual information, listen to their wirelesses, speak with their government members who remained resolute in the battle to safeguard the nation against the threat of Communism.

The government could take comfort a large proportion of the Australian population feared Communism, paranoid of a Communist China invasion supported by the Russian Red Army. Rumblings in the Korean peninsula also assisted the government's case for a Communist free Australia. Stark images on cinema screens of robotic-like soldiers parading past grim faced leaders on podiums high in Red Square. Such images boosted the government's arguments, leaving civil libertarians and unions struggling to counteract the information wing of the Liberal and Country Parties, the major newspapers.

The government could take heart that in America extreme rightwing political stalwarts with courage and tenacity were publicly exposing and expunging Communists and leftwing sympathisers. Writers, actors, film producers, artists, publishers, traitors abusing a public trust and hiding behind their high profiles, exposed and banished. Blacklisted, ridiculed and publicly humiliated.

Sam joined the Adelaide Steamship Company's *Beltana* discharging sugar at Pyrmont, a respite from the frenzy of organising and letterboxing country towns, rallies, demonstrations and street corner leafleting. He saw it in the faces of those he handed his leaflets to on street corners, indecision. With his message and sincerity he thought on occasions he succeeded breaching insecurities, though in the knowledge that when a newspaper landed on a front porch with news of a suspected Soviet spy ring operating in Canberra, or Communist Chinese troops massing on the Manchurian border, his efforts wasted.

≈

Government members worked their electorates tirelessly to convince their constituents the bill to dissolve the Communist Party of Australia would insulate the nation against Communism. The bill did not erode civil rights, instead ensured a continuance of the Australian way of life, a safer and more secure life. A pacifier to calm detractors; when a nation fought to maintain its freedom from foreign aggressors its people should expect some deprivations of civil rights, a small price to pay for freedom.

The prime minister reached heights of popularity usually afforded visiting royalty, a fortress of unconquerable strength. He intoned with persuasive homilies to ignore the orchestrated theatrics of the Communists, the sham civil libertarians who would have the world return to basket weaving and cavorting around maypoles.

The Labor Party endured scorn on the floor of the parliament for having the audacity to question not only the loss of civil rights associated with the bill but its constitutional legality. Communist sympathisers! Weaklings! Puppets of the leftwing union movement! Ingratiating offers of sympathy across the floor of parliament for the unsullied members of the Labor Party who sat in the house of the people cringing and hanging their heads in shame as their leftwing fellows bedded with Communists.

Opposition leader Chifley accepted the ridicule as no more than parliamentary jousting, Menzies and his front bench at their rousing theatrical best. Even so he held concerns Labor's links with Communist trade unions were damaging to the party. Chifley with the numbers in the upper house could reject the bill, but what troubled him and his front bench, Australia constantly endured major strikes in the main caused by Communists officials in the trade union movement. The government argued, and the majority of the population believed, remove the Communist influence and the strikes would end.

Menzies knew exactly where his opposite number stood on the need to combat radical elements in the workforce, dramatic proof with the crushing defeat he wrought upon the miners, though this never lessened the attacks, lies and innuendo. Socialists! Troglodytes! Leaderless! Spineless! Devoid of policy! Dithering! Economic vandals!

The member for East Sydney, at times known to add fire to parliamentary debate, cupped his hands and shouted across the floor: "The Fuehrer has spoken!"

≈

On the 27th of April the Communist Party of Australia Dissolution Bill 1950 came before the parliament amid uproar from some sections of Labor's backbench. The first reading of the bill defined government guidelines of declaring a Communist: *a person who supports or advocates the objectives, policies, teachings, principles or practices of Communism, as expounded by Marx and Lenin.*

The introduction of the bill could not have come at a more opportune time for the government, the release of a damning report from a royal commission into the activities of Communists in Victoria. Menzies thumped the table and glowered. "Communism festering in our midst, exposed in the sovereign state of Victoria! A disease that will be erased from the medical text books with the adoption of legislation with a single objective, safeguarding the people of Australia!"

Labor deliberated long and painfully over the bill, arguments the party should reject it outright evenly balanced with those who supported it. Chifley accused the government of preparing the nation for eventual totalitarian government. His words fell on closed minds that liars and perjurers would file through government doors damning the vulnerable and innocent. The creation of a secretive society, liars and perjurers granted immunity from public disclosure. Removing two pillars vital in maintaining a democratic society, the right of free association and speech.

The government with its majority in the lower house passed the bill, the legislation referred to the senate for review. At first there seemed a faint glimmer of hope for the Communist Party when the legislation stalled in the upper house. Labor saw merit in the bill abolishing the Communist Party, though adamant amendments were required to protect civil liberties. The three factions of Labor debated in the senate chamber, adding amendments which the government refused to accept.

The stalemate came at a price for the Labor Party, an ever widening division, a simmering bitterness between the factions instigated by a diminutive, prematurely balding man. Bartholomew Santamaria caucused regularly with Archbishop Daniel Mannix, their loathing of Communism equally shared with the denizens who dwelled in the netherworld.

The round, pinched face he showed the public projected no charisma, his voice a squeaky monotone. A constant flow of minced words emitted from a small, pursed mouth, never a stumble or mispronunciation. His ultra rightwing religious principles drew him into the embrace of the Catholic Church and its controversial archbishop, an association that would at times be difficult but never lose its purpose, the exorcism of Communism. Santamaria leaned even more to the far, far right obsessed with the union movement which he saw as the womb of socialism.

Santamaria found a multitude of supporters in the ranks of the conservatives, an open invitation to join the Liberal Party, offers of assured pre-selection. Instead likened to a warrior of God he descended into the murky world of working class politics, the nursery of collectivism, seeking out members of the parliamentary Labor Party who believed in the existence of God, especially those who belonged to the Catholic Church.

Menzies hovered in the wings, disturbing events unfolding in Asia as well as dissention in Labor ranks, factors almost guaranteeing the Communist abolishment bill becoming law.

With the bill dormant in the senate the prime minister's first major boost for its successful passage came mid-year when North Korea invaded South Korea. Armies numbering hundreds of thousands of fanatical North Koreans, drilled as a single killing machine, surged southwards, a foretaste of what awaited the democracies as the Communist Bloc made a mockery of peaceful co-existence. Even more catastrophic for world peace as the United Nations offered support to South Korea, a giant across the Yalu River allied itself to its aggressive Communist neighbour, the Chinese Red Army millions upon millions strong.

The democracies under the pale blue flag of the United Nations asked the question of its member states if South Korea fell where would the conquest end? A new catchphrase, short and apt, dominos. The Asian colonies of the European powers falling one by one to Communism. Menzies knew where the last piece would fall, Australia, a fifth column waiting on the beaches.

With United Nations forces in full retreat down the Korean peninsula, rightwing members of the parliamentary Labor Party, prompted by Santamaria, demanded their party support the Communist Party of Australia Dissolution Bill 1950.

An exultant prime minister reintroduced the bill on September 28th, fortuitous as Labor's federal executive met to discuss the widening split in the party. The executive, in an effort to achieve unity, agreed to allow free passage of the bill which became law three weeks later.

≈

Sam thought this indeed the dizzy heights, promoted to bosun of the *Beltana* when the bosun broke his wrist and paid off in Bowen, North Queensland. He eased into his new role, a natural inclination to liaise and organise with other departments. Dealing with the chief mate on a daily basis he discovered a fact of shipboard life, a good bosun almost made the delegates redundant.

Problems on deck usually snuffed out quickly with an informal discussion with the mate, arms draped over the dodger on the wing of the bridge on the four to eight watch. Times when an AB fell by the wayside and missed a square up, the bosun's wrath usually far more effective than the log book.

Sam enjoyed the role, the added responsibly and being part of the ship's planning. He and the storekeeper filled in the gear register book from their grimy notes taken on deck when overhauling and replacing gear. Also a learning experience becoming familiar with breaking strains and safety weight limits of wire, stranded wire formulas, lashing tonnages, load line surveys, gear surveys, lifeboats and the rudimentary of ships stability.

Stability surprised, of a mind like so many seaman a ship sank to her marks and sailed. He learned tons-per-inch submersion, the difference between a loll and a list, metacentric heights, triggers and righting arms. The science of a ship, to most seamen no more than a piece of rusty iron in need of constant attention to remain afloat, fascinated him. On the bridge one morning discussing changing a quarter block with a badly worn distance piece, he made an admission to the chief mate; never again would call a mate a shipowners vacuum.

"Like to join us?"

"Good God no! I'm happy where I am with my merry band of schemers, lunatics and revolutionaries. I even have a defrocked priest on the eight to twelve who takes confessions from a couple of Irish firemen."

Sam felt an affinity to the *Beltana*, Aboriginal for running water; heavy on deck and uncomfortable in a sea with her gear housed on the foremast and mainmast, but a happy and efficient ship run by teamwork and little interference from management. Three sugar trips completed the original Colonial Sugar Refinery charter, the *Beltana* re-chartered for an additional two to clear the previous year's harvest from the sugar refiner's North Queensland facilities.

Emily at home in Pyrmont suffered a severe asthma attack, in hospital her frail body fighting for life. Her face porcelain white he wished she would open her beautiful eyes and look at him, whisper not to worry she would soon be well. To take her to Stanwell Park and sit together on the veranda and watch ships sail by.

Young and recently migrated from Belfast, the Irish doctor sat on the end of Emily's bed. "Mr Wright—"

"Sam, please call me Sam."

"I don't need to tell you how sick your wife is," he said, his rolling Irish accent subdued with the gravity of the situation. "Over the years I have seen too many cases like Emily's in Belfast and the British industrial heartland to be tempted to believe in full recoveries. Children born on the very doorsteps of industries whose emissions should have their directors sent to prison. Growing up in that environment, themselves bearing children to keep the wheels of industry turning."

"The cycle of life for people like me and Emily."

"The way it is for so many in the world, yes. Nutrition plays an important role in how our bodies cope, an odd fact that during the war rationing actually benefited the health of Great Britain."

"Strange."

"Remove all the harmful stuff, which by corporate design is the best tasting and long lasting, and leave only what nature intended and you have longevity and good health. Governments should take note, save them a lot of money for hospitals and my wages."

"Doctor, will Emily ever get better."

"I wish I could give you a positive answer, but I can't. I can though advise you and Emily should have a long look at your life and where you live."

"Our home is in Pyrmont, but we spend a lot of time in Stanwell Park."

"I've heard of it, south of here. The tang of salt air, sand underfoot, hair blowing in the wind, the ocean cleansing and exhilarating. Though not for your Emily. Paradise is killing her."

Sam watched his peacefully sleeping wife, her soft and even breathing assured by medical technology.

The doctor took his hand and shook it. "You have a big decision to make, Sam."

≈

Within twenty-four hours of the Communist Party of Australia Dissolution Bill 1950 passing without amendment in the senate, barely even time to pop the champagne corks, the Waterside Workers Federation issued an injunction against the government in the High Court as to the bills constitutional validity. The union engaged as their counsel, attorney general in the Chifley government, Dr Herbert Vere Evatt.

A fuming prime minister ignored the injunction; he would not suffer defeat at the hands of the very people the dissolution bill aimed to remove permanently from society. He ordered the immediate appointment of an official government receiver to seize Communist Party assets, an order for the federal police to raid every Communist Party office in the country, names taken and files impounded.

The government would not be able to declare individuals as Communists, but would with police intervention and seizures effectively close them down.

The High Court in its deliberations of the Communist Party of Australia Dissolution Bill 1950 seemed to those uninformed of legal processes to be a judicial institution of extreme slowness. The dissecting of the bill clause by clause by the finest legal brains in the country not a cursory browsing. The seven esteemed justices would take until November before finally handing down a decision, six judges to one, that the bill deemed a defence bill and under the constitution invalid because the Commonwealth could not prove the Communist Party a threat to the nation's security.

There were no celebrations for the Communist Party existing under constant police surveillance, their offices under threat of raid at any hour of the day. Similar with the leftwing unions who worked hard in mustering their members and resources to make boring legal deliberations workplace debate. For the government the ruling came as no more than a glitch, the prime minister shrugging off the pall of rejection in conservative ranks with his usual aplomb, and with a clear plan in mind gathered about him a task force of similar mind. To formulate a trigger for a double dissolution of parliament, win control of the senate and prepare a referendum to remedy a constitutional matter.

Lessening the dejection afflicting the coalition party rooms some sterling news members should prepare themselves for a long period of occupying the government benches, the ever widening schism in the opposition most heartening.

41

T HE PERIOD OF RELATIVE calm both political and industrial proved
short, the prime minister taking the scenic drive from his Canberra
residence to the governor general's more regal mansion to inform his
lordship, Sir William John McKell, of obstruction in the senate which made
governance untenable.

A three month period of negative negotiation with the Labor controlled
upper house failed to pass the Commonwealth Bank Bill, the legislation
an election pledge and the government unwilling to have the bill referred
to committee, the government as such requested a writ, Section 57 of the
Constitution, to dissolve both houses of parliament.

Labor, like novices in a game of chess, allowed the old master to take their
queen in the first few months of their occupying the opposition benches, the
board decimated by the Commonwealth Bank Bill, a socialist relic from the
Chifley days, of no real importance except as a trigger for a double dissolution.

The governor general agreed with the prime minister and in his official
position as head of state would ask His Majesty to grant a double dissolution of
parliament, Mr Menzies installed as caretaker prime minister.

Menzies rallied his party, barnstorming the hustings with an invincible aura
that strengthened with each inspiring speech, each grasping handshake, each
time his resonant voice echoed through cavernous halls filled to capacity. His
government demanded the right to govern without obstruction from socialists!
To govern for those who entrusted and honoured him with a mandate to
remove the festering canker of Communism and repeal Marxist legislature
inherited from Labor!

He negated with a cutting tongue criticism of having a fanatical fixation with Communism, a battery of verbiage for those who dared question his vision of a Communist free world to cast their doubting eyes north! Waiting to erupt from their borders in their unstoppable millions, battle-hardened Communists! A mere few thousand miles and welcomed by traitors festering among us who have sworn an oath of allegiance to their Soviet Union and Chinese commissars.

My government, he wafted from thousands of mantelpieces, will not be intimidated with endless strikes, go-slows, industrial sabotage and pigheaded Communist unions who hold our industries to ransom. Seamen, waterside labourers, coal lumpers, ships painters and dockers. Unions under the domination of Communist officials with sworn allegiance to the Soviet Union.

During the election campaign a disgruntled group of members of the parliamentary Labor Party received special attention, Menzies with outstretched arms welcoming the rightwing faction into his conservative embrace. He sympathised of the suffocating miasma of old world socialism forced upon those trapped in a dying party of no consequences, a dinosaur from the darkest realms of the industrial revolution. Even courting political enemies, his focus rarely strayed from the main battlefront.

Strikes! Go-slows! Sabotage! Industrial thuggery! Cronyism! Menzies implored an answer to the question does the nation need any further proof of Communist control of the trade unions? Where did the first challenge to the Communist Party of Australia Dissolution Bill 1950 come from when supported by Labor in the senate? The Communist Waterside Federation of Australia! In his armoury more disturbing questions of who supported that challenge? A Labor government attorney general! A man honoured as a minister of the Crown a Communist sympathiser! Count the Communists and their sympathisers entrenched in the union movement who support and finance the Labor Party, the number mortifying. Accordingly what is the Labor Party's debt? The obligation no doubt repaid with political favours. Is their loyalty to our sovereign monarch or the Soviet Union?

The member of East Sydney countered with his own barrage, his attack equally as compelling. In the last election from whose coffers did large sums of money flow to elect a Liberal Country Party government? Overseas extreme rightwing bigots who based their creed of hatred on Red Army soldiers looting churches and excreting in baptismal fonts.

Lies! Utter nonsense! The conservatives won government on a platform of reward for hard work! Initiative! Freedom! A new direction for Australia!

What did Labor promise for the decades to come? Austerity and suppression of industry and commerce. Rewarding comrade mates with government jobs and contracts. Companies gutted by mercenary unions and stripped of resources to compete in foreign markets.

The coalition represented family values, the prime minister a welcomed guest in Australian homes no matter how prestigious or humble. Wise and warm hearted, a man who would not bend to the avaricious dictates of minority groups.

≈

Menzies elation showed in his jovial face, the glow of triumph in his eyes beneath his bushy eyebrows. Why not indeed, the price of absolute victory the sacrifice of only three seats. The final tally gave the Liberal Party in the lower house equal numbers of seats as the Labor Party, fifty-two. Of course the Country Party's seventeen loyal members of the coalition ensured his government of a comfortable majority. The senate result though brought the most satisfied smile.

Labor lost six seats, its majority and control of the senate blown away like discarded how-to-votes in a chilly autumn wind, the returned government in command of both houses of parliament, guaranteeing swift and unimpeded passage of legislation. Celebrations would only be short, the next and final step to absolute power, a constitutional referendum.

42

T HE MAN WHOSE SEDUCTIVE vocal cords swayed the indecisive, came to the conclusion the nation finally realised their security and prosperity relied on capitalism and not the fanciful dreams of utopian socialism.

Having control of the senate smoothed passage of legislation passing to the house of review that otherwise would have resulted in the attachment of disagreeable amendments, even deals that galled the spirit of elected government. The Country Party gained an extra seat in the senate, no doubt seeking reward with a junior ministerial portfolio, possibly tax incentives for agricultural fuels.

The prime minister envisioned Australia as one nation, not a large continent divided by states and territories, capital city jealousies, football codes and a strong almost tribal bush and city mentality. One nation, the strongest and most trusted link in the British Empire.

He held grave fears the war raging on the Korea peninsula would escalate and set in chain the domino theory feared by the democracies. This not only troubled Australia and the United States, but more so the United Kingdom, France and the Netherlands with Asian colonies in peril of Communist incursion.

The horrendous slaughter of the Korean War, the possibility of another world war erupting in Europe as the Soviet Union tightened its vice-like grip on its satellites, Communism flourishing and growing in strength in every corner of the country, never failed to achieve a phobic reaction in those captivated by the prime minister's rhetoric.

Menzies pondered long and hard over the wording of his referendum, the final screw driven home and countersunk in the Communist coffin draped with the flags of the Soviet Union and Communist China. In the end the wording could have come from anyone with a basic knowledge of English: *Do you approve the proposed law for the alteration of the constitution entitled 'Constitution alteration' [powers to deal with Communists and Communism].*

The date set for the referendum, September 22nd, 1951.

≈

The unions rallied their forces and returned to the streets, parks and racetracks, letterboxing and organising meetings in halls. Those questioned on street corners almost divided equally as to how their vote would be cast, worrying for the no campaign.

The government saturated the country with their argument for the yes vote, supported overwhelmingly by the print media and air waves. A successful battle for a Korean mountaintop designated by a single digit number, a senseless bloodbath, exhausted marines their faces caked with mud and blood barely able to smile weakly for the camera, made the front page of morning newspapers. Next day the enemy, division after suicidal division, recaptured the peak, their losses in the thousands. So the war raged on with the damning word Communism rarely off the front page or opening news bulletins.

≈

Sam joined BHP's *Iron Yampi* in Port Kembla, her sailing board Cockatoo Island, the company's newly developed Western Australia high grade iron ore project. Built in the company's Whyalla shipyard in 1948 and over 12,000 tons, the *Iron Yampi* ushered in a new era for Australian shipping. The first build of four ships, already completed the *Iron Derby* and *Iron Kimberley*. Four hatches and a large bunker hatch amidships, her powerful steam turbine engine gave her a service speed in excess of twelve knots burning sixty-eight tons of coal a day. Without graceful lines or fashion plates she looked a workhorse with four of her eight five ton derricks housed on the foremast, the other four on sampson posts at No.3 and No.4 hatches.

The amidships crew accommodation block and single bunker hatch, black funnel with two blue bands, engine room ventilators and skylights and four lifeboats, were accessed by ladders from the shelter deck, inboard by two long port and starboard alleyways. On the port side in two berth cabins firemen, four ABs and messroom. Bathroom, drying room and laundry in the tween decks. On the starboard side ABs, ordinary seaman, messroom, recreation room; replicating the port side, bathroom, drying room and laundry. The boat deck accommodated the bosun, donkeyman, two greasers, two deck boys, cooks and stewards. The galley aft of the accommodation block serviced both messrooms through slides, eliminating the old kit system. The messrooms glimpsed the future with a refrigerator, steam urns for coffee and hot water, hot press, hotplates and griller. Also looking ahead, the Seamen's Union of Australia negotiating with shipowners the prospect of older less agile members reclassified as crew attendants, two for each ship.

Seventeen men on deck squaring up the shelter deck and tween decks rolled king and queen beams and tossed and stacked 1200 single hatch boards each weighing an average 120 pounds. With the building of the Yampi class Australia entered a new era of shipping dormant since 1916 when the Labor government of Billy Hughes snubbed its nose at British shipowners and shipbuilders and initiated the largest shipbuilding program in the country's history.

With large cargo capacity, economical steaming, these ships were competitive worldwide, and what might be considered by maritime perfectionists a disadvantage burning coal, her engineers could changeover to oil firing in twenty-four hours. On the coast with a large bunker hatch the ships need only bunker in their terminal ports of Newcastle and Port Kembla, coal mined from BHP mines, cheap and accessible.

Shifting ship in Whyalla and Yampi Sound with fixed loader heads required the removal of only the centre section hatch boards, the queen beam rolled aft. Except for stores the gear remained housed during loading and discharging, when discharging the main and emergency aerials and triadic stay lowered.

From Port Kembla and Newcastle the ten day voyage north navigated through the Whitsunday Islands and the Great Barrier Reef under Torres Strait pilotage to Thursday Island, west across the Gulf of Carpentaria and Arnhem Land, setting a final course for the Buccaneer Archipelago and Yampi Sound. The ship's blunt bow cleaved a passage through oily rivers of yellowish green plankton alive with basking sharks and sea snakes. Lookouts relieved each other on the focastle head in three man watches, the night sea aglow with phosphorous, the decks littered with the silvery bodies of flying fish.

Normally warm northern weather favoured maintenance, two days out of Yampi Sound the decks swamped with fish oil hand pumped from forty-four gallons drums and applied with abandon by mops. Many, many drums, the chief mate hoping for an especially dusty load to form a protective skin.

Sam felt at ease with the mixture of Port Kembla, Sydney and Newcastle seamen, though as delegate peeved as always at the company's strict adherence to the award and hours of duty. Apologists could argue BHP employing thousands of more compliant workers in steelmaking and associated industries could show no weakness or favouritism to the small and highly militant maritime section of their operations. Company policy strictly administered by their loyal masters and mates insured most free spirited seamen did not remain long in BHP ships, a trench warfare attitude prevalent with the first footfall on the gangway.

Sam, a day out of Port Kembla, gave his notice, for no other reason but Emily's letters filled with her loneliness, wishing him home. Also it would give him a few weeks to work for the union in the no vote campaign, and where better than Stanwell Park.

43

SAM STOOD BESIDE THE rusty wire mesh and paint peeled hardwood rail fence of the Stanwell Park public school, his VOTE NO banner secured with seizing wire, by his feet a hamper packed by Emily of ham sandwiches and a flask of water. She would come later in the morning for an hour, Sam expecting a relief by a Labor Party member from Wollongong sometime in the afternoon. Liberal Party strategists assessed Stanwell Park as a positive outcome and not worth allocating thinly spread human resources, last election figures recording a high conservative vote.

Briefly making eye contact with those passing through the gate and returning soon after he found difficult to gauge positive or negative feelings. Some smiled, those who knew him nodded, many ignored him while others shuffled by with heads lowered as if confused by the impending stroke of a pencil.

Emily arrived at 11:00pm dressed in a light summer frock smelling of mothballs. His heart went out to her as she waved from a distance; today a good day, even a spring in her step, her breathing not too laboured even with the walk up the hill from the beach.

She lifted on her toes and kissed him, her lips lingering on his. "Busy?"

"Slow. I am supposed to be relieved later on but it would seem the bloke's bike has a busted chain and he has no links and has to walk from Wollongong which should get him here by tomorrow morning if he's fast on his feet. Even riding his bike would take him forever, but I have to give him top marks for dedication. Seems I'm here for the duration."

"Want me to stay with you?"

"That would be nice, but no use two of us standing here. Spoke with the returning officer and most of the locals on the roll have voted. I won't stay the entire time, leave what I have under a rock."

"How do you think it is going?"

"There is a feeling that won't go away that I am the underdog. Don't know really, it just seems people want to keep what's in their minds to themselves. I think many are bewildered by it."

She kissed him again. "Two thick steaks and fresh eggs from our neighbours, hurry home."

"The old couple voted earlier. Got to admit their eggs are good, though not so sure about their feelings towards our comrades in peril."

≈

Sam and Emily heard the news the next morning over the wireless, the failure of the referendum to pass, the government's vision for a cleansed nation now no more than a mountain of crumpled paper. A strange feeling came over him as he listened to the ABC announcer's refined voice, not of elation but more a subdued relief the outcome a victory for the thinking man and woman.

On the veranda with Emily in his arms he listened to the boring monotone: "New South Wales recorded a no vote margin of six percent while Victoria registered a no vote margin of three percent. South Australia also rejected the referendum with the no vote margin of five percent. Queensland supported the government with a yes vote of twelve percent as did Western Australia with a yes vote of eleven percent. Tasmania carried the yes vote by a slim margin of only a few votes. The final tally of no votes cast, 2,370,009. Yes votes, 2,317,972, a margin of one point one percent. Failure to carry the referendum has dashed at this time any hopes the federal government held of abolishing the Communist Party of Australia."

Sam could feel the gentle beat of her heart against his chest, her soft breathing a pleasurable relief for both. Stroking the thick, soft hair that fell around her shoulders he thought of his fellow Australians. Half of them supported Menzies obsession, while the other half resisted and that reluctance probably no more than a possible abhorrence to referendums of any nature. Of concern to civil libertarians, half the country voted for a state that gave immunity to liars and perjurers, succumbing to lies heaped upon lies and the spurious spiel of the conservatives and religious right.

The announcer's voice droned on: ". . . an interesting note on the referendum is the armed forces vote of 6478 yes to 2197 no."

So one third of the army on standby to defend Australia against the Communists, with mates in Korea under fire, voted the Communist Party's right to exist in a free society.

44

THE DECISION CAME EASIER than he expected, the life change. A myriad of conflicting emotions coursed through his mind as he watched a blazing slither of sun peak over the horizon, sitting on the veranda with Emily, a pot of coffee and tray of buttered toast and marmalade on a side table. Making the decision easier, secondary to Emily's deteriorating health, council were about to carry out proposed demolition of illegal dwellings on the beach. Stanwell Park would become the sole domain of surfers, beach fishermen and strolling couples.

Sam at sea Emily suffered a severe asthmatic attack, and if not for a neighbour with a gift of a half dozen eggs who found her unconscious on the floor she would have died. A subscriber to the adage fate moved in ways not planned by man their future plans came about with the chance encounter with a shipmate in the Commercial Hotel in Port Kembla.

Paying off the *Iron King* he called in the hotel with half an hour to catch the bus to Wollongong and saw his old mate holding the bar up. Clive Morrison could easily be mistaken for a jockey, or at least someone with a beer-belly who rode track work and gave the impression early rising made for heavy eyes and not what he poured down his throat. Clive existed in a world of imagined persecution, his nerves constantly on edge and a non-existent fuse obvious by the shape of his bent nose. Sam sailed with him on three ships, a tireless worker and a good seaman when sober though prone through binge drinking to loggings and instant dismissals.

Sam bought two beers. "Haven't seen you around, Clive."

"Why would you when the fucking shipping master gave me six months?"

"Wonder why I'm not surprised. How?"

"Took a few swings at the second mate of the *Iron Derby*. Lucky for me I missed, bastard kept ducking, would have got me life otherwise," Clive snorted through the twisted gristle of his nose and performed a nervous two-step shuffle, his furtive eyes darting around the bar.

Sam thought maybe looking for somewhere to crawl under to wait in ambush to smite a second mate. "So you're still taking on the world."

"Not a case of taking on the bloody world at all, just sorting out a few arseholes who are not worth being in it."

"Like the second mate?"

"BHP dog, always having a go at me and Gussie," Clive's high pitched voice whined. "The bastard got the apprentice up at 2:00am to sneak up on the focastle with Gussie on lookout. Jesus, on a freezing night in the Bight what do you expect the farmer to do? Those two hours in the middle are bloody rough. Only needed a nip of rum to warm him up, keep a good lookout and the strength to survive the huge seas breaking over the focastle."

"Huge seas breaking over the focastle? One nip?"

"Ought to be charged with attempted murder the bastards, yeah, huge seas. Maybe a couple of nips, Gussie sometimes underestimates these things. Then he took shelter to save his life under the apron wrapped in his blanket, what any bloke would do in the Bight in winter to keep warm. Can't blame a bloke for that. Bastards should be shot for putting a bloke on the focastle head in the Bight!"

Sam fought hard to restrain himself from laughing.

"Fucking shit of an apprentice reckons he could hear Gussie snoring from the break of the bridge, and when he shook him the fumes near knocked him out."

"So you sorted the second mate out?"

"Yeah, told you the slimy bastard kept ducking. Instant dismissal, a baddie and six months. Shafted Gussie as well. Bastards."

"How did you survive six months on the beach?"

"Used the old noggin and said to myself this is not the end of the world, son. Don't let the rotten bastards beat you. There's more to life than rolling your guts out sailing with shit. What's going to sea if not like being in jail with the added risk of drowning, read that somewhere? Believe it, too. Got a job on the railways."

"Get away with you! Clive, I can't picture you working for the railways. No way."

"A few quaffs while in deep meditation might have helped, don't know for sure. Read about jobs in the railway and took a train to Adelaide."

"South Australia? Why not closer to home?" Sam finished his beer and Clive stabbed a shaking finger in the barman's direction, then the empty glasses.

"Not South Australia, Commonwealth Railways. Read about the Trans-continental changing from steam to diesel, some shit like that which caught my interest. Do you know if you travel by train from Brisbane to Perth there are five different gauge changes?"

"You're a font of information, Clive. I knew a few but not five." Then Sam did laugh at the earnestness in his battered face. "Did you learn all that in the railways? What did you do?"

"Fettler."

"What's a fettler do?"

"Keep trains from falling off the tracks."

"So you worked your suspension off working for the Commonwealth Railways. You're amazing, Clive."

"Worked on the Trans-continental, Port Augusta to Kalgoorlie, not that I ever got close to Kalgoorlie. Tell you what, it's a bloody good job. No one gets worked to death and after awhile the bushies you work with ain't much different from a bunch of Port Kembla drunks squaring up at midnight."

Clive needed to get comfortable, grabbing a bar stool and kicking one in Sam's direction; he shook his head, his bus leaving in ten minutes.

"So you did the whole six months working for the railways?"

"On the Nullarbor Plain. Can you imagine how many sleepers there are in over a thousand miles of track? A mix of red gum and ironbark from Victoria, Western Australia jarrah, turpentine from New South Wales, but no matter where it comes from it's bloody heavy. The old sleepers have been laid since 1912, most of them still in fair nick but others feeling their age."

"Where did you live?"

"Pimba, out from Port Augusta."

"I didn't think there were any towns on the Nullarbor."

"Railway towns, roadhouses, post office and general stores. What I liked about the job you only ever got to see the ganger maybe once a week. The job ran itself, you did it and no one made a fuss."

"The ganger's the foreman?

"Yeah, this old coot would flop down on a pile of sleepers and roll a cigarette, give us a work list and a schedule of trains so we wouldn't get run over."

"Good serang."

"The best. We knew our job and did it. He knew his, too."

"Hot?"

"Bloody hot and freezing at night, flies thick enough to carry you away. Flies, Christ the flies! Stop for a smoke and thousands of the tiny bastards fed on you. Didn't seem to bother the locals much, strange that."

Sam finished his beer and shook Clive's hand, five minutes to catch his bus.

≈

The sweet lavender scent of soap from their showers, looking out over a dark sea, Sam told her of his meeting with Clive. She stirred against him, drew away and looked into his eyes.

"Sam, I would never ask you to give up the sea."

"You wouldn't need to, because I would without hesitation if it benefited you. I think about it when I am at sea, you being sick and alone. A half dozen eggs saved your life, Emily. Think about that."

"You are a seaman, Sam. That's all you know."

"Firstly, I am a man who shares his life with the woman he loves. Who grows even more beautiful and makes his yearning for her an ache that makes his life a misery. So why would a man with such a blessing want to leave her to go to sea?"

"Because it is his life."

"Life is about change and if the wellbeing of another depends on making adjustments then it should be pursued. Emily, I still have most of my working life in front of me, and it might be a long one if the union can't change shipowners minds that your last payoff is your retirement."

"Would you be happy working ashore?"

"There would be a regret, losing membership of the greatest union in the world."

Her face flushed with excitement. "Sam, could we give it a try? Oh, Sam, could we?"

"All I need do is hang my book up for six or twelve months."

"Can you do that?"

"Yes. We catch the train to Adelaide and treat it as a holiday. Apply for a job at the Commonwealth Railways head office, and if I fail the application or medical, holiday it is."

"According to your friend the weather is warm."

"Warm and dry which might be an understatement."

A frown of indecision crossed her face. "What about our home?"

"Dave's paradise has been claimed by council and the environmentalists and your mother has her own little place close to ours. She can move back to Pyrmont and save rent. Emily, we won't be cutting ourselves off from your family, a simple move across the country."

"Sam, do you really, really want to?"

"Emily, we both should have realised the need for change much earlier."

"Would you miss sitting on our veranda at night and watching the sea, the lights of ships and fishing boats? Your shipmates?"

"Firstly our veranda, or more correctly Dave's, is destined for a council bulldozer. Emily, my shipmates will be with me for life."

"Oh, Sam, wouldn't it be beautiful to be together. No more nights alone, the dread of you sailing."

"More importantly my girl strong and healthy."

She nestled against his chest. "Not so much a girl anymore."

"We have probably reached a tipping point in life, I don't know, a junction in the road. Our future life without separation, it sounds good."

"Only one thing missing."

"I know, but then I would have to share you."

≈

For Emily it might have been a trip around the world, her excitement a continuous hugging of her husband. The longest train she could ever imagine lay alongside Central Station platform No.1, the engine appearing as a distant cloud of smoke and steam; the Sydney Albury express with sleeper and dining cars, mail and guard's vans.

"We're travelling in style, Emily. Sleeper and informed apologetically we will be woken from slumber sometime after midnight to change trains at Albury. Why, because two obstinate colonies couldn't agree on railway gauges. We then board the flagship of the Victoria Railways, the Spirit of Progress for an early morning arrival in Melbourne. Stretching the legs we have most of the day to ourselves before catching the evening Overland Express to Adelaide. Emily, we have embarked on an epic journey."

At the border of New South Wales and Victoria the most impressive railway platform in Australia, 1400 feet of it, stretched the full length of two trains, a buffer in the middle to separate standard gauge from broad gauge. The Sydney train arrived on time at 2:15am, the entire train disembarking to stumble bleary-eyed from one train to the other, shivering in the biting cold. Reflected in powerful marshalling yard lights haloed in mist idled the Spirit of Progress resplendent in blue and yellow livery; a full head of steam engulfed her massive drive wheels, the S-class engine able to speed the engineering marvel 190 miles south to arrive at Spencer St Railway Station at 6:15am.

Those forced to endure New South Wales Government Railways second class, eight to a compartment, rigid and upright, tried hard to forget the experience, the discomfit of changing trains in the early hours of the morning a welcomed respite and chance to stretch cramped legs. Those without the comfort of railway blankets, sheets and soft pillows, their only means of warmth came through their footwear, foot warmers, unwieldy metal canisters on the floor.

Emily thrilled to the experience, dinner in the dining car and called from a deep sleep by a conductor with a polite knock on the door, harder when no immediate reply came from within. Even the long cold walk along the platform with the benumbed multitude and whimpering children, her energy still abounding.

"What's changed in this world? Even the colonial politicians couldn't get it right, agree on anything. With their ridiculous rivalry leaving a legacy that forces people to walk along a freezing railway platform at an ungodly hour. Are we one country, I sometimes wonder?"

≈

Emily marvelled at the bustle of Melbourne, trains and trams seemingly everywhere, its wide boulevards so different from the narrow and congested streets of Sydney. The latest fashions in the shop windows of Bourke St and Collins St, exclusive hotels with liveried doormen commandeering the footpath to usher guests into a world of exclusivity. This city's growth came from gold, tons of the precious metal dug from the ground in Ballarat and Bendigo, slightly lesser amounts panned in steams and even stumbled over in fields.

New millionaires, brash, crude, dressed in fancy threads, once swaggered the opulent streets of Melbourne and casually tossed sovereigns to following bands of urchins. Larrikins in tight bell bottom trousers, short jackets and bowler hats cocked rakishly on their heads, their gaudily attired donahs swathed in feather boas in tow, roamed these streets and caused riot with less outlandish folk.

Their afternoon train to Adelaide departed from Spencer St Station. The Overland Express though more subdued in streamlining than the Spirit of Progress still embodied the Victorian Railways progressive administration. A distinctive long-haul express train between Melbourne and Adelaide with dining, passenger and sleeping cars painted maroon with stainless steel fluting, a reprieve for passengers, the entire 480 mile journey laid with broad gauge rail.

Two S class engines in tandem, between them weighing 450 tons and twelve driving wheels powered by super-heated steam, sped the train across a flat and treeless plain to Bacchus Marsh thirty-three miles west. Then the two powerful engines showed their true engineering mettle, climbing an ancient and treeless remnant of the Great Dividing Range to Ballarat 1427 feet above sea level. At the border of Victoria and South Australia two 500 Mountain class engines hauled the train over another gradient challenge, the Mt Lofty Ranges, before descending to the Adelaide coastal plain.

$$\approx$$

The clerk behind the counter looked quizzically at Sam. "You are a seaman and you want to apply to work on the Commonwealth Railways, that seems a little implausible."

"Seamen at times find themselves in odd places, doing strange things. Yes, I do."

"Labouring jobs are hard work and the climate out west not inductive to ideal working conditions. Have you worked ashore?"

Sam shook his head. "Excluding childhood, going to sea is all I have known."

"Skills?"

"Just about everything I suppose. Supporting fellow workers a skill which should be transferrable to any workplace. Then there's initiative and ingenuity."

"Come to think of it I remember a seaman here before."

Sam grinned. "Yes, you would remember him."

"Somewhat wild, but he left of his own accord."

"Wild describes him, though some of the skippers and mates he's crossed paths with might say deranged as well."

"What do you know about the Trans-continental?"

"That it crosses the Nullarbor Plain and is hot and dry."

"We are also a railway that looks after its own, staffed by reliable men and women who take pride in their work. We rightly consider ourselves a family."

Sam turned his head to look at Emily sitting on a bench against the wall beneath a huge railway clock; pale of face, their journey taking its toll and the excitement which early buoyed her waning. A thought this is only a trial, six months or even less and at the first sign of distress he would take her home.

"When I say family I do so for good reason because in an outback environment with scarce resources you must be self-reliant and intuitive. The Trans-continental and the arid plain upon which is laid is an exceptional world. It holds a world record of which we are justly proud."

"The longest straight stretch of railway line in the world?"

"Even the Americans and Canadians building their trans-continental railways couldn't beat 297 miles of dead straight track between Ooldea and Loongana. The Trans-continental spans the plain from Port Augusta South Australia to Kalgoorlie Western Australia, 1052 miles and crossing not a single creek or waterway. Nothing extraordinary about that I suppose when you consider the entire plain once millions of years ago formed part of the Southern Ocean, 77,000 square miles of solid limestone which doesn't seem to deter the fossickers."

"Does it ever rain on the Nullarbor?"

"Records say eight inches a year, but no one remembers when it rained last. Water has been the Trans-continental's bogey since its inception. Steam trains needed to carry water and coal which of course infringed on their cargo carrying capacity. Steam trains use a great deal of water and coal, but of course now replaced with diesels."

"It must take a lot of people to maintain the railway," Sam said, watching the clerk reach in a pigeonhole behind him for two forms, then under the counter for another. "Aren't there artesian bores in the outback, wouldn't that solve the water problem?"

"For the size of the system not as many as you would think, but it is the dedicated team spirit of those working in a harsh environment that more than counts for numbers. To answer your other question, yes there are bores on the Nullarbor, but brackish and hazardous for boilers and of course undrinkable. I will need you to fill in the application, medical and pay forms. Also I need at least one reference."

"Would discharges stamped VG do?"

"VG?"

"Very good. Character and ability."

"More than enough for me to countersign your application forms. Can you see the doctor this afternoon?"

Sam again turned to Emily; he raised his thumb, then turned back to the clerk and nodded.

"When you return from the doctor I will give you a folder of information concerning your employment, award conditions and pay scales. Your pay is fortnightly, the paymaster travelling on the tea and sugar. Also he can arrange banking details after you have settled in. Your connection to Port Pirie is not until tomorrow which is not problem as we can arrange accommodation in a city hotel."

≈

The railway ran down the middle of the street; on both sides of the train the thriving township of Port Pirie. Cars parked at the kerb, people going about their business unperturbed their main commercial thoroughfare a railway roadbed. A long shadow cast over the railway tracks, the concrete chimney of the lead and zinc smelter.

Sam helped Emily alight, their two suitcases and Sam's seabag sitting in a half inch of talc-like grey dust. "We have three hours before the Trans-continental connects from Broken Hill."

"Sam, what's that awful smell?"

He pointed at the chimney rising from a cluster of buildings a hundred yards down the street. "Sulphur. You can see that chimney from Whyalla. I feel like a beer. Hungry?"

She nodded furiously which changed the course of a swarm of flies about to descend on her; she drew a deep breath which brought a smile to his face.

≈

The Trans-continental stopped to disembark two passengers, tucked in Sam's pocket his starting note for the ganger. Pimba, 148 miles west of Port Augusta, straddled the Sturt Highway, the junction for Woomera in the north. In a shimmering heat haze, rising on a cushion of hot air a roadhouse and general store, hubs in a chain of isolated maintenance depots. In streets little more than twin ruts edged with saltbush fenceless railway workers homes, corrugated iron boxes sitting on polished clay pans testament to the absence of water.

The searing heat of the Nullarbor Plain bore down on them the moment their feet crunched on fine gravel by the hard beaten shoulder of the roadbed, a forlorn look up at the smiling conductor closing the door of the carriage to keep the heat and the flies out. Not so for Sam and Emily with the first beading of sweat, descended upon by a swarm of tiny bush flies.

She might have been in her early forties, her once white skin charred to a leathery hide by long exposure to the outback sun; she knew the conductor and guard by name, draped over her shoulder a mailbag. She stared at Sam and Emily suspiciously, then their luggage and immediately wondered what secrets both harboured. The woman clung to the young man, pale and sickly looking and if she didn't cover her alabaster skin she would burn to a cinder; she thought far too thin to be healthy. The man looked capable enough, tall, good looking and in need of a haircut.

The diesel locomotive blew its siren and a hand waved out the driver's window which the woman acknowledged as she approached Sam and Emily.

"Did you get off the train by mistake?" Her voice matched the texture of her skin.

Couplings one by one took the strain as the locomotive from idling increased power before settling into a steady drumming throb, the train with the faint whir of metal on metal beginning to move. Sam flinched, a tensing of muscles in his stomach, a thought its departure sealing their fate.

"My name is Sam Wright and this is my wife Emily," he said, offering his hand.

Her hand might have been coarse sandpaper. "Jesus mate, what the hell are you doing here? Joyce Broughton, I own the general store and post office. Would have owned the roadhouse as well, but the petrol company wanted too much. Bloody thieves!"

"I have a piece of paper which says I have to see Mick Boyd."

"Yeah, he and Cheryl don't live no more than a hundred yards from here. Might catch him home if he's doing his paperwork, if not possibly a hundred miles east or west of here. You're here to work?"

"Fettler."

She cocked her head to one side and narrowed her eyes. "Been a fettler long?"

Then Sam laughed, reached for Emily's hand and drew her close. "Ah yes, maybe Emily and I might not be what we want to portray to the world. We have nothing to hide east of here, and not that long ago I never knew what role a fettler played in this world. I am a seaman."

"Might find the going a bit rough, but you look strong enough."

"A first tripper, but I am willing to learn. We have come here for Emily's health."

The leathery wrinkles disappeared in an instance, years falling from her face as she smiled. "We are a healthy lot out here, and thank goodness for that because the closest doctor's in Port Augusta. Welcome to Pimba, and I gotta say it, what you see is what you get."

"The man at the office in Adelaide said a house would be available."

"Yeah, there's a house. All the married folk got houses, the single ones bunked in together with one of them elected cook. Of course there's the roadhouse which is known at times to cook up a decent feed and a cold beer in the beer garden."

"Beer garden?"

"Wouldn't exactly call it a beer garden like them ones back east, more a lean too tacked on the side of the roadhouse with tables and chairs. Could call it the best place to be in Pimba on weekends. Can get lively if there are caravans parked overnight, truckies taking a break. I did say what you see is what you get, it's a bit better than that. We are a close society and we all get on and make do. Friday and Saturday nights are special."

"So you're not totally isolated?"

"No way, not like some of the other railway towns across the Nullarbor. We get cars, trucks and caravans coming from Port Augusta to top up, them from the other way to fill-up."

Sam made a frantic swipe at a buzzing mass of flies, half of which settled on Joyce who blithely ignored them crawling up her nose. "Does it get hotter?"

"Summer will bake you." She made no effort to brush off the feasting insects, a slight movement of her head dislodging some but sending those around her ears into frenzy. "Your house hasn't been lived in for awhile so you might need to visit the carpentry shop. There you'll find everything you need to make the place liveable."

At last she brushed off the flies which only rose a few inches above her head before descending again. She dropped her mail bag on the ground and closed the distance between her and Emily; completely out of character she looked closely into her eyes, then put her arms around her. "Girl, you ever need someone I'm never far away. I've got all sorts of concoctions and bush remedies in the store. As well it can get boring alone here and I'm always in need of someone to help out in the store. Don't pay much, but it sure beats doing nothing with your hubby away." She pointed to an overgrown track that led away from a cluster of housing and railway workshops close to the mainline and loop line, a chuckle in her voice. "Track's a bit rough so follow any power pole still standing. Your house is not far. Got a big front yard, stretches all the way to Western Australia. Welcome to Pimba."

≈

"Emily, I don't blame you right this minute if you say we catch the next eastbound train." Sam thought the home more a one room hut constructed entirely of warped and rusted roofing iron, in comparison Stanwell Park a mansion. He stepped it out, thirty feet by thirty feet, the ceiling barely above head height and optimistically lined with hessian for insulation. Twice the width of the front door an awning leaned precariously on flimsy sapling posts, of particular interest another lesser structure of the same roofing iron standing by itself its purpose obvious. The awning served as protection from the sun but also to hang an old railway tarpaulin for privacy when bathing in a concrete tub, the tub also for washing clothes and hanging on a line strung from the house to the outhouse. Their water source, two forty-four gallon oil drums.

A double bed stood in the middle of the room, the last occupants having washed and folded sheets and pillow cases, a quilt and two blankets. A small round table with three wooden chairs stacked on top made him think someone went to the effort to sweep the wooden floorboards and make the place habitable, also to clean the small electric stove beside the cupboard and refrigerator. Paint chipped and dented, unsteady on three castors, he sighed with relief when he turned it on and it hummed into life.

"Sam, there's no sink or taps."

"Or water tank or guttering on the roof which says something about rainfall. I suppose we get our water from town. Emily, I didn't expect it to be this rough, I truly didn't." He looked at her expecting her to agree, but instead she wiped the sweat from her brow and placed her hands on her hips with a determined look on her face.

"Sam, we can make this our home. Another Stanwell Park."

"My god I wish I could believe that. Emily, do one thing for me. Breathe."

She drew a deep breath and released it, then another. "Do I pass?"

"We'll see, we'll see. Emily, it's rough. Not rough, primitive doesn't even come close to describing it. This is pioneering in another century. We're back in the days of plague and high infant mortality. Joyce did say there's a carpenters shop and I have a few skills learned from Stanwell Park. Do you want to give it a go, of course with a few gallons of fly spray?"

She never answered, flicking a switch by the door; a low wattage bulb in a batten holder affixed to a ceiling joist in the middle of the room turned on. "See, you are wrong. We are in modern times and when we both start work we can order all the good things of life. Sam, it doesn't matter where we live as long as we are together. Tomorrow and the day after and the days after that you will be here. Not sailing, that's all I want to be happy."

"The train's hardly out of sight and you have a job."

"Do you mind me working, or whatever work it is?"

"Two incomes, we'll be rich. Without a doubt I will be away most of the day, sometimes even camping out who knows. Emily, I want you to understand this, I brought you here, my idea entirely because of a conversation with someone in a pub who could easily be certifiable. All you need do is say the word and we go home. No questions, no argument."

"Why would I do that?"

"Isn't it obvious?"

"We will make this our home. Sam, I have a feeling about it, I really do."

He wondered what he could do to make this hovel liveable, and he could, like most of his kind boasting a seaman could do anything, no obstacle or challenge impossible. To keep sane he needed to keep in mind three avenues of escape; their home in Pyrmont, a working holiday in the outback, and his union book in a pigeonhole in the Sydney branch office. Then his spirits lifted as he saw the wiry figure of Joyce labouring hard through saltbush and low scrub, an onion bag in one hand and a four gallon drum in the other.

"The stores should last you a few days, the water I don't know, but you can fill up at the depot. Don't drink the stuff in the drums. Me, I'm open anytime but if you have a special order give it to me on Monday for the tea and sugar train with guaranteed delivery on Friday. There's tea and powdered milk and there might be an electric jug in the cupboard. I could do with a strong cup of tea."

"The tea and sugar train?" he queried, completely taken with Joyce, setting the chairs around the table; Emily found the electric jug and Sam filled it from the drum, plugged it into the only power point and heard the reassuring whirr of the element.

"Our umbilical cord. Without it life along the Trans-continental would cease to exist, well for the whites anyway. The Aborigines would simply go back to being Aborigines wandering and surviving on the plain these people have for 40,000 years."

Emily found crockery in the cupboard and mixed powered milk in a jug, made tea in a white China pot and set both on the table.

"Mick's back in town which got me to thinking about you being a seaman, you might know a fellow who also called himself a seaman. Trying to think of his name which makes me mad because he blew this place apart for a few months."

"Clive Morrison."

"That's him! Ranting and raving and generally causing chaos. That man could drink a gallon of wine most people would polish their brass with and not blink an eye. Mad!"

"Many are the skippers and mates who think likewise."

"Mick hit him over the head with a shovel one day to shut him up. Then Mick put him on the black at the roadhouse and general store for booze, but this cagey little fellow takes that in his stride because he's got a mate on the Trans-continental, a fancy steward. Now the crazy bugger's into all the top shelf stuff, bottles of rum and whisky from his mate when the train stops, which it always does with that steward onboard."

"He never got the sack?"

"Mick reckoned when sober he got a good day's work out of him, and smart, but that ain't the end of the story. One day this pretty lass in a figure hugging red silk frock and a huge fashionable hat floats off the train with two suitcases, one light and the other extremely heavy and making these clinking noises. Curious as we are in Pimba we have a closer look, it's the steward on holidays and staying with Clive in the single quarters. That steward went to sea, too."

"I would probably know him as well, Joyce," he said, both he and Emily laughing. "A lot of marine stewards switched to the railways. Now I know how Clive survived six months on the Nullarbor. Booze and love."

After Sam left with Joyce to meet Mick, Emily checked her stores; potatoes, onions, tinned peas and beans, butter, flour, yeast, salt, pepper, tea, sugar, and four pound cut of beef. A docket in the general storekeeper's neat script said she could pay direct or be debited by the railways, another note she could start work whenever she felt like it.

≈

Mick Boyd, even though he habitually wore a battered sweat stained felt hat jammed on his head, some said even when he showered and slept, the years matured and the outback sun baked him. Some even hinted there could be a trace of Aboriginal blood in his bark-like hide, Mick quick to assure what flowed in his veins originated in Ireland. He also inherited the sturdy and work tolerant body of his Irish forebears, generations of canal diggers, five foot seven inches tall and broad of shoulders. He did remove his old hat at times to wipe sweat from his head with a piece of cheesecloth he wore around his neck, patting dry a few remaining wisps of hair.

The old and dented Bedford truck painted in faded Commonwealth Railways colours he drove loaded with crates of fishplates, soleplates, spikes, bolts and tools, like the man himself a victim of a harsh working environment.

"The going's rough along the roadbed why the old girl looks past her prime, but don't believe it. She's a credit to our mechanics and will see most out around her, including me. Mick Boyd, son." Thick ridged calluses dug into Sam's hand. "Got word about you and let me tell you it didn't please me none remembering someone else who claimed to be a seaman here a little time back. Worked his heart out when sober, but when the booze flowed the man went mad. His bloody girlfriend worked on the train, but not the real thing if you know what I mean. You got a real wife?"

Sam gagged. "My Emily is all girl. She suffers from asthma and it's a medical opinion a drier climate might alleviate her condition."

"Well, you can't ask for much drier than here. It last rained here four months ago, or maybe six. Pretty rare stuff. As a seaman have you ever done any hard labouring?"

"Not what I envisage laying sleepers and rail."

"It's hard and gruelling work set to a rigid timeframe so as not to interfere with train schedules. You won't see me around much as I have faith in my gang, men who know as much about keeping trains on the tracks as I do. According to ongoing track surveys I allocate the work, have the necessary materials on site and a time when I will be inspecting the finished work. No one, especially fettlers who do it tough and never get the recognition so deserved of their skilled profession, wants an old grumpy ganger standing over the top of them. My system suits them and me fine and I get the work done with the least fuss."

Sam wished he could have worked with some masters and mates with a similar philosophy. "When Emily and I stepped off the train this afternoon I came close to panic, and probably still am teetering on the verge. Not my wife though which makes me feel this sick girl is far stronger and resilient than me. Maybe, just maybe, I haven't made a bad blunder."

"Women adapt out here, sometimes easier than men. That place of yours is in bad shape, but don't worry about building materials, we got plenty in the depot. You only have to fill in the correct form."

"Thanks, Mick."

"Also I'll be able to stir up some carpentry labour hanging about, call it essential maintenance. Working for the Commonwealth Railways on their frontline the going can get tough at times, probably most of the time, so we do need our creature comforts. Making do with no running water, decent bathrooms, the sun shining through the holes in the roof and walls, is no fun."

He reached for Mick's hand again. "Emily might like a bathroom, but first a front veranda to watch the trains go by. That project I think I am capable of."

≈

Sam made up a gang of fourteen men based in Pimba, all of them hardened, or as Joyce would put it, thoroughly seasoned by the arid plain which bore a single railway line stretching into infinity. The Bedford and two other trucks headed west on the Sturt Highway for a few miles, the road running parallel with the railway line until it veered to the north. A week earlier Mick's gang offloaded hundreds of sleepers along the track in need of major replacement, iron hard and exuding a thick resinous sap, so heavy each sleeper took two men to carry them.

He fell into the routine easily, his period of learning over in the first few hours as he became part of a team jacking up sixty feet stretches of line, with fourteen pound hammers removing the condemned and replacing with new, base plates and spikes. Drilling and spiking, gauging, working with barely a word, not even stopping for a smoke. Only when tampered, the section regauged did the gang stop to boil the billy. Mick arrived later in the day to sign off the work.

As the day progressed, his hands raw and blistered and ingrained with purple-red sap, his back aching and barely able to stand erect, he came to realise why his gang worked without a break; noted in their work schedule a passenger train from the west due at their worksite at a given time and Mick, fearsome of his reputation, forbade even the slightest notion of putting a train's schedule in jeopardy. It never happened in the past and it most certainly would not in the future.

Emily boiled water on the stove and soaking a towel compressed it on his back, gently massaging and cooing her sympathy, especially for his poor hands. Even though exhausted sleep evaded him, his mind filled with one damning thought, Pimba and stepping from the train and subjecting Emily to an outback existence of abject misery.

"Emily, I have done the wrong thing."

She gently caressed his shoulders. "Not by me, Sam."

"Today I learned what a navvy is, and no matter what fancy title I am given, that is what I have become. Worked near to death because a train might be delayed, placed bleeding and splintered sleepers that would test the strength of four men. My God, there isn't a muscle that doesn't ache!"

"My poor Sam," she said, pressing her lips on his warm skin. "While you were suffering I stocked up with essentials and worked for Joyce in the morning. She goes out into the plain to collect rocks which she polishes and sells. Sam, if you want to go home I understand."

"It's me, the strong one, what wants to go home! From you I want one breath. One deep breath to vindicate bringing you to hell!"

"What about something else?" she said huskily, placing soft kisses on both his shoulders.

"Spare me, Emily!" Though every muscle ached in his body he felt a flush of relief, her soft breathing and the tone of her voice, also where her hand now rested.

≈

The schedule next day took the gang eighteen miles east to Wirrappa, greasing points, replacing sleepers, working on the loop line and signals. The day not as intense as the previous, able to boil the billy three times and eat a leisurely lunch, a chat with the driver and fireman of a goods train idling on the loop line giving way to a westbound passenger train. Sam even got to sit in the driver's seat and relive a childhood dream.

Each new day became an improvement on the previous as he felt his muscles lose their tension, able to straighten and flex his shoulders with only a momentary twinge. His hands toughened and wearing gloves protected them from sap and splinters, though his fellow fettlers showed a disdain for any means of protection except for hats and boots, Sam wearing an old army slough hat he found hanging on a nail on the back wall.

"Joyce is driving to Port Augusta tomorrow and I am looking after store by myself. Me in charge, Sam!"

"She better watch herself or you'll end up owning the place. I have heard say women of the outback are caring and trusting and Joyce is all that. You have made a good friend there." He felt relaxed after a meal of braised steak and onions, Emily's bread using Joyce's recipe a success. He experienced a glow of satisfaction watching her as she hummed to herself clearing away the dishes in anticipation of their bath. Naked on a duckboard dousing each other with water, soaping, then rinsing off. The best part of his day, fly free and wondering where the maddening pests went at night. Another thought, a bathroom before a bedroom, but most definitely no change to communal bathing.

Emily ordered a wireless from Joyce, able to listen to the news and classical music on the ABC, the only station Pimba could raise. A week later she accompanied the bush nurse based in Pimba on her rounds of the Wangai Aboriginal communities, and the week after a trip with Joyce who locked up the general store and headed north collecting rock samples to polish and sell to tourists. Emily thrived and rarely left anything on her plate, she breathed easy and slept well. She adapted to the heat and the flies wearing a large floppy hat strewn with corks. Her pale face which she protected from the sun glowed with good health and Sam knew at last his decision the correct one.

Her respite came about not only because of the drier climate but in the contentedness of having her husband by her side; even though he left at dawn and returned late afternoon, the dread of learning the name of a newly joined ship and its departure buried with her sick past.

≈

Within a month Sam's body rippled with hardened muscle, not an ache and his hands healed. Emily's health not only improved but a new outlook put a spring in her step and a laugh never far away. Her man home each night, visits to Port Augusta, the hours spent in the general store, excursions with Joyce into the even greater wilderness of the Nullarbor Plain searching for rocks, and the heart-warming experiences assisting the bush nurse in the Aboriginal communities. The veranda came first built with material ordered under the heading of repairs and requisitions to Commonwealth Railway property; hardwood posts, timber, facia, roofing iron, and a spare key to the carpenter's shop. Items not required, guttering or downpipe.

Sam surprised himself with the finished result, the veranda rigid and true. He used old sleepers soaked with sump oil to create two garden plots for Emily to sow petunias and daisies, pansies or whatever caught her fancy visiting Port Augusta. His next project, a bathroom.

Mick found him outdoor furniture, scavenging the wreck of an abandoned Ford sedan on the Sturt Highway for its front and back seats, perfect for watching trains go by on the new front veranda. Flies, he felt an urgent all consuming need to combat the flies; he knew he could never defeat them, the tiny insects breeding in their hundreds of millions, but he could keep them out. With two inch by one inch battens and rolls of fly mesh he enclosed the entire veranda; with filtered sunlight through the closely woven mesh came the added benefit of cooling. Their time spent on their new outdoor setting bliss.

Trains were a welcomed diversion. A glance at the clock and knowing if on time a passenger train would soon be passing. The first sound barely broke the intense silence of Pimba and from afar as if in practice the driver would sound his siren twice as a warning for Pimba's the only road crossing. A low guttural rumbling of GM class diesel power preceded the train, the train at full speed, another two blasts of the siren as it roared through the town. Gone in an instance in a rush of polished steel on rail and flexing timber, the sound soon fading in the hot and dry air.

Mick's maintenance train consisted of nine flattops shunted to the loop line loaded with sleepers, when allocated a locomotive offloaded along the mainline, mile after mile. Sam enjoyed this work, sliding the sleepers not strenuous as the train moved at slow speed. With the flattops unloaded, sometimes thirty miles from Pimba, the train would enter a loop line, the locomotive uncouple and re-enter the mainline for the return to Pimba. Sometimes hours were lost waiting for an eastbound goods train; ample time to boil the billy and add a nip of rum from the flask Mick carried in his gladstone bag for medicinal purpose, or so he said. He began to compare those he worked with, men he shared beer with in the roadhouse beer garden, like shipmates. These men supported each other and were well aware of their vital role of keeping fast and modern trains on the tracks, allowing clearly defined work ethics to guide their working lives.

Closely watching a new Emily he knew he would never leave her again. Regretfully when the time came he would let his union book lapse, a hard decision made easier joining a union of fettlers and railway men. Not a union of militant comrades hammering down the doors of industry and storming the countryside like fire-breathing missionaries of old, but still a union of workers.

It took time to adjust to the awesomeness of the great plain that white men and women in trepidation named the Ghastly Nothing, but home and sustenance for the Aborigines who wandered the land and the desert to the north for tens of thousands of years. He wondered how long he would survive if he left the line and strayed into the saltbush and spinifex, the flat featureless plain the same everywhere you looked, the silence forbidding.

At times he worked alone on sections of track checking fishplates and soleplates, marking sleepers in need of replacement, more often as he became proficient in the tasks allotted him. He painted signal boxes and greased points and drove railway vehicles, handy for weekend runs into Port Augusta, the luxury of overnighting in a hotel.

One day checking a section of track he saw a group of Aborigines in the distant haze to the north; four men and two women, one carrying a small child in a sling. He watched with increasing interest as the group approached, their bodies cut at the waist in a shimmering silvery mirage. The elder of the group came forward, holding out both hands.

Emily's baked bread, a small block of cheese and a jar of mustard pickles. "Haven't got much, but what I have we can share."

The man's origins reached far back in time, so black he shone like polished onyx, a pronounced forehead and a bone ledge that protected his deep set eyes; he stared at the meagre contents of Sam's lunch box, then forlornly at the woman and child. He asked Sam with gestures to cut two slices from the loaf, cheese and add mustard pickles. The woman wolfed the sandwich, sticking a crust in the infant's mouth.

Sam offered his lunch, the man averting his eyes as he took the food, a few words to the group. In moments their presence might never have existed as the saltbush and scrub closed around them, not even a sign of their footfalls in the stony, arid soil.

Sam watched the approach of the diesel locomotive, the modern world and the ancient, its maroon and silver paintwork glittering in the midday sunlight, at seventy miles-an-hour transporting 144 passengers westbound in luxury and comfort.

≈

A beloved king died and his daughter, a beautiful young princess, ascended the British throne, and a vast continent half a world away sang with passion God

Save the Queen. Even though the nation knelt in reverence to its new monarch and pledged allegiance to the British Empire, it now looked to another more powerful ally for its future security in an increasingly hostile Asia.

New Zealand with the same self-preservation in mind with Australia became members of the Australian New Zealand United States Security Treaty, ANZUS. Prime Minister Menzies could muse on a changing world with boosted confidence, though still miffed at having failed to crush the Communist movement in his homeland.

Sam read in a two day old *Adelaide Advertiser* that the federal government gave permission for the British government to test a nuclear device on the Monte Bello Islands off the far northwest coast of Western Australia. He wondered about the nomadic tribes of Aborigines on the nearby mainland, drinking from waterholes and eating their food off the land. Which way the wind blew, or did the intelligentsia in white coasts who created and exploded atom bombs worry about such mundane matters?

Putting the newspaper aside, listening to Emily singing under her breath as she prepared dinner, he should be angry. In the streets with chanting mobs condemning, burning effigies of a gloating prime minister who could now count among his many achievements ushering Australia into the Atomic Age by radiating thousands of square miles of Western Australia.

Show resentment against a political minion bowing in the presence of royalty, even lower if the regal personage wore a feathered hat and ceremonial sword. No more than a puppet on the world stage who supported a foreign country exploding nuclear devices in Western Australia.

He felt only resignation, and that troubled him. Pimba might have allayed his political and militant past, and when he raised his concerns with Emily she burst into tears. "Sam, Pimba is our home! Please don't take us away and go back to sea!"

Shocked at the tears streaming down her face, he took her in his arms. "I'm not taking you away. Leaving here never entered my mind."

"You say you are not the same person. Is it because of here? Is that why?"

He lifted her face, his lips muffling her sobs. "The old hatreds must still be inside me, but buried deeper and maybe harder to find. It's just that I don't feel the gut wrenching desire to vent it in clenched fisted militancy. Pimba might have taken that from me, but it will never be the cause of me destroying your happiness."

≈

Sam asked Mick a question while boiling the billy alongside a section of railway line he recently finished surveying. Mick never usually stayed long, but this day he did, deciding to eat his egg sandwiches with Sam.

"Mick, you can tell me to go to hell and you probably will talking politics, but as a working class man who has risen through the ranks what are your thoughts on a prime minister called Menzies?"

"You're right, son, politics can make bad friends," he said dismissively.

"Only asking a simple question."

"Here a million miles from nowhere? Why would you ask me that?"

"It's just I have always felt since my first ship as a boy a fire in my gut when I witnessed those elected by the people destroying the essence of what this country is, a nation bound together by a working class with no equal in the world. Who have achieved a dignity of labour through their unions, the banding of comrades on the factory floor not on the glorious battlefield of other peoples wars. Is Pimba quenching that, Mick?

"There a Communist inside you, Sam?

"Mick, I haven't the courage or the conviction to be a Communist. No, I am not. I am though and always will be a unionist."

"Not long after we first met you asked me is there a delegate on the job and what union do I join. Kept that in the back of my mind, is this fellow going to cause trouble among an easy going lot of country blokes even though every one of them belongs to the Australian Railways Union. You've kept your peace as a tactful man would which made it easier for you to adapt to Pimba. I will answer your question, I don't give one damn for Mr Menzies and his city politicians. Most of us here voted for the man we considered best for the job, who makes his presence known around here and is contactable. I know for a fact you wouldn't vote for him, but then your vote just possibly might be the only one on the Nullarbor Plain for the left side of politics. That's how it is."

"That's how it is," Sam sighed. "I thought we humans at the age of enlightenment cast ourselves in concrete that remained unbroken all our lives. God, I hope I am right."

"You seamen get into this philosophical mumbo-jumbo at sea?" Mick squinted at him and thought it time to break out the medicinal rum. "Put that billy on the boil again, Sam. I've something in the truck to make the brew drinkable."

"Seamen in moments of melancholy are known to explore the meaning of life," Sam said, then with a grin of pure pleasure: "You're a good doctor, Mick, one of the best."

≈

Sam excelled in writing official procurement forms for a Commonwealth Railway property in need of repair, renovation, maintenance and required labour. He raised the roof and lined the interior of the home with tongue and groove boards and replaced warped sash windows with louvers. Learning even greater skills, he assisted two carpenters and their offsiders build a bathroom and bedroom on stumps and bearers.

Coats of ceiling white, walls lilac blue to match scatter rugs on the floor. Running water proved another successful project, a salvaged water tank on piers by the side of the house filled by the depot's small tanker and fed by gravity over the sink, bathroom and laundry tubs. Precious water not wasted, every drop recycled for Emily's flourishing flower and vegetables plots.

Their life in Pimba revolved around a social world both Sam and Emily could never have imagined living on an arid plain of saltbush and stunted scrub, flies and oppressive heat, strength sapping northerly winds from the Great Stony Desert on a slow southward march that would one day reach the Great Australian Bight.

Friday and Saturday nights in the roadhouse beer garden with every man, woman and child in town stamping their feet to an accordion, mouth organ and a fiddle. Even the dogs joined in the activities in their own way which meant noisy barking, snarling and mainly stirring dust. A treat for the overnighters in their caravans and trucks, Pimba a pin in the map well remembered.

Sam witnessed a depressing side to the merriment, the clear division of the races evident by Aborigines who observed from the sidelines, spectators, uninvited guests. Supplying alcohol to the Aborigines a criminal offence, heavy fines and loss of liquor license. An itinerant people who walked the land of their own freewill, this vast spiritual plain their home for eons, now with their pride and dignity threatened under white man's tar and concrete, even worse, white man's laws.

These people, these survivors with their rich culture and beliefs in the land, did not exist. Census ignored them. Government claimed the entire continent under the British Crown, then appeased their conscience with money doled to missions.

He wondered if the Aboriginal families who sat outside the luminescence of the roadhouse and general store on Friday and Saturday nights, their wide-eyed little children between their legs, babies asleep in arms, their dogs strangely quiet, felt anger at this segregation. No so much the denial of alcohol, but the absence by government decree the basic right to choose. To be treated as an inferior species in superior white society. No more than a relic of the days when a dark skin meant bondage and subservience.

≈

The community of Pimba came close to civil dissent; the British government detonated another nuclear device in Australia, not on a cluster of remote islands off the Western Australia coast, but in Pimba's front yard!

Maralinga!

Approving the United Kingdom to test its nuclear weapons on Australian soil posed no dilemma for the government; in fact pride played a major role, permitted to participate with lightly dressed military personnel in tropical attire marshalled to view the explosion, of course protected with appropriate glasses. Only those who opposed a free world and supported Soviet Union nuclear supremacy would condemn the contamination of thousands of square miles of useless desert. Some scattered groups of Aborigines needed rounding up, transported to safe areas, or at least where the prevailing weather patterns would give upwind future generations a fair chance of survival and limit the number of birth defects.

Australia entered a golden age under what seemed a permanent conservative government, its prosperous population able to fulfil the dream of home ownership on quarter acre blocks, an Australian built car in a garage against the back fence. Australia grew and prospered and its affluent workforce began to believe those voracious unions branded by the government as Communist would have the nation return to the grim days of endless strikes and shortages encouraged by Labor's socialist policies.

The conservatives in an amicable coalition looked confidently into a long tenure in government with an opposition split into two clearly defined parties. Labor voters now able to choose between two Labor parties, Australian Labor Party or Democratic Labor Party. Confusing which party represented working class values, supporters of both parties not long in having their answer when Santamaria instructed his Democratic Labor Party members to move to the crossbenches and support the Liberal Country Party government.

With a splintered Labor Party assured of keeping him in power, an election pending, Prime Minister Menzies courted a drunken Soviet envoy hinted to have some alarming information about a Soviet Union spy ring operating in

Canberra. Critics of the headline grabbing drama were bemused what secrets of earth-shattering importance the Soviet Union could garner from a lowly nation such as Australia, possibly the number of naval vessels laid up in Sydney or how many men and women marched on Anzac Day.

The master tactician finetuned manipulation into an art form. Sam read and listened to the ABC of Soviet envoy Vladimir Mikhaylovich Petrov's defection. Expelled Russians, high drama of the envoy in hiding and his petrified wife, Evdokia, struggling with broad shouldered KGB agents in trench coats forcing the hysterical woman to board a plane for Moscow. Certain execution for the crimes of her traitorous husband. The nation breathed a sigh of relief, their prayers answered, saved by courageous federal police officers before the door of the aircraft closed.

Well done, he thought, a conniving prime minister about to go to the people to renew his mandate. How could the government fall with the cross benches filled with Labor rats, a Soviet espionage ring smashed? He sat alone on the front veranda; his solitude would be broken by a westbound goods train expected in another twenty minutes, an eastbound idling on the loop line for its passing; Emily in Sydney for four weeks visiting the family.

Miserable and alone he now knew how Emily felt when he sailed.

≈

Mick's retirement came with the expectation of a well-earned rest from the rigors and responsibilities of working all his life for the South Australian and the Commonwealth Railways; he and Cheryl planned to buy a small cottage close to the beach in Port Augusta.

Sam thought Mick might have imbibed too much, his retirement party on Saturday night boosted with additional revellers from a convoy of caravans heading west and five truck drivers keeping the booze flowing. Taking Sam aside he asked him what he thought about becoming a ganger.

"Bosun on the railways? Never gave it a thought, Mick."

"More money, and of course responsibility. I could recommend you with a clear conscience and knowledge you'd serve the railway well."

"Mick, thank you, thank you so much. I feel privileged for your confidence, but I am happy with what I do right now. Happy, Jesus, I never thought I would ever say that when we first stepped off that train, but when I see the glow in my girl's cheeks I know I did right."

"Got no idea what happiness has to do with promotion, but Emily does look fine."

"Pimba has been kind to her." Sam saw Emily sitting with Joyce and a few of the other women. "I never thought we'd make it, I really didn't. I think I came as close to panicking as I have ever done in my life. I looked at Pimba with horror, appalled, and thought my God how is my Emily going to survive this horror."

Cheryl brought two frosty bottles of beer in an ice bucket to their table on a tray, sat beside her husband and took his hand. "You two talking shop? Well, I suppose I can forgive him this time because soon he'll only have me to talk to as we walk along the beach. Right, Mick?"

"Will you miss Pimba, Cheryl?" Sam said.

"Don't know about that. Nothing ever happens here worth mentioning, except of course births and comings and goings."

Mick suddenly burst out laughing, slapping his thighs; with tears streaming down his face, he blubbered: "Nothing ever happens here you say! What about Sam's seaman mate and his girlfriend? Now didn't that stir the locals!"

Cheryl puckered her mouth in a gesture of distaste. "The least said about those pair and their shenanigans the better. Sam, when Mick said you were a seaman I admit most of us around here were filled with reservations."

Wiping his eyes Mick spluttered: "Cheryl took a sneak peek at your Emily looking for an Adam's apple. Right, Cheryl?"

≈

The long serving prime minister felt comfortable in his astute stewardship of the nation, and accordingly received the highest recognition from the young visiting queen, the Most Noble Order of the Thistle. Sam received the news the hard way, hit in the face with a copy of the *Sydney Morning Herald* tossed from a westbound passenger train. The nation basked in pride and editorial writers searched their thesauruses for appropriate accolades, their prime minister rewarded with the queen's personal honour. The nation felt privileged and honoured to have at its helm a knight of the Most Noble Order of the Thistle, fitting tribute for his years of public service to the nation.

Sir Robert Gordon Menzies.

The train gone he might have been the only person in the world and he raised his head and gazed into a clear blue sky. Near midday and the sun bearing down on him, he twisted the bulky broadsheet in his hands, then threw it on a bundle of sticks gathered to boil his billy.

45

THE PRIME MINISTER IN great solemnity led his nation into another war, his third in twenty-six years. His government introduced conscription when young Australia showed reluctance to wear kaki and volunteer to fight a new Communist threat in the jungles of Vietnam. The youth of Australia with more world savvy than their predecessors questioned supporting a corrupt regime in Asia financed with democratic dollars, pounds and francs, for them a future studying for degrees in science and engineering, excelling in sport and preparing to join their lives to others.

Conscription would be subject to a ballot, a marble in a barrel to decide a young man's new career. Saigon begged for support as Communist insurgents from the north engaged in a bloody civil war. Newsreels in vivid colour, and an even more convincing medium for the demonization of an enemy, in every living room a television set, gave irrefutable proof of peasant families fleeing burning villages, the innocent dead floating in rice paddies. Editorials condemned the atrocities of brutal and merciless Communist aggression from the north armed and supported by the Soviet Union and Communist China.

Those who dared query Australia's questionable invitation by the South Vietnamese government for military support retreated under a barrage of vilification from the government and media, accused as Communist sympathisers. Those who referred to Vietnam's history as a struggle for liberation decades old against invaders and colonisers, Chinese, French, British and the United States, branded a threat to national security.

There were also those who pointed out the Vietnamese were a formidable foe, hardened by years of foreign occupation and exploitation, driven by a nationalist fanaticism to command their own destiny.

A new type of soldier departed Australia to wage war in Vietnam, regular and conscript. Highly trained, brave and wholly committed in the war against Communism. Politics played no part in their heroic actions in a difficult field of battle, men who took the fight to their enemy and won through sheer courage and determination. The young continued to give up their lives while the real truth of the struggle remained in sealed secret cabinet papers.

Scribes accused of being on the far left asked the government to table the South Vietnamese government's request for military support. The government in contemptuous rebuke announced its support for South Vietnam, written or not, originated in its obligations to ANZUS.

Sam searched for a chink in the prime minister's armour, a weakness that an opponent could exploit, probe and expose. For too long this man succeeded in spinning fantasies to the working class, endless spin of golden years and unbridled prosperity. Those who wove the myth of Australian affluence as good governance conveniently forgot the years the nation and a world sunk into abject poverty. Also if the world prospered so did the great southern continent.

46

ALL REIGNS EVENTUALLY COME to an end and Australia's most successful prime minister announced his retirement from office and public life. The great man, weary from a long and burdensome journey, would retire at the time of his choosing, January 26, 1966.

He would leave office at the height of his powers, unassailable by the electorate or his colleagues. His legacy of leadership, accomplishments, diplomatic triumphs, electoral victories, the Liberal Party he founded, would continue far into the future the man personally mapped for Australia.

Many young Australians at the time of his retirement knew no prime minister other than Sir Robert Menzies, and a nation would mourn his loss in the public arena. It would though bask in the glories heaped upon him by his peers, world leaders, and additional honours bestowed by Queen Elizabeth. The supreme statesman felled the forces of socialism seven times in the federal arena, with a contemptuous sweep of his hand banishing demoralised opposition leaders into obscurity.

He strode the world a larger than life figure, the embodiment of the British Empire and Raj, an example of white superiority. A revered senior statesman of the British Empire hierarchy, with the term empire symbolic of suppression and colonialism, the British Commonwealth of Nations.

Sam found one flaw, the prime minister's role supporting the United Kingdom's dispute with Egypt over nationalisation of the Suez Canal, a fiasco relegated to the middle pages in small print.

Sir Robert acquiesced to changing pounds shillings and pence to decimal units. Though not without discord when he requested the changeover committee name the new unit of currency royal in honour of his queen. Common sense prevailed, also public condemnation and even ridicule, the committee opting for dollar.

47

FOR SAM THESE WERE the times for reflection under a canopy of blazing stars, a serene world bathed in starlight of even greater intensity than that at sea, walking with Emily along a well-worn track which took them deep into the plain. Here one wondered why people once thought the world flat and to sail out of sight of land the oceans cascaded over a mythical precipice to disappear in a bottomless abyss.

Above their heads a perfect half sphere of heavenly brilliance. With low scrub barely waist high, to turn a full circle a world so vast it must have no end. Over each horizon another began, on and on.

Emily found it more difficult to walk long distances and her medical check-up in Port Augusta found a profound deterioration in her lung capacity. She would squeeze his hand and say she felt fine, but he knew different. Even their annual visits to Sydney failed to lift her flagging spirits. Claire in a nursing home under government investigation, the sale of their Pyrmont home the money needed to enter a first class facility. He visited the union rooms in Sussex St to renew old acquaintances but found only new and younger faces, the old guard no more than memories in waterfront pubs. Seaman wore designer clothes and manned specialised ships, tankers and oil rigs and enjoyed conditions only dreamed of in his time.

He should have felt a yearning to reach out to these seamen and talk of good ships and bad, fighting for conditions now taken for granted. Ask questions of what the future held for Australian seamen in a changing world where the flag on the stern rarely represented the country of ownership. Instead he found he wanted to leave the old narrow streets he knew from his past and feel hard packed arid soil under his feet.

≈

Emily no longer walked, losing even more weight. With no appetite for solid food Sam fed her a rich meat broth, wholegrain bread soaked in the heavy residue. Medication that normally eased her condition took increased dosages, this affecting her kidneys. She missed Joyce who sold the general store and now lived in Adelaide, also the bush nurse who because of government funding cuts now based out of Ceduna with her territory doubled.

New families settled in Pimba and Sam and Emily counted themselves as the oldest hands. A day unusually cold caused Emily to remain in bed and as Sam looked down at her, her shape barely making a dent under the quilt, he knew a time he dreaded would soon be upon him. He sat on the bed and took her hand, a hand as small as a child's. She closed her eyes, those beautiful blue eyes that so long ago captured his heart.

He willed them to open just once more, for her lips to say goodbye until we meet again. Where he did not know, but Emily would. He kissed her lips as if fearful of bruising them, her face wet with his tears.

"Goodbye, my Emily. Goodbye."

≈

He cut the stone from a limestone outcrop guarding the entrance to a subterranean system of caves; with a crow bar he located a fissure and dislodged a chunk measuring around three foot by two, the stone almost the shape he desired. For weeks he slowly worked the stone with a finely honed chisel, smoothing the surface with a paste of stone dust and water applied with a steel wool pad.

The inscription took even longer, his nerves on edge as each delicate tap of his hammer on the chisel followed a stencilled outline: EMILY WRIGHT

1920-1980. His craftsmanship proved true and he wondered if a guiding hand might have helped. This stone would mark the place where their lives truly joined, never again the agony of separation and months at sea. The Pimba years were the years when he came home to his girl each night, their parting in the morning a kiss, another at night.

Pimba extended Emily's life. A life that gave him the joy of her smile, her love, her laughter and her tenderness. His girl would have a stainless steel plague in a wall in Port Augusta, but here among the straggly garden plots she tended, starved of water and nutrients, is where her passage through life would be marked. Here once lived Emily Wright, and the man she loved would stay by her side.

≈

Trains, sleek and modern, containerised and sterile, did not stop in Pimba with privatisation, and the teams of men who worked the line east and west made redundant and their railway homes written off the asset books. Frequent flights from Sydney to Perth in four hours made transcontinental passenger trains redundant, now an expensive tourist attraction.

Slick glossy brochures tempted people of the therapeutic and relaxing ambience of modern train travel, crossing the mysterious Nullarbor Plain and reliving the more unrushed days of a bygone era.

Complex machines kept the trains on the tracks, skilled professionals who wore reflective vests and hard hats, team members versed in occupational health and safety and rarely if ever swung a heavy hammer. Modernisation brought redundancy and Sam no longer needed to rise early, his days never spent alone, always a voice in his mind to make the hours pass.

Pimba's role changed as did the communities scattered across the Nullarbor Plain; with centralisation of resources old depots closed. The roadhouse remained a beacon on the drab plain painted in canary yellow and red with modern fuel pumps, incorporating the general store and asphalt parking for caravans and trucks. Sails to shade vehicles from the sun. Permanent residents numbered less, their work mainly drilling holes in search of minerals.

Sam in the evenings would sit on a bench seat he made in Emily's garden; he still called it Emily's garden though nothing grew in except encroaching saltbush and spinifex. The plain would one day reclaim what man scratched from its inhospitable surface, but not Emily's headstone which he kept free of weeds and dust drifts.

He did not miss the things people took for granted, having to cook a meal on an ancient woodstove by candlelight, the power poles reduced to wafer-like shreds by white ants. A Coolgardie safe fooled the flies and kept the sparse contents inside reasonably cool.

Emily appeared to him in dreams and spoke of many things, things he forgot when he awoke but knew she would remind him next night. He looked forward to lying in bed and looking up at the ceiling waiting for sleep to overcome him so he could talk with her.

≈

Walking to the roadhouse took most of his strength, thankful of the owner's young son who delivered his basic needs on his bicycle, a cheerful ten-year-old who took great delight in asking did any spiders live in the tangled thatch of grey hair that grew on his head and down his chest. He relished these small reprieves, his legs not always saved a trip to the roadhouse when the need arose to draw money from his bank account.

He developed a dry cough which he vaguely remembered might be an indication of a heart problem, then he supposed excluding twinges of rheumatics the years lenient. The boy who imagined spiders living in Sam's hair brought his fourteen-year-old sister for a second opinion. An aspiring artist, she asked could she capture his image in pencil and charcoal. He liked her, freckled and studious in glasses, her long hair in pigtails. Caitlin, he thought her name Caitlin.

Caitlin scoffed at her brother's wild fantasies and in her artist's eye saw an old man of the Nullarbor Plain, possibly an Aboriginal elder. She thought at first he might have been Aboriginal, his skin so dark and coarse, but no, her mistake. She captured him in her sketch book when he came to the roadhouse, sitting at one of the outdoor tables. A motherly tenderness when he nodded off, brush the flies away and wake him with a cold drink. Once when she deputised for her brother to deliver groceries, she asked him did Emily rest beneath the headstone in the garden. He never answered, and he seemed so far away she never bothered to press her inquiry.

Caitlin's portfolio promised a bright future in commercial art, and she never tired of her favourite model, a visit to the old man when she came home on holidays from boarding school in Adelaide. On one such occasion she found him on his bed, a skeletal old man staring wide-eyed at the ceiling.

She shook him gently. "Mr Sam?" Then she cried out in anguish.

≈

"He's like a hundred bloody years old! What's his name again?"

He heard the voices as if echoing in a hollow chamber, swirling around him a grey fog that at times exposed shapes in human form. Objects doing things, busy, a familiar young voice competing with one more authoritative.

"Mr Sam," Caitlin said tearfully.

"Mr Sam who?"

"Mr Sam Wright and wife's name is Emily."

"Christ, is she as bloody old as him? Anyway, she's going to have to sign forms. We've got him stabilised so he's going to make it to Port Augusta." Then the voice tittered. "Continue to live a long life thanks to modern medical science. Where's his wife?"

"She's dead."

He felt her presence, her small hand covering his. "Goodbye, dear old Mr Sam."

48

THE WIND WITH A northerly aspect rustled through the more slender branches of the oaks and elms, the trees now completely bare; Sunday and autumn sunshine continued to attracted visitors to Mt Osmond.

Paul and Wendy took advantage of the mild weather, Wendy anticipating a special lunch today, her man obviously a favourite with someone in the kitchen. A celebration for his last rostered Sunday and a well earned rest on weekends.

He saw her red Kia in the car park, dressed in a long flowing floral dress and baggy cardigan in deference to the unreliability of autumn weather in the Adelaide Hills. He waved and she waved back and he bent close to his patient's ear. "Now isn't she a sweet something on the eye?"

The old man gave no indication he heard, eyes closed and breathing softly through his nose. He called out as she neared: "Virginia ham and Merseyvale cheese on freshly baked poppy seed buns, for afters cherry pie and whipped cream. There's also chocolate milk."

Rising on her toes she offered him her lips. "Though I thoroughly enjoy our Sunday lunches, I really am glad you will be free for awhile."

"Which might be permanent with the hospital board threatening to outsource services in a stoush with the union over penalty rates."

"Don't spoil what is promising to be a nice day with talk of union. I just wish you didn't have to belong one."

"I don't."

"Of course you don't. Mr Howard with his Work Choices spared you that."

With the grass dry he spread a blanket and set out three plates, napkins, ham, cheese and butter in plastic containers, the buns in a wicker basket. "Good old John Howard. Now there strode a man who couldn't be kept down."

"Thankfully for Australia his twelve magnificent years as prime minister worthy of a knighthood," she said, buttering a roll and heaping it with ham and crumbly cheese.

He broke off a small portion of buttered bun and fed it in the old man's mouth; the eyes remained close, but the mouth worked as if on hinges, more so by instinct.

"Tony made a very important statement this week."

"That he will stop the asylum seeker boats by turning them back?"

"Which of course he will on taking office. Tony is saying go to the people now. Bring the election on and let's get rid of you."

"Will she agree?"

"Of course she won't. She'll hang on and take us even deeper into a sinkhole of debt and broken promises, laying out the red carpet to the boat people in their thousands. Though I think she would be taking a prudent glance behind her back with Rudd becoming more vocal and lurking in the background. She might have got rid of him, but he's still got plenty to say."

"Hmm, you're right. Things certainly are more expensive under Labor, or since the days of John Howard and Peter Costello, especially petrol." He broke off another chunk of roll, this time with sliver of ham and cheese.

"With victory guaranteed in September, Tony has stated outright he will not work with the Greens and independents. He will govern alone and have the country behind him cheering after suffering three years of their self-opinionated posturing."

"Wendy, no sympathy for prime minister of the same gender?"

"Of course I am for a woman prime minister, women in cabinet and selected on merit for foreign postings, but stab your own in the back and lie, no."

"With this constant talk of leadership challenge she might not lead Labor to the September election. Rudd could topple her if the polls continue to indicate a catastrophic loss."

She scoffed. "With that lot who would know who will lead them day for day, also who in the current parliament is of leadership calibre if the knife gets stuck in her back? A saint walking on water could lead that rabble to the next election and it will not make a skerrick of difference. The people have already made their judgement without going to the ballot box, and it is goodbye and good riddance Labor."

Paul opened a carton of chocolate milk for his patient. "Hear that, Old Union? Wendy says even a divine figure leading the Labor Party will see it thoroughly routed."

He sucked through a straw and opened his eyes a little and thought the day hazy; probably not, more his failing eyesight.

"Oh Paul, victory will be so sweet."

As if the sun passed behind a dark cloud the light faded even more; he felt lightheaded and the constant nagging pain in his lower back and legs disappeared.

"Polls are intimating we will win over forty seats."

"The *Adelaide Advertiser* is predicting the same," Paul said, handing her a plastic plate of cherry pie smothered in whipped cream. "Their editorials are continually lambasting the government."

His withered hand went slowly and deliberately to the base of his neck, through tangled hair and gripped a chain and tiny anchor. It came away in his hand, the links of the chain worn tissue thin with great age. He did not believe in God or life for the soul after death, but believed when two humans shared a profound love somewhere in the universe their spirits would be united.

The light gradually grew dimmer, the cause he knew not his eyesight but the closing down of his life, a good body that rarely failed him in the past and served him dutifully. He felt no pain or fear, a smile slowly growing on his old, old face as he pressed the anchor against his mouth.

He tasted her sweet lips on the cool metal, and then closed his eyes with a single word: "Emily."

The end